DESTINY'S EMBERS

ELEMENTAL

DESTINY'S EMBERS

BRADLEY WARDELL

BALLANTINE BOOKS NEW YORK

A Del Rey Trade Paperback Original

Copyright © 2010 by Bradley Wardell

Published in the United States by Del Rey, an imprint
of The Random House Publishing Group,
a division of Random House, Inc., New York.

DEL REY is a registered trademark and the Del Rey
colophon is a trademark of Random House, Inc.

Elemental and the Elemental Logo are registered
trademarks of Stardock Entertainment Inc.

Map: Paul Boyer

ISBN 978-0-345-51786-9
eBook ISBN 978-0-345-51788-3

Printed in the United States of America

www.delreybooks.com
www.stardock.com
www.elementalgame.com

2 4 6 8 10 9 7 5 3 1

Book design by Elizabeth A. D. Eno

I'd like to dedicate this book to my mom and my aunt Barb. Their encouragement to read science fiction and fantasy at a young age opened new worlds for me. I can never thank you enough.

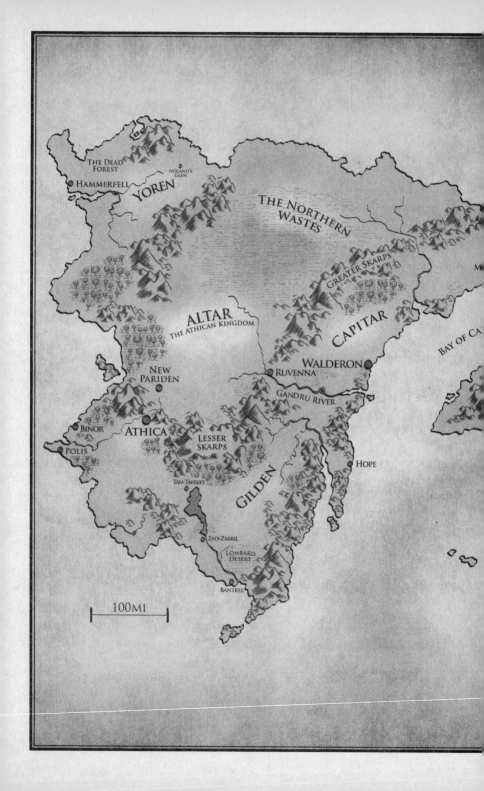

ELEMENTAL
DESTINY'S EMBERS

DESTINY'S EMBERS

PROLOGUE

Once, legend says, the world of Elemental was filled with magic.

All peoples made use of this sorcery. With it, they built great kingdoms—Malaya in the South, Hallas in the West, fabled Al-Ashteroth in the East—raised splendid palaces, magnificent civilizations.

Then came the Titans, immortal beings who sought control of Elemental and the magic contained within it. They waged war among themselves and in the process turned men into their vassals—or worse. Seeking control of the world's enchantment, in the end they all but destroyed it. At the last of the great battles they waged, the land itself was broken. Civilization perished and the Titans vanished from the world entirely.

What remains now is a single continent—Anthys. The western half belongs to mankind and is ruled by the last of the world's great sorcerers, King Galor. Eastern Anthys is peopled by beings known as the Fallen—creatures that were once men but were long ago twisted into other forms by sorcery. A thousand years ago, there was a war—the War of Magic—between the Kingdoms of Man and the Empires of the Fallen. In the end, the Fallen fled into the distant east. For many years now, there has been peace.

No longer.

The East is stirring once again. Rumor of a dark force rising has reached King Galor. To assess its intent, to gauge what threat it may pose to the west, he has sent his most trusted warriors, the Azure Knights, across the Great Bridge that joins the continent's two halves to seek out Ambrose, Lord of the Keep of the Henge.

BOOK ONE:
XANDER AND GENI

*The Destiny always seek to thwart our kind;
for they despise the nature of the immortal.*

—Kir-Tion, Lord of the Dred'nir

Chapter One

He shouldn't be so far outside the walls.

He shouldn't be away from work so long.

He definitely shouldn't be wasting so much time on what was probably a fool's errand; it was stupid to expect that he'd find any more of the stones out here, even if he looked for hours.

He could hear Saren now: *Stupid boy. Stupid Xander, where were you? What were you doing? I had messages for you to carry, money for you to earn, money to line my pocket, money to feed you and me. You let me down, boy, you let us down, and now what will we have for supper?*

The old man had been like a father to him, Xander reflected. Best to cut his losses now and get back to the Keep while it was still light out. How much longer did he have? He looked up. The afternoon sun, peeking between the leaves of the forest canopy far above, was going down already. Another hour or so of light. He ought to get back. He could hear Saren's disapproving voice in his mind.

He could hear Geni's, too.

Oh, Xander. You shouldn't have.

Five more minutes, he thought. If I don't find one in five more minutes, I'll turn back. He noted the trail markings, and took a few hesitant steps deeper into the forest. The Keeper's Wood. He'd roamed it since he was a boy; knew every one of these trails like the back of his hand. There was no reason to be afraid of anything in here, was there? No reason to be hesitant about what might lurk around the next bend in the path, or behind the massive tree trunks that blocked the way in front of him?

No. No reason at all.

Except that Lord Ambrose had declared the wood off-limits a month earlier. On the day the Knights had ridden in from the West, the Keeper—and his Council—had issued several proclamations. Times have changed, Lord Ambrose had said. Things are no longer as they were. In order to ensure the safety of the Keep and all its residents, I hereby make, in the name of the King, the following proclamations. The wood, off-limits to all but those on the Keeper's business. Etc., etc.

Well, Xander thought. He intended the stones for Geni. So by the strict letter of the law, he was, in fact, here on Lord Ambrose's business. Because Geni was Ambrose's business, wasn't she?

He sighed. Somehow, he didn't think the Lord would see it that way, if Xander were caught and brought before him.

Best to finish here, and get out.

The trail narrowed; it led him downhill to the banks of a small stream. The spring rains had been falling pretty hard for the last week; the little stream had overflowed its bank. He left the path, walked alongside the water for a while, heading back upstream, in the direction of the Keep, using the roots and limbs of some of the trees to keep his balance, to keep from falling in. He was wearing the boots he'd found the other day, and if he got them wet . . .

Treat these well, boy, you could work for a year and not earn enough to buy another pair like them, the devil's own luck you have, finding them in the first place, having them turn out to be your size in the second, boy, boy are you listening, boy?

There'd be hell to pay, he knew.

He walked for a while longer, was about to give up when he saw a glint on the far side of the little stream; something reflecting the last light of the dying sun. It looked like . . . it might be . . . no way to be certain, of course, except to get closer.

It was a good ten feet to the other side of the stream. He was no athlete, Xander knew. He was small for his age, fifteen, and barely a hundred and twenty pounds, and not blessed with the coordination other boys his age were already displaying—the kind of coordination that made for a good warrior. What he was, though, was fast. Nimble. That was what made him such a good messenger.

Closer. How to get closer?

With a running start, that kind of speed might let him jump across the bank. Might. Only one way to find out, wasn't there?

He took a deep breath, a couple of steps back, and leapt.

He didn't make it. But luck was with him. Just as he jumped, he caught sight of a flat rock in the middle of the stream. A dry-looking rock, sticking up out of the water. The jump took him to that, and from that a second jump took him to the other side. And the thing he'd seen glittering in the sun. He bent down and picked it up. He smiled.

It was a small black stone, shaped like an arrowhead—triangular, smooth to the touch on one side, like crystal, rough on the other. A midnight stone—the second one he'd found in the afternoon's searching. Geni would like this one even better than the first; he was sure of it. The shape of it, the way it sparkled . . .

Oh, Xander. You shouldn't have.

He smiled to himself, picturing her. The look on her face.

If my father found out you were in the wood . . .

Who's going to tell him? You?

No. Of course not. But it's not safe.

I was careful. I stuck to the trails. Don't worry about me.

But I do.

Xander pictured himself handing her the stone. Their fingers touch. Their eyes meet.

His stomach rumbled. He pictured another scene.

You let me down, boy, you let us down, and now what will we have for supper?

He blinked, came out of his little reverie, and saw that the shadows around him had lengthened even further. Saren would kill him. And rightfully so. Too dark to run any more messages today, by the time he got back to the Keep. Too dark, even, he realized, to use the trails, overgrown as they'd gotten in the last few weeks. The stream, though, would lead him out. A longer route, but he would end up at the same place when he finished. Everything would be fine.

Except it wasn't.

When he came up out of the wood, when he got to the gate, the three of them were there, waiting for him.

Morlis, Vincor, Oro.

He didn't understand why they hated him so. Geni said it was because they were jealous of him, because he was smart and they weren't, but Xander doubted that. Saren said they were jealous, too, though not because of his brains, but rather because of the fact that he had made friends with Geni and they hadn't. That was probably closer to the truth, Xander thought, but the real reason they tormented him, he'd decided, was that he was an easy target. He was alone. Always alone. An orphan, with no family— no brothers, no cousins, no father, no uncle or grandfather even—to protect him.

"Well, if it isn't the skeleton boy." The biggest of the three youths, the one standing in the middle, took a step forward. Morlis had been a bully for as long as Xander had known him. Had always been big for his age, too. Big, and stupid. He was wearing a stable boy's uniform: tan trousers and jerkin, worn black leather boots. Xander could smell him from where he stood. Morlis had been working in those clothes all day, no doubt. He'd probably work in them tomorrow, too. Probably he'd die in them as well. Xander almost felt sorry for him. Almost.

"What do you want?"

A second boy stepped forward as Xander spoke.

Vincor. He was smaller than Morlis—a year younger than him, too. Fifteen, Xander's own age. The two of them had been friends for a few days, when Xander had first gone to work for Saren. Now . . .

"You hear that, Mor?" Vincor said. "Skelly acts like he don't know what we want. You know what we want, skelly. We want to know what you been doin' in the wood."

"None of your business."

"So you say." That was the third boy speaking. Oro. He was the oldest of the three—and by far the most dangerous. Not as big as Morlis, maybe not even as smart as Vincor, but nastier than the two of them combined. "I say different."

"Let me pass," Xander said.

Oro shook his head. Over his shoulder, in the fading light, Xander saw the walls of the Keep, and the outlines of the South Gate. Safety. It seemed a long way off.

"What you got in them pockets of yours, skelly?" Oro asked. "What you been stealing from the wood, hey?"

"Move," Xander said.

Oro ignored him. "More of them little black stones, I'll bet. Going to give 'em to the princess, ain't ya? Going to try and impress her again."

"None of your business," Xander said again. He thought about turning and running for a second—no way any of these three could catch him. Except that he was tired of running from these three, almost as tired as he was of getting beaten up by them.

"That's it, all right," Oro said. "Ain't it? You got more of them stones?"

"Hand 'em over, skelly." Morlis stepped up alongside his friend. "They belong to us now."

"I don't think so."

"You think wrong, skelly," Oro said. "They're ours now. Rightfully so, in fact."

"How do you figure that?"

" 'Cuz we belong here, and you don't. You're just a little skeleton boy—a little orphan living off the goodwill of others. Scurrying around everywhere, taking what don't belong to you."

"It's not scurrying, Oro. It's called working. Maybe you ought to try it sometime."

"Funny," Oro said.

"True," Xander shot back.

Oro glared at him, and took another step forward, and to his left. Vincor moved forward, too, only to the right. Morlis, in the middle, hung back just a bit.

"Listen, skelly," Oro said. "I—"

And then he charged—in mid-sentence—straight for Xander. A surprise attack, Xander supposed, only he'd seen it coming a mile away. Xander knew how Oro expected him to react, too. He was supposed to turn and run, or try to, anyway. Except that when he turned, Vincor, who had started moving the second Oro did, and was even faster than the other boy, would be right behind him. Then Xander was supposed to turn again and run the only way left for him to go, which was straight ahead, straight into Morlis's arms. That's when the beating would start. That was their plan, he knew, and he wasn't having any of it.

He didn't back off, like Oro expected. He charged straight at Morlis, who was only just getting set. Morlis, Xander knew, was not only a bully, but a coward at heart who would not stand his ground. The boy saw him coming, his eyes widened, and he took a sudden instinctual step backward. Coward.

Xander darted past. Morlis recovered and lunged for him. Xander twisted his body out of the way, and ran free, straight for the South Gate.

That was the idea, anyway.

Unfortunately, Xander wasn't quite fast enough. Not quite flexible enough.

Morlis grabbed the tail end of his shirt and yanked him backward.

"Nice try, skelly," he said, and shoved Xander to the dirt. Xander hit the ground hard; his elbow slammed into a stone, and pain shot up his arm.

"Yeah. Nice try," Oro said, and then kicked him in the stomach.

Xander had seen that coming, too, and hunched over to protect himself. Not fast enough, though—Oro's boot dug right into his gut, and he gasped in pain.

Vincor kicked him in the leg.

"Cough 'em up, skelly," he said. "Cough up them stones."

And then Oro kicked him in the head—or tried to. Xander moved just in time, and the tip of the boy's boot caught him in the back of the neck. Hard.

He cried out in pain.

"Think that hurts, skelly? Try this," he heard Oro say, and then he felt the boot kick him again. Square in the back of the head. Tears came to his eyes.

"Yeah, Oro," Morlis said. "Yeah. My turn."

Xander felt a hand grab his shirt, and was vaguely aware of getting dragged to his feet. Then Morlis's hot, steamy, stinking breath was in his face.

"Here you go, skelly," Morlis said, and then Xander saw the bully pull back his fist and prepared for the inevitable blow.

"Stop," a voice commanded.

Morlis's arm froze.

"Hell," the boy said. "Now we're in for it."

"Finish him," Oro hissed. "Now."

"Not me." Morlis shook his head. "I'm not having her mad at me."

He let go of Xander's shirt; Xander fell to the ground again, a smile on his face.

Her.

Geni.

"You three are lower than worms!" the voice—now recognizable—yelled again. "You had better hope he's all right, or I will have you and your families thrown off the cliffs, do you hear me?"

"We didn't—"

"He started it. We—"

"It's just a friendly little—"

"Leave. Now!" Geni shouted, overriding the attackers' objections, in a voice that demanded obedience.

Xander heard the sound of mumbled excuses, and the three boys backing away.

He sat up, and it was only then that he realized that the stone his arm had slammed into was one of the massive slates belonging to what remained of the Lord Protector's Road, most of which was now overgrown with the scrub and grass. In the old days, Saren had told him, the road had been a gleaming highway, running from the heart of old Imperium in the East to the very shores of Lycea, through jungle and desert, over mountain and river. The road had been a place of refuge, of safety, of safe passage guaranteed not just by treaty, but—some said—by enchantment.

If he believed in magic, Xander would have said that enchantment seemed to still be working.

"Are you all right?"

He looked up and saw Geni standing over him.

She was wearing a long cloak. Underneath it, he saw, was a dress.

Geni never used to wear dresses.

"Sure," he said, getting to his feet. "Never better."

"You don't look it." She reached out a hand and touched his cheek.

"Ow."

"That'll be a nasty bruise in the morning."

"I've had worse. Probably will again, if the three of them have anything to say about it."

"Oro's the problem," Geni said. "The other two are idiots."

"They're all idiots." Xander sighed. "Did you mean that—about throwing them off the cliffs?"

"I did. Unfortunately, I don't think my father would approve. And speaking of my father not approving . . . you went in there again, didn't you?" She gestured toward the wood behind him.

He shrugged. "Maybe."

"Xander . . ." Her face darkened. "It's dangerous."

"I can take care of myself."

"Really?" She stared at him. At the bruise he felt growing on his cheek.

He felt himself flush with anger, and embarrassment. "In the wood, I mean. I know the wood."

"Of course you do. But may I remind you, my father has issued a proclamation—"

"I know about the proclamation," he interrupted.

"But you went in anyway."

"Yes."

"Why?"

"Because," he said, and pulled the stones out of his pocket, and held them out to her.

She looked down at them, and then back up at him. For a second her eyes shone with pleasure.

In that second, she was Geni again, not the princess. The girl he'd met the very first day he'd started working for Saren, the girl who trailed him around the Keep for a good week before he'd found out who she was, Lord Ambrose's daughter, Princess Angenica herself, the Lady-of-the-Castle-in-waiting. Not that she acted like a princess—not back then. The two of them spent hours together, exploring, playing, getting into places—the shopkeepers' quarter, the orphans' quarter, the little warren of streets that made up the Armorer's Way, places none of the other girls who had been Princess of the Keep before her had ever been, Xander was sure. Geni was right at home in all of them; she got along with everyone she met. Better than he did, to tell the truth. People liked her, right off. They didn't really like him. Or rather, they didn't notice him. He was pretty easy to ignore, Xander had to admit. Not that imposing physically, no special talent to make him stand out in the crowd. People looked at him and looked past almost like he wasn't even there. Unless he was with Geni.

Which hadn't been quite so often, these last few months. Not his fault; hers. She couldn't get out of the Keep as much to ride, or explore. She had lessons all the time—the ways of the court, the history of the world, music. She wore makeup. And dresses.

She was becoming a princess. And he was staying a messenger.

She was pulling away from him.

That was why he'd gone in search of the midnight stones—last week, and now today. Never mind Ambrose's proclamation, once he saw how heavy the rains had been he knew some of the old stones would be showing up in the river, and he wanted her to have them. Wanted her to have the reaction she was having this very second.

And then that second passed.

"You should bring these to the observatory," she said. "To Mirdoth. My father's mage. He will want to examine them—"

"I know who Mirdoth is," Xander snapped. "I got them for you."

"Oh, Xander." She shook her head. "You shouldn't have."

The two of them stared at each other for a moment.

There was a line of trees leading back along the path to the Keep; over Geni's shoulder, in the shade of the nearest of those trees, Xander saw that there was a man standing. A man in armor. Leeland. Geni's guard. Of course, he thought. Geni wouldn't have come here alone. She couldn't go anywhere alone these days.

"Saren was looking for you, too, you know."

He wasn't surprised. "Okay."

"It's not okay. That old man depends on you, Xander. You don't work, he doesn't eat. You don't work, he doesn't have a place to live. You know that, don't you?"

"Don't lecture me."

"I'm not lecturing. I'm reminding you of your obligations. And the law."

"Thanks so much."

"Xander." She drew herself up. "We're friends. You know that. But I'm more than your friend. I have to be. I'm the—"

"Princess," he snapped. "I get it. Your Majesty."

She glared at him for a second. Then she held out her hand.

"Here. Take your stupid stones."

She dropped them into his outstretched palm, then spun on her heel and stalked away.

Xander watched her go. When she reached the guard, she turned for a second and looked back at him.

He turned and threw them back into the wood.

CHAPTER TWO

"Idiot," Geni said, shaking her head.

She couldn't believe what Xander had just done. Did he know how rare those stones were? How important they might be? How much Mirdoth would want to look at them?

Of course he did. She'd told him so herself. Did he care? No. Obviously not.

"Everything all right?" Leeland asked.

"Fine," she snapped. "Let's go."

The captain fell into step alongside her; she barely noted his presence. All she could see was Xander, glaring at her. Like she was the one who'd done something wrong.

Princess. Your Majesty.

As if she ever treated him like anything but an equal.

"The boy's not hurt too badly?" Leeland asked.

"No. He's fine."

"Good thing you knew where to look for him."

"Hmmmphh." Good thing. She wasn't so sure about that. Xander was so predictable; five minutes after he hadn't shown up for their rendezvous ("You want to know more about what I've been doing these last few weeks? You want to see what I'm learning? Then meet me at the observatory after the fourth watch"), she had a pretty good idea where he was. What he was doing. She hadn't told Leeland her suspicions, of course. She just asked the captain to escort her—not that she could have stopped him; her father had forbidden her to go outside the walls of the Keep alone. He had stated, quite explicitly, in a tone and manner he had never, ever used with her, how important it was that she not go out alone. Thus Leeland had followed her—through the South Gate, to the edge of the wood. She'd told him she was expecting to meet Xander there; he hadn't disappointed.

The three others—Morlis, Oro, and the third, whose name she could not even recall at the moment—had been a surprise. A temporary distraction. Which had prevented her from delivering to Xander the speech she had been planning the last few days.

The speech she had memorized; you have to understand that things are changing for me now, Xander, you heard what my father said, you heard the stories the Knights brought with them, villages burned in Kraxis, traders and caravans attacked within sight of Outpost, murder in Red Spring . . . I don't have time to go roaming in the tunnels with you anymore. I have responsibilities; things to manage. To learn. People who depend on me. I can't be just Geni anymore, I'm a—"

"He was in the wood, wasn't he?"

"What?" Geni shot back automatically, though she'd heard well enough.

"The boy. He wasn't meeting you on the road; he went into the wood itself."

She gave Leeland a worried look.

If the captain told her father, Xander would get the lash. He might even get sent to the dungeons. Much as she felt like hitting him herself this second, Geni didn't want that.

But she couldn't lie. If there was anything she'd learned from the lessons Mirdoth had been giving her, it was the dangers of that first lie. The little one, which led to bigger and bigger falsehoods, bigger and bigger problems.

"Yes," she said. "He was. But it was my fault."

"Your fault."

"Yes."

"How is his being in the wood your fault? Unless you deliberately told him to break your father's laws . . . ?"

"No. Of course not." She explained then how she'd made such a fuss over the first of the midnight stones, when Xander brought it to her. How that fuss had encouraged him to go back into the wood seeking more.

"I see," Leeland said thoughtfully.

"You won't tell him, Captain. My father?"

"No. I won't." A smile flitted across Leeland's face and was just as quickly gone. The captain—head shaved, iron-gray beard, blue eyes that sparkled for her but burned for everyone else—seemed ageless to Geni. He looked the same to her now as he had when she'd first seen him, come to fetch her five-year-old self to a ceremony of some sort her father had requested she attend. Leeland had arrived in the middle of an argument between Geni and the long-gone (and much-despised) Lady Mircella, who to Geni's way of thinking (at the time, at least) was no lady, but a protocol-obsessed, pinch-faced old hag who insisted on making Geni comb her hair, bathe regularly, and wear, if not dresses, then at least clean clothes. Mircella had lasted only a few months before quitting, removing herself and her whole family to the court at Athica, where presumably she'd found charges more to her liking. Poor woman.

Leeland had interrupted Geni's tantrum by clearing his throat, and speaking directly to her. Looking her straight in the eye as he did so.

"I wouldn't have that sort of behavior," he had said, loud and clear. "Not in your father's guard."

Geni had frowned. Geni had stopped screaming. Geni had put on new trousers and gone off to the ceremony without another word, Leeland trailing a step or two behind.

He'd been with her ever since. Much more frequently these days.

"Midnight stones, you say?" the captain asked.

"Yes."

"And he found two more of them tonight, Xander did? That's what he threw back into the wood?"

"Yes."

"Shame." Leeland shook his head. "Those things are hard to find. Valuable."

"I know that," Geni said with a trace of irritation. She knew what those stones were, what they represented. Xander hadn't. He'd thought they were just shiny rocks. Pretty rocks. Unbelievable.

Rocks. She'd shaken her head. *These aren't rocks.*

Well, what are they, then? he'd asked. *Tell me.*

And so she had—legends of times thousands of years in the past, the time of the Titans, the creatures they'd made, golems constructed from the stuff of Elemental itself, massive, monstrous, monstrously powerful beings who had fought alongside men and the Fallen in the final, epic battles before the Cataclysm. The golems, so Mirdoth had told her, had been—like so many other things—destroyed in that last conflagration. Their very bodies splintered into thousands of pieces, scattered across the ruined land. You can find them from time to time, Mirdoth had said. If you're scrupulous about looking; if you're patient. Midnight stones. The King himself was said to collect them; she knew Mirdoth had sent the handful that he possessed to Galor, in far-off Athica, long ago.

She also knew her father had a half dozen of the stones as well that he had kept secret from everyone. They were strung into a necklace that had belonged to her mother, hidden in the drawer of the bureau that had once belonged to her, too.

The one Xander had given her that she had passed on to Mirdoth was the only other that she knew of. Except for the two that Xander had just tossed back into the wood. Idiot.

"Still. Brave lad. Go off all alone, into the wood like that," Leeland said.

"Stupid, is more like it."

"No. He's a smart boy," Leeland said. "Just not thinking clearly around you these days."

"What?"

"Not really my place to talk about these kind of things with you, Princess," Leeland said. "But he likes you. Xander."

Under her cloak, Geni flushed.

She didn't know what to say.

" 'Course, he needs to have the law laid down for him. Have things spelled out," Leeland continued. "You and him . . . like that. Not gonna happen, is it?"

"No," Geni snapped. "Of course not."

"Of course not," Leeland repeated. "You'll want to let him down easy, I expect. Seein' as how the two of you have been friends such a long time."

"Yes." She nodded. "Let him down gently. You're right."

Leeland stroked his beard. "I could do it if you want."

"No no no no no," she said quickly. "I'll handle it. I can do it."

It was Leeland's turn to nod.

"I think you're right. Best you do it." He cleared his throat. "That's if you want to let him down, of course."

"Of course I do. He's a messenger, Captain. That's all he'll ever be."

However, she knew Xander had other ideas. Other plans. He wanted to see the world; they had talked about going to Zabril, the painted jungle, to Athica, to see the King, and the library at New Pariden, and even—when they were older, of course, and stronger, and had the money to hire an army of their own to go with them—braving the Wastes, and making their way across the Spine, up to the ruins of fabled Imperium itself. Being the first citizens of the Kingdom since the Empire of Sorcery to stand inside its walls. Assuming those walls were still standing, as Xander had pointed out. After the last war, the lands to the east were desolate. Nothing lived there now. At least, that was what she had been told.

She sensed Leeland's eyes on her for a moment, studying her. She felt herself flush again.

"Mmmm," the captain said.

" 'Mmmm.' " Geni frowned. "What does that mean?"

"Nothing, my lady," Leeland said. "You're right. The boy's just a messenger indeed. A very fast one, though."

"Yes. He is that. Quick."

"He'd be good with a sword."

"Xander?" Geni almost laughed. "With a sword? Captain, you can't be serious."

"Just thinking out loud, Princess. The boy is fast, like I said. And smart."

"That won't make him a good swordsman."

"Of course not. He'll need training for that."

"You'd take him into the guard?"

Leeland shrugged. "When all this passes . . . when things settle down again . . . I might. I was ward myself to Captain Grader, once upon a time. In fact—"

Leeland, all at once, stopped walking.

"Captain?" Geni said.

He put a finger to his mouth.

"Shhh."

Geni looked ahead. Leeland was scanning the road in front of them as well. Smaller trees—isolated patches of wood, and shrub—lined the path to the South Gate. They were designed as ornament, not cover. But the sky was cloudy, the moon obscured; the way ahead was dark.

"Heard something," he said.

"You think there's someone out there?" Geni whispered.

He nodded.

"Something," he said quietly, and drew his sword. "Probably just one of those boys. Thinking to scare you and Xander."

She nodded. That made sense. Probably so.

But there was a little tingle of foreboding at the base of her spine.

Leeland listened for a moment longer, then pointed with his sword toward a copse of evergreen, up ahead and to the right. "There," he said. "Something in the patch of wood there."

He took a step forward. "Boys!" he shouted. "Come out now. No fooling."

There was no response.

The three of them wouldn't be stupid enough to attack one of her father's guard—they probably thought she was with Xander, Geni decided. Walking back to the Keep with him. They'd changed their mind; they weren't scared of her anymore, they were looking to put a little fright into her and Xander. Now that they'd heard Leeland's voice, though, they'd surely slink back away, run back to the Keep on their own. Any second now, she and the captain would see the three little cowards break free of the trees and head off down the road to safety.

But nothing moved.

Leeland didn't move, either. The captain stood motionless, eyes focused like a hawk's on the road ahead.

Geni came up behind him and stood at his shoulder. It had gotten so dark, so quickly. She couldn't see a thing ahead of her save the Keep itself.

The wind blew. Geni wrinkled her nose and frowned.

"What is that smell?" she asked.

"Ey?" Leeland asked. "What smell? What—"

His sword, all at once, fell to his side.

"Gods," he whispered, and Geni sensed something in his voice that she had never heard from the captain before, not in all the years she had known him.

Fear.

"The Knights—they were right," Leeland said, taking a step backward, simultaneously sheathing his sword. "They have crossed the Wastes. Run, girl. For the wood. The gatehouse—"

"What are you talking about?" Geni asked.

"The Fallen," Leeland said, turning to face her, and in his eyes she saw mirrored the fear that she heard in his voice. "Back to the wood," he said. "Now."

The captain took her by the shoulder and physically spun her around. Then he said something else, something she couldn't quite make out.

"What?" she asked, turning to face him.

He was clawing at the tip of an arrow, coming out of his throat.

Blood was spilling down his hands.

Geni took a step backward and screamed.

CHAPTER THREE

Living in Walderon wasn't cheap. So Saren kept telling him.

"That's where the merchants live, boy. The Lords of Capitar. That's their city. Where they keep their houses, their businesses, their families. Their mistresses." The old man cackled. "What do you want to know about Walderon for, anyway?"

Xander had mumbled some excuse or another—something about being curious. He would never tell Saren the truth—never share with him what he'd shared with Geni, the desire he had to get out of Outpost altogether someday, as soon as he was able to afford it. The old man would make fun of him, never mind that Saren had lived half his life away from the freezing cold of the Northern Lands, had been born and grown up in one of the villages just south of Capitar's most famous port, had lived in the shadow of the great city until his wife died, and had then decided to see what the rest of the world looked like. Crossed the western continent, and then headed east.

The old man had seen the world. Xander wanted the chance to do that, too, before he got old. At one point he'd thought maybe he and Geni would be able to do that together. He'd been foolish. Naïve. She was a princess, and he was—well, not a prince, that was for sure.

Whatever exploring he wanted to do, he'd have to do on his own.

Which meant getting together money before he left Outpost. Enough to live on for a few weeks at least, before he found his way—wherever it was he was going to go. He'd gone hungry enough nights to know that he didn't want to do it again—not ever. If Saren's figures about what things cost in the West weren't an exaggeration, that meant it would be about four times as expensive to live in Walderon as it was here in the Keep. That would mean a job other than messenger, though he didn't know what else he was qualified for. Could he apprentice to a smith, or a tailor? A stonemason? Could he be a soldier? He was fast. Why not?

He'd asked that question of Geni once, when she put the question to him—what are you going to do with your life? She'd burst out laughing—you, a soldier? Why not? Because you're eighty pounds soaking wet, Xander. I weigh more than you do.

He'd flushed redder than the crimson on the Keep's carpets, largely because it was true. Geni was bigger than he was; at least she had been back then, and probably as strong, if not as quick. Better trained, too—they'd had a few mock duels before Captain Leeland put a stop to them; it was only because he was faster that he'd been able to fight her to a draw. Of course, he'd grown since then. A lot, over the last few months. His shirts were getting tight across the shoulders, his pants a few inches short of his ankles . . . Gods, he'd need clothes, too, wouldn't he, if he were to go to Walderon? He couldn't walk around in these old rags forever. And how much would those cost him? Where was he going to get all that money?

He sighed.

In the distance, someone screamed.

Xander, who'd been walking in circles around the long-abandoned gatehouse that marked the official entrance to the wood, kicking at the dead branches on the path in front of him, stopped short.

The someone screamed again.

The someone, Xander realized, was Geni.

In the observatory—along the curving wall opposite the great scope that Mirdoth used to scan the skies, and make his observations—there were shelves stacked with books, volumes that over the last few months had formed the subject matter of her lessons.

There, Geni had seen histories written by the great scholars of the West; journals of the world's most famous explorers; scientific treatises by the thinkers of times past. Some so old that the paper threatened to disintegrate in her hands. Books written in languages that bore no resemblance to modern-day tongues, and that Mirdoth had to translate for her. Books that purported to tell the true story of the Cataclysm, the Titans, and the various changes they'd wrought on the world—including the creation of the creatures collectively known as the Fallen.

According to some accounts, the Fallen had arrived on Elemental with the Titans, had been brought along from whatever ethereal realm those beings had come from. Other historians wrote that the Fallen had been raised by the Dred'nir Lord Curgen from the mud and vines of long-vanished Al-Ashteroth, or that the Titans had constructed them piecemeal from the uncounted dead armies of men who had fallen in battle, fighting for the likes of Curgen and the Lady Umber.

"All of which is nonsense," Mirdoth had told her when she'd come to him, troubled by the conflicting accounts she'd read. "The Fallen—Urxen, Trog, Sion, Edar—all of them, they are different versions of man and woman."

"Different how?" she had asked, and Mirdoth had proceeded to go into great detail then, to show her anatomical drawings of creatures that curdled her blood, shaped like men, yes, but different, unnatural, creatures that looked wrong to her somehow, not just because of the color of their skin but because of the way they were put together.

Like the creature that stood before her now, pulling its arrow out of Captain Leeland's neck. It had the shape of a man, but stood half a foot taller. Its neck seemed somehow elongated, its head perched at a slightly different angle than she was used to seeing.

This particular Fallen, unless she was mistaken, was an Urxen.

"Look what we've found," it said, and a smile crossed its lips. "A girl-child."

From behind the thing two more of its kind stepped forward.

All were dressed similarly—in vests of chain mail that left their corded, hairless arms bare. They wore loose-fitting trousers whose color Geni couldn't make out in the dim light, and boots that raised their height to well over six feet. Their hair was long, and white, and even in the darkness Geni could see that it was matted, and unwashed. The Fallen, by all the accounts she had read, cared little for personal hygiene. That much at least was true; she could verify it firsthand now.

They stank to high heaven. The same smell that had put fear into Leeland's heart.

She glanced at the captain's body and shivered.

"A girl. Yes, indeed, Fened. Looks like a ripe one, too, from what I can tell," said another of the creatures.

The one on her right—was it a he? Geni assumed they were all male—stepped forward. The one who had killed Leeland, she guessed, as it had a bow in one hand, a quiver of arrows slung over its shoulder, and a leer on its face. She shivered a second time.

There were stories in some of the histories she'd read about what the Fallen did to women. Geni tried awfully hard to block those words—and the images that went along with them—from her mind.

Escape, she thought. But how? The South Gate was too far

away for anyone to have heard her scream—that was why Leeland had turned her for the wood, toward the gatehouse. It would have taken a siege engine to break through the walls of that structure. The two of them could have held off an army of Fallen until help arrived.

No help was coming now, though.

She was going to have to manage this on her own.

"Mercy," she said, taking a step backward, trying to look as panicked as she could. Not a stretch. She was terrified. Her heart beat wildly in her chest as she held her left hand up, palm outstretched in front of her, as if to fend off her attackers. "Please—don't hurt me."

The one that had yanked the arrow from Leeland's throat—Fened, the other had called it—laughed and lunged forward. It grabbed her wrist. Its grip was strong; ungodly strong. Its fingers felt like chains tightening around her bones. It drew her closer.

With her free hand, she reached beneath her cloak and drew the knife from the sash of her gown. She stabbed the creature holding her in the gut. The plan was kill it and run.

The blade hit chain mail, though, not flesh; hit it hard enough to numb her fingers. The knife fell from her grasp and hit the ground.

The Urxen holding her laughed.

"Teeth," it said, turning to face its brethren. "The little one has teeth. She tried to stab me."

"Careful, Fened. Perhaps it bites as well," another said, and then they all laughed.

Geni reared back with all her strength and kicked the creature holding her in the shins. The Urxen—Fened—snarled and loosened its grip. She turned to run, and saw then that there were two more of them, right behind her. Urxen as well.

She was surrounded.

"You will pay for that, little one," Fened said, and took a step forward.

Geni took a step back. What could she do? Scream? Surrender? Neither of those things would do her any good in the long run, would make any difference.

She might as well go down fighting.

She eyed the knife that had fallen to the ground. Fened stood practically on top of it. How she was going to get the blade back in her hands . . .

"Take that cloak off, little female." Fened leered. "Let me make sure you have no further weapons."

She took another step back.

Hands shoved her forward, at the same time yanking her cloak free, revealing the fact that she was wearing a dress.

Her mother's dress. Deep green silk, with an inlay of diamonds along the neckline.

Fened saw it and stopped short.

"Well, well," he said. "What have we here?"

"It's a dress, idiot," she snapped.

One of the Fallen snickered; Fened silenced it with a glare.

"A very nice dress." The creature took a step forward and ran a finger over the jewels sewn into the collar. "A very shiny dress. A very expensive dress, I think. Yes?"

Little doubt of that, Geni thought. This was one of the dresses her mother had worn for affairs of state, when the Lords of Capitar, or Kraxis, or the King's ambassadors came calling. A dress designed to show that the Keep possessed wealth and standing of its own, that—

Her train of thought came to an abrupt, crashing stop.

In the copse of trees the Fallen had first emerged from, she saw movement. Someone darting from tree trunk to tree trunk. A thin, lithe, familiar form.

Xander.

"This is no commoner's dress, I think. What is your name, girl?" Fened asked. "Who are you?"

She looked at him, and then—for a second—back toward the

copse. Toward Xander, who was half crouching, half striding toward them.

No, Geni thought. No, no, no. Run, you idiot. Run back to the Keep. Get help. Run. What good are you going to be against five Urxen soldiers?

But Xander kept coming.

"Answer the question, girl," Fened said, and suddenly there was something sharp pressing into her neck. "Who are you?"

Geni looked down and saw that the Fallen leader was holding a knife to her throat.

"Mircella," she said without thinking. "I am handmaiden to Saren, a great merchant of the Keep."

"A handmaiden. With her own personal guard." Fened shook his head. "I doubt that. Your real name, girl. And the truth now, or my blade draws blood."

The tip of the knife dug deeper into her throat. The creature leaned closer. Its breath smelled worse than even its body.

"You stink," she said. "You need a bath."

"Perhaps you can give me one. After our conversation."

"Perhaps you can drop dead."

Fened froze.

The voice was Xander's. He stood behind the circle of Fallen, facing Geni, next to Captain Leeland's body. He was holding something at his side that he raised as all turned to face him. A large stone.

"A boy," Fened said, and laughed. "And a rock."

The others laughed as well.

"Kill him," Fened said, and in that instant, Xander, who had stood motionless, let fly the stone.

Geni heard a whooshing sound, and then a loud thwop!—the sound of something hard hitting something softer—and watched in astonishment as Fened toppled over backward and fell to the ground.

The other Fallen looked shocked, too.

Xander screamed and charged, picking up another stone.

Geni picked up the knife and screamed as well, charging the nearest of the Fallen soldiers.

It blinked, and then smiled, and smacked the weapon out of her hand. Then it backhanded her across the mouth; she staggered backward, and sat down hard on the ground.

Xander was also on the ground. Another of the Fallen stood over him, its boot pressed in his gut, spear in hand.

"Last words, manling," it said. "Have any?"

"The Destiny take you," Xander said, spitting at it.

The creature laughed. "I think they take you first, boy," it said, and raised its spear over its head.

"Not so fast," a voice said. A man's voice. For a second, Geni's heart lifted. Guards—from the Keep, she thought. Rescue. Salvation.

And then she saw that the man who had spoken was alone. A single figure, walking toward them, not from the Keep but from the east. He carried a sword stranger than any Geni had ever seen in her life; it had only a single edge and was slightly curved.

One man. Against five of these creatures?

Then the hilt of the blade caught the moonlight for a second, long enough for Geni to see embedded within it a band of gems, each colored the same shade of blue. No, she realized. Not blue. Azure.

For a second her heart lifted.

And then the Urxen—all five of them, moving with deadly, coordinated precision—charged. They never stood a chance.

CHAPTER FOUR

"I will have his head," Lord Ambrose said.

"Undoubtedly, my lord."

"I am serious, Mirdoth."

"I understand, lord."

"What was he thinking? For the sake of the Gods—for the sake of the Destiny itself . . ." Ambrose pushed back from the table and got to his feet. "I gave specific instructions. Did I not give specific instructions?"

Mirdoth, Ambrose's chief counselor, had served his family for eighty years and looked much the same as he had when he assumed lordship over the Henge after his father had passed. Thin as a rail, with a short silver-gray beard, Mirdoth sipped at his wine and nodded.

"You did indeed, my lord."

"I will have his head," Ambrose said again. "Mounted on my wall. So I can curse at it as often as I like."

Ambrose walked from the table to the fire warming the Hall. It was still cold enough outside to make the blaze necessary, though they were past the dead of winter, when having the fire—and the wood to keep it going—had been a matter of life and death. For now it was just ornamentation, like the ornate tapestry above it of the King, Galor himself, as he had looked in his prime, centuries ago. A larger-than-life Galor, twenty feet tall, a veritable God among men, sitting on his throne, smiling beneficently down on the Great Hall, as if all were right in the world.

But all was not right.

It was an hour past table, and the princess and her guard were not only late, but missing. Nowhere in the Keep itself, nor in the village of Outpost surrounding it. One of the guards on the South Gate thought he had seen someone resembling Leeland leaving shortly before dusk, but couldn't swear to it. Ambrose had a mind to put the man in irons—what sort of guard was it that couldn't recall exactly what had passed in front of him not more than an hour earlier?—but the look on Mirdoth's face as he questioned the man had stopped him. Patience.

Ambrose turned to his counselor in time to see the man stab another potato from the tray in front of him and pop it into his mouth.

"How can you eat at a time like this?"

"Should I waste the cook's efforts, Lord? Best not to let it go to waste."

Ambrose growled.

"I am going to check with the watch commanders."

"Lord." Mirdoth set his napkin in his lap, and sat. "They would be here instantaneously, were there any news."

"You advise me to sit here and do nothing?"

Mirdoth sighed. "There is nothing more that can be done in this matter, Lord. You have sent out patrols. You have questioned the watch. You—"

"I cannot just sit here and wait!"

"Then let us use the time productively. Summon the generals, summon the watch commander. Let us review the mustering rolls the villagers have sent us, to begin better assessing the size of the force we can field. We need to choose officers, we need to send to Minoch for arms—and armorers, for that matter; you heard what

Hulwain said about the capabilities of the smiths here. Their intentions may be good but—"

"I cannot think of these things, Mirdoth! Not while Geni is out there." Ambrose slammed his fist down on the dining table; glasses and plates trembled and rattled with the force of his blow. "He should have known better. Leeland."

"Agreed."

"I'll have his hide. His head."

"So you have said."

"I'll say it a thousand times, damn it! Leeland should never—"

"I suspect the captain had little choice in the matter, my lord. Your daughter can be most insistent when it comes to freedom of movement. I recall long ago a young lad who was much the same way."

"She needs to be told no once in a while. That's all it takes." Ambrose turned and found himself looking up at the tapestry of Galor once more.

If Geni were lost, the King would have words—more than words—for him as well. His daughter figured highly in Galor's plans for the future. As Ambrose himself had, once upon a time.

Mirdoth came and stood next to him.

"You are worried what the King will say."

"I am more worried about Geni."

"She will be fine."

"How can you be so certain?"

"I have a sense for these things." Mirdoth smiled.

At that instant, there was a rush of voices from the corridor outside, and the door to the Great Hall burst open. The guards moved to block the door, and then stepped aside.

Geni burst into the room, sobbing, and ran to Ambroses's arms.

She was also, he saw, wearing one of Odona's dresses.

"Daddy," she said, and squeezed him tighter than she had in a long time.

"Geni," he said, stroking her hair. "What's happened? What . . ."

He saw blood—a thin red stain—on her throat, and a red haze of anger clouded his eyes.

"Who did this to you?" he asked. "Who—"

"Fallen," she said, and pushed back from him abruptly. "They killed Leeland."

"What?"

"He's dead," she said, and started crying all over again.

"The Fallen? Here?" He looked over at Mirdoth, who wore the same stunned expression Ambrose knew was spread across his own face.

"I'm afraid so, Lord." A man stepped into the Hall now. It took Ambrose a moment to recognize him. Tandis. Captain of the Azure Knights. A month ago, he had ridden through the Keep with a hundred of his men, all of them wearing cloaks of dark, shimmering blue. "And there is worse news still."

Tandis's cloak was gone now. His tunic was torn, filthy, and stained with blood.

"Worse news," Mirdoth said. "Have you lost your knack for specificity, Captain?"

Tandis turned to the old man. "Not at all," he said. "I can be very specific indeed. The Fallen have crossed the Wastes. They are burning Kaden's Harbor as we speak. They will be here in the morning."

CHAPTER FIVE

"We killed six of them. An advance patrol." Xander, who had come in behind Tandis, stepped forward. "They were attacking Geni. Well, I killed one. He"—Xander pointed toward Tandis—"killed the rest. Two with one stroke of the blade. I—"

Tandis lay a hand on his shoulder.

"That is enough, boy," he said. "You have done well."

"But—"

"The Lord and I have things to discuss. Wait outside. We will call for you." The knight, Tandis, frowned down at him. The same way he'd been looking at Xander ever since the fight had ended, as he'd been pulling his sword from the body of the last of the Fallen warriors. As if Xander had done something wrong. What? He'd wanted to kill all of them himself? Admittedly, his stone throw had been an incredibly lucky strike.

He'd have to find out later, Xander supposed as Ambrose's guards escorted him out of the room. The great oak doors slammed shut, leaving him alone in the corridor. There was a bench of sorts, a rough-hewn slab of oak with two squat logs at either end for support, backed against the wall opposite the door to the Hall. With a sigh, Xander went to it and sat down.

Wait outside. We will call for you.

How long would they be? He was starving. Xander wondered if he had time to run down to the kitchen. Elana would sneak him some food, for sure—day-old bread, some of the leftovers from Ambrose's table . . . he could maybe even get enough to take back to Saren. A peace offering. The old man would be furious with him now. Probably, he'd be locked out of the hut tonight; have to find someplace else to sleep. Thank the Destiny it was spring; anywhere he could find to lay his head without paying for a night's rest would most likely not have a fire. The thing to do, Xander thought, would be to bring Saren something besides a peace offering; get the old man where it really mattered. In the purse. The promise of more business from Lord Ambrose. Geni might be able to make that happen, if she was so inclined. He doubted she was mad at him anymore; he'd saved her life, right? Well . . . he and Tandis. Besides, their fight earlier—about the stones, about Geni's comings and goings—probably seemed as stupid to her as it did to him now. The Fallen had crossed the Wastes. Everything was different now.

"Hey, skelly."

Xander turned, and looked, and shot up off the bench.

Oro was walking down the corridor, right toward him.

"What are you doing here?" He took a step back defensively, glancing quickly behind him. Nobody. But Morlis and Vincor— where were they? The three of them went everywhere together, although surely they couldn't be so stupid as to attack him here in the Keep . . .

"Easy, skelly." The other boy smiled. "Relax."

"So you can jump me? Not likely."

"I'm not going to hurt you. I brought you a present."

"Right. A present. I'll bet—"

Oro held out his hand. In it was a piece of paper. A present?

"What's that?" Xander asked.

"A message."

"For me?"

"Yeah. For you." He gestured with the paper. "Come on, take it."

"Who's it from?"

"Saren."

"Saren?" This had to be a trick of some kind. Why would Oro have a message from Saren?

Xander looked at the smile on Oro's face, and the glint in the boy's eye, and down at the paper in his hand, and got a sudden, sinking feeling in the pit of his stomach.

He snatched the paper away and unfolded it.

> *Xander:*
> *Your services are no longer necessary. My boy has*
> *your things.*
> *Saren*

My boy. Oro?

"What's this mean?" Xander asked, holding up the little slip of paper.

"Just what it says, skelly. He don't want you working for him anymore. Saren." Oro's smile widened. "On account of he's got me now."

"What?"

"Yeah. I'm his new messenger. Got me a whole stack of important papers to deliver right here." Oro was wearing a pouch, Xander saw now, a pouch that hung from a strap over his shoulder, a pouch full to bursting with paper, a pouch that, as he swung it around from back to front to show him, Xander saw was the same one he'd been using the past half-dozen years, the brown leather one with the King's own insignia pressed into it, the one Saren had given him a few weeks after he'd started working for the older man.

"That's mine," Xander said.

" 'Fraid not. The old man handed it over to me once I said I was ready to go to work."

"You, a messenger? Ha!"

"You can do it, I figure I can do it better. Beats working for Hulwain, I can tell you that right off. Saren's place, he's got a nice soft bed out in the kitchen . . . ah well, but you know that already, don't ya?"

Xander glared. "I don't know what you told Saren, but once I talk to him—"

"Just told him the truth, skelly. What I seen."

"What you seen."

"Yeah. We ran into him when we came through the South Gate. He was looking for you. I told him where you was: lounging around the wood with your little princess . . . Never heard so many curse words in my life." Oro's smile widened. "Anyway. I better get going. Work to do, you know. Responsibilities. Just wanted to deliver that." He gestured toward the now-crumpled-up piece of paper in Xander's hand. "And so . . ."

No, Xander thought. This wouldn't last; he'd talk to Saren and get everything straightened out. In fact, he'd go to the old man right now. This second. "Saren," he'd say. "I apologize. I let you down. I know it, and I'm sorry. I promise—"

All at once he heard Tandis's voice in his head.

Wait outside. We will call for you.

He'd have to deal with Saren later, Xander realized. Probably tomorrow.

"Somethin' the matter, skelly?" Oro asked.

"My things," Xander snapped. "Saren said you had my things . . ."

"Your things." Oro screwed up his face, pretending to be lost in thought. "Oh yeah. Your things. Must've dropped 'em somewhere. In all my messengerin' around."

"Stolen them is more like it. Where are they, Oro? My clothes. My books—"

"Dunno." Oro frowned. "Gee. Maybe your little princess will buy you new ones."

"Where are they?" Xander took a step forward. "Morlis and Vincor have them, don't they?"

"And if they do?" Oro sneered. "What are you going to do about it?"

"Why don't I start by beating some answers out of you?" Xander asked.

"You don't have the guts to do anything without your little princess around, skelly, and you know it." Oro poked him in the chest with a finger. "Do you? Do you?"

The two of them glared at each other for a moment.

"I didn't think so. Well, I better get back to work." Oro tapped the pouch he was wearing. "Good luck finding yourself another job, skelly. And another place to sleep."

He smiled.

Xander yelled, and charged.

He tackled Oro around the waist, and took him to the ground. He started swinging.

"Hey!" Oro shouted, holding up his arms to defend himself. "What are you, crazy? Get off me."

"Soon as you tell me where my things are." Xander reared back to punch him again; Oro backhanded him across the face. Xander fell sideways. Oro rolled him off and got to his feet. For a second he looked like he was about to start swinging at Xander.

Then, all at once, he started backing away.

"Please. Please don't hurt me," Oro said, sounding scared, and not like himself at all. "These messages belong to my master—I can't give them to you, no matter what."

"What?" Xander snapped. "What are you talking about?"

Oro glanced past Xander, and behind him.

A hand closed on Xander's shoulder. He turned and saw Tandis standing behind him.

"Hmm," the knight growled. "I said 'wait.' Not 'fight.' "

"But . . ." Xander pointed at Oro. "He started—he stole—"

"Come. Now." Tandis turned and spun on his heel, and walked through the open door. Behind him Xander could see Mirdoth, and Lord Ambrose, and a whole bunch of other men he didn't know standing at a long table, on top of which lay spread out sheet after sheet of paper. All the men were glaring at him.

He saw Geni then, standing next to her father. She was glaring, too.

Great, Xander thought, and a step behind Tandis, he entered the room.

CHAPTER SIX

Fallen. Here, in Outpost, in the very shadow of the Keep. Fallen, laying hands upon his daughter. Ambrose would not have thought such a thing possible. Had they not learned from the past? From the harm he had visited upon their kind a decade earlier, when the Wastes had coursed scarlet with their blood? Did they need that lesson taught again? If so, he was more than ready to give it.

"Lord." He looked up and saw Mirdoth gesturing toward the doorway as Tandis stepped back into the Hall, followed a moment later by the boy. Geni's friend. The urchin; the messenger. Dressed in the scruffy tunic and leggings he always wore. The lad's name escaped him for a moment, the way it always did, despite the fact that they'd been talking about him just a moment earlier. What was it again . . .

"Xander," his daughter said, stepping forward, wearing a look of displeasure. "What were you doing out there?"

"Nothing," the boy—Xander—answered.

"You were fighting," Geni said.

"I was not."

Tandis looked at him.

The boy's mouth opened, and then shut again.

"Yes, I was." He nodded.

Ambrose stepped forward. "I understand you were in the wood."

Xander's face colored; he looked to Geni, equal parts embarrassment and anger showing on his face.

"Just tell the truth," Geni said. "It's not—"

"Sir . . ." Xander began. "My lord. I intended no harm, I—"

Ambrose had to keep a smile from his face.

He had no intention of disciplining the boy for violating his ordinance; that was intended to keep people from hunting out of season. Geni had, somewhat reluctantly, already told him why Xander had been in there, to gather jewels for her. He'd had a hard time keeping a smile from his face then as well; the fact that the boy had a crush on his daughter was no surprise to Ambrose. It had been obvious to him for years, though a worry only the last few months, as Geni blossomed into a woman—Gods, to see her in Odona's dress had almost stopped his heart. Would that his wife were still here, alive. She would take the girl in hand and teach her the ways of the world—though that concern of course had to take a backseat now to the more serious business at hand.

Leeland was dead. And the bodies of a half-dozen Fallen—Urxen, Tandis had told them—lay a few hundred yards away from where he stood now.

"Tell us what you saw," Ambrose said.

"What I saw." The boy looked confused.

"In the wood," Ambrose said. "You were in the wood for several hours, as I understand. Did you see anything unusual? Anything out of the ordinary?"

"Apart from the stones you decided to toss away so casually, that is?" Mirdoth asked.

The boy flushed again.

"My lord, I don't understand . . ."

Tandis stepped forward. "The Fallen we came across were

part of a larger force. The wood is extensive, boy. It is quite possible there may be others of their kind hidden within."

"I saw no signs of Fallen, sir," Xander said. "Nothing out of the ordinary."

Tandis shook his head. "Too quick an answer, Xander. Think on what you observed."

"Lord, I—"

"Think," Tandis said calmly. "Concentrate."

"Yes, sir. I will try."

"Good." Tandis folded his arms across his chest, and considered the boy.

And as he did so, Lord Ambrose considered him.

Tandis. The commander of the Azure Knights, Galor's most trusted warriors. Named for his father, fallen in battle half a century earlier in service of the King. Ambrose had heard stories of this Tandis for years; he was supposedly the most fearsome warrior on both continents and a renowned strategist as well. Judging from what he'd been able to gather about the skirmish outside the castle, the former, at least, was true. And yet . . . Ambrose was still, frankly, unsure what to think of the man. He recalled the first time he'd seen him, nearly a month ago. Ambrose was sleeping in his chamber when the Guard of the Watch had summoned him. *The Azure Knights: they've crossed the Bridge. They're here, Lord. In the Hall. Waiting.* Ambrose had taken a moment to prepare himself, to change from his sleeping robes to more appropriate garb.

Based on the stories he'd heard—the stories Galor himself had told him years ago, when Ambrose had visited the King in Athica—he'd expected to find men like those out of the pages of history waiting for him in the Hall. Great Knights. Larger-than-life figures. Instead Tandis and his companions struck him, on first glance, more like a motley band of characters out of some playwright's imagination. A handful of them looked almost as old as Mirdoth; there was one—a boy named Calis—who seemed as young as, if not younger than, Geni. Some had the look of thieves, frankly: the shiftiness in their eyes, the way they looked around the Keep, as if judging the value of the possessions they saw, what the paintings, tapestries, and bowls might be sold for on the open market. Some even bore the mark of the King's Warden, proof positive that they had at one time been lawbreakers. And these, Ambrose wondered, were the best of Galor's men?

Ambrose had to admit that Tandis at least looked the part of a knight—tall, rangy, with broad shoulders, and a swiftness to his movements that instantly let Ambrose know how good he would be with a sword. But from the lank, unkempt hair that fell to his shoulders, and the tattered state of his clothes, Ambrose had his doubts, frankly, about the man's intellectual capacity. In Ambrose's experience, the outer man was almost always a reflection of the inner. Tandis had said little to dispel his first impression; during the first meeting, he had let his second in command, an older knight named Hildros, do most of the talking, and now . . .

He seemed to have made up his mind about the state of things before the evidence was entirely in.

General Neral, commander of the Kingdom's permanent expeditionary force in the Henge, did not appear impressed with the knight. He was looking coolly at Tandis while seeming to listen intently to the boy's story.

"Nothing, my lord," the boy, Xander, said, shaking his head once more. "I can recall nothing out of the ordinary in the wood."

"And you were in there how long?" Neral asked.

"A couple of hours, sir."

"Hmmpphh. Long enough to cover a great deal of territory." Neral—an immense man, a good few inches taller and a good hundred pounds heavier than anyone else in the room—turned to Ambrose. "It is as I said, sir. The Fallen may or may not have crossed the Wastes in force, but they are no immediate threat to us within the Keep."

"Nor will they ever be." Jarak—Commander of the Keep Garrison, who stood across the table from the rest of them, his short, spiked, reddish hair still mussed from sleep—nodded. "Need I remind you that these walls have stood for a thousand years, Lord Ambrose? They will stand for a thousand more."

"These walls are but rock and mortar, Commander," Tandis said. "As were those of fabled Imperium, you will recall. Those walls fell. These can, too. Need I remind you of that?"

Jarak glared. "Forgive me, Captain. But you speak from ignorance. These walls are thrice fortified, mortar and stone yes, but constructed in such a way—"

"You speak from arrogance, Commander," Tandis said. "And an ignorance of your own. An ignorance of history that in my experience—"

"Gentlemen," Ambrose interrupted. This was the last thing they needed right now, fighting among themselves, with the Fallen at their very doorstep. "Regardless of how strong the walls of the Keep are, they will do the villagers no good. Should the captain's reports bear out, we will need to bring them inside the walls . . . yes?"

"My lord speaks true," Neral said. "First thing in the morning, I will send out a force to scour the wood. And in the meantime—"

"The wood will be burning by morning," Tandis said. "We must evacuate now."

"There are near to a thousand in the village, Captain," Ambrose said. "To take them inside without adequate preparation—"

"It must be done," Tandis interrupted. "As soon as possible. Or they are all likely to perish."

Geni's eyes widened. "You believe the situation that dire?"

"I do."

"My lord." Neral shook his head. "Aside from those of Jar-ak's watch, we have five hundred men here. Five hundred more to draw on from Red Spring and Kaden's Harbor. A thousand all told, surely enough to—"

"Those men will never get here," Tandis said. "Have you not been listening? An army lies between us and them. Here."

He stabbed at the map on the table: a map of the Keep and the area surrounding it. The sea, to the north; the bay, and the bridge that was the fortress's purpose for existence, to the west. The wood to the east, and beyond that the mountains of Dirdoth. To the south, Outpost—the village that housed the majority of Ambrose's subjects—and beyond that, the Wastes. The map also showed the very northern regions of Kraxis, the country on the other side of the Wastes, whose northernmost villages—Red Spring, and Kaden's Harbor—contained men who were in theory, at least, bound to the Keep's defense.

Almost as soon as Mirdoth had laid out his map, Tandis sketched a line atop it. A line that ran from the easternmost por-tion of the Wastes to the coast itself. A line that represented the position the Army of the Fallen had taken up. A line that effec-tively sealed off Outpost and the Keep from the rest of the conti-nent.

"You made it across the army's lines, did you not, Captain?" Neral asked Tandis. "Is it not remotely possible that others could as well?"

"No," Tandis said.

"You have a high estimation of your abilities," Neral said.

"Yes."

Someone laughed. The boy again. Xander.

"Lord Ambrose." Neral turned to him. "With your permis-sion, I will send birds to General Yaig and the counselors at Red Spring, instructing them to reconnoiter, to determine an accurate picture of the Fallen Army and its size."

"No," Tandis said. "Lord Ambrose, you must command all villages south of Outpost to begin hardening their defenses. To prepare for siege."

"It seems early for such action, Tandis," Ambrose said.

"It's almost too late now, Lord."

"Speaking as your military adviser, Lord Ambrose," Neral said, "I'd say we need a more accurate picture of the strength of this Fallen Army. Their intentions. For all we know, they number in the hundreds, not the thousands that Tandis here assigns to them."

Ambrose had his mouth open to answer, but Tandis beat him to it.

"Their intentions seem to me obvious," the knight said. "As for their numbers . . . my count is accurate, I assure you."

"Forgive me, Captain." Neral shook his head. "But you crossed the lines at night. At a single point. Accurate observation under such conditions seems unlikely at best, more like braggadocio than—"

"Enough!" Tandis shouted, slamming his hand down on the map on the table.

Ambrose heard the sound of wood cracking, and then to his complete and utter astonishment, the table itself snapped in two. The pieces crashed to the floor with a resounding thud.

"Wow," the boy said.

No one else spoke for a good few seconds.

"Forgive me," Tandis said. "But time is short, and the situation is dire. Lord Ambrose, I must speak with you in private."

"All here are my closest advisers," Ambrose said, gesturing to the others. "If there is information you have for me—"

"I beg your pardon, Lord, there is, but it is for your ears alone. These others must leave us—now."

"Have a care, Captain." Ambrose's voice hardened. "It is I who give the orders here. This is my keep."

The guards—one on either side of the door—shifted position, moving hands to the hilts of their swords. Neral and Mirdoth moved as well.

Tandis's eyes met his; in them, Ambrose saw defiance. Then the knight bowed his head.

His words, however, were anything but conciliatory.

"Again, forgive me, Lord, but you operate under a misconception." Tandis looked up and then nodded toward the tapestry on the wall behind them. The tapestry of King Galor, at the court in Athica. "The Keep—and all who dwell within it—are his. And the message I have for you comes directly from the King, and is, as I said, meant for your ears alone. Now . . . will you dismiss these others, sir, so I may discharge my duty?"

Ambrose glared a second longer, then nodded reluctantly.

"Go," he said. "All of you."

"Lord." He became aware of Neral coming toward him. "Whatever this knight has to say—"

"Go!" Ambrose said again, and Neral took a step back.

"As you wish, Lord," he said, and bowed, and with a final glare at Tandis, exited the room.

Jarak exited as well. Geni stepped forward and laid a hand on Ambrose's shoulder. He put his on top of hers for a second and squeezed it.

Then she, too, was gone, and he turned to Tandis.

"All right, Captain," Ambrose said, straightening. "This had better be good."

CHAPTER SEVEN

Her face, Geni knew without looking, was bright red. Flushed with shame for her father, and anger at Tandis. She muttered a series of curse words—not the polite ones the wives of her father's men used with one another when they thought no one was listening, the euphemisms for the private parts of this lady or that lord. No, these curse words were the ones she and Xander heard the traders from Kraxis or Capitar screaming early in the morning at market, when they were haggling with the vendors. The curses her father would blanch white at if he ever heard them escape her lips.

Tandis. Half an hour ago, she'd been half in love with him, the way he'd cut down the Urxen . . . saved her life. And Xander's.

Now she was furious at him. Talking to her father the way he had . . . *you are King Galor's*. No, he wasn't. Well, all right, maybe he was, technically speaking, but in point of fact, Galor was a thousand miles away, and the man people looked up to here—the man people obeyed and took orders from—that wasn't the man on the tapestry. That was her father. Nobody knew Galor from a hole in the wall here. Except her father. And Mirdoth, of course. Though she could never quite figure out what they thought about Galor. Sometimes, listening to one or the other of them talk, she thought they admired him. Sometimes they seemed to despise him. Definitely they feared him. Geni supposed she feared him, too. The thought of journeying to Athica to stand before him, to be judged by him . . .

"Hey, wait!" She turned and saw Xander striding hurriedly down the corridor toward her. His face was flushed as well; not, however, with shame or anger. He looked excited.

She waited for him to catch up before starting forward again.

"Did you see that?" he asked, falling into step beside Geni. "Did you see what he did? He broke the table. With his hand, he broke the table."

"Yes," Geni snapped. "I saw it."

"Gods." Xander shook his head. "It must have been cracked, don't you think? It was solid oak, that table. Impossible that he could have done that with one blow. Don't you think?"

"I suppose." Geni didn't really want to talk about it. Or think about it, for that matter. So Tandis was strong. He was still an ass.

"Where are you going?" Xander asked.

"To my quarters," she said, without breaking stride. "To sleep. It's late."

"Oh."

She stopped walking and turned to face him. "What?"

"Aren't you curious? About what they're saying?" He nodded in the direction of the Hall. "Don't you want to—"

"Oh, no." She shook her head. "No, Xander. My father will tell me what he thinks I need to know. He'll tell all of us."

"But—"

"No. I know what you want to do, and no."

He frowned at her and opened his mouth to say something. Then he shut it.

"What?"

"Nothing." He shook his head. "Never mind."

"What?" she said.

"No. It's not important."

"What?"

Xander shook his head again. She glared at him. He wasn't going to try the tunnels without her, was he? She couldn't allow that. What was he thinking? She was seized by a sudden desire to know.

And then she remembered something. Her lessons. Something she and Mirdoth had been working on in private; something only the two of them knew about. Something for her to show Galor, when she was summoned.

"A simple thing, really," Mirdoth had said. "A way to demonstrate your capabilities. If you indeed have them."

"I don't know," she had said. "I don't know if I do."

"The blood runs within you," Mirdoth had told her. "We will see if it runs true. Your family has a history of Adamants in it—those whose words are impossible to defy."

And then he showed her. It was a matter of concentration, he said. Of aligning the wishes of the mind with the mechanisms of the body. Lending power to the voice; channeling the energies of the world around you, and then bending those energies to your will. Imposing that energy on the lesser energies of those around you.

"The gift of command," Mirdoth had said. "With it you can coerce others to do your bidding. Only an Adamant can do it."

She'd been working on it the last few weeks, with him and on her own. She'd even tried it on Elana, and a few of the other staff here at the Keep. It had worked; at least it seemed to work at the time, though obviously since the staff had to obey her anyway, it wasn't a true test of her powers. She hadn't been sure she was ready for such a test then.

Well.

She'd see if she was now.

She took a breath, and focused. Concentrated. Just as Mirdoth had told her.

She looked Xander in the eye.

"Tell me what you're thinking," she said.

He blinked. "Uhh . . ."

It was working, she thought, putting her hands on his shoulders, and leaned forward.

"Tell me," she said again.

"Why do you want to know?"

It wasn't working. She had no talent.

"Please. Tell me."

He shrugged, then looked her up and down.

"Your breasts," he said. "They're getting bigger."

Geni flushed.

She slapped Xander in the face.

Xander blinked.

"Geni! Wait!"

She'd turned her back and strode away from him at top speed. She didn't break stride now, either. If anything, she sped up.

"Wait!" he yelled, and started to run after. "I didn't—"

She turned a corner, which was when Xander realized that they were already deep within the Keep. That in fact, they were already . . .

She reached the door to her quarters and opened it. Then she turned and glared at him for a moment.

"I'm sorry," he said. "I—"

She slammed the door. A second later he heard the bolt sliding into place.

"Geni . . ." He came and stood at the door. "Come on. I'm sorry. I—"

"Go away," she said through the door.

"I'm sorry. I didn't mean . . . I mean, I did mean, but I didn't mean to say . . ." He was flushing now, too, Xander realized. He didn't know what to say.

"Go," she said.

"Not until you accept my apology."

Silence.

"I'll stay out here all night long if I have to!" he yelled.

The second he finished speaking, he became aware of someone standing behind him.

He turned and saw one of Ambrose's guards.

"What are you doing here?" the guard said.

"I'm a friend of Geni's. The princess. I was just talking to her."

The guard frowned. "No. You are talking to her door."

"Well, yes, but . . ."

"You do not belong here. Come."

"But . . ."

"Come. Now." The guard drew his sword and waved it at Xander. "The master at arms will want to talk to you."

"Hey. Take it easy," Xander said, holding up his hands. "I'm not—"

The door behind him opened, and Geni poked her head out.

"Don't kill him," she said to the guard, ignoring Xander entirely. "Just take him home."

"As you wish, Princess." The guard sheathed his sword, and bowed. "Where is home?"

"Outpost," she said. "The village."

"No, it's not," Xander said. Geni, for the first time, turned and looked at him directly.

"What?" she asked.

"I can't go back to the village."

"Why not?"

"Saren fired me."

Her eyes widened. He told her what had happened.

"That's ridiculous," she said.

"I know. I—"

She turned to the guard. "Take him to the south quarters. Give him a room and some food. Please."

"Of course, Princess." The guard bowed again. "This way, boy."

"Sure. One minute." He turned back to Geni. "Listen, I just wanted to say again I'm—"

"Good night, Xander," she said, closing the door, looking— at least it seemed to him—a little bit less angry than before.

CHAPTER EIGHT

The south quarters turned out to be nowhere near what Xander conceived of as south, although it was quite possible that his sense of direction was completely turned around by the time they got there. The guard had taken him into a part of the Keep he'd never been before, up one flight of stairs, and then down another, and then another still before stopping in front of one of several small wooden doors set along the corridor they'd entered.

"Here," the guard said, kicking the door open. "This one ought to do you. Breakfast is at six, but if I were you I'd get there earlier. Cook don't like strangers showing up uninvited."

"Uh . . . okay. Thanks." Xander frowned. "Where is the—"

Dining room, he'd been about to ask, but the guard had already turned his back and was marching away. Breakfast. Xander supposed he'd find his way there—find his way back out—by smell.

Inside, the room was bigger than it looked. It had a fireplace, and a dresser and a table, and a real bed. With a carved oak headboard. There was another door in the room as well; most likely a storage closet of some sort. He crossed to the mattress; it was plump and firm to the touch. Goose feathers, he thought. Could it be?

He kicked off his boots and lay down.

The mattress gave beneath him, but retained its shape. Supporting his back. His shoulders. His legs. Goose feathers. They made the nice soft bed in Saren's hut that Oro had teased him about feel like it was made of stone. Never mind the Fallen, or getting fired, or the unbelievably rude thing he'd just said to Geni. He would sleep well tonight.

First, though, he wanted to wash off. But he didn't see any place to do that. Maybe there was a washbasin out in the hall. He stood and started across the room again.

And stopped in wonder.

The cobblestone floor was covered in rugs. The sensation of his bare feet touching the carpet beneath them . . . it was unlike anything he had ever felt before. The red strands of fabric softly cushioned his callused feet.

Was this how Geni lived? Gods. Why would she ever want to come out of her room?

Someone knocked on the door. The guard, he thought. Come to fetch me. Come to tell me it's all a big mistake, a misunderstanding, I can't stay here, this isn't the right room, boy, you don't belong here, boy, the princess meant these rooms, he'd say, and march him someplace else in the Keep, into a little cell with a hard stone floor and a draft and a straw pallet.

Ah, well. Goose feathers. At least he could say he lay on them once before he died.

He slipped his boots back on and opened the door.

Two girls—maybe ten, eleven years old, dressed in servant's robes—stood there. One carried a bronze tray the size of a knight's shield, covered with a gray cloth. The other carried a pot of water—steaming water—bigger than she was.

"Beg your pardon, sir," the one carrying the tray said. "Supper."

"And water. For sir's bath," the other added.

"Uh . . ." Xander stood in the doorway for a moment, frowning. "Sir?" It took Xander a second to realize she was talking to him.

I think you must have the wrong room, he was about to say, and then the one carrying the tray pushed past him.

"Excuse me, sir," she said.

Xander watched in amazement as she walked to a table in the corner of the room and laid the tray down on it. She pulled the cloth off.

Xander saw bread. Meat. Cheese. A bowl of fruit. Fresh fruit. An apple. A banana. A calivar, the brightest green color he had ever seen in his life.

"This is for me?" he asked.

"If it does not meet with sir's approval," the girl said, "I can return to the kitchen and bring something else."

"Oh, no. No." He shook his head. "This is great."

He walked over to the tray and picked up the bread. A half loaf. Warm to the touch. Fresh out of the oven. The bread he usually had was cold. Bought at night, from the baker's back door. Leftovers; bread that none of the baker's other customers had wanted. This . . .

"Sir's bath is ready."

Xander turned and saw the other girl standing in the door of what he had thought was a closet.

Behind her he saw a tub, and a washbasin.

"Bath?" he said.

"Aye, sir." The girl bowed. "The water will be hot only a few moments, but I can return with more if sir needs it."

"No. I'll be fine. Thanks."

"Thank you, sir," the first girl—the one who had brought in the tray—said, and then the two of them backed out of the room, bowing as they went.

The door had barely shut when Xander ripped off a hunk of bread and shoved it into his mouth. He chewed two hunks that way before eating the apple and then some cheese. Then he went into the other room, stood next to the tub, and inhaled the steam rising from it. A bath. He'd never taken a bath before. His experience in getting clean largely amounted to being in the rain, swimming in a stream, or wiping off filth with a chunk of snow.

He undressed and carefully lowered himself into the tub. The hot water brought relief to a myriad of aches and pains that he was so accustomed to that their absence was startling. The pain from his run-in with Morlis's gang, the cuts and scratches from his work all began to fade away.

He felt like he could fall asleep, right here, right now.

And then Tandis's face appeared before him. Evacuate. Was he serious? He was that scared of the Fallen? It didn't make sense to Xander, for a number of reasons. First of all, Tandis had taken care of five of them by himself, with scarcely any effort. With all the other Azure Knights at his side, along with the troops here at the Keep already, and the others who would come from Outpost . . . surely they'd be able to handle them. And the Keep itself— why, that was like having another thousand men on your side. It was like Commander Jarak had said. The walls had stood for a thousand years. It was inconceivable to think that they'd fall in his lifetime.

And yet, Xander couldn't get the look on Tandis's face off his mind.

Evacuation. Across the bridge. Considering that he'd lived here all his life, Xander had never actually seen the structure, except from a height, from Geni's room. It looked small to him. Insubstantial. Like it couldn't support more than a single person at a time, though obviously that was not the case. Tandis and his Knights had ridden across it just a few weeks ago. Caravans from Capitar made their way across the span every day, from Walderon itself.

Maybe, Xander reflected, he was headed there sooner than he thought.

The bath was starting to cool down. Xander stood up out of

the water and noticed that the girl had thoughtfully placed a towel on the table next to the tub. He took it and began to dry off.

He stepped out of the tub and wrapped the towel around himself. So many new experiences. First the bed, then the tub, now a big soft piece of cloth to dry himself. Wonderful.

He went back into the other room, and on a whim, opened the dresser.

There was a robe in it; a gray, soft robe of the same material as the towel. He put it on and sighed in satisfaction. He picked up the calivar, peeled it, and took a bite.

He looked down at the fireplace and wondered if someone would be bringing wood for it shortly. Probably not. Probably that would be pushing his luck, to go looking for someone to help start a fire for him.

And then, just as he thought that, he heard a loud click. The door, he thought, and turned toward it, expecting to see someone walk in carrying a cord of wood.

But it was closed. There was no one there.

He heard a click again and turned back to the fireplace.

The wall at the back of it was moving. Up, and out of sight.

Geni's face appeared where the brick had been.

"There you are," she said, and stepped forward, out of the fireplace, and into the room.

First thing Xander noticed: Geni was no longer wearing a dress.

She had changed into trousers and a tunic. Dark brown, the both of them. She had her hair pulled back, too. If it weren't for the fineness of her features, she could have passed for a boy.

He suspected his earlier comment had something to do with the wardrobe change.

"What?" she asked, frowning. "What are you staring at?"

"Nothing."

"Hmmphh." She brushed dust off her trousers and looked up at him again. "You took a bath."

"Yeah. Was that wrong?"

She shook her head. "No. It's just that . . . you look different."

"Yeah," he said. "I'll bet."

He didn't think he'd ever been this clean in his life. Probably his skin was an entirely different color, considering how many layers of dirt had come off in the bath. Xander frowned, suddenly aware that he was wearing nothing but a robe. A loosely tied one, at that.

He pulled it tighter around him.

"So why are you here?"

"I live here, remember."

"I remember." He looked past her, toward the fireplace, and the tunnel she had emerged from. He hadn't realized the tunnels reached this part of the Keep; the two of them had spent a great deal of time exploring the passages that honeycombed the fortress, at least up until a few months ago.

"Hey." He turned and saw Geni frowning at the platter of food. "They gave you my astrafan."

"Astrafan." Xander shook his head. "What's astrafan?"

"This." She picked the hunk of cheese off the platter and held it up. "My father ordered this from Walderon especially for me."

"Well, I'm sorry. I didn't know."

She glared at him again and put it down on the tray.

"Is something the matter? Is it what I said before? I'm—"

"Don't say a word about that." She pointed a finger at him. "Do you hear me? Not a word."

"All right. But I just want you to know—"

"I don't want to hear it," she snapped. "You understand?"

He nodded. "Yes. I understand."

The two of them looked at each other.

"I want to know what they're saying," Geni blurted out. "My father, and Tandis. I want to know what's happening."

Xander nodded. Of course she did. Why else would she be here?

"So do I," he said.

"Good. Then get dressed. We should hurry."

"The tunnels?" he asked.

"The tunnels." She nodded.

CHAPTER NINE

King Galor: Staring at Tandis, and the tapestry on the wall behind him, Ambrose realized it had been nearly twenty years since he had last seen the man. The last—and, some would say, greatest—of the world's channelers. They had met when Ambrose had been summoned to Athica for the testing. Galor had looked on him with favor then, and even after Ambrose had failed at the channeling—even after he'd proven that though the blood ran within him, the blood did not run true—the King had still smiled, and confirmed his succession to command of the Keep. He sent Ambrose home with words of well-wishing. And over the years, Galor had sent him other messages as well. Congratulations on his wedding day; congratulations on Geni's birth. Condolences on Odona's death. Permission to invade the Wastes; thanks for clearing the Urxen from there. Words of warning regarding possible vengeance-seekers. And most recently, a request for Geni to attend him in Athica, to be tested herself, just as he had.

Ambrose had a sudden, awful sinking sensation in the pit of his stomach. Galor's message—was now the time—could it be. . . .

"Captain," he said to Tandis, his voice sounding shaky, at least to his own ears. "Does this concern my daughter?"

"Your daughter?" Tandis looked surprised. "No. Of course not."

"Well, then . . ."

Someone cleared their throat; Ambrose turned and saw that Mirdoth had not left the Hall yet, that he was still bent over the wreckage of the table, picking up his maps, folding them neatly into a pile.

"Forgive me, gentlemen," Mirdoth said. "I will be but a moment longer. My fingers are no longer as dextrous as they once were."

Ambrose studied his old friend—who did seem to be moving a bit more slowly than usual—and suspected that Mirdoth's speed, or lack thereof, had more to do with a reluctance to leave the Hall than anything else.

He was about to say so when Tandis cleared his throat.

"The minister may stay, Lord Ambrose. If you so desire."

"I do."

"Then please"—Tandis gestured toward the now-empty dinner table across the room—"let us sit."

They did: Ambrose at the head, Mirdoth at his right hand, his back to the door, Tandis on his left, his back to the tapestry of Galor.

"Before we begin," Tandis said, "I owe you an apology, Lord Ambrose, for the way I spoke earlier. I have been too long away from courts, and generals, and the ways of civilization. I am too used to speaking my will and having it done."

Ambrose nodded. "I understand. I know you have only the King's interests at heart."

"As your father did before you," Mirdoth said. "Indeed, you seem to me much like him, Captain."

"You honor me by saying so," Tandis replied. "You knew my father?"

"I cannot say I knew him. I saw him on occasion," Mirdoth said. "He was named after his father as well, was he not?"

"Indeed. Such has been the tradition in my family. All the way back to Procipinee's day there has been a Tandis serving the interests of the Kingdom."

"You do not have children, however. Do you, Captain?" the minister asked.

"No." Tandis frowned.

Ambrose frowned, too. He did not see a point to Mirdoth's questions, and this was no time for idle chat.

"The message, Captain."

"Of course. Forgive me, Lord." Tandis turned back to Ambrose. "I must make it clear: The King left it to my discretion whether or not to share this with you. Now it seems to me I have little choice."

Ambrose frowned. "The King left it to you."

"Yes."

The Lord kept his face impassive, but inside he felt just the slightest bit of pique. No. More than the slightest bit. He was annoyed. Did Galor not trust him any longer? What possibly could the King have been thinking . . .

"Forgive me, Lord," Tandis said, and Ambrose realized that some of the anger he felt must have shown on his face. "But it was necessary for me to assess the situation first."

"And the situation is dire, you said."

"Yes."

"This is concerning the Fallen, obviously," Mirdoth said.

"Yes, Minister. Or rather, yes, and no."

Ambrose frowned. "What does that mean?"

"You have a map of the eastern continent? In its entirety?"

"I do," Mirdoth said. "An old one."

"That hardly matters. The older the better, in fact."

Mirdoth rummaged through the stack of documents at his right hand, and pulled out a large, worn sheet of paper. It was a fairly detailed map of the eastern half of the continent. With the Keep, and Outpost at the upper left-hand corner. And to the south, and east . . . the empires of Umber, Ithril, Kraxis, Resolyn, and Magnar. This was an old map; the borders were different than those Ambrose was used to seeing, Ithril larger, Kraxis smaller, Umber still in possession of half of Imperium. The basic outlines of the territories, though, were much the same.

"Galor maintains a network of spies," Tandis said. "Informers. Within each of the territories. Over the last few years, rumors have reached the King. Rumors of Urxen and Trog cooperating. Tales of Sions operating within armies of both. Of old treaties being shredded; of new alliances forming. Of armies, massing in the shadow of Imperium itself."

"This is not news," Ambrose said. "We have heard those rumors as well. Traders from Kraxis. Edmund has sent messages—"

"Have you heard that these armies march under the Dread Lord's banner?" Tandis asked.

"Curgen?" Mirdoth said.

Tandis nodded. "Indeed. One and the same."

The mention of Curgen's name gave Ambrose pause.

The Dread Lord had lived a millennium ago. Or longer, if some of the histories were to be believed. The most fearsome of all the Titans, the demigod who had used magics long vanished from the world to create the Fallen, in all their shapes and all forms. Curgen perished in the same Cataclysm that had split the world in two. Gone these thousand years, and yet worshipped still by those who believed the prophecies, who thought that the Titans would one day return to Elemental. For the Fallen to deliberately call to mind a time when men were little more than cattle, and had been slaughtered as such, by the thousands . . .

"Galor believes he has divined these armies' intent," Tandis said. "They have designs on uniting the eastern continent entire, beneath the Dread Lord's banner."

"A single empire," Ambrose said.

"Exactly."

"It will not work." Mirdoth stood. "Any cooperation between the races of the Fallen is certain to be short-lived. Based on
money, no doubt, I suspect. And there is not enough money in
the assembled trading houses of Capitar to pay the sums necessary to keep Trog, Urxen, Edar, and Sions from turning on one
another."

"It is not money that stays their worst impulses, but fear,"
Tandis said. "Fear of this new leader. A well-deserved fear, based
on what I have seen."

"Go on," Ambrose said.

Tandis nodded and turned toward the fire, and the tapestry of
Galor once more. As if to commune with his King, so far away.

"We crossed the Wastes first," he said. "We visited Kraxis, we
touched Ithril, and there we came upon the site of a great battle,
between the forces of this leader and a Sion lord who had dared
challenge him. This field, my friends . . ." Tandis turned back to
them. "I saw destruction on a scale that I have not seen in—" He
stopped, as if correcting himself. "Well, destruction on a scale I
think you would find difficult to believe."

"And who is this leader?" Ambrose asked. "Sion? Urxen? A
channeler, or—"

"His name is Talax," Tandis said.

"Who?" Ambrose frowned. He was familiar with the leaders
of all Fallen territories—the leaders, and their generals, and their
heirs as well. This was not a name he had ever heard before.

"Talax." Mirdoth was frowning as well. "An auspicious name,
my lord."

"How so?" Ambrose asked.

"In the Hiergamenon, Talax was footman to the Dread Lord
Curgen. His most trusted servant. His deadliest executioner. And
a Titan as well."

Ambrose nodded; the Hiergamenon was one of the oldest,
most sacred books in all of Elemental. A collection of stories from

before the Cataclysm. Those who worshipped the Destiny—who believed in the prophecies—considered its words akin to scripture. Ambrose didn't, and yet . . .

"He evokes the Titans. He evokes Curgen. He seeks to restore the Dread Lord's empire." Mirdoth sat back down and began to fold his map. "This Talax is dangerous indeed."

"Yes. More dangerous than even Galor suspected, I'm afraid." Tandis remained seated.

"What do you mean by that, Captain?" Ambrose asked.

"What I have to say to you now, my friends, must not go beyond these walls. At least until I have had word from the King." Tandis looked at each of them in turn, Ambrose first and then Mirdoth. "Do you swear this?"

"I do swear," Ambrose said.

"As do I," Mirdoth added.

"Very well." Tandis leaned across the table. "Mirdoth, what you said earlier about Talax, that he evokes the name, is only the half of it. I have heard stories of those who have encountered him, fallen into his path, and been brushed aside, and I now fear that he not only evokes the name, but he in fact embodies it."

"I do not understand," Ambrose said.

"I believe I do." Mirdoth looked up at the knight, in a voice suddenly gone cold as ice. "Take care with what you say, Captain. To spread rumors such as this . . ."

"This is no rumor, Minister," Tandis snapped, his own voice changing tone to match Mirdoth's. "This is truth. This Talax is no pretender. He is the thing itself."

Ambrose suddenly realized what the man meant, and barked out a laugh. "Oh, come now, Captain. You cannot be serious."

"Do not mock me, gentlemen. I am quite serious indeed." The man's eyes flashed fire, and for a second Ambrose feared he would pound this table as he did the other, and crack it as well.

"This creature—this Talax who leads the Fallen armies, who has them on the edge of the Western Kingdom itself—is the same

Talax written of in your Hiergamenon, Mirdoth, and a hundred other stories as well. From the time before Cataclysm, before the War of Magic, before the Keep was even a dream in Amarian's head. He is an immortal." Tandis stood then, and looked down on the two of them.

"The Titans have returned."

CHAPTER TEN

"Titans?" Xander whispered, eyes widening as he turned to Geni. "Did he say Titans?"

"Shhh!" she said, shooting him a glare. The two of them stood side by side, barely a foot apart, ears pressed to the seam in the stone wall through which they could hear Tandis and Ambrose—and Mirdoth—talking. Geni's glare was all that was visible to him, though, in the darkness of the tunnel. They had doused the torch they'd used to find their way here a few minutes earlier, as the very cracks that gave them the means to listen to what was being said could also be their undoing, were someone to spot a flickering light where there should have been none.

Xander suspected he could have found his way through some of these tunnels in pitch darkness, he and Geni had been playing in them for so long. It was almost the first thing they'd done together that they could agree on after they'd met. After Geni realized that unlike most of her other friends, Xander wasn't going to do her bidding automatically, just because she was a princess. Maybe that was why they'd become friends so quickly, he thought. Because even after she'd threatened, and yelled, and even cried, Xander hadn't given in to her. Finally, she'd learned that if the two of them were going to play together, she was going to need to learn the art of compromise.

These days, that word didn't seem to be in her vocabulary.

Xander peered through the little crack in the seam of the stone; the tunnels ran along the back wall, behind the fireplace. He and Geni stood next to that fireplace now, between it and the great tapestry of Galor. About twenty feet away from the three men who were talking, with a head-on view of Mirdoth, Lord Ambrose's profile, and Tandis's back. Which was frustrating, as the knight was doing most of the talking. Something about prophecies, written in the Hiergamenon. About the Titans, and the Destiny.

Ambrose was shaking his head. "This is the stuff of fairy tales, Captain."

"I assure you," Tandis said. "It is true, all of it."

The knight leaned forward and began talking once more, in low, urgent tones.

Xander leaned forward as well, straining to listen.

"Captain. Prophecies written in ancient books do not concern me," Ambrose snapped. "What concerns me is the intent of this Talax. You said earlier he seeks to unite the East, under his banner."

"Yes."

"Then why not let him do it?" Ambrose suggested.

Tandis frowned. "I do not understand."

"Evacuate, as you suggest. But all of us, not just the civilians. Evacuate from Outpost, from the Keep itself. Cross the bridge, and once across, destroy it."

"You cannot be serious, Lord," Mirdoth said.

"And why not? Let the Fallen, and Talax, and those who support them have the East. Men will have the West. Would it not be simpler that way?" To Ambrose, it was basic strategy. What purpose did the Keep serve? The King had implied to him, long ago, that the reason Outpost had been settled in the first place was to perhaps strengthen ties with the Fallen. To make certain that there would be no more wars between the two races that shared this world. Whether Galor believed that himself, the lord did not know, but if Ambrose's experiences with the Fallen had taught him anything, it was that the only language they understood was the language of the sword.

Build a fence, he thought. Build a fence, and keep them all inside it. And in the absence of a fence . . .

The ocean would do.

"It is not that simple, Lord," Tandis said.

"And why not?"

"A bridge can always be rebuilt."

"Not with an army on one side of it, ready to tear down whatever structure they begin to construct."

"Perhaps. But there are other ways across the bay."

"Not from Outpost. Or the cities of Kraxis for that matter," Ambrose said. "There are no harbors the length and breadth of the eastern continent until one reaches the northern borders of Ithril. And for Talax to march his army that far—"

"It is an intriguing suggestion, Lord," Tandis said. "Under other circumstances, the strategy would be worth considering. But not here. Not now. We cannot leave Talax and his army to roam the East at their leisure."

"And why not?"

"Because it is not just our defeat the Titan seeks," Tandis said.

"I don't understand."

"There is something else he desires."

"Something else," Ambrose said. "What?"

Tandis was silent for a moment.

"I will tell you," he said. "But first—you must swear to me that what I say will not escape this room."

"Of course," Ambrose said, and looked at Mirdoth, who nodded.

"You have my word as well, Captain," his counselor said. "Go on."

The knight leaned closer then.

"What Talax is after—why he has forced the vanquished Empires under his banner—is an object from the time before this one. The days before the Cataclysm. Before the world took the shape it has now."

"An object." Ambrose frowned. "Could you be more specific? What kind of an object, exactly?"

The knight rose from his chair. "It can take many forms. Lord Avalan wore it on his arm, as a bracelet, when he would do battle. In the Hiergamenon, in the story of Tylan and Tandis, who was my namesake, it was used to—"

"The orb," Mirdoth said. "Gods, Captain. Are you talking about the orb?"

Tandis nodded. "I am."

"The what?" Ambrose said.

"The silver orb," Tandis said. "The bane of the Dred'nir."

Ambrose frowned. "The who?"

In the tunnels, Xander frowned as well.

"The what?" he said, turning to Geni.

She glared at him. "Shhhh!"

"But—"

"Shhh," Geni said again, louder than the first time. "I'll explain in a minute."

In that instant, Mirdoth started, and looked up. Straight at them.

Xander froze, heart hammering in his chest.

*   *   *

"Mirdoth. Have you heard of these Dred'nir?" Ambrose turned to his chief counselor, who for some reason was staring at the wall behind the knight. Focused on something else entirely.

At Ambrose's words, he blinked, and turned.

"Yes. The Dred'nir are the Dread Lords," Mirdoth said. "Dred'nir, and the Arnor. The Titans who tried to enslave mankind, and those who tried to help it. This is written in the Hiergamenon. The orb was lost millennia ago, however. It has not been seen on this world since the time of the Emerald Sorceress; since the rooting of the shards."

"It has been hidden," Tandis said. "But I know where it is."

Mirdoth, for the first time, looked confused. "You know where the orb is?"

"I do. The King's Knights were the ones to hide it, long, long ago. The knowledge of its location has been passed down through our leaders, from generation to generation. This is why you must hold the Keep, at all costs—to allow my men and myself time to retrieve the orb."

"And where exactly is it you must go to accomplish this task?"

"Calebethon," Tandis said. "And from there—"

"Calebethon?" Ambrose interrupted. "I have never heard of it."

"It is within the Spine of the Empire," Tandis said.

Ambrose's eyes widened. "What?"

"Within the Spine of the Empire," Tandis said. "In the shadow of Imperium itself."

"Halfway across the continent," Ambrose said.

"Yes."

"In the heart of Fallen territory."

"Indeed."

Ambrose looked over at Mirdoth, who stood in front of the fireplace, one arm stretched across the mantel. "How in the name of the Destiny will you reach there?"

"My thoughts exactly, Lord," Mirdoth said. "And we have another problem as well."

The man moved his arm then, touched something with his hand—one of the bricks at the back of the mantel.

"This," he said, as the wall to the right of the fireplace suddenly slid to one side.

Geni and the boy stood there, wearing expressions of complete shock on their faces, expressions Ambrose was sure mirrored his own.

CHAPTER ELEVEN

Xander didn't think he'd ever seen anyone look so angry.

Lord Ambrose couldn't even seem to move. He just kept staring at them. Tandis's expression was unreadable—the knight's gaze moved back and forth from Geni to him—but there was a touch of something else in his eyes as well, each time he looked at Xander. Curiosity?

Mirdoth looked at Geni and shook his head.

"Hosten's name, girl, did I not tell you months ago that I knew of the tunnels as well? That they were not a safe place to wander?"

"Uhhh . . . ," Geni said. "Yes, but . . ."

"Yes. And yet you thought to spy undetected? How—"

"Enough, Mirdoth." Ambrose got to his feet. He looked even angrier than he'd been a minute ago. "I will deal with this. You." He pointed at Geni. "To your quarters. At once."

"Father, I—"

"At once!" Ambrose snapped. Then he turned to Xander. "And you. Guards!" he yelled. A second later the door to the corridor opened and two of them entered.

"Take this boy to the dungeons," Ambrose said, and pointed straight at Xander, who felt suddenly, awfully, sick to his stomach.

"Chain him. Give him water only, for the next week. Then come and remind me he's down there."

One of the guards stepped forward and took hold of his arm. Not gently.

"My lord," Xander said. "I am so sorry. I—"

"No!" Geni said. "You can't do that, Father. It wasn't his idea, it—"

"Silence!" Ambrose roared, and stepped forward so that he and Geni were practically face-to-face. "I am the Lord of the Keep, and we are at war! I will do whatever I deem necessary. Is that understood?"

"But—"

"Is that understood?"

"No," Geni said, and tears began to stream down her face.

Xander felt like crying, too. And smiling. Geni was standing up for him.

"No, I don't understand," she said. "You can't think that Xander is such a threat that—"

"My lord Ambrose!"

Everyone in the room turned at once toward the door, where General Neral stood, looking even more upset than Ambrose.

"Gods!" Ambrose snapped. "Does everyone in this castle feel they have the right to invade my chambers?"

"Forgive me, Lord," Neral said with a bow. "And I must ask you to forgive me as well, Captain. My lord, may I have permission to enter and speak with you? It is most urgent."

Neral, Xander saw now, wasn't alone. There were at least a dozen other men standing in the hall behind him; soldiers, dressed in the uniform of the Keep.

"Enter." Ambrose waved the general forward. "You have news, I assume?"

"I do. A bird, from Red Spring. The town is even now surrounded by the Fallen Army."

"The Destiny protect us," Mirdoth said. "They are so close."

"As are my Knights," Tandis said. "Before I left, I tasked them with the town's defense."

"Your Knights." Lord Ambrose, who still looked furious to Xander's eyes, turned to the captain, shaking his head. "If memory serves, you have a hundred men."

"Eighty-three now, Lord." Tandis said.

"Eighty-three or a hundred, it matters not," Neral said. "What matters is that moving at this speed . . . the Fallen may reach here by afternoon tomorrow. Perhaps . . . perhaps we should reconsider our strategy, Lord Ambrose. Evacuate the village now, and—"

"Enough." Ambrose held up a hand to stop Neral from talking, then turned to one of the men standing in the doorway. "You. Find Commander Jarak. Bring him here. Gentlemen, we must talk. Consider this latest information, and—"

"Forgive me, Lord, but the time for talk is past," Tandis said, getting to his feet. "And you, General—forgive me as well."

"I don't understand," Neral said.

"Yes. What do you mean?" Ambrose asked.

"Can you not smell it?" Tandis said, and crossed the room to the windows. He drew aside the curtains then, and Xander knew instantly what he meant.

By the look on his face, Ambrose knew, too.

"Fire," the Lord said.

Tandis nodded. "Fire. The wood is burning." He turned back to Neral.

"The Fallen are here. Now."

CHAPTER TWELVE

Nym loved the night.

It enhanced his natural advantages: the gifts the Destiny had granted him, the gifts he had been born with. His vision, capable of seeing as easily in darkness as in light. His sense of smell. And his speed, above all. In the day, he was unnaturally quick. At night, on the hunt, in the . . .

He was unstoppable.

His love of darkness did not prevent him from appreciating daylight as well, however. The power of the sun. To make things grow, to make things warm. To make them burn. Another thing Nym loved was fire. The way it moved. How quickly it danced and destroyed. He loved to watch fire at work.

Which was why he was so happy now, standing in the foothills above the village. Looking down at the edge of the Keeper's Wood to his right as it blazed, at the peacefully sleeping village directly below him. The place had a certain calm about it. A peaceful, settled air. The little manlings and their women and their runts, tucked safe in their beds.

They had no idea what was coming.

"Commander."

Nym turned, and his good mood instantly disappeared.

Urxen. A whole cadre of them, soldiers, dressed in battle armor. They had questions for him; he could just tell by the way they stood. Gods, they were so unbelievably thick. Would that he could convince Talax to let some other of the Sions deal with them—or better yet, that the Urxen were entirely unnecessary. A burden on him, a burden on the world entirely. Like the race of men.

Ah well, he thought.

One thing at a time.

"Speak," he said, and one of them—the largest—stepped forward.

"We are ready, sir," it said. "All troops."

"Any sign of him?" Nym snapped. "The knight?"

"Not for a few hours, no."

Nym frowned. The knight had cut through their lines like butter; come up from the south, come up through the heart of their camp, and killed a good dozen of them—if you counted Urxen as "them"—and then disappeared. On his way to the Keep, obviously. Nym supposed he was there already.

"So . . . ," the Urxen said.

"So what?" Nym asked.

"Well. We await your order, sir."

"My order?" Nym frowned. "Your troops are here, aren't you? You're ready to go?"

"Yes, sir."

"Well, then." Nym dismissed them with a wave of his hand. "Have at it. Kill them all."

"The village."

"Yes." He couldn't help but roll his eyes; how many times had they been over this?

"And stop."

"That's right. Stop. Form a perimeter around the Keep, and—"

"Wait for orders. Yes, sir." The Urxen snapped off a salute. Nym returned it halfheartedly, and watched as the soldiers moved away, revealing a single figure standing behind them. Another Sion, like him—pale gray skin, long wiry limbs, and tall—a good half foot taller than the Urxen who'd just left.

Lork. About time.

"You brought it," Nym said.

"I did." Lork stepped forward and held out a cloth, though of course it wasn't the cloth Nym was interested in, it was the thing the cloth was wrapped around. The arrow.

Nym unwrapped it carefully and held it up to the moonlight. It looked no different from any of the others in his quiver: a shaft of wood, a tip of metal, feathers on the vanes . . .

"Commander." Lork cleared his throat. "With your permission, sir, I would like to fire it myself."

"You would like to fire it." Nym had been half expecting this. Lork apparently thought that carrying the thing across the Wastes entitled him to some sort of say in its disposition.

"Yes, sir. I would like the honor."

"Well." Nym lowered the arrow and smiled. "I was thinking about that myself."

"You were?" Surprise—and traces of a smile as well—played across Lork's face.

"Yes. And you know I would have allowed that, save for your injury," Nym said.

"My injury?" Lork looked confused.

"Yes," Nym said, and drew his knife. "The unfortunate accident you sustained to your shoulder. I believe it occurred during training."

"I sustained no accident—"

Nym moved then, faster than lightning.

Lork gasped in surprise, and pain, and then shock, as he saw the blade embedded in his shoulder.

"See to that," Nym snapped. "Before it gets infected."

Lork managed to lower his eyes, and withdraw, clearly in agony.

Nym shook his head, watching the Sion walk off. *I would like the honor.* Idiot. No better than an Urxen, really, when you got down to it.

He unslung his quiver and carefully placed the arrow within it.

It felt as it looked, no different from any other, but he had seen Talax work the enchantment on it with his own eyes. The arrow held power; were he to merely scratch another with it, his master had said, that other would die quickly, and horribly.

But the arrow was meant for the knight. Who waited even now, in the Keep. Soon enough, though, the fire—the fighting— would draw him out.

Until then, Nym would keep watch. On the wood, and the village, and the fields, and the world burning before him.

Chapter Thirteen

Ambrose grimaced.

There had been fires in the wood before; a dry spring, a humid summer, and lightning had set off one such blaze almost twenty years ago, destroying a good forty acres of prime southwest forest. Another fire, much smaller, had sprung up just two years previous; a band of thieves, on the run from Kaden's Harbor, camping deep in the wood, a cooking fire gone out of control, prevented from spreading deeper into the wood by the Mill River, swollen a good foot above its normal level by out-of-season summer rains . . .

Ambrose had drawn up plans, after that incident, for a series of firebreaks within the wood itself; a way to quarantine some of the prime hunting areas within the forest so that even if one were destroyed, the others might survive.

Those plans—even if he'd had a chance to implement them—would have done no good against the blaze now spreading through the forest.

"The Destiny save us."

Ambrose stood at the window, Tandis at his left shoulder, Geni, who had just spoken, at his right.

He looked down at his daughter and shook his head.

"I don't expect any help from that quarter," he said, and then turned to face the others: Tandis, Mirdoth . . . Neral and his men. Jarak, who had just entered, boots in hand, hair mussed from sleep. The boy, and the guards holding him.

"We're evacuating," Ambrose said. "Outpost, and the farms around it. All the civilians in the Keep. Commander."

Jarak stepped forward.

"Sound the alert. Wake the villagers. Send a hundred of your fastest men, your best riders, to organize them. Get them moving. They are to bring nothing but the clothes on their backs. No possessions. No pets, no farm animals, no—"

"Understood, Lord," Jarak said, bowing. "Speed is of the essence."

"Exactly."

"With your permission . . ."

"Go!"

Jarak left the room at a trot.

"That may not be entirely safe, Lord Ambrose," Tandis said. "They will be racing the Fallen to the village."

"I know that, Knight," Ambrose snapped. "As does Jarak. All we can do is hope they win."

"Sir. Lord Ambrose. I—oww!"

The boy—Xander—had spoken. The second he had opened his mouth, one of the guards holding him had jabbed him in the gut with the butt end of his sword.

"Stop it!" Geni said. "Father . . ."

Ambrose held up a hand. "It's all right," he said to the guard, and then glared at Xander. "What is it, boy?"

The boy gulped and took a step back. "I want to help, too, sir."

And how are you going to do that from the dungeons? Ambrose almost asked, and then remembered something else about the boy. Xander.

His parents had been killed in the same attack that had taken Odona.

"You want to help," Ambrose growled.

"He knows the village as well as any man, Father. Better." Geni stepped forward to stand between the two of them, Ambrose and Xander. "He has been messenger to Saren for years."

"Been everywhere in Outpost, sir," Xander nodded. "I could—"

"Yes, I remember," Ambrose said. He'd made inquiries after the boy, of course, when Geni had first befriended him. An orphan, a bit of an outcast, but a good enough worker, according to Leeland, who had spoken directly to Saren and then reported to Ambrose, more favorably about the boy than about his employer. The old man's a skinflint. Wouldn't trust him to hold the door open for me, Lord, Leeland had said, and as proof had offered up the fact that as soon as Leeland revealed that his questions came from the Lord of the Keep, Saren had offered to sell Xander to him for the rough equivalent of a week's worth of provisions. Never mind the fact that the boy was no slave, only the old man's helper.

Leeland, Ambrose thought, remembering his daughter's guardian, and those who had slain him, and the situation at hand.

He didn't have time for this.

"Let him go," he instructed, and the guards holding Xander stepped back.

"Thank you, Father," Geni said.

"Thank you, sir," Xander said, bowing. "I promise—"

"The most remote parts of the village," Ambrose said. "The most infirm. Those who won't hear the alarm, those who won't be able to form up with Jarak's men. Find them and get them to the Keep. You think you can do that, boy?"

Xander looked uncertain; it seemed to Ambrose he was considering the actual implications of the job he'd volunteered for. Run into harm's way, and help others escape it.

Then the boy set his jaw and nodded.

"Yes, sir," he said.

"Then go to it," Ambrose said, then turned to Neral. "General," he said, and began relaying instructions regarding the disposition of Neral's forces within the castle walls, and the arrangements that would need to be made with Jarak's men for the two to work together most efficiently.

He could not, however, fail to notice the looks that passed between the boy and his daughter as Xander left the Hall.

A messenger, he thought, shaking his head as Neral fled the room as well, his men in tow. A whole village to choose from, and Geni picks a messenger. An orphan, at that. Ah, well. She was young. Ambrose had been young, too, once. His first crush had been one of his own mother's maids—an older woman, or at least she'd seemed so to him then, probably all of twenty years, he realized now. Cassandra. Gods, he'd been smitten. Deeply in love, though it turned out to be only lust that, once sated, faded quickly. The only love of his life had been Odona. First crush. That's all this boy Xander was. Soon to be forgotten, once Geni reached Athica. She would find others there, of her own kind, her own station, her own more refined upbringing.

"Lord," Mirdoth stepped forward. "There are certain things I think would be safer across the bridge. Items from the observatory. Some books. Certain artifacts that if the Fallen were to somehow obtain possession of . . . the consequences would be dire indeed."

Ambrose's mouth almost fell open.

"You wish to leave with the others," he managed to say. "Evacuate?"

Mirdoth nodded. "I think that would be best."

Ambrose studied his old friend, who had served as first mentor, then minister to him for all the years he had himself served Galor at the Keep. Mirdoth had never shied away from danger before; Ambrose had not expected him to now. True, the man was no warrior, there was not a warlike bone in his body, but to turn and run like this . . .

"If you must," Ambrose said.

Mirdoth nodded.

"I will require assistance, my lord," he continued. "The packing. The transporting."

"Of course."

"Ideally, I would have someone who is aware of both the value and fragility of certain of these items. If I might suggest . . ."

Mirdoth turned and gestured toward Geni, and it was all Ambrose could do then to keep from laughing out loud.

So that was the old man's game. Getting Geni across the bridge, and out of harm's way. If Ambrose had suggested that she leave the Keep, had even brought the possibility up, Geni would have fought, kicking and screaming, every step of the way across the bridge.

To have her teacher request her help, however . . .

"I had hoped to have her with me," Ambrose said, nodding. "But you make a good point, Minister. Geni . . ."

He turned to his daughter, who was already shaking her head.

"No, Father," she said. "I'm staying."

"You can't." Ambrose put his hands on her shoulders. "These things of Mirdoth's—they must not fall into the wrong hands. Now, more than ever. You understand?"

Geni nodded. "I understand. This Talax. But—"

"The King, Geni," Ambrose said, meeting his daughter's eyes. "He will want you safe as well."

"Your father is right, child." Tandis stepped forward. "Galor would have my head if I failed to protect you."

Geni, about to open her mouth to protest further, shut it again and nodded.

"All right," she said, looking absolutely miserable. "I'll go."

"There's my girl." Ambrose pulled his daughter closer and took her into his arms. A moment's embrace, a few words of good-bye, and then she—and Mirdoth—were gone, and it was

just the two of them—Tandis and himself—remaining in the
Hall. The knight, who had never moved far from the window,
walked to it once more.

"The attack. It's begun," he said.

Ambrose walked to his side and peered into the darkness.

The window faced to the southeast—Tandis was looking
more directly south, toward the hills in the distance, the hills that
overlooked the village. Ambrose squinted in the same direction
but couldn't see a thing.

"I can't—"

"There." Tandis pointed toward the hills. "They're coming in
waves. A few hundred of them at a time. Urxen. Moving slowly.
Your men should easily reach the villagers first."

"You have keener eyes than I do, Knight," Ambrose said.

"I have trained for these things," Tandis said.

At that second, bells began sounding throughout the Keep.
Seconds later, Ambrose saw movement, as well as an isolated
flame or two in the village. Torches being lit. People wondering
what was happening. Now he could pick out forms in the street—
shouts came to his ears. Surprise, and panic. It was only the beginning.

He had hoped there was time enough to evacuate the villagers before the Fallen had struck.

"And you, Captain?" Ambrose asked, turning to face the
knight. "What do you intend to do now?"

"Return to my Knights, first," Tandis said. "Do some harm to
the enemy's lines along the way."

"I will send men with you," Ambrose said. "A small force.
Just enough to—"

Tandis interrupted. "I work better alone, Lord. No offense
intended."

Ambrose frowned and studied the man for a second.

Somehow he didn't doubt the truth of Tandis's words, which
he supposed to some would have sounded arrogant.

You have a high estimation of your abilities.

"And then the Bane," Tandis said.

"The thing you spoke of earlier."

"Yes. It must be found. Recovered. Before it can fall into Talax's hands."

"The Bane of the Dred'nir," Ambrose said aloud to himself.

"Avalan's Bane." Tandis turned at last from the window. "Let me finish telling you about it."

Chapter Fourteen

They went to her quarters first. Geni packed a bag: a change of clothes, a few things of her mother's, the practice sword Leeland had given her. Mirdoth raised an eyebrow at that but said nothing.

They headed for the observatory, Mirdoth giving her instructions along the way: You will find a trunk here, you can use that to pack these things there, and when it is full, there will be a bag here, etc., etc. Geni started in as soon as they arrived, running from one side of the great round room to the other and then back again, taking things down from shelves, wrapping them, boxing them as Mirdoth made note of what she was doing and busied himself in a hundred other ways as well.

She found little logic to the things he chose to pack, and those he chose to leave behind, though she had little doubt that there was a method to his madness. And no doubt whatsoever that she knew at least part of the rationale driving his choices.

"Mirdoth—this Talax," she said. "Can Tandis be right? Can he truly be an immortal, one of the Titans?"

"Hush," Mirdoth said. "We will not speak of this now. Focus on the task at hand."

"It's packing," she said. "It doesn't require a lot of brain-power."

"These things must not be misplaced," he said.

She frowned, and was about to complain when she looked up and saw that the sky was lightening. It was dawn already—where had the time gone?

The tower stood at the northwestern corner of the Keep; its uppermost story was a good twenty feet taller than the fortress around it. From that top story—where Geni and Mirdoth were now—there were windows one could look through in all directions.

Geni crossed to the far end of the room, the eastern end. Through the window there she saw the sky, already lit a burnt orange by the flames consuming the wood, taking on an even paler shade: the yellow glow of morning.

To the south, the sky was lightening as well, behind the hills, themselves to the south of the village proper. Movement on those hills made her squint into the gray morning; it looked as if the hills themselves were moving for a second. Then she realized that what she was really seeing was a steady stream of people pouring down the hill, covering nearly every piece of available surface. No. Not people.

Fallen.

Some of them had already reached the outermost regions of the village and disappeared below her sight lines. She had little doubt of what was happening there, as she could also make out the sound of screaming. The noise level had been increasing steadily since she had arrived in the tower: noises from the court-yard below, horses galloping, commands being barked out, foot-steps running past . . .

Noises coming, more and more, from the north. She turned in that direction now, and saw the Great Bridge in the distance. People were moving across it already.

The evacuation had begun.

She turned back toward Mirdoth and saw, to her surprise, that he was removing the cover from his scope.

For all that he claimed to use the instrument for his observations, Geni realized that up until this second, she had never actually seen him use it.

"Mirdoth," she said.

"A moment, child," he replied, bending over his instrument.

"Mirdoth." She crossed the room and stood next to him. "This is not really a good time for stargazing."

"I would agree," he said, without looking up.

"Then what . . ."

Are you doing, she was about to ask, when Mirdoth took hold of the scope's main assembly and swiveled it toward the hills overlooking the village. He then began turning, in rapid succession, three small knobs that protruded from the underside of the scope's assembly.

"Can I ask what you're doing?" Geni said.

"I am adjusting the prisms."

"The prisms?"

"Yes. There." He stopped moving his hands then, and peered intently through the lens.

Geni was completely confused.

"Mirdoth . . ."

He cursed under his breath—once, and then a second time, much louder. Not one of the polite curses, either, but one of the marketplace ones. One of the worst of those, in fact.

Geni had never heard such language from him in her life.

Mirdoth straightened up. He looked pale to her, clearly shaken by what he'd seen.

"What's wrong?" she asked. "Mirdoth, what's the matter?"

"Look for yourself," he said, and gestured toward the scope.

Geni did. She leaned over the scope and looked through its lens as Mirdoth had been doing. One end was pointed toward the hills south of the village. The sky there looked even lighter than it had a second ago. Lighter, and . . .

Redder?

"By the Gods, it's on fire. They've set the village on fire." She straightened up, eyes widening. "We have to—"

Mirdoth laid a hand on her arm. "The village is fine. For the moment."

"Then what—"

"What you are seeing is the Titan."

"The Titan."

"Talax. The immortal that Tandis spoke of. The glow you see is his. His essence. The fire of magic that burns within him. He waits in the hills to the south."

"The red glow."

"Exactly. We must tell your father immediately."

"I don't understand," she said. "How do you know—"

"The Elemscope was not designed to look at the skies, Angenica, but instead at people. The glass, here"—he gestured toward the near end of the device—"is from ancient Imperium. Created, it is said, by the hand of Curgen himself. Under the right circumstances, it can reveal the magical essence of all living things."

"Magical essence." She shook her head. "I don't . . ."

"Every living thing in this world possesses magic, my child," Mirdoth said. "The animals, the trees, the very rocks of the Keep . . . ."

"Rocks possess magic," she said dubiously.

"Everything." He ran his hand along the length of the brass tube that formed the bulk of the Elemscope's body. "Differing only by a matter of degree."

"Ordinary people?"

"Indeed."

Geni bent over the scope again. As she did so she noticed the glass Mirdoth had spoken of: a shining disc held separate from the main assembly. Curious; it seemed for a second to actually reflect a small portion of her image as she glanced at it.

She blinked, and the reflection disappeared.

Geni put her eye to the lens and moved the main assembly.

A village street came into focus. One of the main streets—an intersection. There was enough light now to make out individual forms—people, moving quickly through the street. A man carrying a sack over his shoulder, a woman clutching a bag filled with loaves of bread to her chest . . .

There was a faint—very, very faint—blue-green glow around the woman. A slightly brighter one around the man.

"By the Destiny," she whispered.

"Yes," Mirdoth replied. "Exactly. It is the Destiny who brought magic to our world."

In the scope, an old woman appeared, balanced precariously using a cane. She had a faint blue-green glow as well. Every living thing, Mirdoth had said. Geni supposed it was true. Mirdoth had spoken to her of the different kinds of magic before; now she could see those two different kinds directly before her. Death, and Life. The different colors.

A figure ran past, too quickly for Geni to tell whether it was male or female, young or old—and knocked the old woman's cane out from under her. Geni gasped involuntarily as the old woman began to fall . . .

And then Geni sighed in relief as another figure, a boy her own age, grabbed hold of the old woman, steadied her, and handed her back her cane.

Then Geni gasped again.

The boy was Xander.

"What is the matter, child?" Mirdoth asked.

"Nothing," she said. "It's Xander. He's in the village."

"Doing as your father commanded. Good. He's all right?"

"He looks to be," she said, and then blinked, surprised, as

everything went fuzzy, as the glow around the woman—around the people everywhere in her field of vision—seemed to disappear for a second.

"Are you all right?" Mirdoth asked.

"Yes," she said. "Fine. Must have gotten something in my eye."

She stared down at Xander.

He seemed, she thought, to be staring straight back at her. As if he knew she was there.

Impossible, of course.

Xander had just handed the old woman her cane when he felt the strangest sensation come over him: a compulsion to turn and look back toward the Keep.

So he did.

The light of dawn was just now hitting the fortress, turning the amorphous black mass into the structure he was familiar with: the massive stone blocks, the great iron gate through which people, animals, and even the stray cart were now passing through, under the watchful eyes of Jarak's garrison.

His attention, though, was drawn toward the rear of the Keep, toward the observation tower belonging to the King's mage. He thought he saw a flash of light in the tiny speck of a window he could see.

He blinked, and it was gone.

"You're a good boy, Xander."

He turned. The woman he'd helped to her feet—Zayelle, Morlis's mother—was smiling at him.

"You'll come along, too, now, won't you?" she asked.

"I will. In a minute." He steadied her again, and pointed her on the path toward the gate, toward the edges of the crowd streaming to safety. "I need to find Saren."

"That old fool," she snorted, which Xander had to smile at. Zayelle was at least as old as Saren, probably older, he thought. "He's not worth the trouble."

"Zayelle . . ." He shook his head. The two of them—Zayelle and Saren—had fought like cats and dogs ever since he'd known them. At first he thought it was just an act: two old friends putting on a show. It had taken him about a year to realize that the two truly, greatly despised each other.

"Well, he's not," the old woman said. "You are, though. Take care of yourself, boy."

"I will." He leaned forward and kissed her on the forehead. He was surprised to find the old woman shaking; she was nervous, clearly, and when he thought about it, it was easy to understand why. She had, more than likely, never left the sight of the Keep. Probably no one in her family had—not for generations. Zayelle's clan, like most of the village's inhabitants, were descendants of the Kingdom armies, from the time of the War of Magic, a thousand years ago. Descendants who after their victory over the Fallen Army had staked their own claim to the land here, the rich fertile soil between the Spine and the sea.

Now they were being asked to pack up and leave the only homes they had ever known. In their shoes, Xander would be hesitant as well.

Come to think of it, he realized . . .

He was in their shoes.

His parents had lived and died in the shadow of the Keep, just as their parents, and their parents' parents, and back like that a dozen generations, had before them. His mother and father, Kayra and Arn, had chosen to live about as far from the village center as one could get and still remain in Outpost. A two-room house, far to the southeast, within sight of the Wastes themselves. They'd had no desire to interact with their neighbors; no interest in village life, life inside the Keep, or life beyond it, for that matter, in the western lands. They were proudly self-sufficient, happy to be away from the affairs of men, out on their own . . . until the day of Xander's tenth birthday. Or rather, the night of it.

That night had changed everything.

The sound of horses approaching had been the only warning they'd had. They'd been in the middle of dinner; Xander had heard the animals first, the unfamiliar noise barely registering in his brain until it was too late.

"Horses," his father had said. "A lot of them."

Exchanging a glance with Kayra, he'd risen to his feet, and flung the door open.

And almost as quickly flung it shut again.

When he turned back to Kayra and Xander, his face had gone bloodless and white.

"Fallen," he'd said.

Xander's mother had gone pale as well.

"What?" she said.

"Fallen!" his father shouted, much louder this time, and ran for the ax hanging over the fire.

Fallen. Xander, up until that point, had heard the word only in passing. He had thought of them the way he thought of the monsters under his bed. Not real.

But there was something yelling out in the yard. Several somethings. They sounded not entirely real.

"Gods," his mother said.

Xander stood and reached for the carving knife.

His mother's hand closed on his as he grasped it.

"Let me help," he said.

"No," she said again.

"Kayra, let the boy—" his father began.

"No," his mother said, gritting her teeth. "We'll call you when it's safe," she said, starting to cry, and then Xander started to cry, too, as—with a strength he'd never thought she'd possessed—she dragged him from his chair with one hand, and slid the table away from them with the other.

And there was the entrance to the root cellar—a simple trapdoor—in the floor beneath them.

"No!" Xander said.

His mother didn't even respond; she simply lifted the trapdoor and shoved him in. The cellar wasn't even tall enough for him to stand.

The trapdoor slammed shut over him as he hit the ground, knocking the breath from his body. He rolled over onto his back and gasped, trying to recover his wits.

He heard the door fly open and slam into the wall; the sound of heavy boots on the floor; the crashing of heavy objects. Shouts of pain, and cursing, and then laughter that didn't sound quite right to him. Didn't sound like anything he had ever heard before.

Inches from pushing the trapdoor open, his hand froze.

My birthday, he thought. It's my birthday.

He stayed down in that cellar hour after hour after hour. Long after the house above him fell silent.

He came out to find the house a ruin, the door to the back room half open, a trail of blood leading into it. The buzzing of flies came from within that back room. Xander closed that door, and went to feed the animals in the barn.

But they were dead, too.

It took him three days to get up the courage to bury his parents. The first time, he didn't dig deep enough. He woke in the morning to find dogs digging at the graves. The second time he went a dozen feet down, making sure the animals wouldn't get at the corpses.

It took him until summer to scrub the house clean of the Fallen's presence. By that time he'd gotten used to living on his own—he could hunt, he could fish, he could drink water from the little stream out back. He'd be fine, Xander told himself. He didn't need anybody. And for all of that first summer, it was true.

But as the seasons changed, food began to get scarce. The

nights began to get cold. The tasks that his mother and father had always spent time on for reasons he did not understand at the time—the stockpiling of wood and the canning of fruits and vegetables—became clear.

One cold winter morning, the half-starved ten-year-old boy, his ribs clearly outlined against his skin, made his way to a small stable on the outskirts of the village proper. A stable belonging to Zayelle, her then-husband, Roynen, and their son, Morlis. It was Zayelle who'd found him, brought him inside, and fed him. Zayelle who'd made the deal with him to stay—three coppers a day to help tend to the family horses, to sweep up, to run errands as needed. To help her son Morlis, because Roynen was a drunkard. The two boys had even been friends, briefly, right up until the afternoon that Xander discovered his real talent—not cleaning stables, but delivering messages. He'd discovered that by accident; Zayelle had asked him to deliver an item to the merchants' quarter, a tangled web of streets at the very northern edge of the village. By that point Xander had learned the village inside and out and was able to find people in places few would ever think to look. Soon others were paying him to deliver messages; one of those others had been Saren, who—recognizing a good thing when he saw it—had offered Xander a bed in exchange for an exclusive on his services, so to speak. Ever since then, Xander had been a full-time messenger. Morlis had long since become his enemy.

But Zayelle . . .

When Xander couldn't find Saren at his home—it was only later that he would discover that the old man had been among the first to reach the Keep—the next person he thought to help evacuate was Zayelle. As he suspected, Morlis was too drunk to help his mother, so it had been Xander who'd gotten her out of the old house, though he'd been unable to get her to leave as quickly as he would have liked, and she'd insisted on bringing a bag of her most valued belongings.

Watching the old woman walk away from him now, Xander saw that she'd dropped something from that bag when she had fallen. A pan.

"Zayelle!" he called out, reaching down to the ground to pick it up. "You forgot—"

He heard a noise behind him then, and froze in his tracks.

Hoofbeats.

He turned in time to see them make the turn a few blocks distant, to the south. Make the turn and then turn a second time, to the north.

Fallen. On horseback. A dozen, at least. Some of them were screaming—the same scream, the battle cry, that he'd heard the night his parents had been murdered.

"Run!" Xander yelled, turning back to the stragglers in front of him. "Drop your things and run!"

A handful did. Zayelle stood there, frozen in fear. The woman in front of her—fat, fleshy, a horrible scar down one cheek—dropped the pack she was carrying and started to cry. The old man behind her took a step backward, and stumbled, and cried out.

Xander turned once more, and the first of the creatures—Gods, they were fast, to have moved so quickly—was on him.

CHAPTER FIFTEEN

Xander raised the pan to defend himself and found Tandis—on horseback—staring down at him, mouth half open in surprise.

"You," the captain said.

"You," Xander replied. "I mean, 'you, sir.' " The captain must have ridden in from one of the cross streets, seen their plight, and come rushing to protect them. Good thing.

Xander glanced behind Tandis's horse.

The Fallen were a few hundred feet away and closing fast.

Tandis seemed remarkably unconcerned. He was still frowning at Xander.

"This is most strange, boy."

"Coincidence, you mean," Xander said.

Tandis shook his head. "No. I said what I meant. Strange. Unusual." He gestured with the tip of his sword to the pan in Xander's hand.

"You intend to fight with that?"

"It's all I—"

"Have," he was about to say, and then Tandis reached inside his cloak and tossed Xander a dagger.

He caught it with one hand, his right. He held the pan in the other and took up a fighting stance as Tandis swung his horse back around.

The Fallen were almost on them.

"Stay behind me, lad!" the knight shouted. Then he raised his sword high over his head and charged.

A thousand yards away, two streets to the south, atop the tallest structure in Outpost, a temple devoted to worship of the Destiny, Nym drew the bowstring taut.

The knight had fallen into their laps, just as Talax had prophesied.

Gods, it was good to work for someone smart. Not just intelligent—General Relis had been that, undoubtedly, his knowledge of battlefield tactics, his own combat skills second to none, really—but wise. Someone who understood how others were likely to act, and react, and planned accordingly.

The knight will come to the aid of the Keep, Talax had said. *You will simply need to be waiting, in position, when he does. And then . . .*

And then this, Nym thought. The arrow.

He sighted down his bow. The knight would not stay still— thrusting, slicing, chopping . . . The Urxen were falling like dominoes before his attack. Three, four, five of them down already. Tandis would most likely not stop moving until his attackers were all dead, Nym realized. That would be his best shot, Nym decided. His clearest view of the knight's unguarded neck, and throat.

Until that moment came, he would stay ready.

Geni blinked and lifted her eye from the lens.

The sun's glare was making it hard for her to see—to follow the course of the fight. It was distorting everything she saw through the lens of the Elemscope. Tandis—and the knight beside him, for that matter—glittered like a bright blue jewel, the colors flashing and then fading away before her, reflections from the sky, perhaps, or maybe even the bay.

Either that, or the lack of sleep was finally catching up to her.

"Child," Mirdoth asked, pressing at her shoulder, "what's happening? Are they all right?"

Look for yourself, she was about to say, but then realized she wanted to know as much as Mirdoth.

She leaned forward once more.

Xander was feeling fairly useless.

His biggest contribution to the fight so far had been a cry of warning—"Look out behind you!"—which he'd shouted as one of the Fallen who had been cut down on Tandis's initial attack tried to get to his feet again.

Just as Tandis's head swiveled, the creature gasped, coughed up blood, and collapsed.

Tandis turned back around and pressed his attack once more.

There were three of the Fallen left. He was off his horse, on his feet, driving them south, back from the Keep. The attackers were too closely bunched together, Xander thought. If he'd been facing the knight . . .

Two left.

One of the others screamed, raised his sword over his head, and charged. For a second it seemed to Xander that Tandis was genuinely surprised. It seemed that the Fallen soldier might actually reach the knight.

He drew his knife back, and raised the pan, preparing to charge himself . . .

And sensed something.

Something hurtling toward him—no, toward Tandis—out of the corner of his eye. A weapon: a spear, an arrow, something.

Tandis would never be able to move fast enough to dodge it, but in that split second, as he moved from seeing it to reacting, Xander realized that he was in the perfect position, that if he raised his pan just so and—

Clang.

The something slammed into the pan. The impact knocked the pan from his grasp, and it clattered to the street.

The something fell to the street as well. An arrow.

Xander looked at it and frowned.

An arrow, but there was something different about it. It seemed to him to be glowing . . . a faint, reddish-orange glow that was fading even as he watched. Strange.

He knelt down and stretched out a hand to pick it up.

"Stop!"

Tandis was coming toward him, concern etched on his face. The last of the Fallen lay on the ground behind him.

He pushed past Xander and picked the arrow up off the ground. He examined it closely, and frowned.

He touched a finger to the tip of it, and Xander watched, astonished, as the arrow glowed red.

"It's magic," Xander said, more to himself than out loud.

"Yes. Magic." The expression on Tandis's face changed then, to one Xander had never seen from him before.

The knight looked concerned.

"I am in your debt, boy," Tandis said.

"What?"

"I am in your debt. Had this arrow struck me"—he sheathed his sword—"I would be dead even now."

He clapped a hand on Xander's shoulder.

"You saved my life."

Nym stood there for a moment, staring in disbelief. Staring at the knight. At the boy. At the pan on the ground, and the arrow.

Two years of planning undone. By a cooking pan. He could scream.

So he did.

Screamed, and snapped the bow in two over his knee, and threw the two pieces to the ground.

By the Gods, by the Destiny, he'd had the shot lined up perfectly. As he faced the last of the Urxen, the knight had let his sword arm relax, drawing down his armor, and his throat lay exposed for a second, and Nym—the bowstring already drawn taut, the arrow already strung—had sighted, aimed, and fired.

And at that exact instant, the boy had moved. Faster than Nym would have deemed possible for a man, swinging the cooking pan up to block the arrow. The missile that would have pierced flesh, and worked its magic. The missile that had taken two years of work to prepare now lay on the ground in front of the one it had been meant to kill.

Impossible. Unacceptable. And, truth be told, a little bit frightening.

Nym found himself wondering if Talax would think the failure was his fault.

"I guess that makes us even," Xander said.

"I guess so." A smile tugged at the corners of the captain's mouth, and just as quickly faded.

"What's the matter?" Xander asked.

"That arrow." Tandis shook his head. "Its use proves conquest is not the Fallen's only objective."

"What do you mean?" Xander asked.

Tandis didn't answer. He shoved the arrow into his pack and climbed back onto his horse.

"Where are you going?" Xander asked.

"I will clear a few more streets and buy you and these others a little more time to get inside the Keep," Tandis said.

"I want to help."

"You can. Tell these fools"—Tandis raised his voice and glared directly at the stragglers—"to drop their things and move!"

He straightened in the saddle, yanked back on the reins, and with a final look at Xander, galloped off in the direction the Fallen had come from.

"Don't like him," Zayelle said, stepping forward. "Arrogant sonofabitch."

"Maybe so." Xander turned back to the old woman. "But I think he's right: The Fallen are everywhere now. We're better off leaving that stuff and moving as quickly as we can."

"Hmmphh," Zayelle snorted. "Easy for you to say. You got the princess to hit up for money now, I hear."

"I don't—"

She bent down and picked up her pan.

Then she and the others started moving forward again. No more quickly—though, thankfully, also no more slowly—than before.

With a sigh made up of equal parts frustration and resignation, Xander followed.

Leeland had been right, Geni realized.

Xander was fast. Fast as Tandis, even. The way he'd blocked that arrow . . .

With training, he could be a soldier. Training, and food. A lot of food. Gods, next to the captain, Xander looked like a little stick figure. Thank the Destiny he hadn't had to actually fight any of those Fallen; he'd been lucky enough the first time to kill one of them, but he'd had the element of surprise then. In a true battle . . .

She watched as he hurried the stragglers toward the Keep,

taking the bag from the old woman. Morlis's mother, Geni recognized. They'd been introduced once, a long time ago. What was her name again . . .

"Angenica."

She lifted her gaze from the scope.

Mirdoth, once the battle was over, had returned to organizing his things. To packing. He stood now, next to the half-dozen trunks of his things destined to journey across the bridge. He'd slipped on a warmer cloak. And boots. Heavy boots.

"Time to go," he said, and Geni felt her heart sink in her chest.

Chapter Sixteen

The sun was rising, burning off the last of the clouds that had dripped rain on the evacuees and—thankfully—the fire last night. It was going to be a beautiful day.

Ambrose wondered how many of the men standing alongside him would be alive when it was through.

He stood on the outer ring of battlements high above the South Gate, next to the cauldrons of pitch being burned in anticipation of the Fallen attack, and watched the stream of refugees entering the Keep beneath him. A stream roughly equal in volume to that he'd seen leaving through the north, heading across the bridge. Those entering the gate beneath him were moving faster, though, some at a dead run, even. He understood their haste.

At the edge of the village, a thousand yards away, the Fallen were massing.

There were hundreds of them now, dozens arriving every few minutes or so. They'd brought forward large steel wagons as well, positioning them at the end of all the village streets facing the Keep. For what purpose? The wagons had no offensive weaponry; they could provide cover, he supposed, during an attack, but otherwise . . . the formation told him nothing.

The way the Fallen Army moved told him something, though: these soldiers were organized, disciplined, well trained. No marauding warriors here. That was itself cause for worry: Individually, a warrior of the Fallen was far more lethal than a soldier of the Kingdom. Stronger, faster—even the Urxen. The Kingdom had survived the War of Magic primarily due to superior strategy and tactics, and the discipline of well-trained soldiers. This force, however, appeared as professional and disciplined as any army the Kingdom had put together.

As yet none of them had broached the distance between village and Keep. They were operating under orders, clearly, but whose? And why?

"A good two thousand of them, I'd say. Maybe more."

Ambrose looked up to see that Jarak had joined him. The commander was in full battle garb, armored from head to toe, save that he carried his helm in his hand.

"Not enough to truly test our defenses," the Lord replied.

"No sir," Jarak nodded, a frown on his face. Ambrose could hear the "but" in his voice; the commander knew just as he did that there was something else going on here.

The great iron gate below them swung shut; the last of the village's inhabitants were inside now. He and Jarak began to talk strategy: They brought in Neral and a few lieutenants to review the hand signals that would trigger the pouring of the pitch, the firing of the arrows, and a few other nasty traps that had been prepared for the invading army. And yet the whole time Ambrose stood there, listening to his men, occasionally offering comment, he could not shake the feeling that the eventuality they were planning for—the siege of the Keep—would never come to pass. Odd.

The meeting broke up; the Lord began circling the parapets, offering words of encouragement to his men. A pat on the back here; a note of shared remembrance there. The men seemed to share his nervousness. He tried to banish it. The Keep had stood for a thousand years; it would stand for a thousand more.

"So many."

Ambrose turned and saw his daughter walking toward him, Mirdoth a step behind.

"You should be gone."

"Without saying good-bye? Never."

They embraced; she pulled back from his embrace, looked up at him—and then squeezed him tightly once more.

"I wish you would come," she whispered, head buried in his shoulders.

Ambrose shook his head.

"I can't. Tandis made it clear—the Keep must not fall."

"Jarak can hold the Keep," Geni said. "These are his men. They know him, trust him . . ."

"You're wrong. These are my men," Ambrose said, putting a little steel in his voice. "My responsibility. As is this task."

His daughter nodded, pulling away once more.

"Go now, Geni," he said. "Please. If what Tandis said about this Talax is true, then the fighting will be terrible."

"Lord." Mirdoth stepped forward. "It is true. And what is more . . . the Titan is here. Now."

Mirdoth told him then what they'd seen through the Elemscope: the aura of power lurking just beyond the hills. Ambrose had a sinking feeling in his gut then, a feeling that he knew exactly what the Fallen were waiting for before they began their attack.

Still, he and his men had nothing to worry about. The western entrance was sealed, which left the great iron gate beneath them as the only way in. And that gate, Galor had told him long, long ago, was enchanted, designed precisely to prevent an enemy from gaining entrance. The task before them was simply to prevent the Fallen from scaling the walls; to survive the inevitable siege that would follow their attack. And to give Tandis and his men time to search for the thing he had mentioned, the thing Talax must not be allowed, at all costs, to gain control of. The Bane of the Dred'nir.

The Keep must not fall.

He nodded to Mirdoth, who took hold of Geni's arm.

"Come, Angenica," his chief minister said. "We must go."

Geni nodded.

Ambrose took a step up onto the wall itself, turned, and addressed his men.

"Knights of the garrison!" he shouted. "Men of Outpost! On the eve of battle, I salute you."

He swiveled his head from left to right, catching as many eyes as he could.

"Most of you," Ambrose said, "have never seen those things out there in your lifetime. These Fallen. You may have heard stories from your childhood, how these creatures were once men, how they were magically enchanted by the Titans. I do not know whether this is so or not, but I can tell you, they die as easily as men with a sword through their bowels!"

Cheers—and some laughter—greeted his words.

Geni and Mirdoth were moving along the inner battlement now, closer to the courtyards. He caught her eye and she smiled.

"They will burn as easily as men, too, with the pitch you have prepared! Your arrows will . . . ."

His voice trailed off as he became aware of a sudden murmur among the men. They were staring now not at him, but at the village at his back.

Ambrose turned and saw that the Fallen armies had parted ranks.

A lone figure was walking toward the Keep. Dressed in a plain black robe, wearing no armor whatsoever. An emissary, he thought at first.

And then the figure raised its arms and threw off the cloak without breaking stride.

It was a man. Perfectly, almost unnaturally proportioned. Striding toward them like a god walking the earth.

It seemed to be staring straight at him; Ambrose felt an instant of vertigo, and weakness, and a desire to fall to his knees.

And then he straightened, and raised his hand.

"Archers, at the ready!" he shouted, with far, far more confidence than he felt.

Mirdoth gasped, as if he'd been struck hard. He wavered on his feet; for a second Geni thought he might fall from the battlements to the courtyard below.

"I'm all right, child," he said as she took hold of his shoulder.

"That's him, isn't it?" Geni asked, nodding toward the dark figure approaching the gate. "Talax?"

Mirdoth nodded. "We must go," he said. "Now."

Geni nodded as well. But neither of them moved. Geni, for her part, felt paralyzed.

A dozen yards away, her father's hand remained poised, ready to signal the archers. Out of the corner of her eye, she could see a handful of other men, standing on the towers between the battlements, hands similarly raised.

The Titan continued to walk toward them. He was close enough now that Geni could begin to make out his features; there was something oddly familiar about them. About the way he walked. He reminded her of someone, she realized, though she couldn't say exactly who.

When the Titan was a hundred yards away, Ambrose slashed his hand downward, simultaneously shouting, "Fire!"

Even before the motion had finished, a thousand arrows were in the air, flying so thick that Geni could barely see the figure they were intended for. An instant later those arrows fell toward the Titan. She heard the thwack of some of them hitting the ground.

Talax kept coming.

Either the arrows had all missed, or . . .

"Fire again!" Ambrose growled.

A second wave of arrows flew toward the man and again, they simply . . . missed. Around the man arrows stuck out of the ground, seeming to almost paint an outline of where the man had stood.

There was magic at work here, Geni realized. Magic powerful beyond any she had ever seen in her life.

"Stand firm, men!" Jarak shouted. "Stand fast! The time for battle is upon us. Let us do our Lord—our King—our race—proud!"

Shouts of affirmation followed on the heels of Jarak's words—from some of the men, at least.

Most looked as scared as she was.

The man Talax—no, she should not think of him as a man; he was anything but a man; he was of another race entirely—came and stood before the great iron gate. Looked at it, and then up at the figures standing above him.

He said nothing.

Her father's voice rang out once more.

"Stand ready!" Ambrose yelled, gesturing toward those members of the garrison poised near the boiling cauldrons of pitch, poised to dump the flaming contents of those containers onto the single figure before them.

Talax gestured toward the gate, and the stone beneath Geni's feet began to shake.

A split second later, there was a sudden crack louder than anything Geni had ever heard before in her life, and on the heels of that an even louder sound, a rumble and a crash beneath her feet as if the Destiny themselves had fallen from heaven and slammed into the earth. She knew what that sound was without even looking.

The gate had fallen.

A second later, the wall above it began to give way as well.

Geni watched in horror as her father, and Jarak, and their men, and the cauldrons of burning pitch began to topple slowly toward the ground, all screaming and flailing as they fell.

"Princess!"

She turned in time to see Mirdoth waver once more. The battlement beneath her feet began to crack and crumble.

And in the distance, the Fallen Army screamed, and charged.

CHAPTER SEVENTEEN

Xander had found Saren. The old man was standing near the entrance gate of the bridge itself. He was arguing with a soldier about something, wearing a look of feigned innocence.

"For the sake of the Gods. Look at that fool. The world is ending, and he still finds reason to fight." Zayelle shook her head.

She had hold of Xander's arm; he was helping her stand up in the midst of the steady stream of refugees pouring out of the village. They had at last made their way to the Great Bridge. It was only a short way from the Keep to the bridge, but the refugees had made maddeningly slow progress.

Amarian's Folly; Xander couldn't take his eyes off it. The thing looked like it would fall at any second. It was made from timbers out of the Keeper's Wood, built long before there even was a Keep . . . or so the stories went. Built by Amarian himself, in the last of his days, as he and the remnants of his army made the long journey home after their war against the Dread Lord Curgen. Raised in less than a month, a three-hundred-foot span of timber the width of a single wagon, bridging the space between East and West. Raised by magic, Geni had told him; a magic that to this day prevented it from falling into the surf more than a thousand feet below.

Xander certainly hoped magic had something to do with it; he could not imagine otherwise how the bridge would stay up much longer, given the mass of people and wagons and animals now streaming across it.

"Ah!" Saren had caught sight of him now, and waved him forward. "You will see, Captain. Here is one who will bear out my good name. My good intentions. Boy."

He waved again; Xander, Zayelle in tow, reluctantly crossed to the old man's side.

Xander found that he had mixed feelings about seeing Saren; on the one hand, he was happy the old man was alive. On the other . . . Saren had fired him without so much as a word of warning. And for what?

"You know this man, boy?" the soldier—his rank and insignia revealed him as a captain of Jarak's guard—asked.

"I do. I did work for him."

"Work?" the soldier asked.

"Messengering, the like."

"He's a crook. A thief and a scoundrel," Zayelle spat out.

"Mind your tongue, old woman," Saren said. "Or I'll cut it from your mouth." He raised a threatening hand.

"Now, now—none of that." The guard stepped between the two.

"What's the problem?" Xander asked.

"He's offering to take messages from people headed across the bridge," the guard said.

"Make it easier for families to find each other on the other side," Saren said. "Providing a service, I am."

"Hmmm." The soldier didn't look convinced.

"The boy can vouch for me." Saren put his arm around Xander's shoulder. "He's been my right hand for how long now, boy—ten years? Twelve?"

"Five," Xander said. "And you fired me—remember?"

"What?" Saren looked honestly surprised. "What do you mean?"

"Fired. Let go." Xander peeled Saren's arm away. "Oro's your right hand now."

"Oro?" The guard frowned. "Mahor's son? The one who worked at the armory? That Oro? He's yours?"

"Uh . . ." Saren said.

"Yes," Xander said.

The guard glared at Saren. "He's a crook. A thief. Stole the money I gave Hulwain for—"

"Well, I discovered the same thing," Saren said, nodding emphatically. "Why I let him go. Why I'm back with my boy Xander here. Ain't that right, boy?"

He tried to put his arm around Xander's shoulder again; Xander shrugged it off.

He didn't know why he hadn't seen it before; Saren had been using him all these years. Taking advantage of him.

"No," he said. "That's not right."

Saren looked honestly shocked. "But—"

"Let's go," Zayelle said, grabbing Xander's arm. "I want to get across before the fighting gets here."

"So you won't vouch for him, boy?" the guard asked as Xander and Zayelle started to walk away.

Xander turned back and looked at the old man once more, and his heart softened.

They had shared some good times, and it was true that, yes, Saren wasn't truly a crook. He had run a messenger service of sorts, even if Xander had done all the work.

He opened his mouth to tell the guard all that when the ground beneath his feet rumbled, and shook, and then literally moved as a sound like distant thunder came to his ears.

And then he heard screaming, coming from the direction of the Keep. A sound that grew louder, closer, like a wave approaching them.

The guard's eyes widened, and he turned toward the Keep as well.

"Gods," the guard said. "What was that?"

In that very second—even as the guard spoke his question, even before the cloud of dust appeared behind the refugees, even before those refugees, who had been proceeding toward the bridge at a respectable pace, suddenly broke and began to run, men and women screaming, children crying—Xander knew what had happened.

"The Keep," he said. "It's fallen."

The soldier turned to him.

"What?"

"They've breached the gate," he said.

The soldier's eyes widened. "How could you know that?"

"I don't know," Xander said. "I just do."

"Boy has a sixth sense about these things," Saren said. "A way of knowing what's around the corner. That's what makes him such a good messenger."

The guard looked at them for a moment, then nodded.

"The Destiny be with you," he said, and turned and ran in the direction of the Keep, forcing his way through the stream of refugees like a salmon fighting upstream.

"We have to go," Zayelle said, tugging at Xander's arm. "Now."

"The old woman's right," Saren snapped. "Come." He pointed ahead, to the bridge. "We stay to the middle of the path. Otherwise—"

"Who are you calling old?" Zayelle shot back.

Saren glared at her again. "Hush your mouth woman, or—"

"Or what?"

"I'll hush it for you."

Xander looked at them, at the stream of refugees, at the swaying bridge, and then back toward the Keep.

Geni, he thought. She's in there.

"I have to go back," he said.

The two turned and looked at him as one.

"What?"

"I have to go back. Stay together. Take care of yourselves."

He squeezed Zayelle's hand; he nodded to Saren.

He turned and ran.

Chapter Eighteen

"You shall not—"

Nym supposed the guard was going to say "pass," but by then Nym's knife was in the man's throat, and the man gagged and dropped his own sword, his hands going to his neck to try to stem the flow of blood—useless, of course—and he fell to the ground, twitching and gurgling, eyes wide with shock. Nym couldn't blame him for that. One second Nym had been twenty paces away from him, moving languidly in his direction, or at least it may have seemed that way to the guard, and the next . . .

This.

The man twitched once more, and then lay still.

Nym stepped over him and into the Great Hall as behind him a second round of screaming broke out. Men, and some women this time; by the Destiny, he had half a mind to turn around and tell the Urxen who'd followed him into this section of the Keep that they would get far more pleasure out of the females if they used just a little bit less force and a little more tact. A hard-learned lesson that had come to him courtesy of a particularly vile-tempered female in some caravan he'd come across a few years back; a lesson that had stayed with him ever since. And speaking of vile tempers . . .

His seemed to be gone, he realized. The black cloud that had been hanging over him since the arrow's miss. No doubt the killing had something to do with it; nothing like the thrill of mowing down a few dozen or so people to lift one's spirits.

Actually, it could have been more than a few dozen. Quite a few more. When the gate had fallen, Nym had been the first one into the Keep, partly because he'd gotten excited by the sight of all those helpless, flailing guards on the ground, but partly because he wanted to impress his lord, to make up for what had happened with the knight. Nym had quickened himself in a way he hadn't done for years to accomplish that; summoned every bit of the speed he possessed to dart around the injured and the maimed, the whimpering and the wounded, the cowardly and the courageous, and cut them all down. With his knives, with his hands, his teeth, a piece of rubble, a discarded sword . . . whatever worked.

All that killing had helped him work up an appetite. And as he stepped into the chamber the soldier had been guarding, he saw something to sate it. A table full of food—a repast fit for a king, most of it untouched. We interrupted the lord's meal, Nym thought with a smile.

He sat down and began to eat. This he did slowly, with relish, savoring the taste, studying the room around him as he dined.

The first thing he saw was the wall hanging: a king—Galor, he assumed—looking down, with what Nym assumed was supposed to be a beneficent smile. The King of the West, looking all-wise, all-powerful. The thought made Nym smile: powerful. His lord would show the King a thing or two about power before long.

The walls were covered with ornate wooden fixtures; the floors were lined with a red carpet with golden edges. They had money here, these men. Wealth beyond that normally seen in the East. It made Nym mad to think of it, until he realized that that, too, would change before long.

He took a bite of a calivar, a sip of wine. What he wouldn't give for a good piece of meat; they'd been too long on the march, the army had, pushing up the coast from Kraxis through the Wastes, which weren't called that for nothing. Nym had been on the verge of eating horseflesh more than once.

He took another bite of the calivar, and then threw it at the hanging of Galor. The fruit caught the King square in the face and left a stain as it slid down to the floor.

He smiled and walked to the window.

The slaughter outside was continuing and, he suspected, would awhile longer. Unless Talax deemed the battle worthy of joining himself. He wondered where his lord was; what he was doing. If—

"Commander."

Nym turned as one of the Urxen entered the room. An officer of some sort, judging by the uniform. A familiar face, even, as far as those things went. Gods, these things had names, didn't they? Was he supposed to remember their names? Perhaps so, judging from how it was looking at him. Some sort of pretense of equality.

Well, he'd put a stop to that.

"What?" he snapped.

"We've found a girl. The princess, we think."

"Ambrose's daughter?"

"As I said, sir. We think so."

As I said. Nym couldn't believe the effrontery of the creature, to talk to him that way.

He quickened to its side, and the officer started as Nym's knife was suddenly at his throat.

"Have a care how you talk to me, Urxen."

"Yes, sir," the creature snapped.

"And bring her to me," Nym said. "Now."

CHAPTER NINETEEN

Jarak was dead. Neral, too. Xander had seen the commander's body atop a stack of other corpses in the courtyard, though he had no idea how the man had died. The boy had watched Neral's demise; the general surrounded by three of the Fallen, swinging his sword with a speed and dexterity that belied his girth; a speed and dexterity that ultimately made no difference.

When they'd started to cut the general up into little pieces, he'd turned away and moved on down the secret passage—the same tunnels he and Geni had traversed, what seemed like ages ago—that served as his hiding place. He came to another peephole and watched as Lord Ambrose, face scratched and bleeding, was marched off under guard, limping as he went. He followed Ambrose and his captors through a tunnel he and Geni had taken once, down to the dungeons, where he saw the Lord thrown into the same cell with Mirdoth, who lay unconscious on the floor, face bruised and battered. Ambrose rushed to his friend's side as the cell door slammed shut on the two of them, preventing Xander from seeing any more.

A guard took up station in front of that door, and Xander sighed. He'd hoped to get the Lord's attention unnoticed. That wouldn't happen now. Questions burned in his head: Where was

Geni? Was she still alive? He had to assume so; so where was she, then? A captive as well? She'd be here, wouldn't she? So she was on the loose—at least for the moment. Where was she? What was she doing?

She might be in the tunnels, he realized. She might even come here, if she'd seen her father and Mirdoth captured. If that was the case, all he had to do was wait here for her.

He sat down, as quietly as he could, and folded his arms around his knees, and did just that. Waited.

He rested his head on his arms. His eyes began to grow heavy. He blinked and sat up straight.

His eyes began to close again.

He shook his head and got to his feet.

Sit down again, and he'd fall asleep. Probably start snoring, and the guards would hear that, and then they'd find him, and the tunnels, and then they'd find Geni, too, if she was hiding in them. He couldn't wait for Geni to show up. He had to find her himself.

Acting on instinct, he began heading upward. He reached the upper level of the Keep and, waiting until he was certain the hall was deserted, emerged from the tunnels out into the hallway proper. He stood there, letting his eyes adjust to the light, listening. The only sound he heard was the occasional drip of water that was still draining from the recent spring rains. The drops echoed through the hallway.

He took a step forward and froze.

Instinct had led him to a part of the Keep he'd never seen before. In front of him was a staircase—a wide, winding staircase that led up one level and down another.

From around the corner he heard voices. He ducked behind a support pillar.

His eyes widened as he saw Geni appear, flanked by two guards. They were escorting her up the stairs. For a second he thought about darting out to intercept them, but then remembered that not only was he unarmed, he was entirely untrained. The Fallen, by contrast, were armed to the teeth. And huge.

Geni and her captors ascended the stairs and disappeared.

Just as Xander prepared to follow, he heard the sound of voices once more. Voices, and footsteps. A lot of them, coming from the level just below.

He looked down and saw a good dozen Fallen soldiers appear and stop at the foot of the stairs. One of them—the leader, Xander presumed—stepped forward.

"In case you're wondering, the commander himself is going to talk to her. And while he does, we're to spread out and make sure the manlings didn't leave any surprises behind. Understood?"

The Fallen soldiers nodded and broke formation. Some went to the left, others to right. Some began to climb the stairs.

Xander began to panic.

Where to go? What to do? As soon as the soldiers started to search, they'd find him hiding behind the pillar; certainly if he dashed out and ran for the tunnels, they would see him. And even if they didn't . . . they knew about the tunnels now. A dozen different courses of action, a hundred different outcomes ran through his mind, none of them good. He was trapped. He was dead.

The leader was a dozen steps away from Xander's level when he turned his head and yelled something unintelligible to a guard below.

And suddenly Xander saw a way out. A way up the stairs, even.

With the leader's head still turned, he dashed to the next pillar over. It was only a few feet from the set of stairs leading up to the top floor. A particularly huge Fallen soldier lumbered his way to the top of the first flight of steps and now stood no more than five feet away, looking around.

The fat soldier turned to survey the scene below, and Xander crept up right behind him.

Another soldier, on the steps in front of the fat one, bellowed something and pointed. He couldn't see Xander kneeling behind the fat soldier.

The soldier at the top of the stairs turned and walked back down. The fat one turned as well to watch him go.

Xander seized the moment and ran silently up the stairs, and into a long hallway, as beneath him the soldiers continued their search.

He looked left, and then right, and frowned.

Where had Geni gone? There was no sign . . .

A trail of mud on the hall carpet caught his eye. Three sets of footprints. Geni and her two guards.

Taking care to keep as quiet as he could, Xander followed the trail down the hall.

CHAPTER TWENTY

Geni kept her eyes focused straight ahead. She would not show them that she was scared. She would not tell them a thing. She would go to the dungeons with a smile on her face. Especially if she could manage to get one of these things alone. They were all weak-willed, just short of simpletons. If she had a chance to try to command one, she might just succeed, she thought.

They passed a body—a soldier—lying on the floor. Geni tried not to look at its face, but she couldn't help herself.

Miral. One of Jarak's men.

The guard on her left laughed, seeing her reaction.

"Sorry, pretty," he said. "We'll try to avoid those kinds of sights in the future."

She turned away and stared straight ahead.

She couldn't believe this was happening. The Fallen, inside the Keep itself . . .

Images flashed through her mind; images from the seconds after the gate had fallen. She'd rushed back from the battlements as the wall collapsed, as her father disappeared before her eyes. Mirdoth, too . . . One second he'd been standing next to her, and the next he was gone. Possibly she'd simply lost him in the panic;

possibly he lay crushed and broken among the bodies that littered the courtyard, the bodies that—as she watched in horror—the Fallen trampled, and skewered, and slaughtered. She'd tried to fight, too, for a minute, and then realized it was useless. Realized that she would soon be captured, or slaughtered as well, so she had broken free of the crowd of soldiers and headed for the safest place she knew, the place that no one but she and Xander and Mirdoth and a scant few others were even aware existed . . .

The tunnels.

She'd stayed in there a moment and used that time to gather her thoughts. But the instant she'd stepped out . . . she'd been captured. And now . . . well, she was on her way to see this commander, whoever he was.

They had reached the great staircase when a small crash from up ahead stopped the guards in their tracks.

"What was that?" the smaller asked.

"Not sure. Why don't you check it out?"

"Why don't you?"

The two glared at each other for a moment; they were even stupider than she had first assumed, Geni thought.

She frowned.

Command.

Why not?

"I suggest this," she said, and the two guards turned to face her.

She took a deep breath and looked into their eyes.

"I suggest you both go see what that noise was."

They both looked puzzled for a second.

"But . . . ," the bigger one said.

"We have to . . . ," the smaller one began to say.

"Both of you. Go now." She pointed toward the end of the hall. "The noise there. See what it was. I will wait here."

The big one nodded but didn't move. The little one took a single step backward.

She could sense them trying to fight it. Fight her. She channeled her will, just as Mirdoth had told her.

"Go," she said again, deeper, louder, stronger, pointing toward the end of the hall.

They both turned and walked away.

Geni took a step backward, preparing to turn herself, once they were far enough away from her to give her a running head start. She had no idea how long the spell would last; not long, she suspected, especially if they turned around and found her gone.

They were ten feet away from her. Twenty feet. Thirty.

She turned around.

She ran smack into someone and screamed.

She looked up and saw that the someone was Xander.

"Why'd you do that? Scream?" he asked, the smile disappearing from his face.

"Why'd you sneak up on me like that?" she snapped.

"Because . . ." His words trailed off as over Geni's shoulder, he saw the guards at the end of the hall turning toward them, looks of surprise on their faces as well.

"Come on," he said, and grabbed her arm. "Let's go!"

They sprinted straight ahead. The corridor they were in ended in a T.

"This way," Xander said, turning left.

"This way," Geni said at the exact same instant, turning right.

They turned and glared at each other.

"I live here, remember?" Geni snapped. "I know this place better than you do."

"Fine," Xander said, and took a step in her direction, and then something—a movement? He stopped in his tracks.

A knife landed in the wall between them.

He looked up and saw that the smaller guard had stopped for a second to throw his weapon; the bigger one was still coming, twenty feet away.

"Go!" Xander yelled, and Geni took off.

They went straight, and then left, and then left again, the sound of pursuit never far behind. A sound that seemed to be getting louder and louder with each turn they made.

Geni suddenly darted off the corridor into a room; Xander followed her in. They dove behind a bench, and a second later they heard the sound of footsteps thundering by.

"They'll be back," Xander said, getting to his feet when the noise had disappeared. "Once they realize they lost us . . ."

"Of course they will." Geni shut the door gently behind them. "But we'll be out of here by then."

They appeared to be in some kind of library; Geni walked to the fireplace and knelt down.

"The tunnels?" Xander shook his head. "We can't hide forever."

"We're not going to hide," she said. "We're going to escape."

She pushed open a small door and started to squeeze through. Xander heard her cough, and a second later she poked her head back out. "Take a deep breath," she said. "There's a lot of soot."

He followed her in. "A lot of soot" was an understatement; nobody had used this tunnel in years. Xander guessed it was older than some of the other passages they'd been in; there wasn't even enough room to stand up in it. He got a crick in his neck from bending over as they began to walk.

"Where are we?" he asked.

"I'm not sure exactly," Geni said. "Near the kitchens somewhere. The very innards of the Keep. I've only been here once or twice before."

"You said escape. Where—"

"This passage leads out to the northern wall. I think. We should be able to get to the bridge from there."

"The bridge." Xander frowned. "I'll bet they have that blocked off, though, by now. They might even have knocked it down."

"They can't knock it down."

"I don't know about that. It doesn't look very sturdy."

"They can't knock it down." She sounded quite sure of herself. "Mirdoth said so."

Ah. "Magic."

"That's right."

Magic.

"Is that how they got into the Keep?" Xander asked. "The Fallen? Because the walls were supposed to be magic, too."

Geni sighed. "It was him. Like Tandis said. The Titan."

She told him the whole story then—of how Talax had approached. How the gate had fallen, how she'd been captured. How she'd escaped.

He frowned, picturing that scene in his mind, the scene he'd witnessed just a few minutes earlier. The guards had been dragging Geni with them, and then . . .

Turning around and walking away, just like she had told them to.

Magic.

"Geni?"

"What?"

He hesitated.

"Are you a channeler?"

She didn't answer for a second.

"I don't think so," she said. "Maybe."

"Maybe."

"I'm supposed to go to Galor to find out."

He nodded. A lot of things he hadn't understood for the last few months—mostly her behavior, how she'd suddenly seemed to be so distant, so different, under so much pressure, how she was spending so much more time with Mirdoth than she used to, way beyond the normal amount of lesson time—suddenly made perfect sense to him.

"There's a testing," she said. "My father did it, too. I—"

"Your father," he interrupted, realizing that he had completely forgotten to tell her. "I saw him."

"What?" Geni stopped walking. Xander bumped into her and backed up, straightening as he did so, and hit his head.

"Ow."

"Where is he?" she said, and by the sound of her voice, he realized she'd turned around to face him. "Why didn't you say something? When—"

"He's in the dungeons," Xander said, rubbing his head. "Mirdoth's there, too."

"Well, we have to go back. We have to rescue them. Come on." She pushed at him to get moving.

Xander held his ground.

"What are you waiting for?" Geni snapped.

He shook his head. "We can't."

"What do you mean, we can't? We have to. We can't just leave them sitting—"

"There's two of us, Geni. Against a castle full of those things. How in the world . . ."

He stopped talking, because he heard the sound of something behind him. It sounded like footsteps, but footsteps moving very, very fast. Inhumanly fast.

"What's that?" Geni asked.

"I don't know. Somebody coming?"

"Nobody can move that fast," she said, but even as she spoke, something in her voice changed, something that made a little chill run down Xander's spine.

"Geni?" he asked.

"I think you're right," she said, turning around, her feet scrambling on the tunnel floor. "I think it is someone coming."

Someone, he thought. Or something.

"Run!" Geni yelled, and her voice shook now with the fear that Xander already felt.

CHAPTER TWENTY-ONE

Nym had to slow down a little to let Ulon keep up.

Unfortunate, but necessary. Ulon was a Fire Edar—one of what men would have called Fallen. Probably because he had the same build, Nym supposed: lanky and muscular, though Ulon had orange fur all over every square inch of his body save for his face, which had pitch-black skin. Ulon, though, was barely sentient. Incapable of language. Which Nym didn't mind quite so much. After all, those Urxen guarding the princess had been sentient, and look how little good that had done them. Idiots. He hoped their disembowelment served as a lesson to the others. Talax would have been able to use Ambrose's daughter as leverage to get the Lord of the Keep to be more cooperative. Now the girl had escaped, and it was Nym's job to get her back.

Which was why he'd sent for Ulon—whom he'd grown quite fond of over the last few months. For one thing, Ulon was one of the few creatures that could remotely keep up with his speed.

For another, Ulon was powerful in his own right, with a unique ability to manipulate and make fire. Nym and other Sions had tamed him, which put that ability at their command during critical moments. On the battlefield, and now, where Nym was using his ability as a kind of torch, to lead him through the cramped quarters of the little passage the girl had escaped through. Tunnels, inside the Keep. Interesting. He'd have to have them searched thoroughly—later, after they'd caught the girl. Another few minutes should do the trick.

He turned one corner and caught a glimpse of someone disappearing out of sight up ahead. Not the girl, though. Someone else. It looked like the boy, he realized, from the village. The one who'd stopped the arrow. Impossible. He was seeing things.

"More light," he barked to Ulon, who obliged instantly.

The passage lit up, and at that second Nym heard screaming up ahead. The princess.

If something had happened to her, Talax would have his head. Probably other parts of him as well. That wouldn't do.

He quickened, and darted forward, and then came to a sudden stop.

He put out a hand to prevent Ulon from rushing past him as the reason for the screaming became clear.

The tunnel simply ended. In front of them was nothing but blackness—a giant cavern that seemed to stretch on forever.

He looked down, and in the dim light saw nothing as well. His ears picked up a sound then that he had trouble identifying at first . . . at least until next to him, Ulon made a whimpering noise and tried to back away.

Water. Rushing water.

There was a stream of some kind beneath them.

Geni had been unable to stop herself from falling. She'd come around a bend and the path beneath her feet had disappeared, and the next thing she knew, she was in midair, arms flailing. Screaming, though she wasn't really aware of doing that until she heard Xander yell her name, a sound that started out well above her and then followed her down. He was insane. What was he doing? Had he jumped after her to his death? What purpose did that—

Her feet hit water—cool water, cold water—and then she was completely soaked. Underwater. What . . . where . . .

Her feet hit muck; she pushed up off it, and her head burst into the open air again.

She was alive.

Next to her, Xander's head popped up.

He sputtered for breath and flailed his arms about.

The Destiny be praised. Not only were they alive, there was light in here! Light coming from either side of her, to her left, to her right, enough not only to see that Xander couldn't swim well, but to tell her where they were.

Xander came up coughing and spitting next to her.

"What the—where are we?"

Gods, he was a terrible swimmer. He could barely keep afloat. "The Keeper's Spring," Geni said, and pulled him to the side of the channel as she explained. The spring ran from the wood into the Keep, and provided it with a source of freshwater. The tunnel they'd been walking must have taken them in a different direction than she'd expected: down, into the very heart of the Keep. She pointed back in the direction they'd fallen from, where the cave narrowed, and a few hundred feet beyond that, at a light—the kitchens, she told Xander, where the water was collected. Obviously, they didn't want to go that way.

He nodded as they reached shallower water, where he could stand.

"Lucky break," he said, to which she could only nod in agreement. Some of his luck, she supposed, was rubbing off on her. Gods, how had he managed to evade all those soldiers earlier, walk through the Keep in broad daylight with Fallen everywhere, and not get caught?

"So what now?" he asked.

"I'm not sure," she said, looking around, trying to think. They couldn't go back into the Keep, and they couldn't follow the stream out of here, because that led to the wood, and the wood was burning. So what could they do?

Thank the Gods that they had a minute here to collect their wits, that the thing that had been following them—hunting them was more like it; running from it Geni had felt about as scared as she'd ever been in her life—thank the Gods that it hadn't followed them down here.

There was a sudden flare of light above them and the cavern lit up all at once.

Geni raised a hand to her eyes to shield them from the sudden light; as she did so, she saw something orange and something gray, falling together toward the stream.

Nym had a second of wanting to slice the Edar's throat: the thing had what felt like a death grip on his arm. And it wouldn't stop screaming. At least Nym thought it was a scream; he certainly hoped Ulon wasn't crying. He understood that the Edar didn't like water, hated water, didn't want to get anywhere near water, but he was not in the habit of playing nursemaid. He hoped he'd made that clear enough when Ulon had tried to run; it had actually turned its back on him, and he'd had to quicken himself to dart in front of it.

"Now, now," he'd said, holding up a hand, blocking the passageway as the creature cringed, and tried to get around him. "We have to go that way. Talax wants—"

Mistake saying Talax's name; the thing started whining all over again. Frankly, he had the same reaction when he thought about the Titan, but he made a point of keeping it to himself.

"We have to," he'd said bluntly, and put his head right up against Ulon's, looked the creature in the eye so it could understand how serious he was, how furious. Ulon whimpered even louder then, which made Nym wonder if perhaps there was any substance to the things he'd heard about Edars, and the lesser Fallen. That their lack of sentience made them more sensitive to emotion, and situation. Possibly even telepathic. One of the men in Kraxis had gotten excited at the idea—the King, or one of his generals. *A way to coordinate the movements of these creatures on the battlefield, Commander,* the man had said to Nym. *It is of great tactical interest, do you not agree?*

Nym, who had been eating a calivar at the time, as he recalled, did not. Wasn't interested in the slightest.

This was a Fire Edar. If it wouldn't make fire for him, he had no use for it.

"I don't know if you can understand my emotions, but I'm sure you can understand this," he said, and drew his knife, and held the point right up under Ulon's eyes.

And so it was that, a few seconds later, they'd found themselves standing together again, at the edge of the tunnel, poised above the stream below. Ulon had, at his command, thrown a fireball, revealing both the extent of the cavern in front of them—a natural formation, clearly, predating the fortress, one its builders had taken advantage of—and their quarry, swimming in the stream below.

Which was when Nym had taken it on himself to move things along—by pushing Ulon off the ledge, and following a second later. And now they were falling and Ulon was screaming his head off.

It was, Nym thought, a little amusing.

He was very curious indeed to see what happened when the Fire Edar hit the water.

The light from the apparent explosion had almost faded when there was a second, much louder boom (along with a splash, and some cursing), and then the cave lit up once more, even more brightly than the first time.

"Run!" Geni yelled, though of course Xander was doing that already, pushing his way through the freezing water as fast as he could in the opposite direction from the noises behind him.

The cavern closed in abruptly; he almost ran right into its far wall. Geni, a step behind, ran into him.

"Ow," he said.

"Keep moving," she said.

"I can't," Xander was about to say when he saw that the spring came into the cavern through an iron grate, right in front of him. And luck was with them once more. That grate had been wrenched loose on one side, by the force of the gate's fall, was his guess. He and Geni squeezed through and found themselves outside, in the fresh air, knee-deep in the spring, beneath the shadow of the Keep's eastern wall.

Off in the distance, he saw the wood, still burning. And behind that the shadows of the mountains. The Spine of the Empire itself.

An idea popped into his head.

There were villages up there, he knew. Isolated settlements; freemen, who swore allegiance to no king or lord. It might be a safe place for them to hide out, provided they could reach it.

"Come on," he said, taking Geni's arm.

"What?"

"The wood." He turned to face her. "If we can get across it, get to the other side—"

"The wood is burning," she said.

"The stream isn't. And it's swollen, by the spring rains. Remember?"

Geni frowned.

"We get to the other side, we get to the mountains." He looked her in the eye. "We have to get away. You know that."

She turned and glanced quickly over her shoulder. Xander could hear the same thing she did. Cursing. Animal noises. Splashing. Their pursuers, getting closer.

"You have a better idea?" he asked.

"No," she said.

"Then . . ."

She still looked dubious. But she took a step forward anyway. So did he. Out of the shadows of the Keep, into the clearing between the fortress and the wood. Not far, Xander realized, from where the attack had taken place last night. Where Captain Leeland had been killed, and the Fallen first seen. Not even twenty-four hours ago. It seemed like a memory from another lifetime now.

Something whizzed past his shoulder.

He looked down and saw an arrow sticking up out of the ground. What the . . .

He turned just as another flew past.

He looked up and saw that the eastern battlement was covered with archers. Not Commander Jarak's men. Fallen. There had to be a hundred of them. All now looking down at him and Geni, readying their bows.

"Run!" he shouted, and dragged Geni forward.

"Wait, wait!" she yelled, yanking free. "Didn't you see them? All those archers?"

"Sure."

"So how exactly do you expect to get across the clearing?"

"Well . . ." He tried to smile. "The key here is to not get shot."

CHAPTER TWENTY-TWO

Geni put her head down and ran; what choice did she have? A few arrows struck near her; miraculously, she managed to reach the safety of a copse of trees.

It was only when she turned back that she realized why.

Xander was providing a distraction, zigzagging every which way across the clearing as arrows fell all around him. He was insane; he was going to die.

She watched as another volley flew toward him; he zagged again, and rolled head over heels . . .

And stopped moving, for some reason. Paused there, like he was trying to decide what to do next.

"Move!" she yelled. "Move, or—"

An entire volley of arrows, a good dozen or so, landed not a foot away from Xander. Not an inch apart. Incredible shooting. The sight of them striking the ground seemed to snap him out of whatever trance he'd been in; he began running again. The Fallen were firing in waves now, not all shooting at once but actually timing their attack so that arrows were always in the air.

He was going to die. Then what? As if in answer, the grate in the Keep wall—the grate that allowed the stream into the Keep— flew off its hinges and went flying through the air.

And something orange—a creature, an animal of some sort—burst from the Keep, howling in pain and anger.

Ulon practically ran him over; the Edar, once he'd seen the light of the outside world, and dry land, had barreled through the water like a team of runaway horses. Nym, to his embarrassment, had been unable to keep up. He needed food, sustenance, to quicken himself further.

He emerged from the Keep and saw a figure in the distance, dodging a stream of arrows from above.

And then Ulon screamed, and began hopping about madly, as the archers on the battlements began to fire at him, too.

Nym felt like screaming himself.

"Idiots!" he yelled, stepping forward, waving his arms so that the soldiers above could see him, and see who he was.

Even at that, a half-dozen more arrows fell, albeit halfheartedly, before one of the archers above—someone in charge, Nym presumed—looked down and saluted them.

Nym gave a salute of his own right back. Urxen.

He wished for a second that the species was telepathic, or at least able to read his thoughts.

He certainly had a lot to share at the moment.

Xander didn't stop when he reached the copse.

He just kept going, touched Geni on the shoulder, and she followed, without a word. They ran down the path to the gatehouse, where the smoke from the burning wood began to thicken, right at the old Lord Protector's Road—too bad its magic didn't really work, or he would have sat right down on its stones and dared anyone to harm him—where they had to break from the land, and then plunged into the stream itself.

His first step into the water—frigid, far colder here than it had been inside the Keep—hit him like a punch to the chest, knocking the wind out of him for a second. It hit Geni even harder, he saw when he turned to her. No wonder. The tunic she wore was thinner than his; a finer material, yes, more expensive, yes, and probably warmer, too, but once wet, it was nothing more than thread. And not much of it, a fact he was suddenly very aware of, noticing the way the garment clung to her body.

"What?" she asked.

"You all right?"

"Am I all right? No, I'm not all right. That's the stupidest question I ever heard in my life!" she shouted, and moved past him with a series of curses just like the ones Saren always used to use.

Saren. He wondered if the old man had made it across the bridge. If any of them had. If the bridge was still standing.

Not that they were going to find out anytime soon.

They moved through the stream for what seemed like hours. Wading through it, walking along the edge of its banks, even swimming when they came to parts of the wood where the fire was raging hardest. The worst part was the smoke. It got in his eyes, his nose, his throat; soon he was coughing up black phlegm every few minutes. Huge chunks of it. Disgusting. He would have apologized to Geni, only she was doing the same. Worse, even. Her cough seemed to be coming from deeper in her lungs. Zayelle had had a daughter named Sofi, who'd died of pneumonia when she was nine. Died making the exact same kind of noises.

"This is no good," Xander said at one point.

"What?" Geni asked without turning.

"We're going to kill ourselves. Maybe we ought to turn back."

"Shut up," she said, and coughed again.

Ridiculous, Xander thought.

Twenty feet away the woods were on fire, and here they were freezing to death.

They kept on. At one point the fire grew so hot they had to duck all the way under the water; when he surfaced he found that he'd lost most of the feeling in his right hand.

In front of him, Geni looked paler than ever. Her skin was chalk white. Her lips were blue.

"Hey!" he yelled.

"What?"

"Up there." He pointed a few hundred feet up the spring, to a spot where a boulder stuck up out of the water. "We can rest a minute."

"We can't rest." Geni turned and looked back down the stream. "Those things are after us."

"We lost them a long time ago," Xander said, wading up alongside her. "Come on."

She shook her head. "No. We have to keep going."

But when they reached the rock, she let him pull her up out of the water. She sat on the rock, shivering.

He stood up on his tiptoes and tried to peer past the smoke, to look ahead and see how much farther they had to go until they reached the edge of the wood. It was hard to tell: He could see the outlines of the mountains in the distance, but judging how far away they were was impossible. Four miles, four hundred feet . . .

"How long do you think we've been walking?" he asked.

Geni didn't respond.

He looked down and saw that she was huddled into a little ball on the rock, arms wrapped around her knees. Her teeth were chattering.

Without thinking, he knelt down next to her and wrapped his arms around her.

She stiffened. Xander stiffened, too. Gods, what was he doing?

He'd completely forgotten who Geni was . . . who he was . . . what sort of relationship they had . . .

She relaxed then, all of a sudden.

"I'm so cold," she said, and moved closer, her wet hair brushing against his cheek. He didn't know what to say, so he didn't say anything.

A second later, he relaxed, too. It was good to be out of the water, but now that he'd stopped moving, he realized how completely exhausted he was. He imagined that Geni was in a similar condition; maybe even more so, considering what had happened to her father. They needed a place to rest, a place to get out of these wet clothes. His eyes went to the far side of the stream, and at that second some of the smoke cleared.

And he laughed out loud.

Geni started in his arms and sat up straight.

"What?" she asked, pulling away from him, smoothing her hair. "What is it?"

"Look." He smiled and pointed across the stream. "We're right on top of them."

Geni turned her head, and saw what he saw.

The mountains. They were right across the stream from them: a few hundred feet away, across an already-charred expanse of brush.

She barked out a laugh, too . . . which immediately changed into a cough.

"I see," she finally managed to say.

Xander saw something else, then.

A cave, a few hundred feet farther up the stream.

A place to rest, he thought.

Which was when the fireball above his head exploded. Geni screamed and Xander realized that in fact they hadn't lost those things chasing after them at all.

Here they came now.

* * *

The first fireball missed, but Nym had counted on that as more of a warning shot anyway. Ulon was a bit squeamish when it came right down to it, particularly with regard to burning people.

What he hadn't counted on were the mountains; the second that first fireball exploded, the boy and the girl had taken off like a shot, straight across the stream, heading for the proverbial hills. That wouldn't do. Plenty of places to get lost there.

"Cut them off," he said to the Edar, who reared back and threw another fireball; it passed directly above them and caused a section of the tree canopy not already burning to explode in flames. They turned again, which was when Nym got his first good look at the boy's face.

It was him: the same youth who had blocked his arrow. Had saved the knight.

That was either one very big coincidence indeed, or no coincidence at all. Not that it mattered much either way at this moment.

Nym was going to make sure the coincidences—and the boy's life—ended right here.

The rest back at the Keep had done him a world of good. His strength was back. His speed was back. He prepared to quicken himself.

And then he saw the youth and the princess turn again, and run straight for an outcropping of rock. No, not an outcropping. A cave.

"Ulon," he began. "Don't let them—"

The Edar threw another fireball before Nym could finish talking. A much bigger one than before, it hit just above the cave entrance, sending a shower of rocks into the air. The fugitives, hands over their heads, passed underneath it and into the cavern anyway.

Ulon prepared to throw again.

"No more," Nym said, holding up a hand. "You'll probably kill them next time. I'll take care of this."

He darted across the stream to the cave and stepped inside.

There was just enough light to depress him; the cave was big. Bigger than it had looked from the outside; a lot of places to hide. Nym didn't want to go any deeper than he had to; he'd had enough of dark places for one day already.

He took a few steps deeper into the cave, and listened. There. Breathing, up ahead and to the right, he thought. They think they're being so quiet. So careful. Nym smiled. His sense . . .

A powdery dust fell on him from above. What . . .

He looked up, and a few pebbles splattered his face.

A stone the size of his fist narrowly missed his forehead, then another, identical one landed on his foot, and he winced.

There was a crack from the ceiling above, then rushing air and sound of something falling, and then . . .

A boulder the size of a cannon suddenly hit the cavern floor. The cave shook; a stalactite fell and speared the ground.

Ulon's fireball, Nym suddenly realized. The creature's attack had been too powerful, had shaken something loose in the mountaintop itself. He'd better get out of here, Nym thought, before the entire cavern . . .

There was a rumble from all around then, like the sound of a thousand siege engines beginning to roll. Nym stood up and turned for the cave entrance, and saw them. The girl, Princess Angenica. And the boy.

And then the ceiling collapsed, and he saw nothing.

BOOK TWO
CALIS AND TANDIS

*It was the War of Magic that enlightened
me that in time of conflict, Death is a more
powerful force than Life.*

—The Black Sorcerer to Prince Galor

CHAPTER TWENTY-THREE

"How the swamp got its name?" Ty smiled. "That's an interesting story. You want to hear it, boy?"

"Err . . . ," Calis said, looking around the fire at the others. Hildros rolled his eyes; Bili snorted. Kesper sighed. Uthirmancer took another drink; Okuls, already asleep on his blankets, kept snoring.

That was all there was; the seven of them. Out of the eighty-three that had crossed the bridge. Seven Knights left. Seven not including Tandis, who was gone and not coming back. Calis knew it for a fact, never mind that the others tried to tell him that this sort of thing had happened before, that their captain had taken off for days, sometimes without even telling them he was leaving. They would wake up and he wouldn't be there. The rest of them would just sit around and wait for him to return.

Calis didn't know if he could have stood that under any circumstances, never mind the ones they were in now. Maybe it was because he was so much younger than the rest of the Azure Knights—just turned sixteen a few weeks earlier. He was finally filling out in frame, though he still lacked the training and the skills that the others took for granted. He knew he needed more work in armed and unarmed combat, battlefield strategy, and survival skills.

"That will come with time, too," Hildros always told him. "Patience."

Just like the patience to wait out Tandis's sometimes unpredictable movements. The boy wasn't so sure, on two counts. Number one, that he would ever be satisfied simply standing around, waiting for things to happen; and number two (and more important now) . . .

Tandis wasn't coming back this time.

"So, boy?" Ty asked. "You want to hear it or not?"

"As if anyone could stop you tellin' it. You done with that?" Bili asked, gesturing toward Calis's plate, which still contained a sizable hunk of meat. At least Calis thought it was Bili; in the darkness it was hard to tell the difference between him and his twin, Kesper.

"All yours," Calis said, and handed it across to Bili. Or tried to, anyway.

A skinny hand intercepted him. Ty.

"Ah, ah, ah. Not so fast." The little man shook his head. "I would like to lay claim to a portion of that pretty little flesh there myself."

"I thought you wanted to tell your story," Bili said.

"Plenty of time for both. The night is young, after all." Ty smiled. Bili frowned.

Calis frowned, too. The night was anything but young; only another few hours until dawn. Until what Hildros had declared would be a near-certain second attack by the Fallen. One in which they all—the seven of them—would be killed. So would end the great Azure Knights. "You want to fight me for it, then?" Bili asked, standing up, which was when Calis saw the cut on his arm, and realized it was Kesper.

Ty was about five feet tall, and a hundred pounds soaking

wet. Great one with a knife, in a fight, definitely your man if there was any tricky negotiating to be done, and above all, a great one for "getting things."

Hand-to-hand combat, though, was not his strong suit. He glared up at the other man, but said nothing.

"Didn't think so," Kesper replied, and snatched the plate out of Calis's hand. He sat down and began to eat from it.

Hildros—the eldest among them, their leader now, with Tandis gone—shook his head. "Never get between that man and his food, Ty. You know better. Go on now. Tell your story."

The little man's expression softened.

"Oh, very well," he said. "Now you listen, boy, and listen well."

"The story of Imli's Swamp," Calis said.

"Exactly." Ty nodded. "Imli's Swamp. Imli's Folly. How it got its name. This is in the time of Queen Procipinee, lad—a long time ago. Before the Three Kingdoms, even. The very beginning of the War of Magic. Some of the nobles in the West were more wealthy than they were wise and began trying to buy up land on the coast here, not realizing how steep the cliffs were."

Calis nodded; steep was one way to put it. Sheer was another. The cliffs the swamp abutted were a good thousand feet above the waters of Morrigan's Bay.

"There was a man from Gilden—a noble named Imli—"

"A fool," Kesper said.

"A noble fool," Bili added, and laughed, and punched Kesper on the arm, hard enough that Calis's arm ached sympathetically. Kesper glared, set down his plate, and punched his brother back.

Bili stood up, and cocked his fist.

Kesper stood quickly and did the same.

Then they both looked at each other, and burst out laughing.

"Noble fool," Kesper said.

"Aye," Bili said. "That's funny."

The two of them laughed again, and then sat back down.

Hildros rolled his eyes. Calis felt like he could read the older man's mind: The two of them, Bili and Kesper. They were always fighting. When there was no enemy around, they would take on each other.

They were the best fighters among them now—now that so many were dead. Now that Tandis was gone.

"As I was saying," Ty added through gritted teeth, "this man named Imli bought the land thinking it would be valuable. The way Gildish land was valuable, when near the coast. A place to make harbor; a way to import goods from east to west, and vice versa."

Calis nodded. He could picture this Imli now, in his mind; he'd been to Gilden on occasion and it definitely had more than its fair share of overcultured fools. The southern shores of Gilden were among the most beautiful he had seen. This Imli speculator must have assumed that all shores were similar.

"He was wrong, though," Ty said. "Not that it mattered. The War of Magic put an end to Imli's dream to become a great landowner in the East—but to this day, the swamp bears his name as a testament to fools everywhere."

"Fools, aye," Hildros said. "But Imli's Folly is our last chance."

There were murmurs of agreement from those around the fire. The plan was to lure the Fallen Army into attacking across the swamp—sucking them into a terrain where their speed, their superior weaponry, their overwhelming numbers would be neutralized. It was Hildros's plan.

Calis didn't think, honestly, that it had a snowball's chance in hell of working.

"Going for a walk. Clear my head," he said to no one in particular, and then stood up and left the warmth of the campfire behind.

He walked to the very edge of the rocky outcropping that marked the outer boundary of their camp, and looked down on the plains beneath them. Looked off to the east and the campfires of the Fallen Army or at least that portion of it that hadn't marched north to the Keep. That portion of it that had been left behind to lay siege to Red Spring. The town Tandis had charged the Azure Knights to defend—to the death if necessary. Which Calis had a feeling was going to come very soon.

There were dozens of campfires out there; make that hundreds. There had to be a thousand Fallen soldiers, at least. Maybe even more. Against what? The seven of them, and the remaining able-bodied men of Red Spring, those that hadn't been slaughtered in the Fallen's first attack? The odds weren't good. About the same, Calis reflected, as the odds of Tandis ever returning.

The captain had set out north himself three days ago. What were the odds that he'd made it through the Fallen lines to the Keep? And having made it, what were the odds that he'd be able to find his way safely back to them once more?

Slim, and none, Calis thought.

"About eight hours from now, lad. You going to be ready?"

Calis turned and saw Hildros standing behind him.

"What?" Calis asked.

"Eight hours from now. That's when the attack will come." He pointed toward the campfires below. "An hour or two before first light. Better sleep while you can, boy."

"I'm not tired," Calis said, shaking his head.

"Your mind may be racing, but your body needs the rest. You'll appreciate it come the morning; take it from me." Hildros was the oldest of the Knights among them, the only one who predated Tandis in the group. At least, that's what Hildros had told him.

"What's the point?" Calis asked. "That's an entire army out there, Hildros. Doesn't matter how well rested I am, there's a thousand of them, and seven of us. It's going to be a slaughter."

"You're forgetting the men of Red Spring."

"Men," Calis snorted. "The men are all dead. What's left are old men and boys."

"Like you and me, hey?" Hildros said.

"We're fighters. They're not. You know it." Calis turned to face the older man. Hildros was short, and stocky; at sixteen Calis already towered over him by a good half foot. There was more than a touch of the Ironeer in Hildros, Calis thought.

"The Fallen outnumber us by—"

"You want to give up, is that it?" Hildros snapped.

"No. But—"

"Oh. I see. You want us to leave them to die." He gestured behind him, in the direction of Red Spring. "Is that it? You want us to ride off and let the Fallen do what they will with all those villagers?"

"Of course not," Calis said.

"Then what? You think we ought to surrender?" The old man took a step closer, and even though Calis was the taller, the boy gave ground. "The Fallen don't take prisoners, boy."

"I know that."

"Well, what do you want then? What do you think we ought to do? You have a better plan than the swamp? Go on. I'd like to hear it."

"No." Calis turned away from the man, shaking his head. "It's just that—"

"Come on, boy." Hildros pressed. "Pretend you're in charge. What do you think we ought to do?"

He practically shouted the last few words; over his shoulder,

Calis saw that the others, the rest of the Knights gathered around the campfire, had stopped talking and were watching the two of them.

Even here, Calis thought. Even here he always stood a little apart. His blood. His face. His race.

"I don't know," he said. "I guess there's nothing else we can do. I mean, we've been planning this for a while. It should work. I just . . ."

Calis hesitated, suddenly at a loss for words. Or rather, he couldn't bring himself to tell Hildros the words that were in his heart—that the plan the old warrior had carefully dreamed up was going to fail. He, Calis, had a sense of these things. Tandis had told him so, and more than once.

"Ah."

Calis looked up and saw Hildros studying him carefully.

"You wish he was still here, don't you? The captain?"

"Yes," Calis said, drawing himself up straight. "I do."

Hildros barked out a laugh. "I wish it, too. But he's not, and we've got to make the best we can of things till he gets back. Yes?"

"I suppose so," Calis said, trying to look cheerful, though he was, of course, lying once more. Tandis wasn't coming back. Tandis was dead; he was sure of it.

"All right, lad." Hildros reached up and clapped him on the shoulder. "So get some rest, yes? A couple hours, then we start forming up."

Hildros left him then; Calis watched him walk back toward the campfire, then turned back once more toward the Fallen lines.

Maybe it was his imagination, but he thought that now—in just the few minutes that he and Hildros had been talking—their fires had increased in number. Strange. An optical illusion, most likely. He wondered how many of them there were out there— how many Urxen, how many Trogs, how many of the other lesser races that made up the Fallen. Calis had experience with all of them now, traveling with Tandis and the Knights. Edars, Sions, and countless other deformities of man.

He'd memorized their faces, their differences. Studied each of them closely, searching his memory for a match. Searching for the ones that had killed his parents. The memory went too far back, though. He'd been barely more than an infant—a year old, maybe two—when it had happened.

He had dreams about it, though. Nightmares. The details were always fuzzy; not only did he have a hard time picturing the attackers, he could barely remember his parents, either. Their faces had gone blurry over the years.

One thing, though, was still crystal clear.

Once he found out who the guilty party—the guilty race— was, he would make them pay.

And not in money. In blood.

He blinked and came back to the here and now, and frowned. The lights before him, the campfires of the Fallen, were flickering. Why . . .

One flickered, and went out, and then reappeared. Calis squinted into the darkness.

There was movement in the Fallen lines, he saw. Someone sneaking in their direction. Someone trying to make it through the enemy's camp, to their position.

Tandis, he thought, and his heart lifted.

And then saw that he was wrong.

More than one light flickered. More than one form was moving, out there in the darkness.

Calis began backing away from the cliff.

"Hildros!" he yelled. "Hildros!"

The older man was standing next to their own campfire, talking to Uthirmancer and a stranger. It was one of the men from Red Spring. Calis recognized him now, one of their leaders. They were planning the battle and looked up at him with annoyance at being interrupted.

"Boy," Hildros snapped. "Have you no sense? The Fallen . . ."

The old warrior's face fell then, as his eyes met Calis's.

"What is it?" Hildros asked. "What's the matter?"

"They're not waiting till morning!" Calis said, beginning to run. "The Fallen are coming now!"

CHAPTER TWENTY-FOUR

An hour into the battle—Gods, why call it a battle; it was exactly as he had envisioned it, or even worse, a slaughter; the first wave of attackers had come on them so quickly they hadn't had a chance to form up as planned; the Red Spring warriors, those that made it to the lines, were cut down like chaff—Calis found himself fighting next to a familiar form. A large form, dressed mostly in rags. A smelly form.

Uthirmancer.

The man had assumed a position at the highest point of the outcropping, near a stack of large stones. He was heaving them down onto the soldiers scrambling up the hill below, most of whom, from what Calis could see, appeared to be Urxen. Creatures that made up in sheer force what they lacked in finesse. They were slightly larger than men; their grayish skin rippled with muscle.

"Don't you want a sword?" Calis asked, as one particularly brutal-looking Urxen charged directly at him. He stepped aside, using the creature's own momentum against it, and then, before it could stop its charge, swung his own blade.

The thing shuddered, and spat blood, and fell to the ground.

Calis estimated that he'd killed a dozen already. They were stupid, he thought. Strong, but stupid. But there were hundreds of them. And they kept coming.

"Sword? Why would I want a sword?" Uthirmancer said. "When I have these?"

He lifted a boulder over his head—a rock the size of a barrel—and sent it hurtling down the hill. It hit, and the ground exploded everywhere, in all directions.

So did the Fallen soldiers who'd been standing on that ground.

"Look. Flying Fallen."

Calis turned and saw Ty standing on the other side of him.

"That's not funny," Calis said.

"Not true, either. Truly, they are Urxen. Flying Urxen," Uthirmancer said.

Ty laughed; so did the other man. Calis couldn't help but smile as well, just a little. Uthirmancer had that effect on him. On everyone. Except his enemies, of course.

"On your right!" someone yelled. It could have been Ty, it could have been Hildros, Calis wasn't sure, but he turned in that direction anyway, just in time to see another Urxen clear the crest of the foothill and come charging straight for him.

Calis drew his own weapon and with a single thrust slashed its neck.

As the Fallen zealot fell, Calis turned and absorbed the entirety of the chaotic battle taking place.

One of the Urxen had set the camp aflame; Hildros and Kesper were trying to protect the horses. Okuls was struggling with three Urxen soldiers. The huge man made a natural target in every battle. But Okuls wasn't merely big; he was trained. The best trained of all of them, save for Tandis, of course, who had been his teacher. The evidence of how lethal Okuls had become was literally around him: piles of dead Urxen in impossible positions. His prowess in battle had slowly attracted more and more attention from the enemy, who were now simply trying to overwhelm him with numbers. Numbers they had to spare.

The Fallen were still coming. Fewer of them than before, but they were still coming.

"Hhhhyarggghhh!"

Calis turned again and saw that Uthirmancer had picked up another, even larger stone. The man held it balanced over his head for a second, and then, with an even longer, louder, larger grunt, heaved the rock toward the line of Fallen soldiers climbing the foothills.

The screams came even before the rock hit; even in the semidarkness of the predawn hour, the Fallen must have seen that something massive was heading at them.

It hit—Calis was too far off to see exactly where, and how, and who—with a sickening thud. A second later there was a loud skittering, crashing sound; Uthirmancer's throw had triggered a landslide. A second later, accompanying the sound of falling rock came several anguished cries; the landslide had trapped many of the Fallen soldiers.

As Calis weighed the wisdom of charging down the hill to finish them off, one arrow, and then a second, and then a third, shot past him in the air.

He turned and saw Bili perched atop another foothill, a hundred or so feet behind him. The warrior paused, acknowledged Calis with a nod, and then strung his bow once more.

Calis looked back down the hill.

The Fallen were still coming.

The odds had probably been thirty to one before; they were probably closer to five to one now. They wouldn't stay that way long, though. There were hundreds of other Fallen soldiers out there.

Eventually the Knights were going to be overrun.

"This is hopeless!" he yelled.

"Chin up, lad!" Hildros, some twenty feet away, yanked his own sword out of a corpse. "We're ahead as I see it."

"Aye," Ty said. "This is nothin'. Think of the big picture. If we manage to survive this, we still have the main army behind them to deal with."

"You're not helping," Calis growled.

A second group of Fallen soldiers had reached the bottom of the foothills and was beginning to climb, screaming every inch of the way. Maniacs. Some of them had crossbows; some of them, he saw, were Trogs. Not good. Trogs were far better warriors, far better tacticians. The Trogs coming toward them were all clumped in a group, though; a single well-aimed weapon—a boulder, say, he thought with a smile—could take care of all of them.

"Uthirmancer," he said, turning.

The man was nowhere in sight. Looking for more rocks? Gone off to help Hildros?

"Uthirmancer!" he called again, and then his eyes widened.

He saw the man's boot, sticking out from the outcrop. He saw the man's leg, and then the rest of his body.

He saw the crossbow bolt, sticking out of the man's chest, and his wide, unseeing eyes.

"Uthirmancer!" Calis screamed.

Forgetting the Fallen charging up the hill, forgetting the fact that the crossbows were still firing, forgetting everything but the dead man in front of him, Calis dropped to his knees and screamed once more, a wordless, primal shriek of despair.

Dozens of men had ridden across the bridge with them, but the seven he was fighting with now were the core of the Azure Knights. Tandis's men for as long as Calis had known them. They, as much as the captain, had raised him from nothing, from no one. Taught him to fight, and drink, and stand up for himself no matter what the world said. And Uthirmancer . . .

On the morning of his eighth birthday—or rather, on the day

Tandis had told him he was eight years old; they had no way of knowing when his actual birthday was—he'd woken to find the man kneeling over his sleeping roll.

"C'mere," Uthirmancer had said, smiling his gap-toothed grin, smelling like he'd spent the night lying with the horses. "Got a little something for ya."

Calis had blinked the sleep from his eyes and gotten dressed. He'd followed the man out to the edge of the camp—were they in New Pariden then, or Yoren, he couldn't remember, but it had been cold that morning, his breath making a fine mist with every exhale of air, every word he spoke—to where the camp animals were tied up.

There was a horse standing there. A roan, a gelding, one instantly familiar to Calis.

"Saladan," he said, barely able to get the word out.

"Aye," Uthirmancer said, grinning even more broadly now. "Saladan."

They'd been on a mission to the north then, the Knights—an attempt to rein in the revolt of Edamore, the self-styled "emperor" of Yoren. The day before, Tandis had convinced that man that a lifetime of exile in the East was a better alternative than continuing to press his revolt against Galor. What the captain had said to Edamore to change his mind, none of them ever knew, but the morning after their meeting, the gates to the "emperor's" castle had suddenly opened to them, and the man's honest and appropriated wealth—the latter far outnumbering the former—had been theirs to apportion and return to its rightful owners.

Among that wealth was a horse belonging not to Edamore, but to his master-at-arms, a giant of a man named Tomas who had gone and perished in the fighting that had taken place before the "emperor" had agreed to Tandis's offer of truce.

The horse had caught Calis's eye then, during the fight. It had stood over its master's body, and refused all attempts at being handled. Calis had been struck by the fire in its eyes and the determination with which it guarded Tomas. Uthirmancer, apparently, had noticed.

"Saladan," Calis said again. "What—why is he—"

"He's yours, boy," Uthirmancer said.

Calis had been speechless.

He'd been tempted for a second to hug the man, but of course, Uthirmancer's ever-present odor instantly reminded him why that was a bad idea.

So he'd settled for a grin so broad it felt like it would split his face, and a mumbled thanks.

It had taken the two of them—boy and horse—a few weeks to bond. He'd had to lead Saladan by the reins for most of that time, before finally breaking him to the saddle. But afterward they'd been inseparable.

But Saladan, a creature of the North, had perished in the South, in the jungles of Gilden. Fallen victim to a plague of some kind, one that had made the animal's last few hours agonizing ones.

Saladan. Gone more than a year now.

And Uthirmancer . . . now Uthirmancer . . .

He was crying, Calis realized.

"Boy."

He looked up and saw Hildros standing next to him. The old man was glowering.

"Focus, boy. We need your sword."

"He's dead!" Calis screamed, standing. "Can't you see? Uthirmancer's dead!"

"Can't you see?" Hildros shouted back. "He's not the only one!"

Calis looked past him, and saw Bili kneeling next to another body, one that lay in a rapidly growing pool of blood, one dressed in an all-too-familiar cloak of blue, and shirt of mail.

"Kesper," Calis said. "Oh, no."

This couldn't be happening. The seven of them, now down to five.

"Aye," Hildros answered, his voice sounding as if it came from a long, long way off. "Kesper."

The screams coming from below, from the Fallen charging the hill, grew louder.

"We're falling back," Hildros said. "Making a stand at the far edge of the swamp. General Lossander and his men will construct barricades."

"Falling back?" Calis shook his head. "We can't fall back. Tandis never—"

"Tandis isn't here," Hildros snapped. "Now come on, boy. We need you."

Calis looked down at Uthirmancer once more, and saw Saladan.

He looked back at Hildros, and saw Kesper.

He looked down the hill at the Fallen climbing toward them, and saw red.

And then he screamed, and raised his sword over his head, and charged.

As he ran, he heard Tandis's voice in his head.

Control. Keep control. Always.

The very first lesson they'd had together—the very first time Tandis had let him use a sword on his journeys with the Knights, rather than simply feed the horses, or help Avay prepare the food—that was the first thing he'd said to Calis.

Any fool can swing a blade. Any fool can hold a weapon. Judgment is the key. Knowing when—and how—to use it.

It was a hard lesson for Calis to learn, though. He had a temper; slow to boil, as Ty had put it once, but once set off . . . even harder to cool down. And the sense of power the sword gave him, especially when he learned to use it, fed that temper. Fed that emotion.

As his anger was feeding it now.

Uthirmancer dead. Kesper dead. The Fallen Army, on the verge of overrunning their position. This was not a time for control.

This was a time for rage. A time to use the feelings swirling within to his advantage.

The upper portion of the slopes was pitched less steeply than the lower; from the second he left Hildros's side, sword raised, he ran as quickly as he could, screaming as loudly as he could toward the Fallen climbing the hill, whose own screaming, while less constant, less energetic than it had been when they started their climb, was still loud enough to cover the sound of his own approach.

Until that moment when he launched himself into space toward them.

The nearest of the enemy, a Trog—its white hair, gray skin, red eyes, now easily seen by the light of the dawning sun—barely had time to open its mouth before Calis's sword was in its throat, and he was tumbling over it, pivoting over the creature, and his blade, and landing on his feet in the midst of a group of three, no four, other Trogs that were only just becoming aware of his presence.

He yanked his sword out of the first one's throat and swung it at a second, the nearest one to him, gouging it in the shoulder, and the thing screamed, and slashed at Calis's blade ineffectually, and Calis slashed again, and caught the creature in the face, and blood gushed, and it screamed a second time, and stumbled, but that was all Calis saw. By that time he was turning toward another of the Trogs, but too late: The thing's blade caught him on the arm with a force that caused him to stagger, and stumble, and he would have fallen but for the fact that he backed into a rock taller than he was, and used that rock to push off, and swing out again, and his sword met another—whose he was not exactly sure—and his blade rang in his hands with a force that nearly caused him to lose his grip.

One vicious-looking Trog charged directly at him. Calis's sword stabbed out, pierced the creature's armor, and then the thing itself. It gasped and started to fall.

Calis yanked his sword free, or tried to. The Trog had died with its hands wrapped around the blade. And it wouldn't let go.

Calis grimaced, and yanked again. The sword wouldn't come out.

One of the remaining Trogs screamed and charged.

Calis turned to face it and realized he would never be able to move quickly enough to dodge the creature. Suddenly he felt a burst of energy—where it came from, he didn't know, but he shot forward and slammed into the charging Trog before it knew what hit it.

The two of them fell backward and began to roll down the hill. Calis tried to rip the thing's blade away from it; the Trog refused to relinquish its grip. They rolled, and rolled, and Calis's hand found a rock, and he began bashing the thing in the face, in the head, the body, wherever he could reach. Over and over again, faster and faster and faster.

They came to a stop. Calis got up. The Trog didn't.

But there were others to take its place. Dozens of them, here at the bottom of the hill.

A handful turned his way and drew their weapons. Others, though, didn't. The battle was raging here, too, he saw, and for a second he wondered why. A rearguard action by the men of Red Spring? Reinforcements, from Kaden's Harbor?

Then the Fallen began to circle and he had more pressing concerns.

His weapons were gone.

His left arm stung; he glanced quickly at his armor and saw blood welling through the mail. A cut; a deep one. Now that he saw the wound, he felt it as well. A stinging, stabbing pain. The blood was coming quickly.

"What have we here?" one of the Trogs said, stepping forward.

The world lost focus around him. Calis swayed on his feet, and gritted his teeth, and willed himself to stay upright.

"A boy," the Trog said. "A boy, come to provide us with some sport."

"Hegoner," Calis spat, using the Kraxan word for coward.

The Trog's eyes narrowed.

"How do you think you're going to die, boy?" the Trog asked, drawing its sword. "Slowly, painfully, or—"

"I'll die happy. And some of you will die with me."

The Fallen changed positions, moved closer, forming a circle around him. Two of the others had drawn swords as well; a fourth hadn't. The smallest among them. Calis wondered why, and as he wondered, the creature suddenly swayed on its feet, unsteady.

And then its head fell from its shoulders. Sliced clean off.

"Too much talk of dying," a familiar voice said.

Calis looked up and saw Tandis.

"Better to fight, don't you think?" The captain smiled and tossed him a sword.

CHAPTER TWENTY-FIVE

They came for him the day after the Keep fell.

Mirdoth barely had time to awaken before he was dragged roughly to his feet and marched out of the dungeon he shared with his lord. They brought him up into the castle proper to meet this Dread Lord at last.

The Fallen who were escorting him marched him past what had been Ambrose's throne room, which he presumed the Titan had appropriated. Of course, the Titans were not men and it was dangerous to predict that they would act in that manner. Instead, to his surprise, they brought him to his very own chambers. The tower.

That was his first surprise.

His second was that all his things were in it. They had been unpacked, uncrated, and carefully laid out exactly in their proper places. Impossible, Mirdoth thought, though he supposed with the Titans involved nothing was impossible.

He sat himself in the center of his chamber, in the chair he had called his own for far longer than he cared to remember, and prepared for Talax's arrival. He wondered what the Titan knew about him; what the creature wanted.

Dred'nir's Bane—the thing that Tandis had mentioned? It

seemed a logical conclusion, and so Mirdoth put his energies to learning more about this Bane.

He searched his books all that day and on into the night. Found a brief reference in the Hiergamenon, but nowhere else. No reference. He searched the next day and found nothing. And Talax did not come. His only visitors were guards—Urxen, four of them, two of whom stayed well out of range while the other two saw to his needs, food, drink, water for bathing and changing.

Why are they treating me as a guest and not a prisoner? Mirdoth wondered.

On the third day, he turned his thoughts toward escape. Escape not just for him, but for Ambrose, too, who was still in the dungeon. There was also the matter of Geni, who he had not seen but who he felt certain was still alive, and thus imprisoned somewhere nearby. They all needed to be free of here; free of the Titan's influence. Mirdoth began considering the kind of spell he would need, the kind of magic he would need to use.

The Spell of Command seemed the obvious choice. He knew it. It used life magic. It would not require reaching out to the shards. His secret would remain safe.

He could use the Spell of Command on the near guards first, use them to overpower the others, and then make his way to the dungeons. Find his lord, his charge, and escape. Other spells he could make use of as well but he would need to be careful, of course; there were restrictions on his use of magic, and for good reason. The Spell of Command was a simple spell and carried with it no inherent risks.

All during that night, Mirdoth prepared himself. The gathering of the will, the focusing of his energies. It had been a long time since he himself had done these things; showing Geni the techniques was entirely different. Theory, as opposed to practice. The use of power, as opposed to its mere description.

Yet there was theory involved in this instance, too. Command had to be conditioned, particularly given how he needed events to unfold. Mirdoth would want the guards, when the time for escape came, to stand by, to not revert to their own minds when he was no longer in their presence. After some thought, he decided to start with a simple thing: not escape itself, but a suggestion. The guards had been bringing him bread and water; he would ask for something else.

"A calivar," he told the two who brought his meal.

"A what?" the first said, and looked up.

"A calivar," he said, and met the guard's eyes, and then those of the second guard standing next to him. "I would like—if it would not be too much trouble—a calivar. For my lunch."

The two looked at each other and frowned.

There was something wrong. They both knew it, but neither was able to say what that something was. Neither was strong-willed enough, either, to say what they should have said to Mirdoth in that instant. "The Destiny take you," or some equivalent.

"A calivar," Mirdoth said again. "Cook has a carton of them. Had." He corrected himself. The cook was certainly long gone from the Keep; long gone or dead. "They're in the kitchen larder, no doubt."

"The larder," one of the guards repeated, slack-jawed. Urxen. He had to be careful here, Mirdoth realized. Focus too much power on beings with such limited intellect and he would do permanent damage. He'd done such things before, long, long ago. Done them, and enjoyed them. Seeing the Urxen die painfully . . .

He heard movement in the hall then: the other two guards, coming to investigate what was taking the others so long.

"Thank you. That will be all," Mirdoth said quickly to the two before him, at the same instant allowing his will to drift. Relaxing. Letting them go.

"Hey."

The two guards before him turned just as the others entered.

The four were soon engaged in an argument that Mirdoth felt little inclination to pay attention to. What had taken the first two so long, what business was it of the second two. None of that mattered.

A calivar, he thought. And that is how it begins.

At breakfast tomorrow, he would request something from Lord Ambrose's chamber. It didn't matter what. The point was to have the guards obey him. To inculcate the desire to be commanded.

He returned to his books, his search for mention of the Bane. He spent another fruitless morning, a handful of hours scouring scrolls, and parchments he'd forgotten he possessed. He came across one reference that intrigued him: a reference to Tar-Thela, the Emerald Sorceress, and the actions she'd taken under the spell of Kir-Tion, the creation of the shards, the imprisonment of Elemental's magic within those magical forms . . .

Those actions, the writer of this scroll before him declared, had been the bane of all Elemental. Intriguing choice of words. Elemental's Bane. Not quite the same thing, but . . .

The door opened behind him. Mirdoth turned, just as something came flying through the air toward him.

He put out his hands reflexively and caught it.

A calivar.

"As you requested," Talax said, and entered the observatory.

The Titan wore a simple black cloak. Boots, black trousers, and a shirt of some nondescript material.

"I have control of the guards, mage," he said. "I have control of everyone here. Everything."

Mirdoth said nothing. What could he say?

"You do not want the fruit?" he asked, gesturing to the calivar.

Mirdoth set the fruit down on the table.

Talax smiled. Then his eyes widened, and he walked past Mirdoth to the Elemscope.

"In the name of the Mithrilar," the Titan said, under his breath. "Can it be . . ."

He laid a hand on the ceramic tube, then looked up, fire in his eyes.

"Curgen's glass."

"Just so."

The Titan shook his head. "You are an arrogant fool, mortal. To play with such power . . ."

"The glass is a window."

"The glass is many things. But above all . . . not for those such as you to toy with."

Talax touched the assembly holding the glass, which began at once to glow a bright red. Smoke rose from the metal, which began to flow like liquid.

With a horrendous crack, the glass burst, and shattered, sending splinters all across the room.

Talax turned and looked at him.

"You must learn your place, sorcerer. If you wish to live," the man said.

No, Mirdoth reminded himself. It was a mistake to think of Talax as a man, to think of him as being in any way similar to mortal beings, except for the outer shell he wore. He was another thing entirely, an alien creature, though Mirdoth had often wondered if the shell—the skin of man, which this Titan and all the others he had heard of wore—was an affectation, a way simply to blend in while the immortals were here on Elemental, or if it in any way resembled their own true selves. They resembled the races of men rather than the Fallen. He wondered why.

He doubted he would ever find out.

"Have you found anything?" the Titan asked abruptly.

"What?" Mirdoth asked.

"The Bane," Talax said. "You have been searching for reference to it, in your books. Have you found any?"

Mirdoth, for a second time, was too stunned to respond.

Then he cursed himself for an idiot.

Tandis had told them that the Titan would want the Bane, above all other things. And what other reason could the Titan have had for freeing Mirdoth, for putting him with his books, his papers, and records, than to have him aid in that search?

Thankfully he had found nothing, no knowledge he could betray to the immortal. Otherwise . . .

Elemental's Bane, he remembered then, and his eyes went to the parchment, still on the table where he'd been studying it.

"Nothing," he said. "I've learned nothing."

Talax looked at him, and then shook his head.

"I sense differently," the Titan said, and in that instant the immortal's eyes bored into his. "Tell me, mage, what you have learned."

Mirdoth found his mouth opening, his words about to form an answer to the Titan's question.

It was the Spell of Command, he realized, turned back on him. But a dozen times more powerful than he was capable of casting it.

He clamped his jaw shut and tried to resist. Pain seared through his body.

"One way or another," Talax said, "you will tell me."

Mirdoth felt an instant of agony, and then he felt himself falling. He had no control of his limbs; no control of anything.

He hit the floor, and everything went dark.

He woke up sitting in his chair.

There was a cup of tea in front of him.

Talax sat across from him, in the chair Geni had always occupied. The Titan was reading the very scroll that Mirdoth had been looking at before; the one that mentioned Tar-Thela, and the Bane of Elemental.

Gods. What had just happened to him?

"No," Talax said, tossing the parchment aside. He looked at Mirdoth. "You must keep looking."

Mirdoth blinked. "What?"

"This—Tar-Thela, the shards . . . This is not what we are looking for. You must continue to search."

Mirdoth stared, still trying to gather his wits. The Bane. The scroll.

"My mind," he said, staring up at Talax. "You went into my mind."

A trace of a smile crossed the Titan's lips. He gestured toward the tea. "Drink. It will restore your strength."

Mirdoth's anger rose within him; it was an emotion he had not permitted himself for a long time. What Talax had done to him . . . invaded his mind, stolen his very thoughts . . . that was evil, akin to the darkest of magics. He wanted nothing more than to respond in kind.

A wave of energy passed through his body; he tamped it down. Response would be foolish; futile. Suicidal.

And perhaps worse.

"Tea," he said. "Yes."

He reached for the cup and noticed that his hand was still shaking.

"We should not fight each other in this, mage," Talax said. "For the Bane could be your salvation as well."

"My salvation?" Mirdoth frowned. "I don't understand."

"From the tyrant's rule."

"Tyrant? What—"

"Galor. The sorcerer-king."

"Galor?" Mirdoth smiled. "He is no tyrant. He has his faults, but—"

"After what he has done to you?" Talax said. "Still you defend him?"

"Galor is the light," Mirdoth snapped. "The source of all civilization in this world."

"The Fallen have civilization," Talax said.

"The Fallen have—had—an empire. And now an emperor, it seems."

"Me."

"Who else?"

The Titan smiled, a full-blown smile this time. "I am no emperor, Mirdoth. I do not desire to rule men, or Fallen, or any of the things of this world. I simply desire to go home. Finding the Bane will make that possible."

"Explain." Mirdoth frowned. "I don't understand."

"It's not important that you do." Talax gestured around the room, taking in all of Mirdoth's things. "Continue your search. Be thorough. Exhaustive. There is no finer collection of documents on the eastern continent. Somewhere in here . . . there will be mention of it. You must continue to look."

"I will not work for you. For the Fallen," Mirdoth said.

Talax walked to the door. When he reached it, he turned around.

"Don't worry," he said. "You will not be."

Before Mirdoth could ask him what he meant, the Titan was gone.

CHAPTER TWENTY-SIX

Geni's coughing was worse. Her fever was up. And now she was mumbling in her sleep. What was he supposed to do about that? Wake her up? Xander had no idea. When he got sick, growing up, Zayelle's remedy for sickness had always been sleep. But sleep didn't seem to be making Geni any better. She was only getting worse with each passing day. What should he do?

She moaned again. Xander felt her forehead. She was burning up.

Xander sat up, took the wet cloth he'd been carrying—a strip of fabric torn from his shirt, then soaked in a puddle of water they'd found a few hundred yards back in the tunnels—and pressed it to her forehead.

Thank the Destiny for the lichen, he thought. The only bit of luck they'd had since the cave-in. Some sort of plant that actually glowed with light, a purplish aura that at least allowed them to see vague outlines of things in the otherwise pitch-darkness.

Geni turned away and moaned even louder. A lock of her hair fell across her face; Xander leaned down and brushed it aside.

The movement caused the muscles in his shoulder to twinge; he was still sore there, and along his entire right side, where the falling rock had hit him during the cave-in. A few days ago, though of course he had no way of telling exactly how much time had passed since then. It could be worse, he supposed; they could have been killed. Or caught by that thing that had been chasing them. What had it been? Xander had been too far away to get a good look at it, but it was clearly nothing like the other Fallen that had ambushed Geni and Captain Leeland in front of the Keep. He didn't doubt that bad things would have happened to them had the thing caught up to them earlier.

Then again, bad things were happening to them now. About as bad as you could get.

Geni moaned again and began speaking. Babbling. Nonsense syllables; things in different languages, things that made no sense to Xander. A spell of some sort? He hoped not. Magic was dangerous. If Geni really was a channeler and in her delirium she cast a spell on him . . .

He shuddered. He'd heard stories of things that had happened long ago, during the War of Magic, spells cast on men, and women, and places, spells that once uttered, even in jest, could not be undone—spells of transfiguration, of destruction, curses, and plagues . . .

Magic. Xander didn't care for it in the least.

Geni's eyes opened.

"Xander." She stretched out a hand in the semidarkness; he took it.

"I'm thirsty," she said. "So thirsty."

"Hold on. Be right back."

He walked to the puddle once more and soaked the cloth. He returned to Geni's side.

"Here," he said, and squeezed the moisture from the rag over her mouth.

Water. Its presence—there were puddles of it everywhere they went—was the only thing keeping them alive. But they needed more than water. They hadn't eaten since the cave-in. Xander didn't know how much longer he could go without food.

Geni spat, and sat up.

"Blecch," she said. "There was dirt in that."

"I'm sorry," Xander said. "But—"

"How long was I asleep?" she asked.

"I don't know."

"You fell asleep, too," she said accusingly.

"I did."

"You were supposed to keep watch."

"Sorry," he said. "But—whoa."

Geni was getting to her feet. Xander got to his and helped steady her.

"You have to take it easy. You're not—"

"Easy's not going to do it," she said, shrugging off his grip. "We have to keep walking. We have to find a way out of here."

"I know. But you're not in any shape to—"

"Don't tell me what I can't do," Geni said firmly, and started walking.

Xander sighed and followed her.

They walked for a few minutes in silence.

"We going up or down, you think?" Geni asked.

"I don't know."

"I don't think we're going down," Geni said. "I think we're going pretty straight. Running right alongside the mountain. I'm thinking that if we keep our eyes open, we should find a passage-way off to the right. One that'll take us to one of the free villages."

"Maybe," Xander said, though he wasn't so sure about that. They'd been walking long enough, to his way of thinking, that if they were indeed moving parallel to the mountains, they might have crossed over into Kraxis. In which case, even if they found a passageway out, it might not be the greatest of ideas for them to go looking for a village.

In Kraxis, you never knew what kind of village you might find. Something flashed before his eyes.

"Hold it," he said, and stopped walking.

Geni turned.

"What?"

"Did you see that?"

"See what?"

"There was a—"

The thing he'd seen darted in front of him again. Darted back and then forth, and landed on the wall.

It was a light. A purplish fleck of light, the same color as the lichen on the walls.

"A wisp," Geni said.

"What?"

"A wisp." She held out her hand; the light, to Xander's astonishment, darted through the air and settled into her palm.

"It's alive," he asked.

"Of course." Geni stretched out her other hand, as if to pet the light. Xander squinted and tried to make out the thing's shape. What it was, exactly. Some kind of a bug? Or a bird? He couldn't quite tell.

"I read about them in the Hiergamenon," Geni said. "I don't remember exactly where, but they're in there. Wisps."

"Are they friendly?" Xander asked.

"They're wisps," Geni said, as if that answered the question.

At that second, another landed on her arm. Geni laughed, and an instant later, a third settled next to the other two. Where were they all coming from?

Xander looked up and saw an entire cloud of the creatures coming from up ahead, darting to and fro in the air above them.

"Let's go that way," he said, and, pushing past Geni, moved forward through the tunnel.

The light grew with every step he took; pale purple became

bright enough that for the first time in days, he could see farther than a few feet in front of him. And what he saw caused him to take a deep breath, and his eyes to widen in wonder.

For up ahead the tunnel branched out into a cavern. A huge cavern. Filled with hundreds—thousands—millions of the wisps, flitting about in groups. Clouds of them, moving as one above them, like schools of fish in the Keeper's Spring. Slightly different shades of purple, flashing all around.

"Wow," he managed.

"Yeah. Wow." He sensed Geni come up alongside him; she was looking up as well. Looking up in wonder with a big smile on her face, the first smile he'd seen from her in days.

One of the clouds passed in front of the far wall of the cavern, and Xander saw something he'd missed before.

A stone stairway that led from the ground to a ledge high above. To a door-shaped opening. Man-made, clearly.

"Look," he said, pointing. "A doorway. Where do you think it leads?"

"I don't know." Geni seemed more interested in the wisps than the opening.

"Maybe outside," Xander said. "We ought to find out."

The only problem, as he saw now, was that the stairway was in terrible shape. Half the steps were missing. Still . . .

"You're going to climb that?" Geni asked.

"You have a better idea?"

"I think I do," she said.

"Really? Like what?" he asked, turning to face her.

Only she wasn't there.

He looked up then, and saw Geni flying.

The idea had come to her in a flash.

The wisps could fly. They loved to fly. She could sense that

coming from them somehow, their joy in flight. They were beings of joy. Wouldn't they want to spread that joy? Of course they
would.

Geni had held out her arms then, in that instant of realization,
and willed them to come to her. Not the Spell of Command, not
quite, but a similar kind of thing. More of a question, though; do
you want to?

Yes had been the answer. An almost instantaneous answer,
from dozens of them, all at once. Dozens, and then hundreds,
covering her arms, her legs, her back. She felt them, felt their
wings—well, she thought they were wings; she could not be exactly sure, of course—beating against the skin on the back of her
neck, on her arms, her legs, and then another question: can you?

And they had.

And she'd risen straight into the air, as if she were being lifted
by a giant hand.

Flying.

"How are you doing that?" Xander asked.

"I'm not sure exactly!" she yelled back.

She sensed the wisps—not individually, but all of them, a
group within her mind. She could talk to them, could control her
flight easily, almost intuitively.

She had an idea.

"Help Xander fly," Geni said with a giggle.

Xander's eyes widened.

"Now wait a second."

But it was too late.

Another cloud of the creatures surrounded Xander. A second
later, he, too, was in the air.

"Whoa," he said, leaning, lurching, trying to balance himself.

"Relax!" Geni yelled out. "Don't fight them!"

She tried not to laugh as Xander flailed his arms about. For a second she thought he was going to fall. Then, all at once, he balanced, and he was flying, too.

"Wow!" he bellowed. "Yeaaa!"

He stretched his arms up and darted this way, then that. Swooping like an eagle.

"This is fantastic!" he yelled, turning to Geni and laughing.

She did laugh then. Gods, how long had it been since she'd laughed? Days. Weeks. Months, maybe. She'd been studying so hard with Mirdoth . . .

She pictured her teacher then, in the observatory. At the Elemscope. The Keep. The gates, collapsing. Her father.

She closed her eyes.

No, she thought.

I will not do this. I will not—

"You all right?"

She opened her eyes and saw Xander right next to her, five feet away, concern etched all over his face.

There was blood there, too. Dried blood. A streak of it, down the side of his neck. She hadn't noticed it before.

"Fine," she said.

"Good." He smiled. "Now let's—"

"Fly," she could tell he'd been about to say, except he leaned too far in one direction and wobbled, and almost fell. Geni reached out a hand to steady him, and he caught it in his.

Their eyes met, and the wisps, unbidden, rose a little higher in the air.

They were flying together, hand in hand. It was like dancing.

Geni had tried to get Xander to practice dancing with her once. Years ago. Not long after they'd met.

Dancing? He'd looked at her as if she had grown another head. *You must be kidding.*

And now here they were. Dancing in the air. In a cloud of soft purple light.

He was staring at her.

Geni had seen that stare from boys before. Lately, she'd seen it a lot. But this was the first time she had caught herself staring back.

She cleared her throat. "The ledge. We should get to that ledge before the wisps get tired of playing with us."

"Right," Xander said, breaking eye contact. "The ledge. Let's go there."

And so they did.

The wisps dropped them at the door-shaped opening. Geni preceded Xander through it, into another tunnel. The second she entered it, though, she realized there was something different about this one.

It smelled of fresh air.

"Xander," she said, turning to him, "do you—"

"Smell it? Of course. This is the way out," he said excitedly.

Geni was excited, too. Fresh air. The outside world. Food.

They hurried forward for another twenty feet. The glow from the cavern faded; there was little lichen here.

Which explained why she almost walked right into the tunnel wall in front of them.

"Hang on," she said to Xander, who did, stopping himself just in time to keep from bumping into her.

They'd come to a T in the corridor; the darkness was almost complete here. She turned in each direction, sniffing the air. Searching for light.

She couldn't be sure of it, but she thought the smell of fresh air was coming from off to her right.

"Right, I think," she said.

"I think so, too," Xander replied. "Come on."

He turned in that direction, and just as he did, Geni caught the barest glimpse of something etched into the stone wall in front of her. Carvings. Symbols of some kind.

She ran a hand over them, feeling their outlines.

"Geni?" Xander had turned to face her. "Come on. What are you waiting for?"

"There's some sort of writing here," she said. "I can't quite see it . . ."

A handful of wisps lit up on her arm at that second, and all at once she had enough light to show her what she was looking at more clearly.

"Thanks," she said—or perhaps, only thought—to the wisps.

There were *two* sets of carvings on the wall, in fact. One on the right, one on the left. And an arrow, as well, etched above the words on her right. It pointed down the tunnel to her right. A signpost.

"What is it?" Xander asked, coming back up behind her. "What's it say?"

"One second."

She looked at the phrase under the arrow. The carvings appeared to be common tongue, except . . . a little different. Some of the symbols she didn't recognize. Was this an older version of the language? Maybe so.

"Geni?"

"Valcona," she said, reading the symbols out loud. "Those wanderers who would join—"

"Valgona!" Xander said excitedly. "You mean Valgona, don't you? That's one of the free cities. And it's that way?"

She glanced over her shoulder and saw the smile on his face. He had his arm outstretched, and was pointing, once more, in the direction they'd smelled fresh air.

Valgona. She smiled as well. Gods, had they actually made it? Were they going to live, after all? Were they going to get something to eat?

Her stomach rumbled.

She turned back to the set of carvings on the left, and her smile abruptly disappeared.

These were not common tongue.

They were in another language entirely, something older. The carvings themselves were older as well, worn almost to the point of illegibility. Written with more care, however. The script—it looked to her like Avostan, the language of old Imperium. She and Mirdoth had been studying it for some months now. And that word there . . .

"Calebethon," she whispered.

"What?" Xander asked.

"Calebethon. You remember?" She turned to Xander. "When we were listening in the tunnels—my father, and Tandis? That's what he said. Calebethon. That was the first place he had to go. To get to—"

"The Bane." Xander nodded. "I remember."

The two of them were silent for a moment.

"So what's it say, exactly?" Xander asked.

She read off the first few words. " 'By this sign, Traveler, know that you enter Calebethon, the ancestors of your . . . ' Hmmm."

"What?" Xander asked.

"Not sure that's right. 'Ancestors.' " She leaned forward and squinted at the carvings. Almost as if they'd read her mind, a few more of the wisps alighted on her arm, and the light grew brighter.

And in that instant it came to her.

"I remember," she said.

"What?"

"Wisps. Where I read about them."

"The Hiergamenon, you said."

"Yes. In the story of Amarian's escape from Imperium. They're his guide, through the underground city of Calebethon." She straightened up and turned back to Xander. "It's that way." She pointed to the left. Into the darkness. Away from the fresh air. Away from Valgona, and food.

Toward the Bane.

Xander sighed.

"We have to, Xander," Geni said. "Tandis is probably dead. Talax has the Keep, and my father, and Mirdoth—"

"Us, you're saying. We ought to go find the Bane."

"Somebody has to."

Xander sighed. "I'm hungry."

"I know what you mean. Believe me. It's a city, right? They'll have food."

"If people still live there," Xander said, at which point Geni remembered something else that she'd read in the Hiergamenon.

It wasn't people who lived in Calebethon at all.

She decided—for the moment—not to tell him that.

"Come on," she said, starting off down the corridor. "Let's go."

After a moment, she heard Xander's footsteps behind her, following.

CHAPTER TWENTY-SEVEN

Calis sat on a pile of rocks and put his head in his hands.

All around him was death and destruction. The cries of the wounded; the sobs of mothers, and children, old men, old women. How many had Tandis said were left? Seventy-odd fighters, not including the mercenaries. A hundred or so too badly injured to hold a weapon; perhaps ten times that many villagers from Red Spring, and Kaden's Harbor. And four Azure Knights. Four, out of the dozens who'd crossed the bridge.

Himself, Hildros, Ty, and the captain. Against an army of thousands. Urxen and Trogs. Sions and who knows what else.

They didn't have a chance.

Images flashed across his mind. Uthirmancer, hurtling rocks on the Fallen below. Urxen fleeing, screaming, fighting, charging up the hill. Bili and his bow. Tandis's return. The captain and him side by side, fighting their way up the hill, to the burning remnants of their camp. Finding Okuls's body, and then Kesper's. Sounding the retreat; guarding the villagers, and the army, as they moved into the swamp. The screams of those who'd refused to enter, who'd decided to stay behind. Those who'd thought the Fallen would take them prisoner; who didn't believe what Tandis and the others told them.

The Fallen don't take prisoners.

His boots were caked with mud, his feet soaked with the stuff of the bogs they'd had to pass through. Calis took off one of his boots and knocked it against a rock.

A hand fell on his shoulder. He started and looked up.

Ty.

"Lad?"

"What?"

Ty knelt down in front of Calis and tried a smile. The last rays of the setting sun reflected off a golden tooth in his mouth. His lucky tooth, Ty said. One night, when he was drunk, the little man had grabbed Calis's head in an armlock and dragged his face close.

"I want you to have it," he said, breathing foul air on Calis. "My tooth. If anything happens to me, I want you to have it."

Calis hadn't known what to say to that. But every time he saw the tooth now, that was all he could think of. Ty was going to die and the others were going to give him the little man's tooth.

"It's time to eat," the older man said, his voice bringing Calis back to the here and now.

Calis shook his head. "Not hungry."

"You want me to give your share to them?" Ty asked, nodding over his shoulder, to where a group of soldiers—mercenaries from Kaden's Harbor—stood. Kraxans. Calis could tell just by looking at them. Or at least they had Kraxan blood. Darker hair; stronger, more angular features; olive skin; one look at them and he knew where they came from. Same place as him.

"Doesn't matter to me," Calis said.

"It matters to Tandis." Ty gestured toward the campfire, a few hundred feet away. "He wants you to eat. He wants to talk to you, too. He wants—"

"I don't care what he wants," Calis interrupted. "And you can tell him that."

The little man sighed.

"Have it your way." He got to his feet and walked away. Calis watched him go for a moment, remaining seated.

Tandis wanted to talk. What was the use in talk?

The only thing left in the world was fighting.

The only thing left in the world was to die.

The Fallen had them trapped; cornered at the very edge of the eastern continent, on a small strip of land between the swamp on one side and the cliffs on the other. There would be no escape this time, not for any of them. Not even the captain.

"Calis."

He looked up, and Tandis was standing over him.

"What?" he snapped.

"Come," the captain said, and before Calis knew it, he was on his feet and walking.

Tandis led him past the campfire, a good hundred yards out into the swamp. There were patches of solid ground among the bogs; the trick was finding them. Tandis must have had some kind of secret method; Calis's boots didn't sink more than an inch or two the whole way.

Tandis jumped across a small stream and landed among a patch of tall, reed-thin Q'dari plants. The bushes were everywhere in this part of the swamp; Calis had watched earlier as some of the villagers uprooted the plants whole and wove them into baskets to help catch a brief rainfall that had come earlier in the afternoon.

He jumped across the little stream as well, or tried to, anyway. He misjudged the distance and landed with one foot in the water. He grabbed onto one of the Q'dari plants and pulled himself up and out before he could sink farther.

"This should do," Tandis said, and then turned to face Calis. "Well. Speak your mind, boy."

"Speak my mind."

"Yes."

"What do you mean?" They were far enough away from the camp, Calis realized, that the noises coming from it had faded away.

The captain folded his arms across his chest.

"I mean you're angry with me. Speak your mind."

Calis shook his head. "I'm not—"

"Is it because I left? Because I wasn't there to save the others?"

"No!" Calis snapped. "That's not it at all. It's just . . ."

Except that that was indeed it, Calis realized.

"You shouldn't have gone," Calis said.

"I had to," Tandis said simply. "I had to try to save the Keep."

"Why?"

"Why." Tandis sighed. "That's a long story, lad."

"I don't see that we have a lot to do otherwise."

Tandis smiled. "You *are* angry with me, aren't you?"

Calis, almost before he knew he was doing so, took a step forward.

"This isn't funny," he said.

"Indeed."

"But you haven't said a word about them. Uthirmancer. Bili. Kesper. Okuls. The others. Those men served you loyally for decades and died in your service and you—you don't even care!"

He glared at the captain, and in that instant realized something.

The two of them stood eye to eye with each other. He, Calis, was as tall as Tandis. When had that happened?

For as long as he'd known the man, he'd been looking up to him. In more ways than one. Tandis his commander. His hero. The one man he could count on to do right, in a world that all too often seemed insane.

He wasn't looking up to him any longer, Calis realized.

"Do you really think me so heartless?" Tandis put a hand on his shoulder; the boy shrugged it off.

"I only go by what I see. And what I see is that you didn't even take the time to bury them. They died obeying your orders, and you couldn't even—"

"I can assure you that I will remember them very well, boy. With or without a gravestone." Tandis put a bit of snap in his voice as well; he had touched a nerve. Good, Calis thought. He shouldn't be the only one upset.

"Okuls and Uthirmancer. Kesper and Bili. All who die in my service—in Galor's service—are valuable to me," Tandis continued.

"Your service!" Calis shouted. "That's the problem exactly. To you, we're all the same. We're nothing but tools—interchangeable tools—for you to use, and toss away, and forget about . . ."

His voice trailed off. Tears, he realized, were streaming from his eyes.

"If I seem uncaring I apologize," Tandis said. "I have served Galor a long time. A very long time. I have seen many knights come and go. I value them all. I value you, especially."

Calis was taken aback.

"Me?"

"Yes. You are . . . you have great potential, lad. I sensed it from the moment I saw you."

Calis nodded. This story he'd heard more than once. Of how Tandis had pulled him from the burning ruins of his village and saved his life.

He felt some of his anger slipping away.

"I still don't understand why you had to go to the Keep," he said, now sounding petulant even to his own ears.

"It concerns Talax. You will recall him?"

"I recall his name. He's the one they all took orders from. The Fallen Army."

"He's much more than that, I'm afraid," Tandis said. "Talax is a Titan."

Calis blinked.

"What?"

"A Titan," Tandis said. "One of the immortals."

"But they're dead," Calis said. "They all died in the Cataclysm. Everyone knows that."

A slight smile crossed Tandis's face. "No. Would that were so."

"But . . ." Calis shook his head. Talax, an immortal. One of the Titans.

At that instant, a shadow fell across the swamp. Across the patch of Q'dari plants they stood next to. No—not a shadow. It was the light itself going, the very last vestiges of it fading away.

Calis looked up and saw that the stars had come out.

"The world of Elemental seems to be racing toward a turning point," Tandis said quietly. "A pivotal moment in history. The Destiny are at work once more."

Calis had a hard time keeping the surprise off his face. The Destiny? Never in all the years he'd known him had Calis heard Tandis talk about the Gods, or their powers.

"I didn't know you believed in the Gods."

"I cannot help but believe in the Gods," Tandis said. "Their desires—their maneuverings—have shaped the course of history more than once."

Calis frowned.

"I don't understand. What does this have to do with Talax?"

"It is complicated, to be sure," Tandis said. "Talax seeks a certain . . . object. An artifact the Destiny had a hand in creating. He must not be allowed to obtain this object."

"And that's why you went to the Keep?"

"Yes." Tandis pulled at one of the reeds of the Q'dari plant. Pulled, and then let go. The plant sprang away from him, and then sprang right back. He held up a hand to keep it from brushing against his face. "I went to instruct Lord Ambrose on the importance of holding the Keep against the Fallen. The importance of preserving Galor's stronghold, here on the eastern part of the continent, so that we would have a base from which to launch our search. I had not expected Talax himself to travel with the army. To lay siege to the Keep."

"Well, what now?" Calis said.

"Our first priority remains the same," Tandis said. "Keeping that object away from Talax."

"All due respect, sir," Calis said. "Isn't our first priority to stay alive? We can't do much of anything about this artifact if we're dead."

Tandis looked at him for a moment, then barked out a laugh.

"You have a point, lad. But I don't think the two are incompatible."

Calis looked at the captain and realized something.

"You have a plan."

"The beginnings of one, at least," Tandis said, pulling on one of the Q'dari reeds once more. This time he yanked hard enough at the reed to pull it free of its roots.

He held it up for Calis to examine.

"Remarkable plant, don't you think?"

"What?"

"Remarkable plant, the Q'dari. Flexible. And strong. Quite strong." He held the reed up in the moonlight. "Considerably stronger than it looks, in fact. Holds a man's weight quite easily. Several men, in fact."

"What's that have to do with anything?" Calis asked.

Tandis went on as if Calis hadn't spoken.

"Braid the reeds together, you could make rope. And there are enough plants here"—he gestured around the swamp—"to make quite a lot of rope indeed. Several thousand feet of it, I'd guess. Isn't that something?"

He smiled. Calis glared. What was there to smile about in this situation? Trapped like they were, with the Fallen Army on one side, and sheer cliffs a thousand feet high on the other . . .

Several hundred feet of rope.

"Wait a second," he said. "You don't think . . ."

Tandis tossed him the Q'dari reed.

"We'd better get started, don't you think?" he asked.

Calis nodded, and smiled back.

CHAPTER TWENTY-EIGHT

They found the city itself soon enough.

An hour's travel from the fork in the path. Half of that time in a tunnel, half of it climbing a ladder—metal rungs, set into the wall in front of them, very old rungs made of metal that flaked off in Xander's hand as he grasped them.

He had to climb slowly, and not just because Geni was exhausted—the heat and humidity seemed to grow the higher they went, which made absolutely no sense to him—but also because in one hand he held a torch. One of several they'd found earlier, set into a cache in the tunnel wall. Torches, soaking in a puddle of black tar, along with flint to light them. He'd fashioned a sling from his shirt to hold extras; they would need them, he'd suspected.

When they reached a ledge another passageway awaited them. Then another passageway. Finally they came to a circular metal door, which on first glance looked to be rusted shut but then swung open with little trouble at Xander's slightest touch. "Calebethon," Geni said, and stepped around him. Rocks skittered beneath her feet.

"Careful," Xander said, and held the torch up higher. His eyes widened at what he saw.

They stood in the middle of an immense underground cavern, lit by the same dull purplish glow they had gotten used to in the tunnels below. The lichen, Xander thought at first, only as his eyes adjusted to the new combination of light and shadow—the light from the torch, the light from the cavern, the reflections from both all around him—he saw that there were purple plants everywhere, some the size of bushes, others as tall as trees.

"This is crazy," he said. "The plants—everything. It's glowing. Giving off light."

"Magic," Geni said. "Everything in the world possesses magic, Xander."

"Even me?"

She smiled. "Even you."

He waited for her to explain further, but she didn't. She just started off down the path, toward a cluster of buildings in front of them. Some as tall as the Keep, others barely more than huts. Calebethon, he thought, and followed in her wake.

She was moving with purpose, and it soon became clear what that purpose was.

In the very first hut they came to, they found a well. A pit, dug deep into the earth inside the house, with a bucket attached to one end of a chain next to it. The other end of the chain was bolted into the wall.

"Water," Geni said, kneeling down next to the pit.

Xander smiled. She threw the bucket.

It hit far below, with an audible crack. She quickly yanked it back up. The wood was split in two.

The well was dry.

The same thing happened in the next two houses they came to. It was only then that the question occurred to Xander—the question he should have thought to ask long before, immediately after they'd made the decision to come to the underground city.

"Geni?"

"What?" She'd been kneeling down next to the house's well; she stood up now, a frown on her face.

"Who lives here? In Calebethon?"

She opened her mouth to answer—and then quickly shut it.

"No one," she said. "Obviously."

She turned to go.

"Not now, I mean. Before. Who lived here, when all this was built?"

She avoided his eyes. "I'm not really sure. The Hiergamenon talks about some adventures that Amarian had in the city. That sort of thing. But there's nothing in the history books."

"Geni," Xander said impatiently. "Come on. Who lived here?"

She was quiet for a second before answering.

"Fallen," she said. "It was part of the empire."

Xander was quiet then, too. Fallen.

The empty city—the long shadows, the dusty, uninhabited ruins surrounding them—took on a whole new meaning then.

"Come on." Geni put a hand on his arm. "That was a very long time ago. There hasn't been anyone here for ages. Right?"

Xander nodded. Reluctantly, but he nodded.

"Right," he said.

"Good." Geni smiled. "Let's go find some water."

The path they'd been traveling widened into a road and then dove down deeper into the earth. The buildings grew larger. The road led them right up to the biggest one of all, taller by half than the Keep, or anything Geni had seen in Capitar.

Fifty feet in front of that building, the road narrowed and split into thirds. To the left and right it led around the building. Straight ahead it led up to the structure's front door.

"What do you think this place is? Or was?" Xander asked.

Geni shook her head. "I have no idea."

Xander's torch was dying down; as they approached the front of the building, he paused and used the flickering torch to light another from the sling on his back.

The building leapt into sharper focus. It was all stone; a single, dark piece of it. The walls were smooth to the touch. *Obsidian*. The word leapt unbidden to her mind. In one of Mirdoth's parchments, there had been reference to that type of stone. A drawing. It looked much as the building before her did.

Obsidian. She remember something else about it now as well.

It was used by Morrigan, the deceiver. The betrayer. Hosten's son, who had turned his back on mankind and embraced the ways of the Fallen. There was an epic poem, written sometime in the years after the Cataclysm. *Procipinee's Lament,* written by Sudesh. Mirdoth had made her memorize the whole thing; part of it came back to her now.

> *And in his lair*
> *Beneath the Mountains Deep*
> *Morrigan the base betrayer*
> *In obsidian depths do monsters keep*

Or was that last line "his monsters sleep"?

Geni couldn't remember exactly.

"This place gives me the creeps," Xander said.

Geni, lost in thought, almost jumped a mile high at the sound of his voice. Luckily he didn't notice.

"I know what you mean," she said.

She decided not to tell Xander about the rhyme. Just like she'd decided not to tell him some of the other stories in the Hiergamenon, about the things that Amarian had met inside Calebethon besides Fallen. Cannibals. Dragons. Golems. Etc., etc. She was certain most of those stories were apocryphal.

Fairly certain, anyway.

The important thing was the Bane. Dred'nir's Bane, Tandis had called it. That wasn't in *Procipinee's Lament*, that she could recall. She couldn't recall anything else about what he'd said, though, other than that. And the fact that the way to find it began in Calebethon.

They followed the path up to the door, and then—Xander leading the way, with an audible deep breath—they stepped inside.

Xander gasped.

He stepped backward and landed on Geni's foot.

"Ow," she said. "What's the matter . . ."

Her voice trailed off as she saw what Xander had recoiled from.

Skeletons. Everywhere.

The interior of the building was one vast, empty chamber. And the floor of that chamber was covered with skeletons.

There had to be dozens of them. Maybe even hundreds. Skeletons of men. Skeletons of Fallen. Some clad in armor, some lying bare. All, or at least the majority of them, were clutching weapons of some kind. Or lying next to weapons. Swords. Knives. Spears. Some of them shattered, some of them whole. All of those weapons looked discolored to her; rusted, she thought at first, until she got closer and saw that the discoloration was not reddish brown, but black. As if the blades had been singed, somehow. Burned.

"Gods," Geni said. "What happened here?"

"A battle," Xander said. "A great and terrible battle."

Battle. Geni frowned, looking closer. She wasn't so sure.

There was no order to any of the bodies; no formation. And though they were all skeletons, they were of widely different ages. Different states of decay.

She knelt down next to one of the skeletons. A man. It was wearing clothes: the tattered remnants of trousers, and a belt. On the belt was a pouch. Curious, she pulled at it. It came apart in her hands, splitting in two. The contents spilled out onto the floor: rocks, coins, and parchment—a folded-up piece of it. Geni pulled the edges apart and spread it wide.

A map. A very, very old map, she could tell instantly by looking at the countries that were on it. And those that weren't. The western continent consisted only of three: Gilden, Ruvenna, and New Pariden. No Altar, no Yoren, no Capitar. And the eastern continent . . .

There were no countries at all. Just a single word emblazoned across an oddly unfamiliar landmass.

Calebethon. It stretched from east to west, from north to south. It was huge. Immensely larger, even, than the massive cavern outside this building.

What did that mean? she wondered.

"Hey! Geni! Look!"

She lifted her eyes from the map.

Xander had walked into the center of the room, carrying the torch with him. The flame lit up portions of the interior she hadn't seen before; the first thing that caught her eye was a pile of rubble at the back of the chamber. A huge pile, massive, irregularly shaped, with rolls of—what, fabric? carpets? cloth of some kind, multicolored, shiny cloth—scattered atop it.

Xander wasn't gesturing toward the rubble, though. His attention was focused on a long, stone table in the very center of the room, a table at least twice the size of the one back in the Great Hall, in the Keep.

The table was covered with food. Platters of it—meats, breads, fruits, pastries . . . a feast.

"It can't be real," Xander said, taking a step closer.

Geni rose, too, folding the map back up. No. The food couldn't be real; they had to be carvings of some kind. Wood, or stone; her mother had a platter of calivars—carved rock—on top of her dressing table. When she was little, Geni had more than once picked up one of those calivars and tried to eat it.

Xander was about to do the same, reaching for a piece of bread with his left hand while his right held the torch.

At that instant, Geni noticed a faint blue glow around the entire table.

She thought immediately of what she'd seen through the Elemscope: the blue glow around the people in the village of Outpost. The bright red glow of the Titan, Talax, approaching the Keep. Magic.

"Xander," she said quickly. "Hold on. Don't."

He reached down and picked up the bread.

The blue glow pulsed brighter for a second.

That pulse shot like an arrow—like one of the wisps—along the length of the table and then down to the floor.

"Ha!" Xander shouted, and laughed. "It's real! Geni, the food is real!"

He turned around and held it up for her to see.

Her attention, though, was focused elsewhere. On the blue pulse of energy, which now shot along the floor and into the pile of rubble at the rear of the chamber.

There was a bright blue flash of light, and then darkness returned.

"What was that?" Xander asked, spinning around.

"I don't know." Geni watched the pile of rubble for a second. Watched, and listened.

Nothing happened.

"You think it's safe to eat?" Xander asked.

"I don't know."

"I'm going to try," he said, raising the bread to his lips. "Just a little taste."

He took a hesitant nip with his mouth.

"Tastes all right," he said.

The floor beneath them rumbled.

"What was that?" he asked.

Geni shook her head. "I don't know."

But she did. Or at least she had a general idea.

"I think we ought to leave," she said.

"What?"

"Right now. We ought to leave." She took a step backward. "Come on, Xander."

"But the food—"

"We'll find food, don't worry. We need to—"

The pile of rubble erupted, sending a huge cloud of dust billowing into the air. The floor shook at that instant as well. Geni stumbled and fell backward, landing on her butt.

A gust of wind blew so powerfully it sent her hair flying back from her face and snatched the map from her grasp. It quickly disappeared from sight, and then, all at once, everything disappeared from sight. The torch. It had gone out.

"Xander!" she yelled.

"Geni! I'm here!"

The voice was still coming from right in front of her. She took a step forward and bumped into something.

"Ahhh!" she screamed and stumbled backward, only just then realizing that the thing she'd bumped into—

"Was that you?" she heard Xander yell.

"Yes. Me. I'm right here. Follow the sound of my voice."

She kept talking until she sensed Xander close by once more. Then she reached out a tentative hand and touched him.

"That's my nose," he said.

"I can tell that," she snapped.

"What happened?" he asked. "What was that noise?"

A roar sounded—a roar loud enough that she felt a rumble in her belly, a sympathetic vibration.

"Something came out of the rubble," she said. She told Xander about the blue glow she'd seen around the food, then some kind of magic alarm.

"We have to get out of here," he said.

He wasn't going to get any argument from her.

"I have the torches," he said. "Hang on."

The roar came again. Closer this time.

"Hurry, Xander."

"Going as fast as I can." He cursed under his breath. "I think the flint is getting worn. We're going to have to—"

The wind came then, along with an ominous sound that it took her a second to place.

It was, she realized, the sound of wings flapping. Very, very big wings.

"Xander . . ."

"I'm going as fast as I can. It's not easy doing this when—"

From up above a foul gust of wind blew toward them.

"Oh, Gods," Xander said, the disgust in his voice plain. "What is that smell?"

Something above them roared, and then the floor shook.

It—whatever it was—was close by indeed. Very, very close by.

Two lights had just appeared behind Xander. Glowing green lights, each about the size of the torch that he was still struggling to light.

The lights moved closer.

"Ah," Geni said. "Xander—we—"

"Got it," he said, and in that instant the flint sparked, and the torch lit.

And Geni's eyes widened.

The two lights—each a good three feet across, half again that high—were eyes.

Set into a face that was bigger than one of the towers back at the Keep. Set on a head that was the size of one of her father's galleys. Attached to a body that dwarfed any living thing she had ever seen in her life.

"It's a dragon," Xander said, in a voice about an octave up from where he usually spoke.

For a second Geni could only nod.

"Yes," she said finally. "It's a dragon."

* * *

No, Xander thought. No, no, no. He was seeing things. Dragons were extinct. Everybody knew that. Dragons had been extinct for thousands of years.

"No," he said out loud.

The dragon snorted, and smoke emerged from its nostrils. Billowing clouds of smoke. Xander caught some of it in his lungs and started to cough.

"Little things," the dragon rumbled. "Little, little things. Why have you disturbed my sleep?"

Xander looked at Geni.

"Ah . . ." She cleared her throat. "We . . . um. We didn't mean to . . ."

The dragon opened its mouth and roared.

The sound was incredible. The stench was worse. And deep within its throat, Xander caught a glimpse of fire.

No point in staying around here, he thought.

Even before it finished roaring, Xander grabbed Geni's arm and dove with her under the table. But as he landed, he dropped the torch.

Everything went dark.

"Little things," the dragon said, and Xander knew that it was moving, the way its voice rose in volume. Moving toward them.

In the darkness, Geni squeezed his hand.

"Why do you hide?" the dragon called out. "Do you not want to talk, little things? Have conversation?"

The voice moved closer. Xander heard the scrape of bone against the stone floor, the slither of skin touching it. Gods, it was near. Right next to them. Right on top of them. And then . . .

It moved past.

Xander let out a breath he didn't even know he'd been holding.

"This is impossible," Geni whispered. "Dragons are extinct."

"Yeah," he said. "I know."

"Come out, little things." The dragon's voice came now from far off, from the other side of the room, Xander guessed. "Come out and talk to Magor now."

Little chance of that happening, he thought.

"Let's make a run for it," he said. "The door. That thing'll never be able to fit through. Come after us."

"Wait a minute. Did it just say Magor?" Geni asked. "The dragon?"

Xander nodded. "I think so."

"Magor is in the stories," Geni said.

"What stories?"

"The Hiergamenon. Magor's friendly."

"Yeah. Well, maybe it's a different Magor," Xander said. "It's probably a common dragon name."

"A *common* dragon name?" Geni asked incredulously.

"Could be. Now, come on. We go on the count of three. One—two—"

Geni stood up.

"Magor," she said, and there was a roar, and a flapping of wings, and then a split second later the eyes were back. A few feet away from them.

Xander felt the steam from the creature's breath on his face.

"So little things want to talk now? Tell Magor why they are here?"

"Yes," Geni said, her voice sounding strong and confident. "I will tell you why we are here, Magor."

"And who you are," the dragon said. "Give Magor your names, as he has given you his."

"I am the Princess Angenica, of the house of Aegeon. And this"—she reached out a hand in the darkness behind her, and Xander knew instinctually to rise—"is my friend Xander."

He stepped forward hesitantly.

"Hello. I'm just going to light this torch, if you don't mind."

The dragon grunted then, in what Xander took as assent. He struck the flint and lit the torch. The chamber—the dragon, the skeletons, the table of food, and Geni—all came leaping back into focus.

Magor was staring at Geni. He had an expression that looked very much like a frown on his face.

"House of Aegeon?" the dragon said. "I do not recognize this house."

"We have ruled the Henge for centuries," Geni said. "Since the War of Magic. Since the days of the Cataclysm itself, and the Eternal March."

"War of Magic? Cataclysm? Eternal March?" The dragon's frown deepened. "You will have to explain these things to me, daughter of man."

"I'll try," Geni said. Xander listened then as she talked about the history of Elemental. The wars between men, and Titans, between Curgen and Kir-Tion; between Curgen and Lady Umber. The great army of the West that Amarian had led to the gates of Imperium. The cracking of the world that followed that army's arrival; the Cataclysm. The War of Magic, the Empire of Sorcery and the rise of Galor. The defeat of the Black Sorcerer, and the fall of the Empires of the East.

The dragon looked thoughtful when she had finished. Thoughtful and—perhaps Xander was imagining this—a little sad.

"Much time has passed since Magor has wandered the world. Many years. These places you talk of . . . these people. I know none of them. And the Dred'nir, and Elas'nir—you do not speak of them at all."

"The Titans, you mean," Geni said. "They're gone. Since the Cataclysm. Well, we thought they were gone. Now . . ." She looked over at Xander. "One's come back. Talax. And that's why we're here."

"I understand now, little thing. You think this Talax is in Calebethon. You wish to enter the city to find—"

"No," Geni said. "Excuse me for interrupting, but it's not

Talax we're looking for. We know where he is. What we want is something called the Bane. The Bane of the Dred'nir."

"Bane," the dragon rumbled thoughtfully. "Bane. I do not know this either, daughter of man."

"Tandis said it was in Calebethon," Geni replied. "I was hoping you might—"

"Tandis?" The dragon's voice rose in volume, and pitch. "Tandis the Arnor? This name I know. The greatest of all the Elas'nir. Tandis and I—we are as brothers!" The dragon flapped its wings once, and for a second rose off the ground. "You are Tandis's friends. You are Magor's friend—you are friends to the brethren of the Dragon!"

The dragon's wings sent a cloud of dust up into the air; Geni waved it away, putting a hand in front of her face. "This is a different Tandis," she said, stifling a cough. "He's not a Titan. He's a man—captain of the King's Azure Knights. He's the one who told us about the Bane."

"Tandis the man. Not Tandis the Arnor. I see." The dragon, Magor, seemed to deflate before her eyes. "Of course. The Titans are all gone. This you have said before."

"He said it was in the bowels of Calebethon," Geni added. "The deepest reaches."

"The deepest reaches. The oldest parts of the city itself, then." Magor sighed. "Nit'va'ganesh. The path there is not an easy one, little things. The way is long, and difficult."

Geni remembered something then. She backed away slowly till she reached it.

The map.

"I have this," Geni said, picking up the sheet of folded paper from where it had been blown from her grasp, and spreading it out for the dragon to see. "Maybe you could show us where we need to go on this."

Magor moved his—its?—head closer and squinted. He rumbled once, twice, and then drew his head back.

"Too small for Magor to read," he pronounced. "As I told you. You must find Nit'va'ganesh. This is the oldest part of Calebethon. The oldest, and the deepest dug. First by the Dread Lord Curgen, and then Morrigan the Betrayer."

"Is it far from here?" Geni asked.

Magor snorted. "Can you fly, little thing?"

"Well . . . no."

"Then it is far."

"How far?" Xander asked, stepping forward. "Days? Weeks?"

The dragon turned its immense head, and regarded him disdainfully. "Can you tunnel, little thing?"

"No. But we can walk pretty fast."

The dragon snorted. "Walking. You will be slow. Weeks."

"I don't know if we have weeks," Geni said.

"Do you have magic, little thing?" The dragon fixed its eye on her. "I think that perhaps you do."

"She might be a channeler," Xander blurted out. "She's going to Athica, to be tested."

Geni turned and glared at him.

"It's the truth," he said.

"Indeed." The dragon turned to Xander. "But you, boy . . . in you I sense no magic at all. In fact . . ."

Magor lowered his head and snaked it around Xander once, twice, a third time. Then it snorted.

"I sense nothing at all from you," the dragon said. "Curious. Very curious indeed."

The dragon rose to its full height once more.

"Find Nit'va'ganesh, little things, and you will find the Bane," Magor said. "But be warned. Calebethon is as large as all the kingdoms of man combined. In it you will find men, as well as those races that were twisted from them, and dragons by the Dred'nir. There is much danger."

"Can you tell us how to avoid that danger?" she was going to say, but all at once the dragon roared, interrupting her. It raised its head and looked up.

"I must leave this place and discover what has transpired in my absence. Learn more about these channelers, and shards, and the like." Magor spread its wings and looked down on Geni, its immense mouth curling into a smile. "But if you truly do need me, you may summon me."

"And how do I do that?" Geni asked.

In answer, the dragon flapped its wings, with such force that it was as if a tornado had blown into the room. And then it rose into the air, and with a mighty roar, yelled, "Good-bye, little things!"

It disappeared toward the roof of the immense structure. There was the distant sound of something shattering, and then the dragon was gone from sight.

"Duck!" Xander yelled, and Geni felt him grab her by the waist and drag her underneath the same table they'd been hiding under before.

A moment later, debris—rock, glass, marble—rained down from above. A cloud of dust followed a second later.

"There's a way out up there," Xander said, getting to his feet as the rain of rubble ceased. "If that dragon can get out, so can we."

Geni got to her feet and looked around. There.

She walked over to where a corner of the map peeked out from beneath a huge shard of glass as long as her forearm, and pulled it free.

"No," she said, shaking the dust off the parchment and holding it up for Xander to see. "You know where we have to go."

CHAPTER TWENTY-NINE

Ambrose paced the cell; by this point he knew it well. Five feet wide, ten long, a narrow room, the walls of stone; rough-edged rock, mortared together with clay. He'd gone round those walls a dozen times those first few days, pressing on stone after stone, hoping to trigger a mechanism, hoping to reveal an opening to a tunnel, a link to one of the secret passages that honeycombed the Keep. Hoping even though he knew it was probably hopeless; Mirdoth had shown him drawings of the tunnels years ago, and though there were a few on this level, they were all on the other side of the corridor. Still . . .

In his youth, Ambrose had spent many nights in dungeons of various sorts. He had created a classification for each of them based on how easily he had escaped. When he had taken command of the Keep, he had insisted that his dungeon be impossible to escape from.

There were untold levels to the fortress, dating back to the time of Amarian himself, and the Eternal March. Levels, passages, perhaps predating Mirdoth's map. Ambrose had to hope. He had to find a way out.

He had to find Geni.

Eight days now since the Keep had fallen, and no word of her.

She must have escaped; he felt certain she was still alive. If she had died he would have known it, inside. He was no channeler, Galor's test had proved that, but there was a connection between his daughter and himself, as there had been between him and Odona. When she had perished, Ambrose had been in chambers. In a council meeting. In the middle of addressing emissaries sent from Kraxis, including the Regent Edmund, when all at once it was as if he'd been plunged into a bath of ice-cold water; his heart felt like it would stop.

Something was wrong; he'd known it instantly. Something had happened, and when Odona's face flashed before his eyes, he knew to whom.

He'd had no such feeling about Geni. In his heart, in his gut, he knew she was still alive. All that was necessary was for him to escape, and find her, and then the two of them together could go about setting the world right once more.

The cell door slammed open and Yanos stepped in.

"Lord of the Keep." The Fallen captain sneered. "I have something for you."

Ambrose turned to face him.

Yanos was sergeant in charge of Ambrose's guards here in the dungeon; an Urxen. Far and away the smartest of those vile beings the Lord had ever met. Ambrose's own height, but whip-thin. Gray skin, lanky hair the color of burnt copper, with eyes to match. After they'd marched Mirdoth off, that first day Ambrose had continually badgered his guards with questions, until finally, having given up on satisfying his demands for information, the underlings had turned to the master.

From the third day of his imprisonment onward, Yanos was the guard that Ambrose dealt with. The one who brought him his food in the morning; the one who doled out little bits of information regarding the fate of his soldiers (Jarak and Neral are dead; would you care for body parts as souvenirs?), his subjects (each night we burn another building in Outpost; they make lovely firewood), and his possessions (the portrait of your late wife, in your bedchamber; we have drawn a few embellishments onto it, enhanced certain physical features; I can bring it to you if you wish).

Ambrose hated the creature in a way he had never hated anyone—or anything—before.

"Something for me," he said. "Pray tell, what is it?"

The two glared at each other.

"A visitor," Yanos said. "You'll have ten minutes, Lord of the Keep. Use them wisely."

Ambrose's heart soared. Geni, he thought.

And then Yanos stepped aside, and Mirdoth entered his cell.

This was going to be even harder than he'd thought, Mirdoth realized, seeing the look on Ambrose's face. Seeing the surroundings his lord found himself in. Mirdoth had been in the cells only one day; he had now been in his quarters, in the observatory, for seven. A prisoner, yes, but in comparatively luxurious surroundings. He had forgotten what imprisonment truly meant. And how it smelled.

"My lord, are you well?" Mirdoth asked.

Ambrose arranged his features into the semblance of a smile. "As well as anyone who is imprisoned in their own Keep can be. And you? You seem . . ."

"Yes. They have installed me in the observatory," Mirdoth said.

"To what end?"

Mirdoth frowned, and glared at the Urxen captain, who his lord seemed to have forgotten was in there.

"Ten minutes," the Fallen said. "I will return."

He backed out of the cell and closed it behind him.

"Mirdoth?" Ambrose asked again. "To what end?"

"The Bane," Mirdoth said. "Talax thinks there will be clues to its location among my papers."

"And have you found any?"

"No. Not yet."

"And Geni," Ambrose said, crossing the cell and laying hands on Mirdoth's shoulders. "Have you heard from her? Do you know where—"

"No." Mirdoth shook his head. "Not a word."

"Gods!" Ambrose cursed, then turned away. "What is happening out there, Mirdoth? What have you found out? Tell me everything."

Mirdoth nodded, and recounted—as quickly as he could, since they had but ten minutes, after all—the events of the last few days.

"More and more troops are arriving every day," Mirdoth said. "Many Trogs. Fighters. Far more than are needed to hold this Keep."

"An invasion, you think?" Ambrose asked.

"Perhaps." Mirdoth nodded.

"Any news of activity from the West? From Galor, or the villages south of Outpost?"

"Not that I know of, my lord. Though I do not have free run of the Keep—there is no way to observe what is truly happening." Mirdoth hastened to add this last fact.

"You must find a way to do so, old friend. Your magic." Ambrose's eyes bore into his. "Eavesdrop, if you can. Are there not spells . . ."

Mirdoth shook his head. "I cannot, Lord. I dare not. Do not ask me."

"Dare not?" Ambrose frowned. "What do you mean by that?"

Mirdoth shook his head. "I cannot say."

"What?"

"I cannot say," Mirdoth repeated, knowing that by doing so he was only increasing his lord's curiosity. He was unable to think of anything else to say.

He could think only of Talax. Talax, who had been in his mind. Talax now knew who—what—he truly was. Or so Mirdoth feared.

"Mirdoth," Ambrose said, and now there was concern in his voice as well as anger. "What is it? Something is wrong, I can tell."

"Yes," Mirdoth said. "Something is very wrong, my lord."

"Does this something have to do with the reason you are no longer my cell mate, old friend? Why you are no longer on this side of the bars that imprison me?"

Ambrose grinned. His words were obviously meant as a joke.

Mirdoth, however, found it hard to return the smile.

"The Titan's powers are formidable, my lord. He has been in my mind. Found out things—forced me to confront things . . . I have long kept hidden."

He met Ambrose's eyes.

The Fallen sergeant, Yanos, had come to the observatory barely an hour earlier. At Talax's suggestion.

Talk to Ambrose, was the message the Urxen had brought. A message that came from the Titan himself. Talk to your lord and master. No doubt he misses your company. Mirdoth had wanted to see Ambrose, and so he'd accepted. He had walked into the cell with only that thought in mind: to see his lord, to assure himself that Ambrose was well. The idea of revealing what the Titan had discovered about him had never, ever occurred to Mirdoth, and yet now that he was here . . .

He wondered if that had been Talax's plan all along. Force Mirdoth and his lord together, force Mirdoth to reveal to Ambrose . . .

"Things?" Ambrose frowned. "What type of things?"

Mirdoth opened his mouth, then closed it again.

He dared not speak another word. Dared not tell Ambrose anything, he realized. That path—the path of confession, of acknowledgment for the sins of the past, the things he had done wrong, the thing that he had been—that path was no longer available for him to walk.

He had chosen his road long ago. The road of silence. Solitude. Secrecy.

"They are personal things, my lord," Mirdoth lied. "I should not have mentioned them."

"Nonsense." Ambrose smiled again. "We are friends, above all else. There is not a thing you could tell me about your past that would shake my faith in you. My understanding of the person that you are."

Mirdoth once more had to avoid his eyes.

"Thank you, my lord. I hope to justify your confidence."

"You can, old friend." Ambrose moved closer and put a hand on Mirdoth's shoulder. "Find out about Geni. Where she is. Where she's gone. Where she hides. And find out about—"

The cell door slammed open and Yanos entered the chamber.

He sneered at Ambrose; he turned to Mirdoth.

"Time's up," the Fallen sergeant said. "Let's go."

With a backward glance at Ambrose, Mirdoth left the cell.

CHAPTER THIRTY

The reeds became ropes. The ropes became ladders. And the ladders led down to the sea.

It was a thing the women of Red Spring—and indeed, the children, and some of the less infirm among the old, and the wounded—could all do. Gather the Q'dari plants at the edge of the swamp, and work them into their salvation. Their path down the cliffs, to the bay below. Tandis's idea, which Calis had instantly grasped. A way out from the trap they found themselves in. The Fallen Army, held at bay by the swamp on one side, the sea on the other.

Calis stood now, at the edge of the cliff, and looked down.

It was a sheer drop of a thousand feet to the water's surface; the rock face leading down was nearly sheer as glass. Looking at it, it seemed to him that the world itself must have been snapped in two sometime in the past and a great sea rushed in to fill the gap.

The ropes would get them down to that sea, but from there the way to safety would require boats. And so birds had been sent to Minoch, and its ruler, Baron Mancer. Birds had come back; ships, the messages they carried said, were being sent. And now they were here. A fleet, though a fleet like no other Calis had seen in all his journeys across the world. Hundreds of ships, some large as the great seafaring galleys the men of Yoren favored; others as small as rowboats. Would they be enough to carry the thousands gathered here, at the edge of the swamp—the villagers, the soldiers, the farmers, and their families—to safety?

They'd find out soon enough, Calis supposed.

"Boy. Come."

He turned and saw one of Lord Ambrose's soldiers—an officer; he'd met the man earlier; hadn't noted his name, though—motioning to him. The officer stood a few dozen feet away, next to the first of the great ropes. They'd woven half a dozen of them, nearly as thick as Calis's fist and secured to structures—logs sunk deep into the earth, fifty feet away from the cliff's edge. The more able of the evacuees would use the first two and go down hand over hand. The other four ropes controlled a platform made of two wagon beds, fastened together, with a rail the height of a man's waist circling it, a platform that could carry upwards of a dozen people at a time.

The officer motioning to Calis was one of several standing near that platform, directing people to form up into lines, yelling at them to keep the pushing and shoving to a minimum. It wasn't working; there were people, particularly out of the soldier's sight, who were trying to force their way to the front of the line, to be the first ones down to the sea and the waiting ships. Tandis had warned Ambrose's commanders that that would happen; they had waved him off dismissively.

"These are the good folk of Outpost," one of them had said. "Of Red Spring, Kaden's Harbor. These are our folk, Knight Captain. They will listen, and move respectfully, according to our wishes."

Tandis had shaken his head. "They respect you, yes. But it is fear that will keep them in line. You must prepare for a panic, particularly if—"

"We thank you for your service, Captain," the same man—

Commander Bodain, an officious little prig; Calis had seen a thousand of his type since joining the Knights: the kind of officer who ruled from a tent, or a desk in some castle chamber, never from horseback or the field—had said, "but these are our people, as I said. I expect no trouble."

But the second the birds had come back, the trouble began. People clamored for a favored place in line—my son died at Red Spring to stave off the army; Lord Ambrose is my sister's cousin; I have paid the wealth of a small kingdom in taxes to the Keep's coffers; I deserve this; I deserve that . . .

Tandis, Hildros, Ty, and Calis—all that remained of the Azure Knights—had stood to the side as the jockeying for position began, and watched the spectacle.

"Panic ain't the half of it," Hildros said quietly, shaking his head. "You watch."

"Why don't you do something?" Calis had turned to Tandis. "Why don't you take charge?"

"On what authority?" Tandis asked.

"Galor's," Calis said. "You're his man. He's the King. You can—"

"They would fight me," Tandis said. "It would only make things worse."

"But they're wrong," Calis said. "You know they are. I know they are. We can't just let them—"

"There is nothing we can do," Tandis said.

Calis, however, hadn't been willing to let it go at that.

He'd volunteered his services to Bodain—or rather, one of Bodain's lieutenants; he hadn't actually been able to talk to the commander himself—to be on one of the great ropes, lowering the platform to the sea, thinking that in that way he could at least act as a calming presence.

As he made his way toward his station, though, he realized that he'd forgotten one thing.

He was Kraxan. And the people here—villagers from Outpost, Red Spring, and Kaden's Harbor, as well as those wounded army men unwell enough to descend by their own power—did not like Kraxans. Did not trust them. Did not want them around. Their eyes—their blue eyes, set in their fair-skinned faces, their tall, lean frames—raked over him as he passed. Noted his angular features, his swarthy complexion, his dark hair, all of which marked him as alien. Different.

"Blood traitor," one woman shot at him as he passed, and spat in his general direction.

He took a deep breath to keep himself from reacting in kind.

He reached the platform and took his place.

Bodain stepped forward.

"Everyone." The general cleared his throat. "We'll begin loading the boats now. I want to stress that while speed is of the essence, safety must also—"

His voice was drowned out by a chorus of inarticulate cries from the villagers, who surged forward so fast that Calis was afraid for a second that he was going to get shoved off the edge of the cliff. He tightened his hold on the rope.

"Bleedin' idiot," the man behind him—there were a dozen of them assigned to each rope—whispered.

Calis grunted an affirmative response; luckily for all of them, Bodain wasn't a complete fool. Even if he hadn't entirely heeded Tandis's advice regarding the evacuation, he'd at least had the good sense to listen to the captain when it came to military matters. As soon as the commander had heard Tandis's idea about the ropes, he'd realized they would need time to make the possibility of escape a reality, and so Bodain had ordered a squadron of men forward into the swamp separating them from the Fallen, a feint, a move designed to make the Fallen commanders think that the commander had chosen to make their stand there.

For the moment that seemed to have stayed the Fallen advance, the swamp being a place where superiority in numbers would have less meaning. Still . . . it was only a matter of time before the Fallen moved, Calis knew. A very short span of time, most likely.

Bodain had also taken care to keep himself protected from the mob of villagers, Calis noted, seeing the small knot of soldiers that surrounded him.

That group now massed together, spears raised, and began using those spears to push the crowd back.

"In line, you!" one of the soldiers shouted. "In line or you get hit."

Calis glared at the man. Heavily armored. Massively muscled. There were three much like him standing at his side. No. Not much like him. Exactly like him.

Brigands. Mercenaries.

"They're not Ambrose's soldiers," Calis said.

" 'Course not," the man behind him murmured. "They're Bodain's. His own hires. The finest money can buy."

As he watched, one of them shoved a man backward. The man fell to the ground and cursed at the soldier.

Calis glared. Finest money could buy. He didn't believe that for a second. They looked like bullies to him.

"Boy, get your grip."

Calis turned and saw the man behind him motioning to the rope. A second later he saw why.

The first batch of villagers was climbing onto the platform.

Calis wrapped his hands around the rope and braced himself.

Four hours later, Calis—his hands raw, his shoulders aching—took his first break. He made his way along the back of the line of villagers—it looked just as long to him as it had when they'd started the evacuation—to where Hildros and Ty stood. Tandis was nowhere in sight.

Hildros handed him a flagon of water. "Slow going, eh?" Hildros asked.

"Yes," Calis replied. It was true; loading, and in particular unloading, had taken much longer than they thought. That was because the boats had to make their way through the surf to an area directly underneath the platform, where the villagers could safely jump—or in some cases, be handed down—to waiting seamen. Depending on the skill of the boat's pilots, depending on the size of the boat, depending on the strength of the surf, that was a process that could take anywhere from one minute to twenty.

And already there had been deaths.

A small ship, dashed up against the cliffs by a monstrous wave that seemed to come out of nowhere.

A small boy slipping from a soldier's grasp and into the waiting ocean.

As the sun began its descent toward the horizon, it seemed likely to him that worse was yet to come.

"Never liked the ocean," Ty said. "Won a boat once in a game of Needles. Beautiful boat. Sold it for a dozen cattle."

Hildros looked at Calis and rolled his eyes. "And this was when, exactly?"

Ty ignored him. "Sold the cattle for twenty thousand rigma. Used the rigma to buy myself a breeding stallion out of Gilden. You know what they say about those stallions, boy, don't you?" He grinned at Calis, revealing his gold tooth. "Same thing they say about the ladies in Athica—as long as you're paying for it, you might as well get the best that money can—"

A woman screamed.

Calis lowered the flagon from his lips and turned.

The four soldiers he'd noticed earlier, Bodain's mercenaries, were standing over a sandy-haired villager who knelt on the ground before them. It looked to Calis like the man was crying. The woman Calis had heard scream stood nearby, a child in her arms. A boy a bit younger than Calis stood behind her.

As Calis watched, one of the soldiers raised his arm and cuffed the man on the ground right across the face. The man let out a groan and fell flat.

The woman screamed once more.

"Stop! For the sake of the Gods—stop!"

The soldiers laughed. One spat on the man; another turned to face a crowd of onlookers that had gathered. He growled at them and made as if to draw his sword. The villagers shrank back; the soldier laughed.

Calis saw red, and started forward.

"Easy, lad." He felt a hand on his arm; Hildros, he thought, and tried to shrug free.

The grip became a vise; Calis turned and saw Tandis.

"Let me go," Calis said. "You saw what they did."

"I saw." Tandis, not letting go of his arm, moved closer, dragging Calis with him. "Let's see what it's about."

Calis sensed Hildros and Ty a step behind them as they moved forward.

"They paid money, that's why," one of the soldiers was saying. "Gold. Not coppers, you understand? They paid in gold, and so they get to move up in the line. That's how the world works, my friend. You have gold, we'll move you up, too."

"I don't have gold," the man said. "But I can work. As long as my wife—my children—get to the boats. I just want to make sure—"

"Sorry, friend." The soldier shook his head. "No gold—can't help you."

The man's face fell; the soldier and his companions laughed.

"Although . . ." The soldier stepped closer to the man's wife and poked a finger under her chin. He raised her head so that she was looking at him; the reason for his interest in her became clear a second later, as Calis got his first good look at the woman's face.

She was beautiful. Underneath all the dirt, and the matted hair . . .

"Saying there were certain . . . extras, to be included in the bargain," the soldier smiled at the woman, who glared and pulled back, "I'm sure we could find it in our hearts to move you up. You and the kids. Couldn't we now, lads?"

The soldiers laughed once more.

"Come on," Calis said to Tandis, trying to take a step forward. "Let's—"

"No," Tandis said, not relaxing his grip for a moment. "There's nothing we can do."

"What? Nothing? We have to help these people. We can't let those bastards get away with this." Calis said quietly but with anger rising in his voice. "They're selling places on the line!"

"What would you have us do, lad? Should we go over there and slay them?" Hildros asked.

"We have to do something!" Calis insisted.

"Whatever you do, lad," Tandis said, "you get involved, there will be consequences. Unintended ones, most likely."

"With all due respect, to hell with the consequences! This is about justice!"

"Justice." Tandis shook his head. "In my experience, there is no such thing."

"You can't believe that," Calis said.

Tandis regarded him for a moment, then stepped back, loosening his grip. "All right. Go ahead."

Calis frowned. "What?"

"It's justice you want, is it? Very well, what are your orders?"

"Orders? Me?" Calis was confused. "You're the master; I'm the apprentice."

"Consider this a part of your training. You want us to kill all of them?" Tandis asked.

"No," Calis said. "I don't. But . . ."

He hesitated, and at that moment the soldier interrogating the woman moved a hand down her neck, to her dress. His hand traced the outline of her collarbone.

She looked terrified.

"Leave her alone," the boy behind her said, taking a step forward.

The soldier removed his hand from the woman and shoved the boy backward. The boy stumbled and fell to the ground.

"Aden!" the woman screamed.

The baby in her arms began to wail.

The man, her husband, started to get to his feet. One of the soldiers cracked him across the back of the head and he toppled over.

Calis saw red.

"Bastards," he said, taking a step forward. "Why don't you pick on someone who can fight back?"

Silence, all at once, fell along the line.

"Oh, dear," Calis heard Ty say from somewhere behind him. "This is not going to end well."

The soldier who was talking to the woman turned, eyes blazing with anger.

"And who in the name of the Gods . . . ," the man began, and then stopped as he saw Calis, and Tandis and the others standing behind him.

"Well. If it ain't King Galor's little Knights. What's left of 'em, anyway." He shook his head. "One fighter, one old man, one . . ." The soldier frowned, looking at Ty, unsure what exactly to make of him.

"God Lord of Menace and Pain Giving is the title I prefer," Ty said.

In response, the soldier snorted. And then he turned his gaze on Calis. "And a blood traitor," the mercenary said, his eyes narrowing. "So what is it you want us to do, boy?"

The soldier took a step forward. Calis suddenly realized just how big the man was. How big his friends were.

He took a deep breath.

"I want you to leave them alone," Calis said.

"You're going to make us, then?"

"If I have to."

"You do. Have to, that is." With a smile the man drew his sword, and Calis then drew his.

The others around them gave way.

Attack, Calis thought. Tandis had always told him the best defense was a good offense, particularly in a situation where you were overmatched, up against a superior fighter, as Calis suspected he was in this instance.

He lunged forward with his sword; the man stumbled back, surprised. Calis pressed the assault, slicing left, and then down; the mercenary was able to block him both times. The man set his feet, and now he sliced down; his sword, thicker and larger than Calis's, came down on the boy's weapon with so much force it was all Calis could do to hold on to the blade.

The man kicked out with one leg and caught Calis in the knee. It buckled underneath him. He held up his sword to block the strike he was sure was coming; the man kicked him again, this time square in the face.

Calis saw stars and fell backward.

He was vaguely aware of his sword falling from his hands; vaguely aware of the man rushing toward him, of movement behind him as well. Tandis, he was sure, rushing to his defense, only he wouldn't get there in time, Calis would die unless—

Time seemed to stand still then.

And Calis felt something gather within him. Strength. Power. Energy. Coursing through his veins like he had never felt in his life. He felt invincible, he felt—

His attacker's sword plunged forward.

Calis clenched his fist, and a light—a red light, a bolt of energy—shot out from it. It struck the man standing over him, and enveloped him. The man's eyes widened.

And then he fell to the ground; even before he hit, Calis knew the man was dead.

And there was silence, the same shocked silence that had greeted his own earlier challenge of the soldier.

"Gods, boy. What . . ."

He turned his head toward Hildros, who was staring at him, shaking his head, as if he'd never seen Calis before.

"I don't know what happened," Calis said. "I . . ."

He turned toward Ty, who began backing away from him.

Along with the other brigands. And the villagers. All of them were looking at him with entirely different eyes. All of them were muttering under their breath as they stepped back; not the usual words, either. Not blood traitor; not Kraxan. This time the accusations were different:

Sorcerer. Channeler. Mage.

Calis found Tandis's eyes, and as their gazes met, the captain's words came rushing back to him.

Unintended consequences.

Tandis opened his mouth to speak.

But then from the far end of the line, a horseman came riding forward. One of Ambrose's soldiers. He wore a look of alarm on his face.

"They're coming!" he shouted. "The Fallen! Ten minutes behind me—maybe less! They're crossing the swamp now!"

And the panic began in earnest.

CHAPTER THIRTY-ONE

The fighting had been brief, a lot briefer than Lork had expected. He made his way across the battlefield, surprised at how few of Lord Ambrose's soldiers dotted the ground. There were more corpses of unarmed men and women than fighters. Strange. Where was everyone?

As he walked, he was not unaware of the looks he was getting from his new subordinates. He had heard the whispers earlier, that he was unqualified for the task to which he had succeeded. Lork disagreed; to his way of thinking, he had done exactly as a commander should. He had been cautious with the lives of those under him, not proceeding into the swamp until he was sure of the size, strength, and position of the enemy confronting him. He was no coward; true, he did not have the experience that Nym had had, but Nym was no longer here, was he? And the most important thing, to his way of thinking, was not the villagers. It was Tandis. It was making sure that the knight did not escape them again.

Talax had summoned Lork to his side a day earlier and given him the weapon that would slay the captain of the Knights. No arrow this time—no subjecting the mission's successful strike to the winds of Fate, as it were.

Now the Dread Lord's enchantment was on another type of weapon entirely. Not as potent an enchantment, to be sure, but . . .

Lork felt the weight of the dagger within his cloak. It was a murderous-looking weapon, a handle of pale white bone, a blade of gleaming steel a half foot long. He had unwrapped the cloth it was wrapped in last night, in the safety, sanctity, and solitude of his tent. Had gone so far as to touch the tip of the blade with the index finger of his right hand, which made the world swim before his eyes. Swim with a dull red glow that he knew to be the enchantment—the death-magic—that Talax had laid on it.

"Sir."

Lork looked up as one of his Urxen subordinates rode up alongside him.

"You have news?" he asked. "You have found Tandis?"

"Ah." The Urxen cleared its throat. "Well, we know exactly where he is."

Lork frowned. "I don't understand. He's here, isn't he?"

"Not exactly, sir."

" 'Not exactly.' What does that mean?"

"Best if I show you, sir," the Urxen said. "If you'll follow . . ."

Lork did. The spit of land separating the swamp from the cliffside was a narrow one; it took them less than half a minute to cross.

The last of the fleeing boats was still visible in the distance, by the light of the setting sun.

Lork cursed out loud; the Urxen next to him stiffened. Lork knew why; he had been in the soldier's shoes himself, when Nym was alive. When Nym was in command. Had that still been the case . . . Lork had no doubt that in his shoes, Nym would have gutted the soldier alongside him and tossed him over the cliff. Lork himself had an instant of wanting to unsheathe his blade and use it. But the instant passed. He was not Nym. Besides which, the lord Talax had planned for this eventuality as well.

CHAPTER THIRTY-TWO

Xander woke with a start. With the knowledge that something was terribly, horribly wrong. It took him less than an instant to figure out what that something was.

His foot was touching Geni's.

The two of them had gone to sleep on either side of the small fire they'd made. But somehow during the night, they'd moved, and now . . .

He tried to slide his foot away, which was when he realized the situation was even worse, actually. Geni's foot lay on top of his. Not just her foot, in fact; the whole bottom half of her leg. He was going to have to move that in order to move himself. Great. Wonderful. She's going to wake up and think that I'm . . .

She groaned, as if she could read his mind then, and rolled even closer, so that her face was barely a foot away from his.

He paused for a moment and looked at her.

Her long golden hair was tussled; her gown was thoroughly wrinkled; a little fleck of spittle at the corner of her mouth bubbled up as she breathed in and out. And yet . . .

She was still beautiful. She'd never, in fact, looked quite so beautiful to him.

Quit it, he told himself. Just quit it. You're friends, and that's all you're ever going to be. Friends. She's a princess, and you're . . . well, he really wasn't much of anything at this point, was he? And that was the problem in a nutshell.

In sliding closer to him, Geni's weight had actually shifted, so that her foot was now just brushing up against his. He slid out from under her, picked up the sleeping sack he'd plundered from one of the bodies in Magor's chamber, walked over to the other side of the fire, and lay back down.

He closed his eyes, still picturing Geni.

Just friends, he told himself. Just friends.

He lay that way for a good half hour before realizing he wasn't going to fall back to sleep.

So he got up and stretched. He wondered what time it was. Hard to know exactly without the sun, or stars, to mark the passage between days, and between day and night. His stomach was growling a little, though, which told him something. Time for breakfast, he decided, and walking carefully, he headed back in the direction of the main trail.

They'd camped down in a little hollow, a few hundred yards back from the path they'd been walking; Xander had told Geni it would be a good idea to get into a less trafficked area, and she'd gone along, probably remembering what Magor had told them about Calebethon being such a dangerous place. Xander had more specific reasons to want to get off the path, though; he had had the sense yesterday afternoon—he'd had it for several days now, actually—that they were being followed. Probably his imagination, he thought, but . . .

He patted the hilt of the sword he'd appropriated from the chamber; it was a little long, a little heavy for him right now. But he wasn't entirely overmatched by the weapon; the blade was one he'd grow into, Xander decided.

And hopefully he wouldn't need it before then.

He crested the little rise they'd camped behind, and squinted in all directions. This part of Calebethon was hot, and not a little bit humid. He figured that somewhere among the plant growth there had to be something edible. They'd managed to find a few other things down here that made good eating; Xander didn't see any reason they couldn't get lucky again.

In what he figured had been the equivalent of two days of traveling, they'd passed through landscapes of dizzying variety. Rocky, boulder-strewn hills the size of small mountains; deserts of monstrous dunes as tall as the towers of the Keep. And now jungles of strange vegetation, much of it the same blue-green lichen mass as they'd encountered earlier, jungles as thick and dense, Xander would warrant, as any of those that Saren had told him of seeing in Gilden. It was just the kind of adventure he and Geni had always talked about going on, except these weren't quite the circumstances he'd pictured it happening under.

Still, here they were. Might as well make the best of it.

In and among all the strange, glowing, blue-green leaves, he found some familiar ones. Plutrim; he pulled a few of the pods off the branches and hefted them in his hand. They felt ripe to him; felt like they'd make good eating. A few hundred feet on from there, he found what, if he wasn't mistaken, was a llithac tree. Or a variety of it; the leaves had the same characteristic size and thickness. He pulled off a handful and carried his treasures back to the campsite.

Geni was still sleeping. Xander found a flat rock and built up the fire again. He put the rock on the fire, then he pulled out the plutrim roots, and after a little quiet trial and error, managed to crack the pod fruits open. He poured the contents onto the rock, then rubbed the llithac leaves together in his hands, grinding them into a pungent powder—or the closest thing to a powder he could get under these circumstances.

As the rock heated, it began to cook the plutrim, which after a few minutes made a sizzling sound on the stone.

Geni sat up and rubbed her eyes.

"Hey. Good morning," Xander said.

"Good morning." She smiled at him. "Something smells good."

"Breakfast," he said.

"Breakfast?" Her eyes widened. She scooted to her feet and came closer. "Where did you . . . how did you . . ."

"Here." He used the thickest of the llithac leaves to scoop up some of the cooked plutrim, and handed it to her.

"Are these eggs?" she asked. "Gods, where did you find eggs?"

Xander hesitated before responding.

Scrambled plutrim pods certainly resembled eggs, and they tasted pretty much the same, at least to Xander's way of thinking (he, in fact, found that he preferred the taste of the pods to the "real" thing)—but he was well aware of how plutrim was regarded by the upper classes. And Xander was also quite sure that the Princess Angenica had never eaten the pods of a plutrim tree before. So how should he answer Geni?

Luckily, he was saved by her taking a bite of the food.

"Oh," she moaned in between bites. "Oh, that's good. That's really good."

Xander smiled and helped himself to the rest of the scrambled pods.

When they were done, they cleaned up and broke camp. Each of them had managed to salvage a workable pack from the bodies of the dead, scattered near Magor. Each of them had found a blanket as well.

And Geni, of course, had the map, which so far had been of little use. Almost as soon as they'd left Magor behind, they'd found their way forward blocked by a rockfall, and so they'd had to leave the trail to try to circle around the massive stones. That's where they'd come across the first jungle, one that had overgrown a grouping of single-story, squat buildings that were not marked on the map at all. After passing through that jungle, they'd found what had looked like the main road once more, and had been traveling on it for a while—two sleep cycles, which Xander suspected was fairly close to two days. The map didn't have any scale on it, though, so it was hard to tell exactly how far they'd traveled on it.

The area marked Nit'va'ganesh still seemed to be a long way off, though.

They marched on, side by side, silently. The air got hotter, and thicker; the way forward, on what he certainly hoped was the main road, grew more difficult. Vegetation hung over the trail. Debris—trees, rocks, what have you—blocked it. Geni was moving with even more difficulty than he; was she still waking up? Or still a little sick?

He decided to stop and give her a break.

"Wait a minute," he said. "I want a drink."

No lie there; he was starting to sweat already. He peeled off his pack and pulled out the flagon of water. He took a few sips and held it out to Geni. She shook her head.

"Come on," she said. "We have to keep moving."

He frowned. "I thought you might want a break, too."

"We don't have time for breaks," she said. "My father is in the dungeon, remember? And Talax is going to be looking for this thing, too. We have to find it first."

"I understand," he said. "But it's a long way off. We have to pace ourselves."

She glared.

He reached into his pack and pulled out a handful of llithac leaves. He crumbled them up and chewed a few pieces. He held out a handful to Geni.

"A little sustenance," he said. "Go on."

She looked at the leaves, then shook her head. "I don't need sustenance. I need to keep moving."

"Okay," he said, and got to his feet.

And they were off again.

A little while on, the trail began to climb. The path grew

more rugged. Rockier. The jungle around them began to thin; Xander stopped and gathered more leaves and a few more of the pods. He loaded up his pack, and Geni's, and made a satchel from the sleeping sack as well. It was a lot to carry; Geni said as much. He felt as though he could read her mind; the additional supplies would slow them down. Which was undoubtedly true.

But who knew when—or if—they would find food and water again.

They stopped to sleep; it was much colder than before. It would have made sense for them to huddle together to stay warm, but Xander didn't dare suggest that. He stayed awake a long time, shivering.

By the circles under her eyes when they were eating again, Geni had had a hard time sleeping as well.

A few hours into the next day's journey, the jungle was completely gone. They were still going up; the air got colder still, which didn't make any sense to Xander. They were underground.

"Who built this place, anyway?" he asked Geni at one point.

"Nobody's really sure. Some say Curgen. Some say Morrigan," she replied.

"Morrigan."

The two of them were walking side by side; Geni turned and glared at him. "Tell me you don't know who Morrigan is."

Xander shook his head. "Uhh . . ."

"Morrigan the Betrayer? Morrigan the Usurper? Morrigan who killed his own father, who—"

"Hosten," Xander said. "He was Hosten's son."

"That's right."

"That's about what I remember about him."

Geni went on to tell him all of what she knew about Morrigan. How unnaturally long he'd lived; how powerful a channeler he had been. How strong in the death-magic; how wrong his experiments had been. Breeding men to other creatures; breeding the Fallen themselves for specific traits; creating monsters of his own, deep in the tunnels outside Imperium.

"Wait a minute." Xander frowned. "You're telling me that Calebethon goes all the way to Imperium?"

"I think so," she said. "In the Hiergamenon, Amarian walks through Calebethon to escape after the Cataclysm."

Right. He remembered now.

Weeks. He wasn't sure they could make it for weeks. They were just about out of the pods now, their water was running low, and—he stopped dead in his tracks.

The path suddenly, abruptly, came to a stop.

In front of them was a chasm. A narrow stone bridge; the width of a horse's back, if that, led across it. On the other side was a structure of some sort. A building? Maybe, though it looked to Xander as if it had been carved out of the rock more than it had been constructed.

He took all that in, in an instant.

And then he looked down.

The dim light from above wasn't strong enough for him to see bottom.

"Gods," Geni said, coming up behind him. Her feet, shuffling on the path, kicked a small stone over the edge.

It disappeared into the darkness without making a sound.

He never heard it hit bottom.

Chapter Thirty-three

Geni took another step forward.

The building on the other side of the chasm looked vaguely familiar to her. A second later she realized why. The long, narrow triangular archway that marked the building's entrance looked just like the archway on the palace at old Imperium. Morrigan's palace, the one he'd built during his five-hundred-year reign as emperor. There were paintings that had been made; artist's sketches, based on the old writings, some of which Mirdoth had copies of.

"Geni. Come here."

She turned and saw Xander kneeling down next to a rock near the beginning of the stone bridge; a flat rock. She knelt down next to him.

There was writing on the stone.

"Can you read it?" Xander asked.

"I can try." She moved closer and squinted. The light wasn't quite bright enough for her to make the letters out clearly; the language was Avostan, but . . .

"Amarian." She pointed to the last word on the stone. "See this here?"

"Amarian." Xander nodded. "The Emperor."

"That's right. He's the one that escaped Imperium, after the Cataclysm." She squinted at some of the other words; there weren't many of them. A couple of sentences' worth, at most. Children of man. Men.

She frowned.

"*Grazna.*"

"What?"

"*Grazna.* That word there. I think . . ." She peeled off her pack as she talked, then pulled out the map and spread it out on the ground.

"There." She smiled. "The same word—you see?"

Xander nodded. "I see."

"This must be where we are."

"Not very far."

"But we're on the right path. See?" She pointed again, to Nit'va'ganesh. "That's good news."

It was great news, in fact; instantly she felt better than she had in days. This was the first landmark. A marker, she guessed, one left by Amarian himself.

She stood up, and as she did so, frowned.

"What?" Xander asked.

She looked down at the marker, and across the bridge, at the triangular archway.

Amarian.

The story of his escape from Imperium; the Eternal March, through the underground city of Calebethon.

The worst fight of all—the fight in which more than half his company had died, in which all the Azure Knights who had left Imperium as his escort perished . . .

That fight had come near the very end of his journey, in the last of the palaces Morrigan had built in the underground city. Dozens of his men, slaughtered even as they retreated across the narrow stone bridge that connected the palace to the path to safety.

She turned back to Xander.

"Before we cross," she said, "there's something I need to tell you."

Xander insisted on going first after that. He insisted on drawing his sword, and insisted on Geni carrying a weapon as well. Not that Geni needed much convincing: Magor's words of warning had stayed in her head, too.

As they made their way across the bridge, Geni noted something she'd missed before. On either side of the archway before them, twin streams of water trickled down into the chasm below. That fit with the palace's description in the Hiergamenon, though in that book they were giant, cascading waterfalls rather than just streams.

Nevertheless, it was further proof that they were now retracing Amarian's journey.

Geni decided not to share the information with Xander; he looked nervous enough already. She didn't want him tripping over his sword and disappearing into the darkness below.

Without him she would have been dead a long time ago. She would never have found food or water. She probably wouldn't even have lived past the initial cave-in that had trapped them inside Calebethon.

The knowledge made her feel, for a second, helpless. Foolish.

All this book learning that she'd had had done her no good at all.

They passed across the chasm and, after a moment's hesitation, through the archway and into the palace itself. Into darkness.

"Wait," Xander said. A second later he lit a torch. Their surroundings leapt into view.

They were standing in a great hallway, twice as wide, twice as tall as any within the Keep. There were great candelabra hanging

from the ceiling above; empty now, of course. Covered with cobwebs. The air smelled musty; it felt, to Geni, as if no one had
been here in eons.

Xander handed her the torch, then picked his sword up off the
ground from where he'd laid it down. They started forward again.

"Geni?" Xander asked.

"What?"

"If we do run into . . . trouble here," he said, talking without
looking at her, "I was wondering . . . do you know any spells?"

"What?"

"Spells. Magic. Something we might be able to use against
whatever we might find here."

"Spells to hurt them?"

"Yes."

"That's death-magic," Geni said. "That's too dangerous to
use."

"There's nothing, then?"

Geni hesitated before answering.

"I've read about some things," she said. "Spells of Defense . . .
Spells of command . . ."

Even as she spoke, though, she was shaking her head. Mirdoth had refrained from giving her a lot of information about any
of those things. In truth, she thought she'd be better off with a
sword at this point. Not that it would do her much good if the
things that Amarian had run into were still here, she suspected.
She wished the Hiergamenon had gone into more detail about
the "great battle" that had been fought here; talked more about
the kind of creatures the Emperor had defeated . . .

She was about to tell Xander all that when he stopped, and
pointed up ahead.

"You see that?"

The first thing she saw was that the corridor ended in a set of
immense, ancient-looking wooden doors. But that wasn't what
he was gesturing at.

Along either side of the hallway, set into huge, recessed alcoves in the wall, was a series of immense stone statues. Soldiers,
armed for battle, dressed in the characteristic black chain-mail
uniform of old Imperium. Six altogether, three on either side,
each well over ten feet tall.

They looked amazingly lifelike.

"Must've taken a long time to carve those things," Xander
said.

Geni nodded. The paint had hardly faded on them at all, except for the eyes. They looked ready for battle at that instant,
lacking only orders to step forward.

They moved past the statues to the end of the hall. Geni
couldn't help but sneak a look back as they passed.

"It's locked."

She faced forward and saw Xander pulling at a great wooden
handle, trying to yank the door open.

"That's because there's a bar bolting it shut," she was about
to say, a bar a good three feet above the handle, but Xander had
seen it, too, and he was sheathing his sword, reaching upward to
lift the bar, when Geni saw something else.

A faint red glow, around the bar.

Magic.

"Wait!" she shouted, but it was too late.

Xander lifted the bar free, and in that instant, from behind
her, she heard a faint, barely audible crackle. Like the sound of
sand pouring onto stone.

She turned around just as the first of the statues began to move.

Xander was about to kick the door open when he heard Geni
scream.

He spun to face her, and his eyes widened.

One of the statues—no, two of the statues—no, three, four,
five, six—all of the statues were—

"Run!" Geni yelled, darting toward him.

Run, Xander thought. Good idea. He kicked the door open and the two of them darted through.

He slammed the door shut behind him and barred it.

"What were those things?" he asked, turning to Geni. "How did they—"

He stopped talking, struck into silence.

The room they had entered reminded him instantly of Magor's chamber; it was huge, dome-shaped, maybe even bigger than the dragon's sanctuary had been. Bigger across, at least; maybe not as high. The door they'd come through was one of literally dozens along the walls; the far end of the chamber was filled almost entirely by an immense, wide staircase leading down into darkness.

"Where do we go?" he asked.

Geni shook her head. "I have no idea. Let me see the map."

Xander heard the sound of something smashing into the door behind him, and then the sound of wood splintering.

He turned in time to hear a second smash and see the wood shatter.

A stone fist poked through the hole.

"The stairs!" Geni said, and started to run. Xander followed, the sound of splintering, cracking wood echoing behind them.

The stairs started off wide, and gently sloping, but a few dozen steps down, the passageway narrowed abruptly, and grew steeper. And darker. And Xander began to smell something. A smell he couldn't quite place, but one that made him instantly, extremely uncomfortable. Nervous. Scared.

A step in front of him, Geni slowed as well.

"Wait," she said, holding up a hand. "Do you—"

"Smell something? Absolutely," Xander said. "I vote we go back. Those things—"

"No," Geni said. "That's not it. I hear something."

"Hear something?" Xander frowned. "I don't—"

"Shhh," she said.

Xander listened for a moment. Then he heard it, too.

A kind of rustling, skittering sound, coming from in front of them. Not too far in front of them, he thought at first, taking a step backward unconsciously, but then, as the sound continued to get louder and louder, he realized how far off its source must be. How far down the staircase.

And how loud it must really be.

"Something's coming," Geni said.

Xander nodded. "And I vote we don't stick around to see what."

"I'm with you," Geni said, and turned, and then they were both dashing up the stairs again.

They got to the top to find the stone soldiers fifty feet away and heading right for them.

Geni ran for the nearest door and yanked at the knob.

"Locked!" she yelled.

Xander tried another. That was locked, too.

He turned back to Geni.

And almost got his head cut off by a stone sword.

The statues had split up. Three had followed him, and three were moving toward Geni, trying to cut her off from some of the other doorways.

The statue closest to him raised its sword again. Xander dove between its legs, did a somersault, got to his feet, and tried another door. This one swung open instantly, and he was about to yell to Geni to come on when he saw that it didn't lead anywhere. It had just been hiding another alcove. And another of the statues, this one even bigger than the others. Made of metal, not stone.

He slammed that door shut quickly, not wanting to wake it up and make things worse than they already were.

"Xander! Over here!"

He turned and saw Geni standing in an open doorway about fifty feet away.

He ran toward her, and at that second heard the skittering sound again, even louder than before.

And a second later he saw what was making it.

Fallen. But miniature ones. Dozens of them skittered up the staircase, and then paused. They had deformed, monstrous little faces, and the look in their eyes . . .

Well. His guess was, they weren't exactly rational beings.

They were hopping up and down, like little monkeys. Some of them began screeching. Xander couldn't tell at what—at him, or Geni, or the stone soldiers. He was just awfully glad he and Geni hadn't run into the little things in the passageway.

They had awfully sharp teeth as well.

He ran to Geni's side. She was looking at the little Fallen as well, shaking her head.

"They're darklings," she said. "In one of Mirdoth's books, there are pictures, but they're supposed to be gone. Extinct."

"Clearly not," Xander said, guiding her backward, into the dark of the passageway that had been hidden by the door. It was more to scale; their scale, at least. Maybe a foot taller than Xander; not quite wide enough for the two of them to go side by side. Xander let Geni go first; he jogged behind her, his sword at the ready.

They ran for what had to be a good ten minutes, until the torch began to flicker. Xander stopped and pulled another out of his pack.

"Darklings?" he prompted.

"Yes," Geni said, putting her hands on her hips and gasping for breath. She waited for a moment before going on. "They were experiments, from what I read. Morrigan's first."

"Morrigan. The Usurper."

"That's right."

"And the other things? The statues?" Xander asked. "What were they?"

"Golems," Geni said.

"What?"

"Golems. Creatures made out of earth, or rock—the stuff of Elemental—brought to life by magic. They're pretty single-minded. Pretty simple. They take one command . . ."

She stopped talking.

"What?" Xander asked.

"Command," she said. "I think I could get them to obey me, if I could get close enough."

"I don't understand."

"You have to get them to hear you," she said. "At least that's how Mirdoth explained it to me. You have to look them in the eye."

Xander nodded as he lit another torch and handed it to Geni. Not that he really got it, even now. If the golems weren't alive, how could they hear you? Not that it really mattered. They were leaving the golems, and the darklings, and Morrigan's palace behind them, he hoped. This passage was long enough that it should get them back out into the city again, he suspected, and from there . . .

From there it would be another story. Hopefully one not involving any more of Morrigan's little creatures.

He pulled the drawstrings of his pack closed, shouldered it once more, and stood up. Geni, he saw, had gotten a good ways ahead of him already; she was moving fast.

And curving out of sight.

He stopped, and frowned.

It must be a trick of the light, Xander thought, but just to be sure he took a few steps back, as Geni took a few more steps forward. And now he could definitely see it. A noticeable bend in the corridor. Not much over a short distance, but over the long haul . . .

"Xander!" Geni called out from up ahead. "Hurry! There's a door!"

Door. The word, for some reason, gave him pause.

"Hang on a second!" he yelled, and started to jog.

He got there just as Geni was opening it and stepping through.

Right back out into the chamber once more.

Where the darklings, and golems, were still waiting.

Geni blinked, unable for a second to believe what she was seeing.

"Come on!" Xander yelled from behind her.

She turned and was about to run back to the safety of the passageway when a shadow fell over her.

She looked up just in time to see one of the stone golems reaching for her. She stumbled backward; it stretched out, caught hold of her shirt, and yanked her forward.

The shirt ripped; a whole sleeve came free. So did her pack; Geni fell backward once more and hit the floor, dropping the torch as she did so. She scrambled to her feet and ran without thinking, a decision she regretted a half second later, when she realized she'd run away from Xander and the relative safety of the passageway. Had run toward the stairway, where the darklings had been waiting.

Whatever invisible force had been keeping them from rushing her before was gone now. They swarmed toward her. Dozens of them. Screeching, skittering, clawing at one another in their haste to be the first to reach her. She tried not to remember why; tried, and failed.

The darklings, if memory served, were cannibals.

Xander stepped in front of her. A sword slashed through the air; blood splattered along with it. A screech turned for a second into another, even more hideous sound.

She and Xander backed up toward the wall. The darklings and

the golems moved with them. Some of the darklings attacked the golems; little bodies began flying through the air, with accompanying screeches.

The torch on the floor, fifty feet away from them now, sputtered and began to dim.

"Any ideas?" Xander asked, waving his weapon in front of him, thrusting at the darklings, trying to keep them back. One good thing about there being so many of them: The sheer weight of numbers kept the golems from reaching Xander and Geni just yet.

The golems, though, refused to stop. They stepped on the darklings that wouldn't move; stepped, and sliced, and always, always moved forward.

"The one on the left there," Geni said.

"What?" Xander didn't dare look at her.

"The golem on the left," she said. "I'm going to try to get close enough to it that I can use the Spell of Command."

Xander felt a door at his back and remembered something.

"You want something to command?" he said. "Try this."

He flung the door behind him open.

And there was the metal golem.

Geni screamed.

Xander had to be crazy! But then she saw that the golem in the alcove wasn't moving. Was not about to attack them, which she had feared.

It was even bigger than the others. And it looked to be made of metal of some sort. If she could command it . . .

Wake, she said in her mind. Wake, and help us. Help.

"Aarghh!" Xander yelled, and Geni snuck a quick glance back.

Three darklings had him. One was on his shoulders, clawing

at his face. Another was trying to climb up one leg. The third was dying, stuck on his sword, spitting, hissing, trying to strike at him even as its lifeblood oozed out.

Xander swung his leg around and slammed the one hanging on to it against the wall. It screeched in pain and dropped off.

"Geni!" he yelled. "Help!"

Help, Geni thought. Help!

The word echoed in her mind.

She turned to the giant golem and found it looking right back at her.

Waiting motionless; waiting, she realized, for her command.

For what seemed like the first time in hours, she smiled.

And then she told it what to do.

CHAPTER THIRTY-FOUR

At the edge of the makeshift tent city that had been set up to house the refugees from the East—soldiers and villagers alike—Calis sat alone.

As he'd sat alone, by himself, since the very moment he had killed the brigand, back on the cliffs. Unwanted. Scorned.

Sorcerer.

He had a feeling that if the others could have, they would have left him behind in the East. The villagers he had helped, the soldiers he had fought alongside, even—he could have been wrong about this, he knew—Ty and Hildros seemed to want nothing to do with him.

The lone exception was Tandis. In the instant of his powers' revelation, in the instant of the Fallen attack, the captain had dragged Calis to his feet, and sent him as well as many others to the safety of the ropes. Tandis had seen to it that the boy made it onto a boat; made it across the bay, to the beaches, to this spot here. Tandis had been everywhere in those few hours; now, though, he seemed to have disappeared. Not that it mattered.

Calis intended to disappear, too.

Everything had changed; he couldn't stay where he wasn't

wanted. Being a Kraxan had been hard enough; add to that the fact that he was different in this way, too, now . . .

East was the only place for him. Kraxis. Maybe he would even return to the place he had been born: Pikel, an old river town, a prosperous town, until the day Fallen soldiers had ridden down its streets pillaging, burning most of the commercial district to the ground. The day the captain had rescued him. Calis had heard occasional stories of the town since then. He had run into a merchant from there a few years back, a merchant and his daughter, who told stories of a rebuilding city. A growing city. The girl had wondered at his interest; since he was obviously Kraxan, she wondered if he intended to visit one day. If so, he should find her. Her father's trading house. She'd been a few years older than Calis; probably sixteen or so. He'd just begun to shave. His voice to change. He hadn't realized what she'd really been asking; not then, at least. Looking back on it now . . .

Nurianne. That was her name. Nurianne. He couldn't think of the name of the trading house, but he was sure it would come to him soon enough. When he was on his way. He would have to cross the bridge, of course. That might be difficult. But he'd find a way.

He knew magic, after all.

Calis heard hoofbeats approaching then, and looked up.

Tandis was there, on horseback. Holding a second steed by the reins.

"Come," he said. "We must talk."

"About what?" Calis asked.

"Come," Tandis said again, and a second later, without even thinking, Calis was on his feet.

He had the reins of the second horse in his hand before he even realized what he was doing. It was as if his feet were moving on their own. As if he had no control over them whatsoever.

His eyes widened. He looked up at Tandis.

"You," he said. "You, too. You're a—"

"Come," Tandis repeated. He turned his horse and rode away.

Calis, after a moment, mounted and followed.

They rode along the beach, far from the camp, for a good fifteen minutes, till the horses were lathered in sweat, till Calis's arms ached from holding the reins, till his legs shook from the strain of staying in the saddle. Finally the captain slowed and allowed the boy to come up beside him.

Calis had a hundred questions running through his mind. Before he could ask any of them, though, Tandis spoke.

"The Bay of Calder," the captain said, nodding toward the water on their left. "Can you imagine a time when this wasn't here?"

Calis shook his head. "No. "

"And yet that time was. Before the Cataclysm, the bay did not exist. You could walk from Imperium to Coriopolis. All was one land. A different land."

"What does that have to do with anything?" Calis asked, irritated.

"The Cataclysm," Tandis snapped. "The Dread Lord Curgen. In his desire to control the magic of Elemental, he did this"—the captain gestured again toward the bay—"and nearly destroyed the world."

Tandis looked Calis in the eye.

"Magic, boy. Elemental is filled with it. That is what drew the immortals to this world in the first place. The pursuit of magic, and the power it represents. But in the wrong hands, that magic can be dangerous indeed."

"You're talking about Talax now, aren't you?" Calis asked, a little confused. "Talax, and that artifact he's looking for?"

Tandis smiled ruefully. "Talax? I suppose, although what I was really talking about was you."

"Me?"

"Yes. You have a fire within you, boy. A bright, shining, blue fire. I have walked the world long enough to recognize it for what it is. Hosten's blood runs strong in you, Calis."

"Hosten." Calis frowned.

"The greatest of all channelers," Tandis said. "The mortal who brought the Dread Lord Curgen to his knees."

"So I'm a channeler," Calis said. "Is that right?"

"I believe you are," Tandis said. "I have thought so for a very long time. Since the day I first saw you, in the ruins of that back-water village."

"That's why you rescued me," Calis said.

"That's right."

"Why didn't you say anything, then? About me? About what I could do? Why did you let me—"

"I had to teach you to govern yourself first, boy, for one thing. And for another . . ." Tandis sighed. "I feared for you."

"Feared for me? Why?"

"Because there are those who would regard your very exis-tence—the presence of another channeler in the world—as a threat."

"Who?"

"That does not matter, for the moment. What does matter . . . There are powers here at work I don't entirely understand. The Destiny . . ." Tandis shook his head. "The Keep should not have fallen. Not so easily."

"Not much we can do about it now," Calis said.

"On the contrary." Tandis smiled. "I plan to retake the Keep."

"You want to fight Talax?" Calis was thunderstruck. It sounded like a suicide mission to him.

"I do not wish to fight anyone," Tandis said. "But neither will I run from a battle."

Calis remembered how Tandis had made him take the reins of the horse earlier, and realized something.

"You're a channeler, too," he said. "Aren't you?"

"No. Although I am familiar with certain spells. I can help you understand your power, Calis. Later." Tandis shook his head. "For now, I have more earthly concerns. "

"I don't understand."

"Retaking the Keep, as I said. And to do that we're going to need help. An army. King Galor's army."

"I don't see why you need me for that."

"You will," Tandis said.

Chapter Thirty-five

Xander and Geni retreated into the safety of the alcove, lit another torch, and watched the slaughter. The metal golem—made of iron, he guessed—didn't move very far from the alcove, either; it didn't have to. The stone statues came to it, one after another, mindlessly plodding forward to their destruction, which only proved to Xander how silly magic could sometimes be. You'd think that whoever enchanted these things would've given them at least a little bit of common sense, a little bit of a self-preservation instinct. But no.

The darklings fared a little better. After the stone golems lay in pieces on the floor, they continued their attack for a span of time—ten or fifteen minutes—before tapering off and retreating down the giant staircase.

So Xander and Geni were left all alone with their monstrous protector, who, the instant the last of the darklings were gone, simply stopped moving.

"Wow," Xander said, stepping from the alcove at last. "That was amazing."

Geni nodded.

"So you can do it," he said. "That spell."

"I guess so," she said.

" 'Guess.' Of course you can. What just happened"—he gestured toward the iron golem—"that's proof. You're a channeler."

Geni didn't look convinced.

"We need to get out of here," she said. "Before those little things come back."

"The darklings? I agree. But which way do we go?" He shook his head. "We don't want to end up going around and around in circles."

"No." Geni nodded and pulled out the map. Xander started toward her, intending to read over her shoulder.

The iron golem moved. It spun around to face them and started walking toward Xander.

"What—" he said, but that was as far as he got, because the thing's arm darted out, grabbed him by the collar, and lifted him high into the air.

It was going to throw him to the ground.

It was going to kill him.

"Stop!" Geni yelled, and the golem's arm stopped moving.

"Put him down," she said. "Gently."

And the thing did.

Xander straightened his shirt, then looked over at Geni.

"It thought you were going to hurt me," she said.

Xander looked at her, and then at the golem.

"Well, tell it I'm not going to."

"I can try. I'm not sure it's going to understand, though." She said a few words to it then, under her breath; from the intensity of her expression, Xander also got the feeling she was using some sort of magic to communicate with it as well.

He used the time to survey the chamber. He walked over the broken pieces of the stone golems, over some of the bodies of the little Fallen corpses, and started trying doors. Most of them were locked.

Which, he suddenly realized, wasn't going to be a problem.

"Hey!" he said, turning back to Geni. "Bring that thing over here!"

"What?"

"Bring that thing over here. The golem." He nodded to one of the doors. "Let's see what's behind these."

"I don't think it matters," Geni said, walking toward him, the golem following a step behind. He saw that she had the map out once more and was studying it. "We have to go that way."

She pointed down the stairway.

"What?"

"We have to go down," she said. "Remember? The bowels of Calebethon."

Xander frowned. She was right, obviously, but . . .

"You may remember that's where the darklings came from—right?"

"I remember. I think we'll be okay, though." She smiled, and nodded up at the golem.

"You want to bring it with us? The golem?" He shook his head. "It'll slow us way down."

"Better slow and safe than dead."

Xander frowned. She had a point there, he supposed.

"Besides which, I think he can move a little faster than the others when it comes down to it."

"He?" Xander frowned. "What do you mean, 'he'?"

"I named it," she said, running a hand along the thing's metal arm.

"That's silly," Xander was about to say, when he saw that Geni's eyes were moist with tears.

"Leeland," she said. "His name is Leeland."

Xander swallowed the rest of his words.

"Leeland," he nodded. "Okay. Sounds good."

They moved as a unit toward the stairs.

*   *   *

The darklings followed them, of course, as they went down. Geni could hear their skittering and an occasional screech. But they kept their distance. Kept out of eyesight, at least, which she was thankful for.

She was also thankful for the golem. Leeland. Stupid thing to name him that, she knew, but when their minds had touched, when she'd sensed its absolute devotion to her . . . well, she was stuck with it now. Stuck with the golem, too, and that was a good thing. This one wasn't quite so simple as the others, she'd decided, the stone statues who seemed only to be able to hold one idea in their heads. Come with us, protect us, she'd told it, and from the way the golem—Leeland—kept looking around as they descended the ever-narrowing staircase, she had a feeling it knew exactly what she meant.

At last they reached the end of the staircase; down a short passageway they found a rusted, ruined iron gate, hanging—barely—from one hinge. The golem, almost without prompting—she had merely wished the gate to be gone, and suddenly he was in front of them—pushed it aside.

They emerged into a walled courtyard of sorts; the ground was covered with debris. Dead trees; ruined, random pieces of metal. The blue-green lichen was everywhere; there were vines climbing the walls.

"Wow."

She turned at Xander's words and saw immediately what had provoked his remark.

The gate they'd just emerged from was set into the side of what looked at first glance like a mountain. Only she could see that all the way up that mountain—hundreds, if not thousands of feet—there were indentations in the rock, straight lines that made it look almost as if the peak before them were made of bricks the size of barges. As if it had been built, as if it were an unnatural, rather than natural, formation.

She didn't see how that was possible, though.

"Do you think somebody actually . . . ," Xander began to say, shaking his head as he spoke.

She knew what he was trying to ask. She didn't have an answer, mainly because she didn't have any idea what kind of creature—outside of a Titan, of course—would be able to build something so incredibly massive.

She didn't even, in fact, want to think about it.

"I don't know" was all she said.

They stopped in the courtyard to eat and drink. Then they moved on. They quickly found a stream, one that ran at the bottom of a much larger riverbed. Geni found a river marked on the map that appeared to continue on toward Nit'va'ganesh. She hoped it was the same one they were following; she wasn't sure. Their path continued on downhill, though, which at least meant they were going in the right direction.

She hoped.

Xander, as they walked, kept looking back over his shoulder.

"You think they're following us?" she asked. "The darklings?"

"I don't know. Maybe."

He hesitated, frowning, as if he wanted to say more. But he didn't.

An hour or so away from Grazna, the riverbed dried up entirely. They continued following it, until they came to a wooden dock. Surrounding the dock was a series of low-lying buildings, some made of stone, some of them wood-framed, the latter mostly rotted away.

They walked in and out of a few. All had long been abandoned, that much was clear instantly. All that remained were ruins. Clay watering vases, some plates, and other flotsam from long ago littered the rooms.

The wreckage quickly depressed Geni. It took her a few minutes to realize why. The place reminded her of Outpost. And thinking of Outpost, she thought instantly of her father.

In the dungeon, at the Keep.

If he was still alive.

"Xander!" she yelled.

"What?" He was pawing through a collection of tools he'd found; looking for what, she had no idea.

"Let's go."

"But—"

"We're not going to find out anything here," she snapped. "We need to keep moving."

He looked up from the tools and glared at her.

"Yes, Your Majesty," he said. "Right away, Your Majesty."

"Don't start with me," she said. "You know as well as I do that we're in a hurry."

"There might be something important here."

"Like what?"

"Maybe another map. Maybe a clue to where we are. Maybe a flint, because we're running out of torches?"

"A flint."

"Yes. Like this one." He held up a piece of metal. Geni felt herself flush.

"I'm sorry," she said. "It's just—my father—"

She felt herself starting to tear up, and turned her back on Xander. "Just come when you're ready," she said. "I'll be outside."

"No, no. Wait. I'm sorry." She heard footsteps coming up behind her. A second later, she felt Xander's hand on her shoulder. "I just—I'm nervous, that's all. I keep thinking there's something following—"

The wall next to them suddenly exploded.

The golem walked into the room, heading straight for Xander.

"Call it off!" Xander yelled, stumbling backward. "Call it off!"

He fell to the ground.

"Leeland!" Geni said, stepping in front of the golem. "Leeland! No!"

But her words were unnecessary. The second she had thought it, she realized, the golem had stopped moving.

"That thing is dangerous!"

She turned back to Xander, who sat on the ground, wide-eyed.

"It doubts your intentions toward me," she said. "Just like the original!"

She started laughing.

A second later, Xander joined in.

They moved on.

The riverbed continued to lead downhill. The air grew hotter, and moist once more. Vegetation multiplied; the ground grew muddy beneath their feet.

The golem got stuck. It took them nearly an hour to free it. The effort exhausted Xander, and Geni as well, he suspected, though she wanted to keep going. "I'm not tired," she said, but just looking at her, Xander knew different.

He took off his pack and began making camp.

Geni, angered, took a step toward him.

So did the golem.

She calmed down instantly, which Xander was glad to see. Only he wasn't glad at all about the golem's actions; the thing was starting to worry him. There would come a time, he feared, that he'd do something to make the golem think he was threatening Geni, or hurting her, and she wouldn't be able to convince the monster otherwise.

Any thoughts he had of kissing her were going to have to wait.

"Those buildings weren't built for people," Geni said, as she and Xander gathered wood for a fire.

"What?"

"The buildings back there? In that town? Did you notice how low the ceilings were?"

He had, but he hadn't paid that much attention to it.

"So who do you think they were built for?"

"I don't know." She frowned. "The darklings, maybe?"

"They didn't strike me as the kind of creatures that used buildings."

"No." She nodded in agreement. "But . . . maybe they were smart, a long, long time ago. And now . . ."

"Yeah. Now they're not." Xander shuddered, remembering the ravenous look in the eyes of the little creatures as they'd charged him, back in Grazna.

They ate the last of the llithac leaves, and the pods, though Xander was certain they'd find more easily enough, now that they were back in jungle.

The two of them arranged their bedding on opposite sides of the fire once more; the golem was positioned at the edge of the camp. Geni had told it to keep watch. Presumably that was what it was focused on, but Xander wasn't taking any chances.

After Geni fell asleep, he moved his bedding another few feet away from hers.

The last thing he wanted was their feet touching in the middle of the night. That might be all the excuse Leeland needed.

They woke and drank. Packed up and moved on.

A handful of the darklings that had been following them, unseen, moved on with them. Another handful stayed behind, gathering the scraps left at the campsite. Discarded podshells; uneaten remnants of the evening meal. Two began to fight over a half-rotted pod that Xander had left behind.

Then, all at once, they froze. A second later the two creatures—and all the other darklings scouring the campsite—scattered.

And a second after that, Nym stepped out of the shadows.

Chapter Thirty-six

He thought, for a second, about quickening himself. Chasing down the little creatures and grabbing the fattest one for his breakfast.

But he was tired already of the taste of darkling. Their flesh was stringy, and tough, and not at all tasty. He would rather go back to eating plants, Nym decided, than stomach darkling for another day.

Once he had found the Bane, though—or rather, once the boy and girl had led him to it—he could feast. The girl, in particular, looked tasty to him. In more ways than one. Which was how he planned to enjoy her, when the time came. But for now . . .

He moved on down the path, following in their tracks.

He didn't want to get too close just yet; that thing that was traveling with them looked formidable indeed. Nym had the feeling that no matter how fast he was, if it came down to a fight, and that thing got its hands on him, he wouldn't last too long. He'd have to be clever when the time came; trick it somehow. Or trick the girl, whom it seemed particularly devoted to. The girl, who he now knew had magic within her. At least that's what the dragon had said; that was the closest he'd been to them up until now, a few hundred yards away, having finally caught up to them after the cave-in, about to pounce, when the dragon had emerged. Magor. Magnificent animal.

His shock at seeing the beast, though, was almost as nothing compared to his shock at hearing what the manlings were up to. The little quest they seemed to have taken on unbidden.

They were seeking the Bane.

As Nym knew his lord Talax was; the boy and girl seemed to have some information the Titan did not, however.

Nym had been considering exactly how to get that information—all they had regarding the Bane's location—out of them, when the dragon had, without warning, taken flight. And the roof of the great building had collapsed right on top of him. The second time his speed had failed him. When he woke, the boy and the girl were gone.

And he was trapped beneath a column the size and weight of a siege engine.

He'd lain there for hours on end, with no way to keep track of time, in the green-blue twilight of the caverns, fairly certain he was going to die. Drifting in and out of consciousness. At one point he'd opened his eyes to see that a darkling had come by to hasten his end. He'd let it get close, had feigned sickness, and terror, until it was within reach, and then he'd snatched it up and made short work of it. Eaten its chewy little flesh, gnawed on its bones, and used the energy he'd thus gathered to quicken himself and dig at the dirt around the column until it shifted position and he managed to roll free.

The next time he woke, he was in agony. Pain all up and down the right side of his body, as if he'd broken or bruised something. He couldn't stand; he somehow managed to drag himself deeper into the dragon's chamber, where he found food and water, preserved by the same magic that had apparently alerted the dragon.

And then he slept. A deep, deep sleep that could have lasted for days, as far as he knew. He woke with his side stiff and sore, but he was at last able to move. And so he had, following the same path the girl and the boy had started out on. Nit'va'ganesh; the bowels of Calebethon. He'd never heard of the former before, but it seemed to Nym that if he kept going down, he should eventually arrive at the same place as the boy and the girl.

And now here they were.

The princess, and the boy, whose name, Nym now knew, was Xander, though he had no idea whatsoever who the lad actually was. Not that it mattered. Slicing him to ribbons would be no problem; would actually be a great pleasure, considering how the boy had deflected the arrow and ruined Nym's long-planned attempt to murder the great Tandis.

No, the real problem here was the monster they had with them; getting the girl from its clutches would be difficult. That would require a little planning, a little concentration. All his energies, focused.

Nym frowned.

Maybe he'd better go get another darkling, at that.

CHAPTER THIRTY-SEVEN

Mirdoth could not, despite the opportunities afforded him, bring himself to return to Lord Ambrose's cell. His bond with the man was too strong; only the interruption of the Fallen sergeant, come to fetch him back to his books, to the tower, had stopped Mirdoth from revealing the truth about his past the last time. He feared Ambrose's questioning would pick right up where it had left off before, feared the lord would continue to pry into Mirdoth's history until he blurted out the thing he had struggled so long to keep hidden.

And so he remained in the observatory; remained with eyes glued to page, with body hunched over worktable, pouring through scroll after scroll, book after book, finding no reference at all to the "bane" Tandis had mentioned before his disappearance.

Until on the fifth day after his visit to the dungeons, he did.

In the unlikeliest of all places. A mention in the diary of the Lady Varraine, third consort to Morrigan the Usurper, Morrigan the Betrayer, Morrigan the Damned, the last man to wear the crown as Emperor of Imperium, and all the lands of the East.

The diary had been found years after her death; her execution by the high court of Imperium for crimes against nature. Trumped-up charges, Mirdoth had assumed; by the time of his own death, Morrigan had executed dozens of his intimates, male and female, man and Fallen alike. As one of the most complete surviving documents of the age before this one, the time before the Cataclysm, the book was of immeasurable value in and of itself, though as Morrigan had kept his own counsel in almost every matter of importance, Varraine had little insight to shed on most things historical. Mirdoth had turned to it only because of Morrigan's own well-known connection to Calebethon. He'd first read the diary—a slim volume; the copy he had (the original, of course, was in the library at New Pariden) was but seventy pages long, most of the entries not more than a paragraph in length—when he was much younger, in the first years after his exile from Athica. The contents had mostly faded from his mind, but there were certain passages he recalled having read, things to do with the underground city . . .

He found them at the very end of the book: a series of entries that dealt with the time when Varraine realized that her own days at the court were numbered—though Mirdoth could not read into her words any sense of fear for herself, beyond her loss of position, which made her words all the more poignant.

I cannot satisfy him, Varraine wrote.

> *Not the physical lusts that rage within his body, not the lust for power that rages in his mind. As to the former, it shames me to love a man, and be found wanting. Jule* [one of the Lady's handmaidens, Mirdoth recalled from an earlier entry] *begs me to keep in mind my husband's past. He has lain with a goddess, Majesty, she says, and once having lain with a goddess, what man could be satisfied with a mortal?*

In my mind, I understand, but in my heart, it pains me, that I cannot hold the Emperor to his marriage bed in the way a woman was meant to do.

As to the latter—Morrigan's lust for power—I fear to say that it has near unhinged him. He leaves the governing of Imperium, more and more, to the Dread Lord's lackeys, and spends his time— days, sometimes weeks of it at a pass—in his laboratories. Sometimes in the palace, but more often, in that loathsome sanctuary of his outside the city. Calebethon, he calls it, where he plays with the things of the immortals, seeking to ursurp their power for his own.

You would not understand, Varraine. You are but mortal, Varraine. As if he is other than that. Yet he will tell me nothing of what he does there— nothing of what occurs in those laboratories. Yet one thing I did learn, last night . . .

I should not write this.

And yet . . .

Nothing I do seems to matter; why then, should a mere note be any different?

So. Last night, for the first time in months, the Lord Morrigan shared my bed. The act of congress gave him little pleasure, however, and though it has gone this way for some time, I at last summoned the courage to speak when he had finished.

"My lord," I recall saying. "If there are things you would have me do . . . ways in which . . ."

He turned to me, and for the first time in a long while, I saw something akin to emotion— sympathy—in his eyes.

"Varraine," he said. "My beautiful, beautiful Varraine. The fault lies not with you."

He touched me then, on the cheek, the callused skin of his hand rough against my smoothness, and I felt tears well in my eyes.

"It is me," he said. "It is her."

"Tar-Thela."

He nodded, and turned away from me. I laid a hand on his shoulder, and he groaned out loud.

"Leave me!" he cried. "I cannot bear this. I cannot . . ."

He fell silent for a moment, and when he spoke again, his voice had changed.

It was no longer Morrigan my lord that was speaking.

It was Morrigan the Usurper. Morrigan the Patricide.

"She will bend to me once more. The gift I have found—Aphalan's gift—will see to it," he said, and turned on me eyes of deepest, blackest coal—

Mirdoth shut the book and leaned back in his chair.

Aphalan. That was a name he had never heard before. But there was Avalan, whose name was found in the Hiergamenon, in the story of the Titans before they came to Elemental. Varraine could have misheard, and if that was the case . . .

Avalan was one of the eldest of the Titans, a great leader, a great warrior who had been himself corrupted by the power contained in the circlet he wore into battle. The circlet lost eons ago, the circlet named as Avalan's Bane, the circlet that was also an orb. . . .

It can take many forms.

Tandis's words—spoken that night long ago, or at least it

seemed long ago now to Mirdoth, the days when Ambrose had ruled the Keep—came back to him.

The circlet. The Bane.

Could they be one and the same?

"Counselor."

Mirdoth looked up.

The Fallen sergeant, Yanos, stood in the observatory doorway.

For a second, Mirdoth feared that Yanos had come to summon him at Ambrose's request. He feigned a sigh, as if he were tired. The sergeant paid him no attention.

"Talax commands your presence," he said, then turned his back and walked away.

Mirdoth, clearly, was meant to follow.

And so he did.

Yanos left him outside the Great Hall.

"He will summon you when he is ready," the sergeant said, and marched away.

Mirdoth stood at the doorway for a moment, then walked to a bench and sat down.

He should not have come, he realized. Or at least he should not have come so easily. The Titan would once more invade his mind and discover the things that Mirdoth himself had only just found out. Varraine's diary, Morrigan's experiments . . . a possible clue to the Bane's whereabouts.

He felt something sweep over him then. At first he thought it was just a wave of exhaustion. He had slept fitfully this fortnight, since the Keep's capture. But then he realized the feeling was something else entirely.

A feeling that had not come to him in a long, long time. A sense of emptiness, where he had once been full. A sense of a vacuum, where there had once been power.

The shards called to him.

"No," he said out loud, and pushed himself to his feet.

And at that second he heard voices coming from within the Hall. He walked to the door and pressed his ear to it. The voices were identifiable—at least Talax's; the other was unrecognizable—but the words remained murky and indistinct. And he wanted to hear them.

He felt the shards in his mind, the power waiting there. He could not. He should not, by all the Gods that were. And yet . . .

He reached out with his mind and channeled some of that power into his own body.

He focused on the wall between himself and the Titan, and all at once it was as if the wall were no longer there.

He could see everything happening within the Hall.

Talax was alone, standing in the middle of the Hall, which was completely bare of the furnishings Ambrose had placed within it with such care.

The only thing present in the room besides the Titan was a green crystalline disc, on the floor near Talax. As Mirdoth watched, the disc on the floor began to glow. Talax stepped back from it another few feet. A green cloud of light filled the room. It wavered and shimmered in the air, like something solid.

Mirdoth, in all his considerable years in the world, had never seen anything like it.

The light began to change shape. Slowly, at first, and then more rapidly, it coalesced into recognizable form. The aspect of a man. A man of middling years and unremarkable features.

It was not, Mirdoth sensed instantly, the creature's true aspect.

Whatever this thing was, it was as far away from being a man as a lizard was from a dragon.

The projected figure folded its arms across its chest and regarded Talax.

"And?" it said.

"The knight has escaped."

"The knight concerns me not at all. I seek news of the Bane. Do you have any?"

"Not yet." Talax did not append a salutation at the end of his words—spoke nothing like "lord" or "master" to this mysterious figure—but his manner was that of subordinate to superior.

Mirdoth strained to see more of the mysterious projection.

"I desire to be free," the figure said. "I desire to leave this place. I must have the Bane."

"I desire the same," Talax said. "I would ask—"

"You may ask of me nothing," the figure interrupted. It lowered itself into the suddenly manifested form of a chair. "You must ask of the sorcerer what he knows."

"He continues to look," Talax said. "Even now—"

"Results," the figure responded. "I wish only results."

And with that, it vanished.

Talax stood there for a moment, and for the first time Mirdoth saw recognizable emotions play across his face. Anger. Concern. And something else he could not quite identify.

The Titan strode quickly toward the entrance to the Hall; Mirdoth stepped back just as the door swung open.

"Sorcerer," Talax said. "Come. You must share with me what you have found."

Must. Mirdoth didn't like the sound of that word.

He bowed his head, and at that instant drew once more upon the power of the shards, to form a shield within his own mind. A barrier against unwanted intrusions, such as the Titan's earlier one.

"As you wish," he said, and stepped past Talax into the Hall.

In that second, he saw once more the emotion he had been unable to identify earlier on the Titan's face. Now he could put a name to it.

Fear.

Talax the Titan, Talax the immortal, was afraid.

And that made Mirdoth scared as well.

What in the name of the Destiny could frighten a being of such immense power?

CHAPTER THIRTY-EIGHT

"Rinna." Geni pointed straight ahead, off into the distance. "That's Rinna."

"How can you be so sure?" Xander asked.

They were standing on the banks over the riverbed, which was now a muddy, narrow stream once more. A stream that led into another waterway, this one a great river that ran perpendicular to it, a few hundred yards in the distance.

On the far banks of that other river, directly opposite them, was a fortress. A great stone structure that resembled the Keep more than anything else Xander could think of; a great wooden gate was its sole entrance, apparently.

"Look." She spread the map out and pointed. "This is the only place in all of Calebethon where two rivers come together. Right here. Which makes that—the fortress—Rinna. It has to be."

Xander frowned. "Yeah," he said finally. "I guess."

"You guess?" Geni glared at him. "What do you mean, you guess? There's nothing to guess about. This is where we are."

He shrugged; Geni glared. Xander knew he was being difficult. He didn't quite know why. Maybe he was just hungry; they hadn't eaten for hours. And maybe he was just nervous. That sense he'd had earlier, that they were being followed . . . it was back. Stronger than ever. He hoped he was just imagining things; Geni had told him he was. And the golem didn't seem concerned, either, though he supposed there was no real way to tell about that. It wasn't as if the thing had a lot of facial expressions.

"Which means we're about halfway there," Geni said, head still bowed over the map. "Halfway to Nit'va'ganesh. We have to cross the river, and then on the other side of the fortress we should find a path."

Xander was about to respond when all at once, in the fortress ahead of him, he saw movement. A shadow, passing across a window.

"Wait a second," he said.

"What?" Geni asked.

"I saw something. Somebody in there."

"In the fortress?"

"Yes."

"Darklings?"

"I don't know." He shook his head. "I only got a quick glimpse."

"Could have been an animal."

"Maybe," he said, but at that moment the great wooden gate began to swing open. A second later, figures emerged from within the fortress. Metal gleamed. Even this far away, Xander could tell who and what they were.

"Soldiers," he said.

Geni squinted, and then sighed.

"Fallen soldiers," she replied.

There were a half dozen of them; they came forward from the fortress to the river and walked along its banks until they came to a landing. They got into a boat and rowed away downstream.

Geni and Xander waited until they were out of sight, then

used the cover of the jungle to creep closer, till they were within fifty or so feet of the river. It was a lot wider than it had originally appeared; a few hundred feet. The current looked strong. Getting across was not going to be easy, was Geni's first thought. And speaking of not easy, she now saw something she hadn't seen from farther off.

There were walls extending from the fortress; stone walls stretched out in both directions directly in front of them, paralleling the river and blocking their way forward. Leeland could smash through the walls, she supposed, but the very fact that they were there . . .

"We have to go that way?" Xander asked.

The two of them were squatting down next to each other, peering through the cover of a bush, staring at the fortress. Leeland was farther back in the brush.

"Yes," Geni nodded. "I think so."

"That's a problem. There are probably more guards."

She nodded. A lot more, she was guessing. Inside, on the gate, on the walls . . .

"We'll need a distraction," Xander said.

"Like what?"

He frowned, brow furrowed for a moment in concentration. Then he smiled.

"Like him," he said, and turned and pointed to the golem.

"Leeland?"

"That's right."

"A distraction."

"That's what I said."

"What exactly did you have in mind?"

Xander explained his plan; Geni listened with growing unease. A distraction was one thing; what Xander had in mind sounded like a suicide mission. The golem was powerful, but not invincible, and this . . .

"What's the matter?" Xander asked.

Geni shook her head. She was being ridiculous, she knew. She should never have given the thing a name. Especially the name she had chosen. Leeland was dead; the golem wasn't Leeland, the golem was a piece of metal that someone had enchanted long ago, a thing with no will or mind or memory of its own. A thing she had managed to enchant as well, after a fashion. It cared nothing for her, and she had no business caring for it.

"Nothing's the matter," she said.

"So . . . ?"

She turned and looked at the golem. It looked back at her with its blank, expressionless, unseeing eyes.

"All right," she said, nodding. "We'll do it. We'll go with your plan."

She gave the golem its marching orders, and off it went. Toward the river, toward the gate, toward what Geni was certain would be its eventual destruction.

It seemed to her for a second that the beast had hesitated before marching away.

Ridiculous, Geni thought. She was imagining things.

The golem entered the river. Xander and Geni moved upstream, watching it start across.

"Wait until they notice it," he said. "Then we go."

"I heard you the first time," she snapped.

What's the matter with you? he almost asked, but he held his tongue. Leeland. He shook his head; silly idea to name the thing. It was a tool, like a sword, or a knife. Meant to be used.

The golem emerged on the far riverbank and started for the fortress gate. Any second now, Xander thought, and readied himself. The Fallen would spot the creature and an alarm would sound. Or a cry go out. That would give him and Geni the opening they needed. They'd run to the river and swim across. They'd climb the wall, run for cover, and then, when it was safe, move on. Nothing to it. Straight ahead. Simple. A little lacking in detail, maybe, but . . .

The golem began hammering on the gate. Next to him, Geni's hand tightened on a tree limb. Her knuckles turned white.

They waited.

And waited.

The golem kept hammering; the gate cracked, and splintered, and fell.

The golem froze.

"I don't understand," Xander said.

"That's all I told him to do. Go up to the gate and try to break it down," Geni said.

"No. Not that." Xander straightened up and looked left, then right, behind, and as far off into the distance as he could.

"Where is everybody?"

CHAPTER THIRTY-NINE

The first step in gathering the army he needed, Tandis told Calis, was a trip into Minoch proper. To speak with that city's ruler—Baron Mancer—and to communicate with Galor himself, though exactly how he planned to do that, the knight did not say. It took Tandis two days longer to satisfy himself that the villagers, and the remnants of Lord Ambrose's army, were provisioned with sufficient supplies and shelter to survive, pending his return. But now, at last, after an uneventful journey west, the four of them—Tandis, Calis, Hildros, and Ty, the last of the Azure Knights—finally stood before the city gates.

Unfortunately, the city seemed to be closed.

"Well, what do you think about that?" Ty asked, frowning up at the gates. "Guess they didn't get the word we were coming."

"It's because of the refugees, I expect," Hildros said.

Calis frowned. "I don't understand."

"Not the ones we sailed with, lad," Hildros said. "The ones that came over the bridge. When the Keep fell. There's just enough scum intermixed with the honest folks that after dark it's just not safe to let the riffraff in."

"Like us," Ty said.

"Like you," Hildros shot back, laughing.

Calis pointed to the towers above the gates.

"Guards up there, Captain," he said to Tandis.

"I see them," Tandis said. "And no doubt they see us. The trick is to get them to pay attention."

"I'll handle that," Ty said, stepping forward. "Hey! You up there! This is the party of Captain Tandis, adviser to the king. Leader of the Azure Knights. Hero of the Battle of Drayana. Hero of the Battle of—"

"City's closed!" a voice shouted down. "Curfew. Come back at daybreak."

"Nicely done," Hildros said.

Ty glared back at him.

"Excuse me," Tandis said, stepping forward. "This is Captain Tandis. These are some of my Knights. If you will summon the baron, I am sure he will order the gates opened."

More movement up above. Then a guard appeared in the tower. "I have no way to verify who you are, sir. I'm sorry. You'll have to—"

"We have no time for this kind of idiocy," Hildros fumed. "Lad, if you do not let us in, we will open the gate our—"

"Hush, Hildros. Let me handle this," Tandis said quietly. And then, "Guard! Commander Duncan. Does he still man the night watch?"

"Aye."

"Well, then . . . bring him here," Tandis said. "He will verify my identity."

Moments later, a large guard whose armor barely fit his body appeared at the top of the tower. He took one look at the four of them, and his eyes widened.

"Open the gate!" he called out, and a second later the great doors creaked wide before them. They walked into Minoch.

"Captain! Captain Tandis!" Calis looked up and saw the large guard, Duncan, wobbling down the winding wooden staircase that led up to the guard tower. "Forgive us, sir. Forgive me. Re-cent events—these last few weeks—"

"Have no fear, Duncan." Tandis laughed, holding up a hand to forestall the guard's apology. "I understand completely. Refu-gees. I'm certain you've never seen so many."

"Oh, no, sir. It's not the refugees. They're not the problem at all."

Tandis's eyes narrowed. "Then . . ."

"The Fallen, sir. They're on this side of the bridge."

"What?"

"Aye, sir. Even caught a few of them sneaking into the town the other day. Terrible thing. Wouldn't be surprised if a few of them are inside the gates even now. Skulking about."

"How did this happen?" Tandis looked furious. "Was the pass not guarded? Did Baron Mancer not receive my missive telling him—"

"He sent a patrol," Duncan said. "But—"

"A patrol." Tandis glared. "How many men?"

"A hundred."

"A hundred men to guard the bridge?" Tandis cursed under his breath. "Fool. The Fallen Army numbers in the thousands. They could all be in the West by now. Where is he, then? The baron?"

"Well, sir. He is sleeping. The hour is late, as you know. And—"

"Take me to him," Tandis said. "At once."

The larger man shifted uncomfortably. "Sir, I have orders. Can it not wait until—"

"Never mind. I know where to find him," Tandis said, and turned his back on the man. "Hildros. You'll find us lodging, yes?"

"Of course, sir," the older man said.

"Good. One night only. We'll be leaving in the morning. Re-port to the watch with your location. I'll find you."

Hildros nodded.

"Beg your pardon, Captain," Duncan said. "But it really wouldn't be a good thing for you to disturb the baron now. He's had a hard few days himself, he has, and—"

"And you," Tandis said, ignoring Duncan, turning to Ty. "No trouble. Do you understand?"

"Trouble?" Ty smiled. "Me? Why, Captain, I'm surprised you think—"

"No trouble," Tandis said again. "Hildros, you make sure."

"I'll keep an eye on him, Captain. Don't you worry."

The captain looked at Calis then, and smiled.

"Restrain yourself as well, lad. Yes?"

"Yes, sir," Calis nodded, knowing full well what the captain meant. Keep his emotions, his instincts, his magic, and any displays of it, in check.

"Good," Tandis said, and then, with a final nod to the three of them, started off down the cobblestone street.

Duncan, protesting, followed.

"Anyone up for a game of Needles?" Ty asked.

"None of that," Hildros snapped. "You heard what the captain said. We're to find an inn and settle down for the night."

"I heard the part about the inn." Ty smiled. "Didn't hear anything about settling, though. Don't see as how they're mutually exclusive propositions, to tell you the truth."

Hildros growled.

Minoch was much like most of the smaller cities Calis had traveled to; dirt alleys, a few cobblestone streets. A few nicer buildings made of stone; many more of wood, and thatch. The overpowering smell of urine and human feces, which varied in intensity depending on the part of town.

The first inn they found reeked. They moved on. The second was a little better; the third a step down. The fourth inn looked worst of all, but was the least fragrant. The three of them looked at one another, nodded agreement, and walked in.

The clientele and the décor matched the building, unfortunately. Hildros took one look around and leaned close to Calis.

"Be ready," the older man whispered.

Calis understood.

Normally they were careful about interacting with the locals. Being a Kraxan made for tense encounters during the best of times. With the Fallen having just declared war . . .

He pulled his cloak up around his shoulders and tried to keep his face and his features hidden.

There were a dozen or so customers in the main room; a man was behind the bar polishing its surface. Hildros approached him.

"We need rooms," he said. "Four of them."

The barman looked up.

"Don't know you."

"You don't need to." Hildros slapped a coin on the bar; two of them. Rigma.

The bartender's eyes widened for a moment at the sight of the gold. Then he shook his head.

"Four rooms. And only three of you. And one of you hiding his face. Can't do it. Not now."

Hildros opened his cloak and showed the barman the hilt of his sword. The azure handle. "We're Knights," he said. "Galor's own."

He put another rigma down on the bar. "Your best rooms."

The bartender set the cloth down and sighed.

"Have to see four of you."

"There'll be four," Hildros said. "You have my word."

"And his face." The bartender gestured toward Calis. "Have to see his face."

"Yeah." Another voice rang out from behind them. From right behind them. "Let's see it."

And even as Calis was turning, he felt a hand yanking at his cloak, and a second later his hood was down.

"Krax." The voice that had spoken before—the voice that spoke now—belonged to one of the biggest men Calis had ever seen in his life. A huge, burly man, wearing only a filthy brown vest and rough leather trousers. A man whose massive, muscular arms gleamed in the candlelight, whose head was shaved bald, leaving the only hair on his face a thick, dark mustache.

"Krax," the man said again. "Blood traitor. We don't like your kind here."

"I'm not a traitor," Calis said, well aware that his voice was shaking. He cleared his throat. "I'm a knight. As much of a citizen of the Kingdom as anyone. And I'm no traitor either. I hate the Fallen. They killed my parents."

The big man grunted. "Dead Krax. That's a good start anyway."

Calis felt himself flush. Felt his skin prickling. Felt his anger growing.

Hildros stepped toward the man.

"I'd watch what you say, friend."

"Yeah? And if I don't?"

"Well. That'll tell me a lot about what kind of man you are."

"Really?" The giant stepped toward Hildros. "So tell me then, you broken-down old excuse for a soldier, what kind of man am I?"

"The kind of man that makes fun of orphans. That probably takes advantage of 'em, too. Not much of a man at all, to my way of thinking."

"At least I am a man and not a traitor to my race."

"I told you before—I hate the Fallen," Calis said.

"I don't believe that for a second. Krax are the same thing as Fallen anyway," the huge man said.

"Familiar with the Fallen, are you?" Ty asked. "Seen a lot of them?"

"Enough," the man growled.

"Really? Where? What kinds? Urxen? Trog? Sion?"

The man glared. "They're all the same."

Ty smiled. "Liar. I'll bet you never seen a single one. I'll bet you spent your whole pathetic life in this bar here, ever since you got off your mother's teat. Hiding behind a gate, that's what you been doing, while people like us defend cowards like you."

The man roared, and charged Ty, swinging his fist in a huge overhand arc as he came.

Ty easily dodged the blow. He spun around the big man then and slammed his boot into the man's knee.

A loud *crack!* echoed through the room, and the man fell to the ground, screaming.

Calis couldn't help it. He smiled.

And then the smile, as quickly as it had come, fell from his face.

Something was wrong.

He sensed it then, as surely as he'd ever sensed anything in his life. Before the events of the last few days, he would have called it intuition, but now . . .

He turned around, scanning the room. He saw nothing amiss, except . . . there were more people in here now, he realized. There. By the door. Two men in cloaks . . .

"Calis!"

He turned again at Hildros's words, and saw that the man who had fallen had friends. Three other men, who were now advancing on the three of them. The one closest to Calis had drawn a knife: a wicked-looking weapon, six inches of rusty, jagged blade.

Calis moved slowly and carefully to one side, keeping a table between him and the man.

"Blood traitor," the man spat. "Scum."

He lunged forward and stabbed. Calis jumped back, then forward, and chopped down on the man's wrist. The knife fell to the ground.

Ty bent down and picked it up.

"Nice weapon," he said. "How about a game of Needles?"

The man's eyes widened, and he began backing away.

"No . . . don't. . . ."

He backed right into a half wall, near the bar. As he stumbled back against it, Ty threw the knife.

It caught the cloth of his shirtsleeve, pinning him there.

The other two men, meanwhile, had cornered Hildros, who was shaking his head.

"Stand down, lads. Save yourself pain."

"Us?" The two men looked at each other. "Worry about yourself, old man."

And then they charged.

Hildros brought the first man down with a single straight jab. The second picked up a chair and attempted to smash it over Hildros's head. Hildros caught the oncoming blow in one hand, and with the other struck the man in the gut. He went down, and he stayed down.

The noncombatants in the bar did not make a move but their eyes told the story.

Hate.

Calis's attention was drawn for some reason to a man in a long gray cloak, who sat at the far end of the bar, a man who looked somehow familiar to him, a man whose face—as his own had been up until a moment earlier—was hidden from sight.

"The rest of you," Ty said, looking around, "until you're ready to take up arms yourself, don't lecture us about who's a traitor and who isn't. This boy here is one of the bravest warriors in the entire Kingdom."

He turned to Calis and smiled.

"So we get our rooms, barkeep?" Hildros asked.

The man looked at him, and then at the men lying on the ground, and frowned.

And at that second, Tandis walked in.

The captain looked around and shook his head.

"I might have known," he said, heading toward them, his eyes lit with amusement, belying his words. "I ask you to do one thing, and—"

As the captain walked past the man in the cloak, the latter suddenly stood.

Calis's heart leapt into his throat.

The man was no man at all. He was one of the Fallen. He was drawing something from beneath his cloak, a dagger, but the dagger was glowing, why was it glowing, it—

The expression on Tandis's face changed. He frowned, and turned, and as he did so the Fallen creature stabbed him square in the chest.

The captain's eyes widened. He let out a short, surprised gasp.

"Tandis!" Calis yelled.

The dagger in the captain's chest glowed for a second—a brilliant red.

Then Tandis gasped once more and collapsed.

CHAPTER FORTY

They spent hours exploring the fortress. Cautiously exploring. Xander still had a hard time believing the place could be entirely deserted. And yet, the more they searched, the more obvious it became that the place had been abandoned long ago, that the soldiers they'd seen were just visitors. There were signs of habitation in some of the rooms they came across—chairs arranged into a circle, foot trails in the layers of dust in the halls and rooms—but no evidence of permanent inhabitation.

And no food. No water. The main things they were looking for.

Xander, for once, envied the golem. He wondered if there were any magic spells that would enable him to survive without food or drink.

He met Geni at the bottom of a long, stone staircase. She was coming down, the golem a few clanking steps behind her.

"Nothing." Xander shook his head. "You?"

"The same. I . . ." Her voice trailed off. She frowned.

"Did you hear that?"

"What?" Xander asked.

"That noise. It sounded like somebody yelling." She pointed down the corridor, to a half-open door. "Came from that direction."

They walked to the doorway. Xander swung it slowly, cautiously all the way open, revealing a staircase and a set of steps, leading downward into darkness.

He heard it, too, then.

"Help."

He looked at Geni.

"What do you think?" she asked. "Should we . . ."

He hesitated before answering. In truth, he thought a couple things. Number one: Anyone calling for help in a place the Fallen had just left was more than likely going to be somebody they wanted to help. Number two . . . It was awfully dark down the stairs.

The cry came again. "Help."

"Well?" Geni prompted.

Xander sighed, and pulled another torch out of his pack. Then he gestured to the golem.

"He goes first."

The stairs led down to a dungeon. An unbearably hot and humid dungeon. There were pools of fetid-smelling water everywhere; the whole place stank of rot, of decay.

It didn't take them long to find the source of the cries for help. In the only occupied dungeon cell, a creature—small, slight, clothed in nothing but rags—was chained to the wall, its hands and feet encased in iron cuffs.

It saw them and strained forward.

"Thank the Gods," it said. "Thank the Destiny. Release me, please! Hurry. Before they return."

"Gods. Wait one minute, and we . . ." Geni's voice trailed off as she and the torch moved closer, and the thing's features came into better view.

It was one of the Fallen.

"Hurry!" the creature said. "Did you not hear me?"

Xander and Geni looked at each other.

"We heard you," Xander said. "Who are you? What are you doing here?"

The creature glared.

"What am I doing here? You can see, can't you? I am imprisoned. Locked up. Release me now—hurry!"

"Who locked you up?"

"The others, of course. The soldiers."

"The Fallen, you mean?"

"Fallen. That is your word for them, not mine."

"Them. As far as I can see, you're pretty much the same race."

"Do you not have eyes?" The creature hissed. "Can you not see? They are Urxen. I am Sion. Completely different. They imprisoned me. Left me here to die. Hurry now, set me free!"

Xander frowned.

"We can't just leave him here, Xander," Geni said, stepping forward.

"Why not?"

"Why not?" Geni's eyes widened. "Well, for one thing, he'll starve to death. I couldn't do that to another person, could you?"

"He's not a person. He's a Fallen. And—"

"I am Sion," Nym said. "Not Fallen at all. 'Fallen' is insulting. Would you like it if I called you pinkling for your pink skin?"

Geni giggled.

"You still haven't told us why you're here," Xander said. "Why they locked you up."

"Because I refused to join them. Those others you saw. The Urxen. They had gathered together to aid in the attack on your Kingdom. Myself and many others, we wanted nothing to do with any wars, so . . . I was locked up here. Left to die."

Xander frowned. Something still felt wrong to him here. Why would the Fallen—the Urxen—use this place as a dungeon if they were only passing through?

"Not letting it go is the same as killing it, Xander," Geni said quietly, coming up alongside him so that the creature couldn't hear. "Is that what you really want to do? Kill him?"

"No. But—"

"Mercy," Geni said. "We should show it mercy. That's what separates us from those who captured my father."

Xander looked from her, to the imprisoned Fallen, and sighed.

"Fine. We'll free it," he said.

Geni smiled and turned to the golem.

And a second later, the chains around first one limb, and then another, and then the third and fourth in rapid succession, were no more. And the Sion was free.

It rubbed its wrists, and ankles, and then looked up at Xander and smiled. He got a sudden, queasy feeling in his stomach then. Like they had just done something terribly, terribly wrong.

Geni didn't seem to share his concerns.

"You must need food," she said. "Water."

"That would be wonderful, yes," the creature said. "Thank you for rescuing me. Thank you, thank you. What is your name, may I ask?"

"I'm Geni."

"Xander."

"And that's Leeland," Geni said, pointing to the golem.

"Leeland. Xander. Geni." The creature looked at them and bowed. "I am in your debt."

"What about you?" Xander asked. "What's your name?"

It turned back to face them.

"Nym," it said. "My name is Nym."

BOOK THREE
TALAX AND NYM

If we can crush Hosten the Nemesis, then we will have thwarted the Destiny for all time. Only their embers will remain.

—Lord Curgen, High Dread Lord

CHAPTER FORTY-ONE

They had a map.

Every few hours, the girl kept taking it out and looking at it. It was, Nym quickly discerned, a map of Calebethon. All of Calebethon, including parts he had never seen before. The city's existence was no secret, but its true extent, its shape, its size, were things Nym—and most others, he suspected—were completely unaware of.

It was wrong, in fact, to think of it as a city. It was more like a country—and their destination within that country, Nym gathered, though not from anything that was said. The boy kept casting suspicious glances at him, and gave the girl warning glances whenever she began to speak of the path they were to take. No, Nym's intelligence came more from the way the girl's fingers moved on the map, the way she glanced up, and down, and traced the outlines of the riverbank they were following . . .

Their destination was a place called Nit'va'ganesh. Nym had heard that name before as well. But up until today he had thought it myth.

Nit'va'ganesh; Morrigan's domain. So it was real. Which meant that some of the things he had heard about were real, too. The cave hounds that his uncle had teased him about . . .

He could not help but shudder at the thought.

Shudder, and then chide himself.

The Usurper was more than a thousand years gone; he, and his creations, could hurt no one anymore. Least of all the four of them. Correction, Nym told himself. Least of all Talax. Whom Nym had to now contact. The question was how. He could not leave his "rescuers" for the moment—he still needed to find out exactly what they knew about the Bane, and—

"Nym. I'm curious."

He looked up and saw that the boy had fallen in step alongside him.

The fortress was far behind them. The four of them were now walking along the riverbank, following the water's course, heading south. Nym leading the way, the boy a step behind, followed by the girl, and then the golem.

The path had widened enough to allow Xander to join him; the boy, Nym noticed, had sheathed a dagger on the outside of his shirt. Within easy reach. He was still suspicious. Fool.

Had it come to violence, Nym would have sliced him to bits with his bare hands before the boy had time to draw it.

Of course, given the circumstances, that would have been very counterproductive.

The Bane, he told himself. Talax. Remember what is important.

"You're curious," he said to Xander. "About what?"

"How exactly they captured you. The Urxen. You haven't really talked about that."

"What is there to talk about?" he asked. "I refused to join them. And that's why—"

"Them," the boy interrupted, rudely. "Who is them?"

"The intelligent races that make up what you call the Fallen—the Urxen, Trogs, and Sion gathered together to attack your Kingdom," Nym said. "I wanted nothing to do with their war, so they locked me up. Left me in that fortress to die."

"That's terrible," Geni said.

"Oh, it was. An army of them came to my estate." Nym lied, looking back over his shoulder at the girl. "They demanded food. Horses. They also demanded that I enlist. When I refused—and I wasn't the only one: my father, my brothers, we all refused—they chained us, took us to the eastern entrance of Calebethon, and handed us over to the Urxen who live in the city here, under the mountains. They wrenched my family apart," Nym said, making sure to catch the girl's eye as he spoke. That appeal to family—with her own father left behind at the Keep—would be sure to tug on the child's heartstrings. "They dragged me here and there with them, always on me, always after me to join them, but I refused, and then . . ." He paused, as if overcome by emotion. "Well, then, they chained me in the dungeon. I was there for weeks!"

The girl's eyes misted over. Trusting fool. She would be no problem. And the golem . . .

Well. It had no mind. No will of its own. Nym had seen sorcery enough to realize that the creature was somehow bound to the girl. Something he would have to keep in mind, he realized, when the time came to eliminate her. Separation from the golem.

"Weeks," the boy said.

"That's right."

"How did you survive without food or water?"

"Water," he frowned. That was a good question—how *had* he survived without water?

Nym didn't have a ready answer to that one.

Hmmm. Perhaps he would have to kill the boy now after all. Get the girl away from the golem—drag her through the river perhaps, and then force the answers he sought out of her . . .

The river.

He looked at the water running alongside them, and then remembered something.

"You saw the dungeon, boy," he said.

"I did."

"Water was everywhere there, was it not?"

Xander frowned.

"I suppose."

"Exactly. I was able to drink the puddles. So water wasn't a problem . . ."

"And food?"

Nym smiled. That one was easy.

"There was food everywhere as well."

"Everywhere?" Xander smiled, too, now. A smile of disbelief. "Really?"

"Oh, yes. This part of the underground realm—there is no trouble finding food. Here it is much like a great forest except deep under the mountains. I will show you."

And before the boy—or the girl—could respond, Nym stepped off the path and into the darkness. Once there, out of their sight, he quickened himself. Within seconds he had found what he was seeking. And seconds after that, he stepped back onto the path, holding the thing he had captured in front of him. A small, fuzzy, brown creature, a thing that looked like a huge bat that had lost its wings. It squawked and struggled in his grasp.

"What is that?" Geni exclaimed, disgust evident in her voice.

"We call these Hutins," Nym began. "They live in the dark places and feed off insects. If we can make a fire, they're quite good."

"You eat them?"

"We do," Nym said. Reaching out with his free hand, he broke the small creature's neck.

"You killed it!" Geni cried.

"A necessary first step in eating it."

"We're not stopping now," Xander said, glaring at him. "There was no reason to kill it."

Nym had to repress a smile. The boy's expression made him happy. He still owed the lad much, in terms of anger. He still boiled over at the memory of Xander rising from nowhere, deflecting the arrow meant for Tandis.

"Shame to waste food," Nym said, and pulled his arm back to heave the dead thing into the darkness. "Still, if you're certain we're not stopping . . ."

He paused, because the boy's expression had, all at once, changed.

"Do you hear that?" Xander asked, frowning.

Hear what, Nym almost said, and then realized that he did indeed hear something, in fact.

Several somethings. Hoofbeats.

"Off the path!" Xander yelled. "Hurry!"

They dove into the bushes. Just in time.

A trio of armored riders—Urxen soldiers—thundered past, followed in short order by another dozen of the same. And then another, and another, and another. A whole army of them. Their uniforms were unfamiliar to Nym. Talax's sigil was nowhere in sight. And the soldiers themselves . . . they were unfamiliar as well. Urxen, obviously, but a somewhat stunted version of the same. Did they actually live here, in the underground realm? It was possible, he supposed. In which case revealing himself to them would do no good. They might mistake him for food, the savages. Best to just let them pass. He settled back in the brush to do just that. Settled back, and waited.

And waited, and waited. More and more of the Urxen rode by, obliterating the path as they came. The four of them, hiding in the brush, had to move farther back into the underground forest.

He saw the boy and the girl, next to each other, off to his right, exchanging glances. He felt like he could read their minds; how many of these things are there?

On the other side of him, the golem waited as well. Its attention was focused not on the Urxen, but on the girl. Nym took the opportunity to study it. Metal; it looked to be iron. He reached out a hand and touched it.

The golem's head swiveled, and its eyes locked on his.

For a second Nym had the feeling that there was life behind those eyes. Intelligence. Ridiculous thought.

"You're an ugly bastard, aren't you?" Nym whispered under his breath. "Think I'll melt you down for scrap after this is all done."

The golem didn't respond, of course. It just continued to stare at him. After a while, Nym looked away. The monster unnerved him a little, if he was honest with himself.

When the thundering parade of soldiers at last ended, the four of them crept cautiously back onto the path and continued their journey south.

They didn't get far. A half hour's walk and the forest abruptly ended, trailing away into a vast plain of grass. Calebethon was a world unto itself.

And there were the Urxen who'd passed them on the trail—and many, many more. An entire army—close to a thousand of the beasts, Nym guessed—camped on either side of the river, as far as the eye could see.

Geni shook her head. "How are we going to get past them?"

"We're not," Xander said. "We're going to have to find a way around."

"There is no way around," Geni hissed.

"Then we'll have to double back," Xander said. "Maybe there's another tunnel that leads . . . that goes where we want to go." The boy glanced at him, and then at the girl. Fool. As if Nym didn't already know their ultimate destination.

A little detour was necessary, however. A little question-and-answer session. A private one. Him and the princess.

He cleared his throat and the others turned to face him.

"What?" Xander snapped.

Nym smiled.

"I have an idea," he said.

"What?"

"Perhaps we ought to make camp before deciding. Eat a little something, gather our strength . . ." He held up the Hutin's corpse.

The princess shuddered.

The golem didn't move.

Xander frowned.

"All right," he said. "Let's find a place."

Geni was not going to eat the little Hutin. Not at first. But the smell it made, crackling over the fire . . . the look of it when Nym took it off the spit, and Xander (who refused to surrender his weapon to the Fallen creature) took it and began to do the cutting . . .

She held out her plate just the same. The second she began to chew, she was glad she had done so.

Meat. When was the last time she'd eaten meat?

The night before the Keep fell. No, the afternoon. She and Leeland had eaten together, in Outpost, in the village itself, before her lessons with Mirdoth . . .

Memories suddenly rose and surrounded her; memories of her life that had been, her father, her teacher, her bodyguard, her friends . . . her room in the Keep. Maids, and servants, waiting on her hand and foot. Waiting on her command. She hadn't really liked the feeling, back then, in a lot of ways; the way they treated her, the way they looked at her, as if she was better than them somehow. Or they were worse. She hadn't liked them doing things for her. But now . . .

It sure would be nice to have someone waiting on her now. Someone to rub her back. Comb her hair, clean her clothes . . .

"You like the Hutin?"

She looked up and saw Nym smiling at her. His pointy teeth, in the glare of the firelight, looked very sharp. Sharper than they'd seemed before.

Or perhaps she was imagining things.

"Yes," she said. "It's delicious."

"We eat a lot of it," he said. "Back home. Raise them for food. These wild ones . . . the meat is flavorful, but tough. You can come to my village. My home. I will cook you one from our farm. Twice as big. Tender flesh."

"That sounds good," she said.

"Oh, it is. It's very good." He smiled again and ripped a hunk of flesh off the bone he held. Juices ran down the front of his mouth, and Geni involuntarily shuddered.

"Where is your home?" she asked. "Your farm."

"Far from here," Nym said. "In the far east. And you? Where do you two come from?"

"Outpost," she said. "The Keep."

"The Henge," Nym said.

"That's right," Geni replied. "The Henge."

"You've come a long way," Nym said. "Why?"

"Not your concern," Xander said.

"I am only curious," Nym said.

"Yeah. I noticed." Xander turned to Geni. "Can I talk to you for a minute? In private?"

Before she could answer, he put a hand on her shoulder and dragged her to her feet.

"Hey!" she snapped, just as the golem, who'd been standing guard a few feet back from the fire, moved toward them.

Geni raised a hand to stop it. "It's all right," she said. "Nothing to worry about."

The golem halted, calmed as much, she suspected, by the thoughts she was sending it as by her words.

Xander led her away from the camp they'd made—a little ravine, a half mile or so back from the edge of the jungle and the Urxen camp—and up to the top of a small hill.

"This ought to do," he said.

"For what?" Geni asked. "What's so important you couldn't talk about it back there?"

"What do you think?"

"Nym?"

"Of course Nym," Xander said. "What are we doing, taking that thing along with us? Why—"

"Where else is he going to go?"

"Who cares?" Xander asked. "Geni, it's a Fallen. It—"

"He," she snapped. "Nym is a 'he.' And in case you hadn't noticed, he just made us the first real dinner we've had in days!"

Xander glared at her. "Yeah. It was a good dinner. So what?"

"So stop being so suspicious. You saw where he was. You saw—"

"I saw a lot of things," Xander said. "I heard a lot of things, too. First he lives on an estate, then a farm. First he says he hasn't eaten in weeks, then he doesn't seem at all interested in food."

"He was eating."

"He was more concerned with seeing you eat," Xander said. "I've known real hunger, Geni. He is not acting the way someone who has been imprisoned for weeks would act. He was chained up when he found him. How was he catching food or getting water for those 'weeks' he says he was imprisoned?

"He's more concerned with finding out about us. Where we were from, what we were doing . . . I don't trust him, Geni. Not at all."

She was about to respond when, all at once, a breeze tickled a lock of her hair, blowing it into her face. She brushed it back.

"We don't have to tell him where we're going. What we're going to do when we get there." Not that they actually knew that themselves. Find the Bane. And then what? "But it doesn't hurt to have somebody else . . ."

She frowned and stopped talking all at once, suddenly realizing something.

"What?" Xander asked.

"The breeze," she said.

"What?"

"I felt a breeze. Fresh air. Over there." She gestured toward the other side of the rise they stood on, where, she saw now, the cavern wall suddenly curved inward. Was that natural light she saw? "I wonder . . ."

She heard the rustling of leaves, and a second later someone stepped out of the brush directly in front of her.

A soldier. Dressed in full battle gear. Full armor, including a helm.

He drew his sword and advanced on the two of them.

"Who are you?" he spat. "What are you doing here?"

"I am"—the Princess Angenica, she was about to say, when she caught a good look at the insignia on the soldier's chestplate.

A black helm, on a black and gray chessboard. The armor, she saw now, was black, piped in yellow. The colors of Kraxis.

"Blood traitor," Xander said. He stepped in front of Geni. "Run!"

She turned to go, and a half dozen other Kraxans stepped out into the clearing behind her.

"Bind them," the first said. "And then look around. I have the feeling they're not alone."

CHAPTER FORTY-TWO

Ty was playing Needles. By himself, in the far corner of the tavern. Hildros sat at the bar, a bottle he'd pulled down from the shelf set in front of him, a glass in his hand. Neither had said a word for what seemed like hours. They were content to let the healer and his assistants work.

Calis, though, could not sit still. He must have changed seats a hundred times since the healer's arrival. He had probably paced the length and breadth of the tavern at least that many times as well. Right now he stood at the door, holding it half open, watching the streets begin to fill. Horses riding past; dogs rising from slumber, children playing, women on their way to and from the well in the city square with water for the morning meal . . .

The city of Minoch, coming to life, in the early morning.

And behind him, Tandis dying.

He couldn't bear the thought.

Calis turned and almost walked right into Hildros.

"Lad." The older man looked up at him and frowned. "You should get some rest."

"Go to sleep?" Calis shook his head. "I can't. Not while . . ."

He gestured toward the middle of the tavern, toward the makeshift hospital, where the captain was being worked on. Two large tables had been pushed together, covered by white sheets, now stained red with the captain's blood. Tandis lay atop the makeshift bed, his face obscured from view by both the healer's back and by the objects the man was using in his attempt to save Tandis's life. Two basins of water, pouches filled with various medicinal plants and herbs, a handful of sharp steel instruments . . .

Gods, it might as well be magic for all that Calis understood it.

"Go upstairs. Take one of the rooms. We'll come get you if there's any news," Hildros said.

Calis just shook his head once more and moved past Hildros back into the tavern. The healer had brought two assistants— one male, one female, both not much more than Calis's age. Calis had attempted to engage them in conversation earlier; he would try again now, he decided. Find out what progress they had made. The boy was standing a little ways back from the healer now, looking on. Perhaps he would be able to shed some light—

"Lad. Calis." The innkeeper—the same one who'd started all the trouble last night—stood behind the bar, motioning to him. Calis walked over.

"You all right then?" the man asked.

"Fine. Why?"

"Just wondering." He gestured toward the healer. "How much longer do you think they'll be? I don't want to sound callous, but if I'm to open today, I need to clean the place up. Need to—"

"It'll take as long as it takes."

Hildros came up alongside the two of them.

"But . . ."

"You're lucky we don't burn the place down," he spat.

"Burn it down?" The innkeeper looked incredulous. "Why . . . ?"

Calis knew why; knew what Hildros was thinking. If you and

yours hadn't caused so much trouble last night when we'd let our guard down, hadn't let that Fallen creature sneak past us with its enchanted blade . . .

If only they had the thing in their custody; if only it hadn't, in the confusion and panic immediately following the stabbing, managed to escape the tavern, and no doubt the city, which had in the interim been thoroughly searched.

"Knights."

Calis and Hildros turned as one.

The healer stood before them, face grave. For a minute Calis feared the worst. His heart sank.

"He wishes to speak to you," the healer said, and stepped aside.

Tandis, cushions propped beneath his head, body propped up on his elbows, skin near as white as the sheet he lay on, smiled, and with a single, crooked finger, motioned them closer.

Ty laughed, and stepped forward, and hugged the healer. Lifted him right up off the ground.

"Sir knight," the healer said. "I beg you . . ."

Hildros, Calis saw, was crying. Wiping his nose, and snuffling, even as he shuffled forward toward the captain.

"Stupid," he said, shaking his head. "Even Galor has a body-guard. You need a bodyguard. Stupid. Stupid, stupid, stupid."

Calis smiled, seeing Hildros in tears. He went to laugh and realized he was crying, too.

"Oof," the doctor said, as Ty set him down.

"You'll leave the man alone, Ty," Tandis said, his voice weak and unsteady. "I have need of him still."

"For some time to come, Captain," the healer said. "Your survival, frankly, astounds me. One of our attendants died from merely touching the blade, such is its dark enchantment. That you live . . . it is nothing short of a miracle."

"My survival is a testament to your skills, healer," Tandis said. "Your wisdom."

"If you value that wisdom, Captain . . ."

"I do."

"You will speak with these men but a moment, and then rest."

"You have my word," Tandis nodded.

The healer stepped back. The three of them—besides Tandis, the last three surviving members of the Azure Knights—drew close.

"What of the enchantment, sir?" Hildros asked. "What do we know of who—"

"Can you recall anything of the creature, Captain?" Ty interrupted. "Its face. Any distinguishing marks. What manner of Fallen—"

"The red glow on the blade, sir," Calis said. "What did that mean? Is there—"

Tandis laughed and shook his head. "Listen to yourselves," he said, and the sound of his voice, weak as it was, caused all of them to fall silent. "I suspect I could not answer all your questions were I to sit here through the afternoon meal. And the healer tells me that well before then I must be in bed, upstairs, though apparently I cannot walk there under my own power but must instead be carried like a newborn babe."

"We'll do it, sir," Hildros snapped.

Tandis smiled. "And then laid in bed like a sick woman. Where I must rest, with the aid of a sleeping draft, no less, until such time—a long time, apparently—"

"Indeed," the healer said.

"—as I am well once more," the captain finished.

"We'll see you're not disturbed, sir," Ty said, casting a glance over his shoulder toward the innkeeper, who Calis saw was listening in with a frown. "By anyone."

The innkeeper took a step backward.

"Your concern is appreciated, my friends," Tandis said. "But I have another task for you."

The captain coughed then, and cleared his throat.

"I spoke at length with the baron last night. Baron Mancer. The city's ruler. I told him—as I have told the three of you, separately—of the thing that Talax seeks. The Bane." The captain lowered his voice; at the same time his eyes went to each of them in turn. "I told him of its importance. And the importance of retaking the Keep, that we might have a base from which to conduct our affairs in the East. Our attempt to recover this artifact for Galor. We arranged, he and I"—Tandis coughed again then, a sound that brought the healer scurrying forward, at which point Tandis held up a hand to forestall him—"for a military expedition."

Hildros and Ty exchanged a glance—an expression of concern, Calis noted.

"Across the bridge?" Ty asked. "Sir—"

"Granted, it will not be without its difficulties," Tandis said. "Nonetheless—"

"Difficulties? Captain, speaking plainly . . ." Hildros shook his head. "It's a suicide mission. Whoever attempts to reach the other side—they'll be sitting ducks. That's an exposed crossing, sir. The Fallen'll see whoever's coming and shoot 'em down from a mile away. It's a foolish thing to do, sir, begging your pardon. A foolish way to accomplish the task—better to send an army by ship to the south and move up from there . . ."

"The plan is made, Hildros," Tandis said, his voice taking on a little of its old snap and vigor. "Baron Mancer agreed to commit his armies. I was to command the first of the legions across— but now, obviously . . . that duty will fall on you."

Hildros's eyes widened. "The first legion? But sir—"

"Suicide mission, I know. You said." The captain managed a small, thin smile. "But it must be done. And done as soon as possible. If Talax should find this—"

He began, all at once, to cough, a hacking, wheezing sound that shook his whole body.

The healer stepped forward.

"This is too much. He has overexerted himself," the man said, placing a hand on Tandis's back. He pressed here and there, shaking his head as he did so. "He must rest now."

The healer motioned to the boy and the girl, who stepped forward and—before Calis or either of the others could say or do anything—took hold of either side of the sheet and lifted the captain from the table.

"Upstairs," the healer said. "You may talk to him—"

"Make arrangements with the baron," Tandis said, raising his head. "The invasion must happen soon. As soon as possible."

"It'll be done, sir," Hildros said. "You have my word."

"Good."

"And you." He caught Calis's eye. "Be careful."

But before the boy could ask him what he meant by that, the captain was gone.

The command given, there was no question of sleep. The three of them ate breakfast in the tavern while the innkeeper and two young boys scurried around cleaning, making the inn ready for customers later that day. Probably the same customers they had fought with the night before. What would they say when they saw Calis there again?

Not much, now that his identity had been established. They would not want to make trouble. Or risk another beating.

For his part, though, Calis was itching for a fight. Or rather, he was itching to do something. It took him a few moments to realize what.

Tandis had talked of the Bane, of the necessity of retaking the Keep, of its importance to the West. What he hadn't talked about at all, Calis realized . . .

His attacker. The assassination attempt. And the blade. Magicked.

The question was why.

Ty and Hildros were discussing what they remembered of the territory around the bridge, on the eastern and western continents; how well guarded the eastern approach was likely to be. How naked the western one was.

"They'll see us coming a mile away," Ty said.

"Suicide mission. We already brought that up," Hildros replied.

"I like living," Ty said. "It's my favorite state of being."

"Nighttime assault," Hildros said. "A night without the moon."

"And when's that likely to be?"

"The baron'll know. Or he'll be able to find out soon enough. So—"

"A week or so from now," Calis said. "That's my guess anyway. Based on what it looked like last night."

Ty frowned. "What it looked like last night."

"Yes," Calis nodded. "It was about three-quarter full. It'll take another few days to wane all the way."

"Mmm," Ty said. "Suppose you're right."

"Good thinking, lad," Hildros said, smiling brightly at Calis. It was the first genuine smile the boy had seen from the older man since the events at Imli's Swamp, since Calis had demonstrated his powers.

He smiled back.

"The blade was magicked," he said. "The one Tandis was stabbed with. Why do you suppose that was?"

Hildros frowned now, as did Ty. "I don't understand your question, boy."

"Why did they magick the blade?"

"It was an assassination attempt. They wanted him dead, so . . ."

"Thoroughness," Ty chimed in. "You gotta appreciate that."

"I suppose so," Calis said, not entirely convinced. He understood very little of magic, but it seemed to him that what he'd seen last night—the Fallen creature's disguise, the bright red glow of the blade—spoke of a very powerful enchantment indeed.

He supposed, Calis realized, that despite Tandis's denials, he still hadn't entirely rid himself of the suspicion that the captain was, after all, a channeler.

That suspicion—the questions about the blade, and other questions concerning his own abilities—floated around his head as they finished breakfast and made their way through the town of Minoch toward Baron Mancer's estate, a magnificent house that stood in the very center of the fortress. Its most characteristic feature, they'd learned from the innkeeper, who'd given them directions to it, was an immense, sprawling private garden, centuries old, one that had become more splendid with each passing year. They caught glimpses of it as they made their way to the front gate and rang the bell.

Two guards answered; after Hildros announced the purpose of their visit, another joined them, so that there were three guests and three escorts, the latter preceding the former as they made their way down a long hallway and into a large room, with sparse, albeit tastefully appointed furniture. There were two very comfortable leather chairs set in front of a fireplace; Hildros and Ty took those, leaving Calis standing alone. The guards glared at him—more anti-Krax prejudice, the boy assumed—and turned to leave the room.

"He'll be with you in a moment. The baron," one said, and shut the door.

"Didn't offer us any drinks, did they?" Ty asked. "Wonder if they got anything here?"

He reached toward a cabinet; Hildros slapped his hand away.

"Mind your manners."

"It's good manners to offer your guests a libation or two. A social nicety."

"Yes, well, stealing from your host isn't. If the baron wants to offer us something later . . ."

Ty glared and lowered his hand.

Calis walked toward the back of the room. The entire back wall was covered with walnut shelving, which was itself covered with more books than Calis had ever seen in his life. Most of them, he noticed, were written in other languages. Not Common Tongue, not even any of the Fallen languages that he was familiar with.

"Knights."

Calis turned just as the baron entered from the hall, through the same door they'd come through.

Mancer was a powerful-looking, powerfully built man. Calis put his age at fifty, perhaps a little older, his hair raven black in spots but sprinkled with gray. He wore green velvet robes, woven with the sigil of the house of Aegeon—the same sigil as the Lord of the Keep's had been, Ambrose.

"My Lord," Hildros and Ty said, simultaneously, rising to bow as the baron came toward them. "Thank you for seeing us so quickly," Hildros added.

"Of course." Mancer's deep voice filled the room. "The news of your captain's injury . . . the attack on Tandis. I am greatly saddened that this could occur in my domain. How is he?"

"He lives, Baron," Hildros said. "He is weak, but he lives."

"Thank the Gods," Mancer said.

"Indeed." Hildros cleared his throat. "He charged us to come speak with you, my lord. Regarding the arrangements the two of you had made."

"Arrangements?"

"The army," Hildros said. "I am to command it, in his stead."

"You."

"Yes." The old warrior straightened. "I am Hildros. Lieutenant of the Azure Knights. Longest serving among them, save for the captain. This is Ty, my second"—he gestured to the other man—"and Calis."

Mancer nodded. "The Krax."

"Yes, Lord," Calis said, trying—and failing—not to blush. "I am he."

"I mean no insult," Mancer said. "I have heard reports of you, boy. Certain abilities you seem to possess."

Channeler, Calis thought. Even though he still wasn't entirely sure it was true.

"Have no fear of the lad's loyalties, lord," Ty said. "He may be Krax, but he has lived his entire life with us. Traveled across all the world."

"Impressive," Mancer said, and he managed a slight smile as he spoke, one that told Calis that just perhaps the man meant what he said.

"We are the last of the Azure Knights, Baron," Hildros said.

"Yes," Mancer said, and sighed, and turned away from them to look out the window. "I am familiar with the Azure Knights. There was, after all, a Mancer among you."

"Tandis has entrusted us with the task you two agreed on last night," Hildros added.

Mancer looked down.

Hildros and Ty exchanged a quizzical look. Calis knew just what they were thinking.

Something was wrong here.

"My lord," Hildros said. "What troubles you? If I have misunderstood the captain's words . . . mischaracterized what the two of you agreed on . . ."

"No, Hildros. That is not it at all," Mancer said.

"Then . . ."

"You see my garden, Hildros?" He gestured out the window. "It was started by King Indion, the Lord of Ithul. The kingdom that was, before the dark times. Before the War of Magic, nigh on a thousand years ago now. Nearly all of Ithul was destroyed in that conflict. In that great war, until the West was saved by the hand of Relias."

"Yes, Lord," Hildros said, still sounding confused. Still obviously uncertain what Mancer was driving at. Calis wasn't sure, either . . . but he didn't like the direction the conversation was taking.

"War is not a thing to be undertaken lightly, Knights. I trust you understand that."

"My lord," Hildros said. "All due respect. We are more familiar than most about the costs imposed by war. We are, as I said, the last three of Tandis's knights remaining."

"Yes," Mancer said. "Yes, of course."

He turned to face them then, and cleared his throat. "Regarding the army. The invasion of the Eastern Henge. Retaking the Keep. Those plans, I am afraid, are no longer in effect."

Hildros's eyes widened.

"What?"

"I have had word from the King this morning. Informing me that no action is to be taken against the East without his specific approval."

"The King," Ty said. "Galor?"

"There is only one King, good knight. As you well know."

"Galor is in Athica," Calis said. "How . . ."

"The King has his ways, Calis," Baron Mancer said. "His words—his commands—were quite clear."

"But Lord . . ." Hildros looked stunned. "Did not Tandis tell you of the Bane? Did he not make it clear . . . the danger . . ."

"I understand the danger," Mancer snapped. "As does the King, I am certain. His orders, however, are clear as well."

"Then the King's not thinking straight," Calis blurted out.

Mancer's head whipped around. He glared at Calis.

"Have a care, boy."

Hildros laid a hand on Calis's shoulder. A warning hand.

Calis shrugged it off.

"Baron. If Talax finds the Bane—if he and his army are allowed to retain possession of the Keep—to conduct their search for this thing unchecked, unabated—"

"The King was quite specific in his instructions, Hildros," Mancer said. "I am sorry. I am to make no aggressive moves toward the East without his express permission."

"But we have to return over the bridge now!" Calis said. "We can't wait—"

"Our King has given us a direct command, boy. There is no question of our duty here," the baron replied.

"But the King's not here, Baron," Calis said. "You are. And you know the situation far better than he ever—"

"Enough!" Mancer snapped. "I will not be lectured by a child."

"I'm not a child," Calis shot back.

Mancer turned to Hildros. "Your boy may have traveled the world, knight, but he has yet to learn the intricacies of protocol. Perhaps that is a lesson you can teach him now. The importance of knowing his place in the order of things. Yes?"

Hildros hesitated for a moment before replying.

"Perhaps you are right, Lord."

"And perhaps not," Ty said. "The Fallen would not be trying so hard to kill our captain if there were no merit to his desires, would they, Baron?"

Mancer's face darkened. Calis could see him trying to gain hold of his temper. It took him what seemed like an eternity to do so. Finally, the baron spoke once more.

"You will pass along my wishes for a speedy recovery to your captain, knights. Good day."

And with that, Mancer was gone. Out the door, the way he'd

come in, leaving the three of them standing in front of the fire-place.

The fire, Calis noted, had gone out.

"Well, that could have gone better," Hildros said.

"No doubt." Ty eyed the cabinet over the fireplace longingly. "Guess we're not getting that drink after all, are we?"

CHAPTER FORTY-THREE

Their captor—the soldier who had first come upon them in the caverns—put a knife to Geni's throat. When the golem arrived, apparently summoned by some unspoken command from Geni, and saw the danger the princess was in, it ceased movement.

The Kraxan soldiers bound it in chains and buried it beneath boulders they wedged away from the cave entrance—the door to the outside world, the source of the fresh air that Xander and Geni had smelled earlier, while they were arguing.

Nym was a little more trouble.

The Sion—Xander had to give it credit—fought like a creature possessed. He killed—by Xander's count, anyway—at least a half dozen of the Kraxans before they subdued and then bound him.

The soldiers then dragged the three of them—Geni protesting every step of the way, over their treatment, the soldiers' brutalization of Nym, their destruction of the golem—out into the fresh air.

When they emerged, Xander saw that they were in the shadow of the Spine of the Empire—the great mountain range that bisected the eastern continent.

The brightness of daylight caused Xander to blink. He had almost forgotten how long they had been journeying through the great underground domain.

The soldiers marched them a half mile or so down the foothills, to a great encampment of tents, endless rows of them, stretching out as far as the eye could see. Kraxan soldiers. Their camp was huge; the walk through it, past suspicious glances directed at Nym and himself, past lecherous stares directed at Geni, seemed to take forever. At last they were ushered to a particularly splendid-looking tent, with green and red fabrics emblazoned in intricate designs all across it.

"You will wait here," the soldier who captured them declared gruffly.

"The Sion, sir." Another soldier spoke up. "Should we not . . ."

"Aye." The first soldier nodded. "Cage it. Put it with the slaves."

Nym let fly a fresh round of curses, as did Geni. To no avail. The Sion was dragged away. The first soldier disappeared into the tent. And Xander and Geni were left out front to wait. And wait.

And wait.

Soldiers and other dignitaries came and went, in and out of the tent. Xander watched them go with mounting discomfort; he was used to moving around, not standing still for long periods of time. Geni looked as uncomfortable as he felt, maybe even more so. She wasn't making any attempt to hide her displeasure. Clearly she wasn't intimidated by the circumstances—or her surroundings.

Finally, a huge guard—a good foot and a half taller than Xander—stepped out from the tent and bowed to them.

"His Majesty will see you now," he said, and held the tent flap open.

Geni and Xander looked at each other, shrugged, and entered.

The tent was remarkably spacious. The air smelled of incense.

At the back sat a young man on a fairly impressive-looking chair with two large men on either side.

His Majesty?

"Princess," the man said smoothly, rising from his chair. This close up, Xander could see that he was younger than he'd first appeared—not much older than Geni, or himself. It was his clothes—a long, flowing robe of black and gold—and his hair—elegantly styled—that made him look older than he really was. And was that makeup he was wearing on his eyes?

The first impression Xander had was of a little boy, putting on airs.

He took an instant dislike to the young man.

"I apologize for your treatment. I beg your forgiveness. I have been receiving visitors all day, and the lieutenant here"—he gestured toward the soldier who had captured them—"only just informed me you were here."

Xander frowned. Something about the speech didn't ring true to him. He turned to Geni, expecting to see a similar look of suspicion on her face.

Instead she was smiling.

She ran a hand through her hair, pulling it back from her face.

"Oh," Geni said. "They just told you."

"That's right." The man—the boy—smiled back. "Again, I beg your forgiveness. When my men saw the Sion, they were naturally suspicious."

"Understandably," Geni said. "Your Grace, you have me at a disadvantage. I must apologize, but I do not know who you are."

"There is no need for apology, Princess. One so beautiful never needs to apologize."

Geni blushed again.

"You are too kind," she said, bowing.

"Not at all. Merely truthful." He returned the bow. "I am Jacob of Kintrock, son of Lord Edmund, Warden of Kraxis. It is my pleasure to welcome you to our camp, Geni."

"It is my pleasure to be here, Your Majesty." Geni smiled and bowed her head.

Oh, come on, Xander thought, and took a step forward.

"Listen, Prince," he began, "why—"

A spear point in his chest stopped him.

"Ah." For the first time, the boy—Jacob—turned his attention to Xander. From the look in his eyes, Xander could tell he felt roughly the same dislike as he did. "Your companion here, Princess. Your servant, I assume. Could you introduce us?"

Servant. Xander glared.

Geni spoke before he could.

"Actually, Xander is my friend, Prince. He and I—"

"Why are there so many soldiers here?" Xander blurted out, less out of curiosity than to stop Geni from saying anything about the purpose of their journey.

Jacob's eyes narrowed. A touch of annoyance crossed his face for a brief moment, and then just as quickly as it had come, it vanished.

"Why so many soldiers? Well, boy—"

"I'm not a boy," Xander snapped. "Not any more than you are, at least."

He got a slap in the back of the head for that, from the soldier who'd captured them.

"You'll keep a civil tongue in your head when you talk to the prince, lad," the man said. "Or you'll lose the both of them."

Geni put a hand on his arm.

"You'll forgive my friend, Prince Jacob," she said, soothingly. "But I'm curious as well. All the soldiers we see here—this must be the entire armed might of Kraxis—why . . ."

"Have we gathered together here? Now, at this point in time, in such numbers? For a single, simple reason, Princess." The smile on his face suddenly disappeared. "The armies of the Empire are on the move as well. The Keep has been overrun. I do not know if this is news to you or not, but—"

"I am aware of what has happened at the Keep."

"Then you know this is a dark hour for the Western Kingdom. For Galor."

"I didn't think Kraxis was allied with the Kingdom," Xander said. "I thought you—"

He sensed the soldier who had slapped him earlier and had threatened him with a spear point taking another step toward him.

Before he could even flinch, though, Jacob had raised a hand.

"It's all right," Jacob said to the soldier. "The boy can speak."

The boy. Xander glared for a moment, then forced himself to continue.

"You were allies with the Empire," he said to Jacob. "You fought with the Fallen. Against men. You—"

"That was a millennium ago, boy. Times have changed. People have changed. The Krax have changed." The boy's eyes turned hard. "We side with Galor now. The Keep has fallen. The men of Kraxis, at my father's command, march north to liberate it."

"This is so?" Geni said. "Truly?"

"It is. Our forces plan to hug the Spine until we reach the border, and then strike north and west with a single fist. Expel the invaders, and raise the sigil of Aegeon above the Keep once more." Jacob bowed his head slightly again. "We would be honored to have you join us on our journey, Princess. To be there when we restore your father to command."

"I would be honored to be there," Geni said, and all at once, started to cry.

Jacob stepped smoothly forward and took her in his arms.

Her body began shaking. He smoothed her hair.

Xander opened his mouth, but no words would come out.

"And you, boy?" Jacob asked, looking over Geni's shoulder at him. "Would you like to join us as well?"

"Absolutely." Xander gritted his teeth. "Wouldn't miss it for the world."

* * *

Jacob ordered plans to be made for a banquet that very evening, in Geni's honor. A half-dozen women appeared, maids, maidens dressed in clothes as fine as the prince's. The prince directed them to help Geni freshen up, and to make room for her in one of the finer tents.

"We have hot water, Your Highness," one of the girls said. "Ointments, and soap, to wash your hair."

"A bath." Geni turned to Xander. "A bath! Did you hear, Xander?"

"Oh, yes," he said. "I heard."

She looked happier than he'd seen her in weeks. Not that Xander could blame her. A hot bath, a banquet, a handsome prince doting on her, the same prince on the way to rescue her father . . .

Xander didn't know what to say; was there anything he *could* say? *I don't like the looks of this guy.* Or more truthfully, *I don't like the looks he's giving you.*

Even less, if he was honest with himself, did he like the looks Geni was giving the prince in return.

The women began pulling Geni away. With a wave to Xander and a promise to see him at the banquet, she disappeared.

Xander himself was led to a tent in the middle of the camp. A small tent. With a bowl of dirty, lukewarm water. No bath. He tried to inquire about Nym—he had no particular fondness for the creature, but compared to the way he felt about Jacob, the Sion was starting to seem like an old friend—but his questions were ignored.

He changed into the fresh clothes that were left for him. He stepped outside the tent and saw that his escort had disappeared. He saw something else as well then.

He'd been placed in the middle of the camp followers. Saren had spent many hours telling Xander about them—the servants who supplied an army with everything it needed to survive. Saren had seen them during his years with the legions of Capitar, when that army had marched into Tarth to quell a rebellion against the Kingdom. They were a sight indeed, just as the old man had said; a moving village, literally, with merchants, tailors, shoemakers, and women who seemed to be offering pleasures of every imaginable kind. At least to the soldiers passing through; they were ignoring Xander entirely.

He suspected his lack of a bath had something to do with that.

He began wandering the immense camp, looking for Nym. Put the Sion in with the slaves, the soldier who'd captured him had said, but Xander could find no trace of slaves. No one willing to answer his questions, either.

By the time the sun—had it always been so bright? so yellow?—began to go down, his feet were tired, and he was more than ready to give up on his search and eat. The banquet itself was easy enough to find; all he had to do was follow his nose. The smell of food cooking—meats, breads, and other baked goods—permeated the air.

Tables had been set up just outside the prince's tent. People were beginning to sit; Xander arrived just in time to see a retinue of elegantly clad ladies walking toward the largest—what he assumed was the head—table. Head because Jacob was standing there, talking to a number of his officers.

Geni was in the middle of the group of women. She was dressed in a light blue gown, with a white shawl about her shoulders, presumably to keep the night air from chilling her. Her hair was pinned back; she wore a necklace that sparkled in the firelight.

She looked radiant.

Seeing her cleaned up, wearing new clothes, Xander could tell that she'd lost weight in the tunnels. Not a surprise. What he hadn't noticed, though . . .

The weight she'd lost was like baby fat. There were new lines to her cheekbones, new strength in her features.

She didn't look like a young girl anymore; she looked like a woman.

Jacob, alerted by one of the officers he was talking to, turned toward her. His face lit up with pleasure; so, too, Xander noticed with chagrin, did Geni's.

The prince held out both his hands, and she took them. He said something that made her laugh and then pulled out a chair for her. She sat; he sat down next to her. They began chatting, and laughing.

Xander felt his stomach turn over.

At that second Geni happened to look up and catch his eye.

She smiled at him, and stood.

Xander's heart lightened; he smiled back and started walking toward her.

Jacob caught sight of him and frowned. The prince stood as well then, and whispered something in Geni's ear that wiped the smile off her face.

Xander came closer; she came out from behind the table to greet him, looking, all at once, very uncomfortable indeed.

Xander had intended to compliment her on her clothes, on how good she looked.

The first words out of his mouth, though, when he reached her, were "What's the matter?"

"You're all right?" she asked.

"I'm fine." She even smelled wonderful, he realized, a perfume that made him all the more aware, at that instant, of how he smelled. "You?"

"Great," she said. "Good."

Then she cleared her throat.

"Try not to be angry," she said. "But the Kraxan nobles—the ones that Jacob's been talking to—the ones that he's sitting with over there—"

She gestured over her shoulder, toward a group of men, most of them middle-aged or older, standing near the prince.

"I see them," Xander said. "What about them?"

"Well." Geni shifted her feet. "They weren't happy at the thought of . . . uh, well, Jacob told them the banquet was to honor me, and the honor of sitting with me was to fall to the nobility, not . . . um . . . others, and so—"

Xander got it instantly.

"They don't want me to sit up there. With you."

"Well, yes. That's it."

Xander couldn't keep the hurt—or the anger—off his face.

"I'm sorry, Xander," Geni said quickly. "I don't want to hurt your feelings, but I don't want to upset them, either. The nobles."

"Or the prince, I suppose."

She frowned.

"What?"

"You don't want to upset Jacob, either—do you?"

"What are you talking about?"

"Never mind." He waved a hand dismissively. If Geni wanted to pretend the prince had nothing to do with this, that was fine with him. Sort of.

Not really.

"Listen, Xander. Please. This isn't just about you, or me. It's about Kraxis allying with the Kingdom again. About rescuing my father. Do you understand?"

She looked at him pleadingly. He sighed and nodded.

"Yes," he said. "I understand."

"Good. Thank you." She rose onto her toes and kissed him on the cheek. Xander felt himself blush.

"Come find me when the meal is over. We can talk then."

She took his hand and squeezed it.

Xander smiled, and caught Jacob's eye.

The prince, now, didn't look happy at all.

And that made Xander feel almost as good as Geni's smile.

His good mood didn't last long, though.

There were only a dozen or so tables, and barely enough chairs for the highest-ranking officers—generals and warlords—of the Kraxan army. The remainder of the officers invited to the dinner ate around various campfires nearby; Xander, for his part, settled for a patch of bare ground within eyeshot of Geni's table, where he could both eat and watch what was happening.

The food was passable; he caught snatches of conversation between Geni and some of the others at her table. Many of the lords were quite complimentary toward her father, remarking on how fairly they'd been treated by Ambrose in their dealings despite not truly being members of the Kingdom. He couldn't hear Geni's responses; nor, of course, could he hear the whispered asides made by Prince Jacob to her at several points during the meal.

The food consumed, Jacob rose to announce the presentation of a series of gifts to Geni, most of which came from the very "nobles" who had denied Xander a place at her table. Jewelry; clothing; even a sword. Prince Jacob gave her a golden necklace, which looked quite valuable indeed. As did many of the other items.

Which is why it struck Xander as very odd that no one seemed to mind when a short, grubby little man walked over to the table and without warning began casually picking up some of those gifts and studying them quite closely.

"Hey," Xander said, starting to get to his feet.

There was a small campfire next to him, where two officers were still eating and drinking. Mostly drinking. One of them turned now and glared at Xander.

"What do you want, boy?" he snapped.

"Nothing," Xander said. "I wasn't talking to you. I . . ."

He stopped speaking, because the grubby little man in front of Geni's table had pulled out a linen sack, into which he was now stuffing the gifts.

And still no one seemed the slightest bit concerned.

What was going on here?

Maybe the little man belonged to Prince Jacob. Maybe the prince had told him to keep the gifts safe, once they were given. Maybe he was taking them . . .

The little man picked up the golden necklace, wrapped it around his wrist, and began to walk away.

Xander caught up to him and grabbed him by the wrist.

"What do you think you're doing?" Xander growled.

The little man took one look at him and his eyes widened.

"You can see me," he said.

"Of course I can see you. Now give me that." Xander yanked the necklace away from the man. "This belongs to Geni. And so does all this other stuff."

He reached for the bag the man was carrying.

And at that instant, a hand clamped down on his shoulder.

He turned and saw one of the officers he'd been sitting next to glaring at him.

"Boy," the man said. "What are you doing with that necklace?"

"Saving it," Xander snapped back. "Since the rest of you are apparently too busy talking to one another to notice something getting stolen right in front of your eyes!"

The man frowned and shook his head.

"What in the name of the Gods are you talking about, boy? I saw you, didn't I?"

Before Xander could respond, the man grabbed hold of his ear and yanked his head down, ripping the necklace from his grasp.

When Xander straightened up, Jacob was standing in front of him.

"What's all this, then?"

"The boy stole the princess's necklace," the man said.

"The other gifts are missing as well," Jacob said.

Xander rubbed his ear. "Well. Obviously. The thief took them, too."

"Yes. Obviously," Jacob replied.

The tone of his reply confused Xander even more.

"Xander." Geni suddenly appeared, right next to the prince. She looked confused, too; confused and concerned. "Why did you take the necklace?"

"What?" Xander's eyes widened. What was the matter with these people? "I didn't steal anything. It was him!"

He pointed over Geni's shoulder at the short, grubbly little man, who was now backing away from the rapidly growing circle of people around Xander. Backing away, and still carrying the bag full of Geni's other gifts.

"Him." Jacob, who had turned to follow Xander's gaze, turned back again now. "One of my soldiers? One of these nobles? Who exactly are you accusing of the theft, boy?"

Xander shook his head.

The little man smiled sadly at him, waved, and faded away into the crowd.

"Ask him where the other gifts went, Prince," someone snapped.

"He must have had help," another said.

"A little torture'll loosen his tongue," called out a third voice.

One of the nobles stepped forward then.

"I think, perhaps, the boy took the necklace because he was jealous of you, Prince," the man suggested. "He is the princess's servant, yes? The one who's been traveling with her? All that time they've spent together—perhaps it's given him ideas."

Jacob nodded thoughtfully, an evil glint in his eye. "Perhaps. But we can't let it ruin our evening, can we?"

"But—" Geni began, before Jacob held up a hand to stop her.

"We'll sort this all out in the morning, Princess," Jacob said. "Perhaps it is a misunderstanding. In the meantime, though . . ." Jacob turned to a handful of soldiers who had gathered nearby. "Take him. Cage him with the Sion."

And before Xander could say a word, the soldiers had hold of him and were dragging him away.

CHAPTER FORTY-FOUR

They had burned him.

They had cut him.

They had whipped him, and beat him, and starved him. For three long days, all he'd had to eat or drink was the water in the bottom of his cage.

Now, on the evening of the fourth day, one of the Krax soldiers tossed something through the bars at Nym. It landed on the floor of the cage with a wet smack. He picked it up and studied it. Meat. Flesh, from some beast of burden. Rotten meat. Days old. Falling off the bone it had been attached to; a leg bone, unless Nym missed his guess. A nice, thick, strong bone.

He looked up and smiled through the bars at the soldier.

"Oh, thank you," he said, surprised at how hoarse his voice sounded.

The man let out a guffaw. "Rotten meat," he said to his fellow soldiers.

Nym almost laughed, too. Rotten meat. As if he couldn't tell by the smell. By the white slime oozing out from the crack between gristle and bone. Did he care? No, he did not.

He picked up the bone and dragged it off to the far corner of his cage.

"Thing wants a little privacy to eat its food. Damn." The soldier smiled at him, a cruel, taunting smile. Nym memorized that smile—and the face attached to it.

Then he lifted the bone and took a bite of the rotting flesh. A big bite that went right down to the bone and cracked it. First try. Excellent.

Nym spat the meat out onto the floor and bit down again. Hard. He snapped the bone in two with his teeth. He pulled back, and one half fell to the floor.

He held the other half of the bone up high. Ooh. He'd been lucky. A nice sharp edge. A nice sharp point.

The soldier who'd given him the meat had moved away a little, was talking and laughing with his friends. Nym's guard had moved closer once more, was standing with his back to Nym. Within arm's reach—a stretched arm's reach, anyway—of the cage.

Hiding the bone behind his back, Nym took a quiet step forward. And then another.

The thing to do was stab hard, and quick, get the bone to lodge in the guard's back. That way, he could use it to pull the guard's body closer to him. Grab the keys, perhaps, even before the others knew what had happened.

And then he would kill. Then—

"There you are!"

The unexpected exclamation from behind caused Nym to start and caused the guard to turn around as well.

"Now, hey! Tell them what you did. Tell them it wasn't me who stole the necklace. Tell them—"

"Shut your mouth, boy. Or I'll shut it for you."

That was the guard speaking now; speaking to the boy Xander, who was in the cage next to Nym's, a cage just like his. A cage made of iron bars that rose vertically from a round base and gradually met at a sharp point in its center, a cage about ten feet around, about that high as well.

Xander had been caught, apparently, stealing from the Krax prince a few days ago. They were still trying to decide what to do with him, Nym gathered. The girl was involved. She'd been by several times to talk to the boy—and to him as well, Nym recalled. She'd even intervened—or tried to, anyway—to stop the soldiers from tormenting Nym. Yesterday was a case in point. Men had gathered around his cage and began lighting what appeared to be small packets of flammable material. Once ablaze, the men threw them into the cage in an effort to burn him.

They laughed at his attempts to dodge the flaming packets.

"Leave him alone!" the girl—the princess—had yelled. "His family and estate were burned down for resisting the evil commands of the Fallen."

Her words had only caused the soldiers to laugh harder.

"Princess," one of the guards had said. "He's a Sion, this one. They don't have no families or estates. They're raised in the Sion temple in Imperium. Live there, too."

Geni had looked to him then, confused. Nym, his torture momentarily stopped, had shaken his head.

"Don't listen to them," he had croaked. "They don't know what they're talking about!"

The girl had nodded; Nym wasn't sure whether she believed him or not. One thing she clearly didn't believe: what Xander was telling her. Something about an invisible thief, who was the person who had really stolen the things he was being blamed for.

"Stop it, Xander," she'd told him. "You're really not helping things with this pretense. Listen, I understand. You were angry that nobody wanted to congratulate you for the things you'd done—helping me escape from the Fallen, all that—you were upset at how much attention everyone was paying to me, maybe you were a little jealous—"

"Jealous!" the boy had exploded. "Of what? Of who? Jacob? I'm not jealous of anyone. Anything. I'm telling you the truth. There was someone else there."

The girl had rolled her eyes.

"This mysterious thief you keep talking about."

"Yes," Xander had said. "This mysterious thief."

Which thief, Nym realized, the boy was apparently talking to now.

"Tell them!" Xander yelled, pointing at the empty space straight in front of them. "Will you please—"

"Stop it now, boy," the guard said. "Yer lucky you're a special guest, or I'd have a mind of putting you in there with the Sion!"

The boy glared—at the guard, at the empty air in front of his cage, and then, turning, at Nym.

Then he sighed and sat down in the middle of his cage. The guards moved away. Nym hid the sharpened end of the bone in what remained of his pant leg and sat, too.

"What?" the boy snapped, glaring at him. "You think I'm crazy, too?"

Nym didn't bother responding. He didn't know what he thought of the boy, truth be told. The lad had seemed capable enough, back in the tunnels. Had a good survival instinct, some sound fighting skills, and a healthy degree of suspicion regarding Nym. But this now . . . this business with an invisible thief . . .

Well. It made him reconsider everything. Clearly, the search for the Bane was being guided—and had been most likely initiated—by the princess. Xander's presence here—the boy's presence earlier in the village outside the Keep, when he'd saved the knight, and inside the Keep itself, when he'd saved the princess—that was all luck. The whim of the Destiny, as it were.

"Get some rest, boy," Nym snapped. "Eat some food."

Maybe you'll come to your senses then, the Sion thought but didn't say. Nym needed rest as well—now more than ever. He needed to conserve his strength. He'd need to be ready to seize opportunity when it came.

He felt the sharpened piece of bone digging into his leg as he stretched out on the cage floor and closed his eyes. Now that they were cellmates, as it were, perhaps he could count on the boy's assistance in escape. Or at least count on him not to alert the guards. Perhaps the two of them, Nym thought as he drifted off to sleep, could even make a plan together. Escape, and reach the princess, and return to their quest. They would discuss it the next morning.

But when Nym woke, the cage next to him was empty.

The boy was gone.

Xander, for his part, had been unable to sleep. The rough wooden floor of the cage wasn't the problem; he'd slept on far, far worse. The howls of the camp dogs, fighting over scraps from the cooking fires, the screeches of cats and other animals mating in the nearby woods, the snoring of the guard supposedly watching over him and Nym . . . those weren't a problem, either. The fights Zayelle and Saren used to have were at least as bad. At least as loud.

No, the problem was him. His situation. He simply could not believe what had happened to him over the last few days. He'd gone over the scene at the banquet in his mind a half dozen times; he had not been hallucinating. The man had been there, no doubt—but no one else had seen him. How was such a thing possible? He'd tried to ask Geni about it, whether or not she knew of any spells that would make someone invisible, but she wouldn't listen to him. She just went on and on about how he had abused Prince Jacob's hospitality; how he ought to just apologize, accept whatever sort of punishment the prince would impose on him— probably, she implied, she'd be able to talk him out of that punishment, once pronounced—and move on.

The whole time she was talking, Xander couldn't help but notice the golden necklace hanging around her neck. And the matching bracelet dangling from her wrist. The new dress she was wearing; the way her hair was done up atop her head. The way she smelled. The two guards who stayed a few steps behind her as she spoke to him.

The way she kept referring to "Jacob." "Jacob this," "Jacob that." Jacob's army, which was going to march on the Keep and expel the Fallen. Save her father.

"And deal with Talax how?" Xander had asked.

Geni's face had fallen then. Her tone turned surly. Shortly after that, she'd left.

She'd come to see him a half dozen more times; their conversation had followed roughly the same pattern. Tell him you're sorry for what you did, this'll all be over. But Xander couldn't. He hadn't done anything; there was nothing to apologize for.

He had to find the little man. Correction: had to find the man who had shown up and stared at him on more than one occasion since he'd been imprisoned. It was all starting to seem to Xander like a nightmare. One he couldn't wake up from.

He rolled over on the wooden floor and almost screamed out loud.

The invisible little man stood outside his cage, staring at him.

The man had appeared earlier that afternoon as well. Xander had been shocked to see him then, too. He had almost begun to believe that he had hallucinated the whole thing.

"I still can't believe it," the man whispered. "You can see me."

"Of course I can see you," Xander had told him. "It's not like you're invisible or anything."

The man sighed. "If only that were true."

"Is that it?" Xander asked. "You're invisible?"

"No, no. Not invisible. Just . . . unnoticeable."

"What does that mean?"

The man just shook his head and started to walk away.

"Wait!" Xander had yelled. "Tell them! Will you please—"

That was as far as he'd gotten before the guard had shut him up.

And now . . .

Here the little man was again.

This was the first chance Xander had gotten to really look at him. He was old—maybe not as old as Saren, but well past middle age. He was short. Very short—maybe five feet tall. And his hair, his clothes, every inch of his body was covered in filth. This close to him, Xander noticed something else as well.

The little man stank. As if he hadn't bathed in weeks.

"It's a miracle," the little man said.

"What's a miracle?" Xander asked. "What are you talking about? Who are you? And why can't anyone else see you?"

The little man shook his head.

"Vreen," he said. "My name is Vreen. It's a miracle. The Destiny be praised."

"The Destiny?" Xander glared. "The Destiny don't have anything to do with this. What are you . . ."

His voice trailed off, because the little man—Vreen—had begun to cry.

To sob, actually.

In the cage next to him, Nym growled and shifted in his sleep.

"Hey," Xander said, not wanting the Sion to wake up. He still didn't entirely trust the creature for one thing, and for another . . .

He wanted to figure out what was going on here. Why could he see Vreen when apparently no one else could?

"Take it easy," he said soothingly. "It's okay, little guy. Vreen."

The little man sniffed. "Yes. Yes, it is okay. At long last it is. Come. We must hurry."

And then, to Xander's surprise, the little man reached up and unlocked his cage. The door swung open.

"Come," Vreen said.

Xander didn't need to be told twice.

* * *

He had half a mind to grab the man by the ear and drag him to Prince Jacob's tent. To demonstrate that he wasn't crazy, that he wasn't guilty, either. But that hadn't really worked before; since nobody but him could see Vreen, Xander didn't think it would work now, either.

So he remained silent as the little man led him to his camp, on the outskirts of the Krax army: a small campfire, a cache of food, and—no surprise—weapons, money, and jewelry, hidden in a hollow near the foothills of the Spine. Very near to the spot where they'd emerged from Calebethon. Which reminded Xander of their purpose; what they were supposed to be doing. What Geni was supposed to be doing; not being waited on hand and foot by Jacob's servants; not picking out new dresses, drinking fine wines, eating delicacies; not spending all her time in Jacob's tent, talking and laughing and—

"Here," Vreen said, handing him first a hunk of bread and then some cheese. "Eat. Please."

Xander studied the food. He wasn't sure how much of an improvement it was over what the Krax had been giving him, but it was certainly more than the meager amounts he'd been rationed.

He bit off a hunk of the bread; it was old, and tough to chew. The cheese was old as well. But it was food. He wouldn't argue. He needed to get his strength back up, figure out a way to get to Geni, and get back to Calebethon. The golem, he thought. The Krax soldiers had buried it, but he was fairly certain that if he could get it out from under those rocks, the thing would be okay. With the element of surprise, it would be able to handle Jacob's personal guard.

"Drink," Vreen said, and handed him a mug. Xander raised it to his lips and drank.

And immediately spat out everything in his mouth.

"Bleccchhh!"

Vreen frowned. "The wine is not to your liking?"

"I don't drink wine," Xander said. Which was not completely true; he had drunk wine on several occasions, to his regret. He'd sworn off the stuff since then, at least until he had a higher tolerance for it.

"Then I will bring you water."

Vreen went back to his supplies and refilled the mug. He brought it back to Xander.

"Thank you," Xander said.

"The food is to your liking?" the little man asked.

"Oh, yes. It's delicious. You're being very kind, and I appreciate it."

"It is the least I can do, of course," Vreen said. "Considering that it is my fault that you were in such trouble."

True enough, Xander thought but didn't say.

"I did not realize who you were then," Vreen continued. "Why you were here. But it is clear to me now what is happening."

"Oh?"

"Indeed. The Destiny sent you. There is no other explanation."

Xander, in the middle of chewing, held back the retort on his lips—"the Destiny have nothing to do with it." Instead he merely nodded, and mumbled an agreeable "mmm-hmmm."

"They have decided to lift my curse."

"Curse?"

"Yes. It was placed on me long ago. A curse that prevents people from noticing me."

"You'd think people would notice your stench."

He spoke without thinking, but if the little man was offended, he didn't acknowledge it.

"They do notice the stench; they just don't recognize the

source. Sometimes they even hear me, but since their eyes show them that no one is there . . . they ignore the evidence of their ears."

"How long has it been like this?" Xander asked. "That people can't see you?"

"I cannot tell you the number of days. A long time. A long, long time." Vreen sighed. "I was a burglar back then."

"Seems to me you still are," Xander said.

"Yes." Vreen sighed. "Yes. I suppose I am. In those days, though . . . I was normal. A normal burglar."

"What happened?"

"I wasn't even working that night." Vreen smiled ruefully. "My job, I mean. I was walking past a village. I walked by this hut. It had a window, and through the window . . . I saw these jewels. Dozens of them. Maybe even hundreds. All colors, all sizes . . . so many of them I was sure they weren't real. Except the closer I got . . . well, I saw that they were. And there was no one around, so . . . I decided to help myself. But the minute I touched one of the jewels, she appeared."

"She?"

"Yes. She." Vreen was silent for a moment. "A sorceress of some kind. She called me a thief."

Imagine that, Xander thought but didn't say.

"And she said 'If you wish to sneak through life, then let me help you do so!' And then . . ." He shuddered. "There was light all around me, all of a sudden. A red light. My whole body . . . it felt strange suddenly. I felt strange. I couldn't move for a second, and then . . . then I dropped the jewels I was carrying, and I ran. Fast as I could. I ran till I couldn't run anymore, and then I stole a horse, and I rode until I reached my home village. But when I got there . . ."

He took a sip from his own mug then, a long, slow sip, which told Xander it wasn't water in the little man's cup, but wine. That wasn't a big surprise.

"No one could see me. Or, more to the point, no one noticed me. The only way I could get anyone's attention would be if I grabbed their arm or physically contacted them and even then, they would soon lose interest as if I were simply a wall or other object to be avoided or bypassed. And it's been that way for years . . . gotten worse, really. I can't remember the last time I actually had a real conversation with anyone. Up until now."

He looked at Xander and smiled—a weak, forlorn smile.

And then he started crying again.

Xander didn't know what to say.

"That's . . . terrible," he managed.

"It is." Vreen sniffed. "It was."

"Was?"

"Yes." The little man smiled. "But now that you're here . . . all is well!"

He leaned forward and clapped Xander on the shoulder with his free hand. The stench was overwhelming.

"What exactly do you mean by that?" Xander asked.

"What do I mean?" Vreen laughed. "Come now. Don't joke with me. You have been sent by the Destiny. Is this not true?"

"Me? Sent by the Destiny?" That again? Xander shook his head. "I don't even believe in the Destiny."

"But . . . you can see me. How is that possible . . . ?"

"I don't know how it's possible," Xander said. "I'm not a channeler or anything. Maybe there are others who can see you, too. Believe me, there's nothing that special about me."

Vreen looked like he was about to cry.

"Look." Xander got to his feet. "I'm sorry for your curse. For your situation. If I could help you, I would. But right now, I have to get back to . . . this task I have. This mission."

"The Bane," Vreen said.

Xander's eyes almost popped out of his head.

"How do you know—?"

"The princess, and Jacob. They have been talking about it."

"What?"

"Yes. I have heard them speak on several occasions. He has convinced her to come with him, to travel with his army to the Keep and save finding the Bane for later."

"That's not possible," Xander said. "It can't be true."

"It is," Vreen said. "While they were dancing last night, he whispered to her—"

"They were *dancing*?"

"Yes. The prince ordered his musicians to—"

"Fine." Xander stood up. "She can do whatever she wants. Dance, eat, drink, make merry . . . I'm going to go find the Bane."

Vreen stood as well. "Let me gather my things. I will come with you."

Xander shook his head. "I appreciate the offer, but—"

"The Destiny sent you to me. I believe this. Even if you do not . . . you are a part of their plans."

"I don't think so," Xander said.

"Nonetheless, it is true."

"I don't want—"

"I can help you," Vreen said. "You'll see."

"How? Can you fight?" The little man's expression told him all Xander needed to know. "Look. Vreen. I'm going to get some supplies together, and go complete my mission. Even if Geni won't come with me, she should be safe enough with Jacob until she gets back to her father."

Vreen looked shocked. "You can't leave her here."

"Why not? She seems to be doing pretty well."

Dancing, he thought, picturing Geni and Jacob, arms wrapped around each other. Gazing into each other's eyes. Moving closer . . .

"She is in terrible danger," Vreen said.

"What?"

"The princess. She is in terrible danger."

"How so?"

"Jacob has been lying to her all along. Lying to all of you."

"Lying. What—"

"The Krax army," Vreen said, and he gestured toward the sea of tents behind them. The thousands upon thousands of soldiers and camp followers now bedded down for the night. "They aren't marching north to liberate the Keep. They're reinforcements."

"Reinforcements? What do you mean?" Xander asked, though as his eyes swept over the campground, as he thought back over the events of the last few days, he realized he knew exactly what Vreen meant, exactly what the little man was saying, and that realization caused a chill to run down his spine.

The Krax, blood traitors during the War of Magic, had betrayed the cause of mankind once more.

Jacob's armies had sided with the Fallen.

Chapter Forty-five

Mirdoth studied himself in the looking glass.

The hair at his temples looked gray no longer, but snow white. The circles under his eyes seemed darker, and deeper, the lines on his forehead more pronounced.

All his imagination, of course. It had to be. He had used his powers on but a handful of occasions. Twice, that first afternoon, when he had listened in to Talax's conversation with the Titan's unknown master, and then used a blocking charm to prevent Talax from learning of his suspicions regarding Avalan's circlet and its connection to the Bane. Twice more, the next day, when he'd tried in vain to overhear further conversations between the Titan and the mysterious figure on the green disc who was giving him directions.

And then last night. When he'd used the spell of masking to make himself unnoticeable to the guards outside the observatory, when he'd left his chambers, and gone walking through the Keep unobserved, past the ruined walls, and then out the yawning space where the great gate had stood to the Keeper's Wood. There Mirdoth had entered the gatehouse, where he had sat for hours, thinking about his life, the directions it had and had not taken. The things he had done, and those he had forsworn doing ever again.

He was only just now realizing how much he had missed the exercise of his own natural capabilities. No, not just natural ones: the capabilities he had studied, and practiced, and performed over and over again until they were part of him. The things he could do almost without thinking; he had forgotten, Mirdoth realized, who and what he truly was. The power he had. It was wrong not to use that power to its fullest extent, was it not? To deny himself—and the world—the benefits of those capabilities?

Did the hawk not soar, for fear of killing the snake?

Did the tiger forswear the hunt, for fear of injuring the ox?

No.

In his mind, the shards called to him.

Mirdoth, hearing their song, stepped back from the mirror and sighed.

He needed to drown out that song; he needed to occupy his mind with other thoughts. Lady Varraine. Her diary still lay on his desk, in the center of the observatory. He sat and flipped through its pages once more, seeking further reference to this Aphalan, who Mirdoth believed to be Avalan, or to the circlet, which he suspected was the Bane. He found nothing.

He returned that volume to his shelves and sought another. As he did so, his eyes caught a glimpse of something on the floor, sparkling in the light. He bent down and picked it up.

It was a piece of the shattered Elemscope. A piece of Curgen's glass. A large enough piece—the size of a small hand mirror—that Mirdoth pocketed it instantly, placing it within the inner compartment of his robe.

Morrigan had been fascinated by the glass, or so the Lady Varraine believed, had written in her diary. Had made it the centerpiece of many of his experiments, in fact.

"Counselor."

Mirdoth started.

He turned and saw the Urxen captain—the captain of the guard, Yanos—standing before him.

"I did not give you leave to enter my chamber," Mirdoth snapped.

"I didn't ask for it," Yanos said. "Just came here to bring you a little something."

"Bring me something? What . . . ?"

The words died on his lips.

Yanos stepped aside and two other guards stepped forward, carrying someone between them.

They hurled that someone into the chamber. That someone landed on the floor and groaned.

Mirdoth recognized that groan.

"My lord!" he said, kneeling down at Ambrose's side.

The man lifted his head off the floor and cracked one eye open.

"Mirdoth," he said, and smiled. "Fancy meeting you here."

"Clean him up," Yanos snapped. "Get him ready. Talax will be here in a minute."

Ambrose had been tortured.

It was what Mirdoth had feared, the entire time he was sitting safe in the observatory. It was a large part of the reason he had avoided trying to call on the Lord of the Keep in his cell.

While he hid what little information he had on the Bane from Talax, the Titan's minions were using any and all means at their disposal to pry loose whatever secrets Ambrose had regarding it.

"Amateurs," his lord said. They were in the bath chamber; Mirdoth had helped him out of the filthy robes he had been wearing, after which Ambrose had bathed quickly and changed. Mirdoth was now attending to a series of bruises on Ambrose's lower back and abdomen, where he'd been beaten.

"They hardly deserve the title. Torturers. At least compared to those we came across ten years ago—the brigands. The ones raiding the trade caravans. Remember?" Ambrose grimaced as Mirdoth pulled a bandage soaked in a healing draft tight around his body.

"I remember." How could he forget? It was those brigands—that group of Fallen—who'd killed Odona. Those had been the darkest days of his lord's life, Mirdoth thought. And his. At least up until now.

"What they did to Jarak," Ambrose said. "He was never the same man."

Mirdoth pulled Ambrose's shirt down over his body again; the Lord stood and took a deep breath.

"Thank you, old friend." Ambrose looked at Mirdoth. "They're not altogether unskilled, though. Obviously."

Mirdoth was puzzled.

"My lord?"

"What they did to you. The torturers."

"I don't understand."

"No need to play the fool with me, Mirdoth. Your eyes. Your hair." Ambrose gestured. "Some sort of spell they cast? Did the Titan himself interrogate you?"

"Yes. He did." Which was the truth; Mirdoth allowed his lord to infer the lie, that the interrogation was responsible for the physical changes Ambrose saw.

"You told him nothing, of course," Ambrose said.

"Of course."

"Of course. Nor I."

The two returned to the observatory; Mirdoth was searching for a way to tell Ambrose about the mysterious figure he'd seen three days ago, the figure who seemed to be in charge of the Titan, when Ambrose walked to the shelves and picked something up from them.

"Geni's necklace," he said.

"Yes." Mirdoth recognized it, too. "She must have taken it off, when she was helping me pack."

Ambrose turned it over in his hands and sighed.

"I wonder where she is. If she is safe. If . . ."

The door to the observatory swung open. Talax stepped through, followed an instant later by another. A man. Tall, thin, dark-skinned, with aquiline features. Mirdoth didn't recognize him at first. Not so Ambrose.

"Edmund." The Lord of the Keep sighed. "So. The Krax have sided once more with the enemies of our race."

"Ambrose." The man—Warden of Kraxis, its ruler for nearly two decades now—shook his head. "You still do not understand. Those you call 'Fallen'—they are our blood kin. Different on the outside yes, but inside—"

"The same as you and me. Gods, when will you tire of that speech, Edmund? I almost think you believe it now."

"As I almost think you have convinced yourself that your interests and those of the tyrant Galor align."

"Galor? A tyrant?" Ambrose let out a laugh. "Truly, Edmund—"

"Enough." Talax spoke for the first time. "I did not bring you all here to argue."

"Then why are we here?" Mirdoth asked. Even as he spoke, even as he drew the Titan's attention to him, Mirdoth was raising his guard. Closing the shields in his mind.

"Because I have need of you. Of information you possess, mage. You as well, Lord Ambrose," Talax said.

"I have told you all I know of the Bane," Mirdoth lied.

"Really?" the Titan replied, and in that instant Mirdoth felt the shields in his mind being probed. He resisted, just a little. Not too much; not enough to make the Titan suspicious. Just enough—he hoped—to make it seem as if the empty spaces Talax's probes encountered were the natural boundaries, the limits of Mirdoth's knowledge, and not gates guarding deeper realms within his mind.

"I find this difficult to believe," the Titan said. "Considering what Lord Edmund here has just told me. You, too, Lord Ambrose. You have lied to me as well."

"As I recall," Ambrose smiled, "I haven't even spoken to you."

"Gods, Ambrose." Edmund shook his head. "You would joke at your own funeral."

"Doubtful I'll be in any condition to do that," Ambrose said. "But if you'd like me to say a few things at yours—or perhaps even help arrange the event . . ."

"Enough," Talax snapped. "What does your daughter know about the Bane, Ambrose?"

The Lord's eyes widened in surprise. Mirdoth's widened as well.

"Geni?" Ambrose frowned. "She knows nothing. Why?"

"And now you lie to my face. Do you think me such a fool?" Talax took a step forward and raised his hand.

Before Mirdoth could do anything—before he could even think to draw on the power of the shards to somehow protect Ambrose—the Lord groaned, clutched his forehead in agony, and dropped to his knees.

"She is even now with the Krax army," Talax said. "With Edmund's son and heir. She has apparently traveled half the continent in search of the Bane. She knows where it is, Ambrose—does she not? Do you not, as well?"

The Lord growled, stifling a scream.

Mirdoth started forward—

And all of a sudden found himself flying through the air, in the entirely opposite direction. He reached out a hand to brace himself and heard bone snap as he smashed into the stone wall of the observatory.

"Where is it?" Talax asked. "What did that fool Tandis tell you?"

Ambrose said nothing, seeming to prevent himself from screaming.

Mirdoth gritted his teeth to keep from screaming himself. He looked down at his hand—his right hand—which dangled loosely from his arm. Beneath his skin, there was a bump visible. The break. The two halves of the bone.

He closed his eyes and concentrated.

The shards.

He felt the energy flowing from them; flowing to him. He directed that energy the length of his arm, toward the break. The bone began to knit.

"Make it easy on yourself, Ambrose," Edmund said. "You understand, don't you? It's not worth defending Galor. The old man's gone mad. You know that yourself. Mirdoth?"

Edmund looked across the room; Mirdoth managed to rearrange his features from an expression of concentration to one of (partially) feigned hurt.

"You know it as well," Edmund said. "The King is a tyrant. His commands are erratic, to say the least. He—"

Ambrose fell forward onto the floor, hitting it with a loud thump.

He lay there as if dead. Mirdoth tried to get to his feet and failed, which was when he realized that it wasn't just his arm he'd heard breaking earlier.

The back of his heel—his left one—there was something wrong there as well. It was a mass of seething agony.

He fell back on his rear and fought to keep tears from his eyes.

"This pain is nothing," Talax said. "Just a beginning. Keep that in mind for when I return. Edmund."

The Titan walked out of the room without waiting for a response; Edmund reached the door himself, then turned.

"Just a beginning," he said, and, smiling, left as well.

CHAPTER FORTY-SIX

Geni shook her head.

"Where does he get all these clothes?" she asked. "These gowns. And why does he travel with them?"

"I could not say, milady." The girl who had been dressing Geni tugged on a lace and stepped back herself. "This one fits you best of all, I think."

Geni eyed herself in the glass.

The dress did fit well. It was a pale yellow, not a color that she normally liked on herself. But with her hair put up like this; with her skin freshly scrubbed . . .

"Milady has a choice of perfumes as well." The girl bent to the trunk from which she had drawn the yellow dress—as well as the half-dozen others that Geni had tried on over the last few hours—and pulled forth a small wooden chest. She set the chest down on the bed. Gods, Geni thought, it was as high as her own back in the Keep, and at least as soft. The girl opened the chest and took out a small glass vial. She uncorked it and held it out.

"Here. Sniff."

Geni leaned forward and did.

The smell hit her nose like an avalanche of flowers—too much, too strong. She waved the vial away.

"You don't like it," the girl said.

"No. What is that?"

"Varasay. A flower that grows along the coast here—by the bay. It is a strong scent. Perhaps this will be more to your liking." The girl pulled out another vial. Geni sniffed again, more cautiously this time. Sniffed, and smiled.

"Plumerasol."

"Yes."

"Better." Much better. It was a familiar smell. It reminded her of home. Of her father, and Leeland. Lessons in the Keeper's Wood.

And Xander.

Thinking of him, she felt instantly contrite. Guilty for enjoying all these pleasures while he was out there somewhere. Probably shivering in the cold. Probably hungry. Maybe getting attacked by wild animals. Why, oh, why had he escaped? Why hadn't he done what she'd told him to, apologized for the theft and been done with it? Jacob was an understanding soul; he would have been done with the matter as well then. Instead . . .

"Shall I help you apply the scent?" the girl asked.

"No." Geni shook her head. "I'll do it myself. I'd like to be alone now, if you don't mind."

"As you wish, milady. I will see you at the meal."

"Yes. At the meal," Geni said. The meal meaning dinner—another multicourse banquet. Where she would have to put on the mask of a lady once more. The thought made her grimace, though she understood now how necessary protocol was, sometimes. Jacob had helped her see that protocol reinforced discipline; the men would not listen to him, would not obey his orders unless they feared the consequences. And they would not fear him if they did not know that his words were backed up by a thousand other men, ready and willing to obey his every command.

Geni understood all that, and yet . . .

She was still uncomfortable with it. Court protocol and the like. She supposed it was because Outpost was in so many ways such a backwater. There wasn't much of a court there. When the nobles from Athica came to visit her father, they brought their wives and daughters, who were all frankly astonished at how familiar Geni was with her servants. And her supposedly "lower-class" friends. Like Xander.

She sighed.

What was she going to do? What could she do? Talk to Jacob, perhaps. Perhaps he would agree to send out a small search party for Xander. Bring him back to the camp and at least get him food and shelter. Yes. That was a plan. Or at least the beginnings of one.

She chose a necklace from the chest and unstoppered the vial of perfume once more.

And almost gagged.

What on earth was that smell? It certainly wasn't plumerasol, and now that she sniffed the vial once more, she realized it wasn't even coming from there. It was coming from somewhere else in the tent, but where . . .

She turned toward the entrance, just as a hand pulled aside the flaps and Xander entered.

For a second Xander thought Vreen had the wrong tent.

He barely recognized Geni: the way her hair was done up; the dress she was wearing. Yes, she'd been wearing dresses those last few months at the Keep, but this was different. This was a gown. This was silk or something. A lot more fitted than any of the other dresses he'd seen her in. She looked like a princess.

He opened his mouth to say something, but no words would come out.

"Xander! What are you doing here?" She smiled, took a step toward him, and then stopped. "And what in the name of the Gods is that smell?"

"Didn't I tell you?" Vreen, standing next to him, looked up at Xander and nodded. "She can't see me at all."

"I see." Xander turned and tied the tent flaps shut.

"What are you doing?" Geni asked, taking a step forward, nearly running into Vreen. "Why . . . ?"

"We have to talk," Xander said.

"Where have you been? Why did you escape? Why—"

"The prince has been lying to you," Xander said.

"What?"

"The Krax aren't marching to liberate the Keep. They're allied with the Fallen."

Geni shook her head. "Xander . . ."

"It's true," he said. "We have to get out of here. Now. Grab whatever things you need and—"

"Wait a minute," Geni said. "Slow down. What makes you think the Krax aren't on our side?"

"Vreen," Xander said. "He told me."

"Vreen." Geni frowned. "Who's Vreen?"

"Him," Xander said, gesturing toward the little man at his side.

Geni's face fell.

"Oh, Xander." She shook her head sadly. "Why do you persist in—"

"I'm not making this up!" Xander said. "Jacob is on the side of the Fallen. They all are!"

"That's nonsense," Geni snapped. "Jacob hates the Fallen."

"So he says."

"It's the truth. He promised he'd show them no mercy when they took the Keep."

"Really? Has he told you what their battle plans are?" Xander asked. "What sort of strategy they have? How long a siege . . ."

"Specific strategy?" She shook her head. "No. Of course not."

"Of course not." Xander shook his head. "That's because they don't need any strategy. The Fallen are going to welcome them with open arms."

"So your invisible man says."

"That's right."

The two of them glared at each other.

"Excuse me—Xander?" Vreen said. "I have an idea."

"What?" Xander asked.

"What?" Geni asked.

"I'm not talking to you," Xander said. "I'm talking to him."

"Oh. Of course. Forgive me. Go right ahead. Talk to your invisible friend all you want. Don't mind me."

"I won't," Xander snapped. "What's your idea?" he asked Vreen.

"Put your hand on my shoulder," Vreen said.

Xander frowned. "Why?"

"It's not that I'm invisible," Vreen said. "It's just that . . . she doesn't notice me. If she can't help but notice me . . ."

Xander nodded. He understood what Vreen was driving at. He wasn't sure it was going to work, but they needed to find some way to convince Geni of the danger she was in.

He stepped behind Vreen and put a hand on each of the little man's shoulders.

Geni's eyes widened, and she screamed.

"Gods!" She pointed at Vreen. "Where did he come from? How—"

"Shhh!" Xander said. "Do you want to draw the guards in?"

Geni shook her head. She was still staring at Vreen.

"This is him," she said. "The invisible man."

"That's right," Xander said.

"Vreen," the little man said. "I'm Vreen. Pleased to meet you, Princess."

He held out a hand for Geni to shake, at the same instant taking a step forward. Xander's hands lifted from his shoulders.

"Ahhh!" Geni said, taking a step back. "Where did he go?"

"Nowhere," Xander said, and explained about the little man's curse. When he finished, Geni nodded thoughtfully.

"The spell of masking, it sounds like," she said.

"You know what it is?" Vreen asked. "You know what the curse is?"

"So you weren't lying after all," Geni said, turning to Xander, ignoring Vreen's question, because she could no longer see him.

"No," Xander said.

Geni sighed heavily. "I owe you an apology."

"Indeed you do."

"Wait a minute? Spell of masking?" Vreen grabbed hold of Xander's hand and placed it on his shoulder, moving in between him and Geni.

"Stop doing that!" Geni said, eyes widening, taking a sudden step backward.

"Sorry. But spell of masking?"

"I think so. I'm no expert, but from what Mirdoth told me—"

"You see?" Vreen turned to Xander, smiling. "I told you the Destiny sent you to me. You cannot deny their influence."

"Of course he can," Geni said. "Xander doesn't believe in the Destiny."

"That stuff's not important right now," Xander said. "What is important is getting out of here. Getting back to our mission."

"Yes," Vreen said. "You must find the Bane."

Geni turned to Xander, looking furious. "You told him about the Bane?"

"No. He overheard you telling Jacob about it."

"Well, I had to tell Jacob," Geni said. "I had to tell him why we're here, didn't I?"

"I suppose so," Xander said. "I suppose you had to tell him a lot of things, when the two of you were dancing."

"How did you know that we were dance—" She turned to Vreen. "You've been spying on me. Haven't you?"

"Heh. Well . . ." Vreen lifted Xander's hand off his shoulder and took a step backward.

"Don't run away from me!" Geni snapped.

"Don't yell at him," Xander said.

"He was spying on me!"

"You were consorting with the enemy!" Xander snapped.

"Consorting?" Geni's eyes widened. "Just what do you mean by that?"

Xander flushed. "Nothing. It doesn't matter. The point is—"

"Just because you were telling the truth about him"—she gestured toward Vreen—"doesn't mean I believe a word of what you're saying about Jacob!"

Xander was about to respond when a voice came from behind him.

"Someone mention my name?"

He turned and saw Jacob walk into the tent, followed an instant later by two guards.

The prince looked at Geni, then at Xander, and smiled. A smile with no warmth in it whatsoever.

"Ah," Jacob said. "The prodigal son returns."

CHAPTER FORTY-SEVEN

It turned out it hadn't been her scream that had brought the prince to her tent, as Geni feared.

No, Jacob showing up at that particular instant had nothing to do with her at all, as it turned out. It was Nym, apparently. The Sion had killed a guard in his own attempt to escape. Now they were going to try him for the crime.

They were also, it seemed, going to try Xander at the same time.

"It was just a necklace," Geni said to Jacob as the two of them walked together to witness the trial. "Surely there doesn't need to be a trial for a simple theft? Particularly since I don't even want to press charges?"

"You're right," Jacob said. "Normally we wouldn't need a trial. But there are complicating factors here."

"Such as . . . ?"

Jacob turned to her and smiled.

He was dressed for dinner as well. A long velvet cloak. A white laced shirt. Boots of shiny black leather. His hair had been styled as well; it sat high and magnificent on his head. He was altogether the most handsome boy—man—Geni had ever seen in her life.

She tried not to think about what Xander had said. *He's lying. The Krax are on the side of the Fallen.*

"We're at war, Princess," he said. "Protocol must be followed. On top of which . . . there is the gift giver's feelings to consider."

"The gift giver."

"Captain Adelson. The necklace was a family heirloom. Even though it has been returned . . ."

"I suppose," she said, sighing.

Jacob stopped walking.

"Something is wrong," he said. "What?"

She shook her head. "Nothing," she lied. "It's just . . . Xander . . . he's not a criminal."

"I know you are old friends. But clearly the boy's brains are addled. An invisible thief?" Jacob laughed. "We have been over this, haven't we?"

"Yes." Geni forced herself to smile as well. "We have."

Only she knew Xander hadn't been lying about Vreen. And if he hadn't been lying about Vreen . . .

"Come," he said, and held out his arm. "We shall deal with this unpleasantness, and then eat."

She circled her arm through his and they continued on their way. They soon arrived at a large clearing in the middle of the camp. A wooden table and chairs had been brought forward, at which now sat a tribunal of men: three military officers, all older—her father's age, perhaps. Two rows of chairs had been set up on either side of the table as well; the gathered crowd parted then to allow her and Jacob access to two seats in the front. When they had assumed their places, the prince gave a nod to the officer seated in the middle chair, who cleared his throat and spoke.

"This tribunal is now in session."

"Magister-General Hald," Jacob said, leaning over and whispering in her ear. "He is a very fair man."

Geni nodded. The prince's words gave her little comfort.

Fair? None of this was fair. She had half a mind to tell Jacob that Vreen was real; only she couldn't exactly prove it at the moment, could she? Besides which . . .

He's lying to you.

She wasn't sure that what Jacob had in mind here was justice.

"Bring the prisoners forward!" Hald said, and opposite the table there was a flurry of movement. A second later, a handful of guards appeared. Two handfuls, actually—one group gathered around Nym, another around Xander.

Geni gasped to see them; their condition. They'd been badly beaten. Nym in particular looked as if he'd been abused. There was bruising all about his face.

"Look at them," she said. "What happened? How—"

"Barbarians," Jacob said, and Geni turned and saw a look of anger on his face to match hers. "I will see whoever did this dealt with."

"Good," Geni said, getting to her feet. "Let's—"

"Not now," Jacob said, putting a hand on the sleeve of her gown. "After. We must not interrupt the magistrate during the reading of charges."

Geni frowned and sat down.

She liked this—the trial—less and less.

Two large stakes the size and thickness of a jousting lance had been driven into the ground about a dozen feet apart.

Xander and Nym were each fastened to one.

Hald cleared his throat.

"This tribunal is assembled to consider the charges against you, Xander of Outpost, and you, the Sion Nym. Thievery, and fleeing the Ward's Justice, in the first case. Murder, and espionage in a time of war, in the second. How plead you to these charges? You first," Hald said, gesturing to Xander.

"I am not guilty," Xander said. "Of either."

"Hmmmff." Jacob snorted under his breath. "That won't go over well."

"What?" Geni asked, turning to him.

"Pleading not guilty to fleeing, when he obviously did. Hald and the others won't like that."

"Well, what's he supposed to do, if he's innocent?"

"Innocent?" Jacob turned to her with an amused expression on his face. "Now you believe in the invisible man as well?"

She didn't know what to say to that.

"Guilty of the one," Nym said. "Murder. Which I enjoyed quite a bit. So much that I'm thinking about doing it again. Your Highness."

The Sion met Jacob's eyes then. Geni could sense the prince, next to her, tensing up.

"Jokes do not serve your cause, Sion. You would do well to keep that in mind. We"—Hald turned first toward his right, and then his left, to the men on either side of him—"will now consider the charges."

"What?" Geni said.

"Wait a second," Xander said. "Don't I get to offer a defense or anything?"

"This is a military tribunal, boy. The tribunal considers the evidence."

"But you haven't heard any evidence!"

"Quiet." A soldier stepped up alongside Xander and jabbed him in the belly with a spear.

"No," Geni exclaimed. "They can't—"

Jacob raised a hand and the soldier stepped back.

"This isn't right," Geni said.

"It is the law, unfortunately," Jacob said. "In times of war, the military tribunal must make its own decisions. For the good of the people."

He looked, to Geni's eye, a little frantic. She felt just the same way.

This wasn't going well at all.

The guard raised a spear again; Xander quieted down.

"Nym, Sion of Magnar," Hald said abruptly. "The tribunal has reached a decision in your case."

"Already?" Geni said. "How is that possible?"

"Shhh," Jacob said, turning to her. "Please."

Geni glared at him. He was concerned with protocol—at a time like this?

"We find you guilty of conspiring against the realm of Kraxis, and guilty of the charge of murder," Hald said. "We sentence you to execution, such sentence to be carried out immediately."

"Surprise, surprise," Nym said, his eyes traveling slowly across the table where his three accusers sat. "Guilty. I never would have thought it."

"Shut up, you," the same guard who had jabbed Xander said, stepping toward Nym with his spear. "The magistrate—"

Nym growled low in his throat, and all at once leapt toward the guard. Or tried to, anyway. The ropes held him back.

The guard stumbled backward and almost fell.

The crowd snickered.

Hald cleared his throat and spoke again.

"Xander of the village of Outpost. You have been accused of unlawful flight from the Ward's Justice, and theft of a noble's property. We find you guilty as well."

"Now would be a good time!" Xander said to seemingly no one.

"In determining appropriate punishment, this tribunal has taken into account the gravity of the charges against you, as well as the conditions under which the crimes took place. A time of war. A time when every second taken away from our country's focus on these critical affairs is wasted time; a time when every second can mean the difference between life and death. Accordingly . . ."

"No," Geni whispered, because she knew, somehow, what Hald was going to say, even before he said it. "No. This can't be."

"Death," the magistrate-general pronounced. "Such sentence

to be carried out immediately, concurrent with the Sion's pronounced punishment."

"You have to stop them," Geni said, turning to Jacob. "They can't—"

"Geni." Jacob leaned closer to her; Gods, he was wearing perfume, wasn't he? "I wish there was something I could do, Princess, but the magistrate is entirely correct. The Kingdom is at war; the laws of war must apply."

Geni was too shocked to even respond.

"I am sorry," Jacob said. "But my hands are tied."

She didn't even know what to say to that: his hands were tied? No. It was Xander's hands that were tied.

She stood up.

"I demand a trial," she said, looking toward Hald.

The magistrate shook his head. "This boy is without standing. No family name. He has no rights."

"All have rights," Geni said. "It's the basic law of the land."

"Your land, perhaps," Jacob said. "But this is not Outpost. It is Kraxis. And here our laws apply."

Guards roughly unbound Xander from the stake. His hands were still tied behind his back in rope cuffs. To his left, Nym was in much the same condition except that his feet were similarly tied in rope cuffs to prevent him from using his remarkable ability.

"Take them outside the camp," Hald said. "Summon the executioner."

Geni glared at Jacob.

"If you do this, Jacob, you end any chance of alliance with our people."

"Alliance?" He looked at her strangely—almost as if he had no idea what she was talking about.

And then she realized that he didn't.

Xander was right.

There was no alliance. There never had been.

"Blood-traitor," she said, and slapped Jacob across the face.

His face twisted into an ugly sneer. And then, without warning, he slapped her. A backhand blow much harder than the one she'd given him. It spun her around and sent her hurtling to the ground.

She landed hard and felt the sleeve of her gown tear.

She stood up and ripped it the rest of the way off.

"You want a fight?" she said, and took a step forward toward Jacob.

Behind her, she sensed a guard moving to block her way toward the prince.

And then she sensed someone else moving as well.

For Xander, time seemed to stop, just the way it had back at Outpost, when he'd turned and seen the arrow heading for Tandis.

He saw Geni starting to fall, her mouth bleeding from the prince's cowardly blow.

He saw Jacob sneering even as he pulled back his arm from his strike.

He saw the guard next to him taking out his sword, its sharp, jagged blade gleaming in the sunlight.

And in that frozen instant, Xander saw a way out for him, and the others.

In a single fluid motion, he twirled around, moving his hands just so, so that the blade of the distracted guard's sword cut through the rope that bound him. The rope snapped and fell to the ground.

Xander's hands were free.

He stepped forward and ripped the soldier's sword from his grasp. Now the man moved, turning in surprise, but Xander was already past him, running toward Nym. The Sion, out of all of them, was the fastest to react to Xander's movements. He twisted himself away, spinning himself around on the pole, so that by the time Xander reached him, the ropes binding Nym's hands and feet were facing Xander, who cut through them with a single stroke each. In an instant he was free as well.

Nym moved as if he'd been shot out of a cannon, bolting forward and leaping onto one of Jacob's guards, leaping high in the air, landing, grabbing hold of the man's neck as he did so, and—with an audible *crack!*—snapping it.

He pulled the guard's sword free and raised it just as the other guards surrounding the prince attacked him.

Xander lunged onto the long wooden table that the tribunal had sat at and without a pause kicked Hald, who was drawing an ax of his own, in the face with his boot.

Xander was stalking Jacob, who had taken a step backward. Coward, Xander thought, as the prince's guards moved forward to block his way.

They were on the attack for the moment, Xander thought, but the moment wouldn't last. They were outnumbered by a dozen to one here in this small clearing alone—and once the wider army got involved . . .

"Gods," Hald said at that moment, looking up at Xander in fear. No, not up. He was looking over Xander's shoulder. Xander turned and looked, too.

And smiled.

The odds had just gotten a little bit better. No, a lot better.

Here was Vreen, at last.

And here, too, was the golem.

The creature moved toward Geni.

"Leeland," she said. "Kill him."

She pointed toward Jacob, who stumbled backward, eyes wide.

"Kill him," she said, and the golem started forward.

"No," Xander said. "Leave him, Geni. We have to go."

"Go?" Her eyes widened in surprise. "But—"

"We have to concentrate on what's important," he said. "The Bane."

"The Bane." She nodded reluctantly. "You're right."

They formed up behind the golem then, the four of them, and began fighting their way toward the mountains—and the underground city of Calebethon—once more.

CHAPTER FORTY-EIGHT

"A direct order?" Tandis said.

The captain was propped up in his bed, sipping tea from a cup on the tray in front of him: a breakfast tray on his lap, filled to overflowing with food. Eggs, meat, biscuits . . .

Tandis hadn't touched any of it, Calis noticed.

"Aye, sir. A direct order. That's what the baron said." Hildros stood at the right-hand side of the bed; Ty leaned against the windowsill behind him, keeping watch on the street outside. Calis stood on the other side of the captain, between Tandis's bed and the door. Nothing—no one—not Fallen, man, or sorcerer's trick, would get to his commander without going through him first.

This was the first day the three of them had had a chance to speak to the captain regarding their meeting with Baron Mancer. Calis had expected Tandis to rage at the news of Mancer's refusal to honor their agreement—or at least have some kind of strong reaction.

The captain, though, had simply nodded when informed of the baron's decision. Almost as if he'd been expecting it somehow.

"I don't understand the King's thinking, sir. Truly I don't,"

Hildros continued. "If he knows the importance of holding on to the Keep . . ."

"He does," Tandis replied, picking up the cup. He took a sip from it.

"Well, then . . ."

"The King has his reasons, I'm sure."

"Sure wish I knew what they were," Hildros said.

"I have my suspicions. Nothing definite, however."

Tandis set down his tea. Calis had the sense that he knew more than he was saying at the moment.

"Here. The thing is, we could hire mercenaries, sir. If we had access to the Knights' accounts, wouldn't be much trouble at all. Not here in Minoch. They have mercenaries to spare. Contractors. Mind if I . . ." Ty leaned forward and reached for one of the sausages on Tandis's plate.

Hildros slapped his hand out of the way.

"Enough of that," the old warrior said.

"What?" Ty asked.

"That food's for the captain, Ty. Help him gather his strength."

"I thank you for your concern, Hildros. But I'm not hungry yet. Ty, you may . . ."

The little man snatched up the sausage and shoved it into his mouth.

"Not bad," Ty said. "Not bad at all. Got a taste of something Gildish in there—one of them exotic spices. Good stuff, sir. You ought to try one."

"Perhaps I will," Tandis said, in a way that Calis knew meant "no."

"You have to eat something, Captain," Calis said then. "Doctor says you haven't had food at all these last few days."

"The doctor exaggerates. I have eaten, never fear. I am just not hungry at the moment. And this news from Mancer does not help my appetite at all. Not in the slightest."

"So what are we going to do, sir?" Hildros asked.

"We could send a messenger," Calis suggested. "A fast rider could reach Athica in a little more than a week."

"In the fall maybe. Not this time of year." Hildros shook his head. "The spring melt. The Gandru'll be swollen up something fierce. Some of the bridges will be down."

"They'll all be down," Ty said. "Three weeks, at best." He reached for another piece of the sausage; Hildros slapped his hand away.

"Hey!" Ty glared. "The captain said he wasn't hungry."

"Leave something in case he changes his mind, hey?" Hildros said.

"A messenger." Tandis spoke, looking directly at Calis as he did so. "To what end?"

"Well. All due respect, sir—to the King and yourself—Galor's half the world away. He can't know the situation at the Keep—everything that you do. If you were to write a letter to him, he might change his mind."

Tandis nodded; so did Hildros. "He might at that," the captain said.

"Sound thinking, lad," Hildros chimed in.

"A letter can't make an argument, though," Tandis said. "Better to send someone in person."

"A messenger. Like the lad said." Ty gestured toward Calis.

Tandis nodded. "Actually, I was thinking three messengers."

Silence greeted his words.

Calis was the first to break it.

"Us, you mean."

"Exactly." Tandis nodded. "I would go myself, but I am as yet not well enough to travel. And Galor knows the three of you well. Trusts you."

"Hmmm," Hildros said.

"Would be nice to see Athica again. This time of year." Ty grabbed one of the biscuits and popped it into his mouth.

"Weather warming up. Merchants'll be in, looking to load up cargo. The ladies will be in their spring finery . . ."

"It's a mission, you," Hildros said. "Not a vacation."

"Galor doesn't know me, sir," Calis said. "I'll stay here."

"Here?" Tandis frowned.

"Aye. Someone needs to guard you, Captain," Hildros chimed in.

"I don't think so," Tandis said.

"The Fallen are across the bridge, sir. They're here, in the West, and they have it in for you, Gods know why. So as long as you're not capable of defending yourself . . ."

"Very well." Tandis nodded. "Ty."

The little man's eyes practically bulged out of his head. "What?"

"Ty," Tandis said. "You'll stay here. On guard."

"Why not him?" Ty asked, pointing to Calis.

"The boy needs seasoning. No offense, lad," the captain said. "If I need a guard, I want the most experienced possible."

Ty's chest swelled a little; Calis tried not to let the hurt he felt at that instant show.

"I'll want to talk with you, Hildros. About the arguments to make to the King."

"Aye, sir."

"And I'll write something as well. A letter. For Galor's eyes only."

"Very good." Hildros turned. "Boy, you'll purchase supplies for the two of us. A week's worth. We'll restock in Ruvenna."

"Yes, sir," Calis said. "I'll tend to that now."

Without waiting for another word—with Tandis's words ringing in his ears—he turned on his heel and left the room.

Calis spent the afternoon securing supplies for the journey; he made it a point to frequent the more run-down trading houses, the less-reputable general stores. *The boy needs seasoning.* As he made his purchases, he snuck in questions designed to help him track down the captain's would-be assassin. His plan was to show up at Tandis's door with the creature who'd tried to kill the knight firmly in hand. That would show just how much seasoning he had, Calis thought.

But his search was fruitless. The Fallen might have come across the bridge, they might even have entered Minoch, but no one had the slightest clue where they were.

Night fell, and Calis returned to the tavern to pack the stores for their trip. It was not a long process; the supplies had been packaged by the merchants; he had bought a single change of clothes for himself and saddlebags to carry them in. He had just finished cinching up the last of them when someone knocked on his door.

"Come," he called out, turning as a figure stepped inside his room.

His eyes widened as he saw who it was.

"Captain!"

"Shhh." Tandis entered and eased the door shut behind him. The captain wore a robe that lay open to the chest. His color was still wrong; too pale by far. His hair was matted down and stuck to his forehead by sweat.

Calis's anger softened.

"Sir. You're not well enough to be walking. Your injuries . . ."

Calis's voice trailed off as Tandis stepped forward into the light shed by the room's half-dozen candles. The wound on the captain's chest—a gash with scar tissue the size of Calis's palm this morning, surrounded by a bruise in varying shades of purple and blue—had shrunk by half. Had closed to a single line of pinkish-red skin. It hardly seemed possible. And yet . . .

"I need to speak with you," Tandis said, and sat down on the bed.

"Yes, sir."

"I spoke harshly this morning, Calis. Forgive me."

"Sir?"

"If ever I thought you needed seasoning, what happened at Imli's Swamp has taught me different. You are all that a knight should be."

Calis felt himself flush. "Thank you, sir. But then why—"

"You needed to make this trip, that is why."

"I don't understand."

"The King has ruled now for hundreds of years, Calis. He is as close to immortal as a man can be."

"Yes, sir."

"He wants to rule forever."

"I still don't—"

"It is magic that has kept him alive; kept him on the throne all this time. His ability to access the power trapped in the shards. He is the most powerful channeler of this age."

"Yes, sir," Calis said. "I see."

"Do you?" Tandis asked, staring up at him. Waiting for something.

And all at once, Calis realized what.

The captain's words on the beach—the words Tandis had spoken to him the night they had landed on the western continent—came rushing back to him.

There are those who would regard your very existence—the presence of another channeler in the world—as a threat.

"Me?" Calis croaked out. "Captain, are you saying that Galor is worried—"

"Galor is consumed by fear. These past few years . . ." Tandis shook his head. "The King is a changed man. He fears you. He fears me. He fears the Bane, and what Talax may do with it. That fear is making him act rashly. We must show him that there is no cause for fear. That he has no reason to doubt you, or your loyalty to the Kingdom."

"Gods," Calis said, and sat down on the bed. "Gods."

It was all he could think to say. His mind raced; the King, threatened by him? But he had just discovered his powers. For all he knew, he wasn't even a true channeler. For all he knew . . .

"You have to go to Athica," Tandis said. "See Galor. Convince him to trust you. To retake the Keep. Do whatever you must do to prove your loyalty, Calis—swear to me that you will do it."

"Whatever he asks me to do? I don't understand. What—"

"Just swear it, boy," Tandis said. "Swear it to me now."

Tandis grabbed his wrist and pulled him close.

In that instant, the captain looked barely mortal.

"Yes," Calis said. "Yes. I swear."

CHAPTER FORTY-NINE

None came to help them. Not to see to their wounds, nor to bring them food, or water.

Mirdoth healed himself, and then Ambrose as best he could; the wounds of the body, at least. He did not know what to do with his lord's mind, which was a tangle of chaotic thoughts and impulses, none of which he could read. Mirdoth decided to leave things as they were, for the moment; when Ambrose regained consciousness—if Ambrose regained consciousness—he would see what help he could render.

In the meantime . . .

Geni. On the track of the Bane. Mirdoth did not know what to think; the girl was brave, of that there was no doubt. But if he was right, if it resided where he thought it did . . .

Gods. Mirdoth himself would have second thoughts about entering the Patricide's domain. What had been his laboratories. All manner of creatures were rumored to have lived there once. Perhaps they lived there still.

Mirdoth waited for hours, hoping that someone would come to bring food, or water. No one did.

As the dark gathered, he cast the spell of masking on himself, and went to leave the room. He found that he could not; the way was blocked. There was an enchantment on the door; an enchantment of a kind that he could not lift, not without expending so much of his energy that he would surely draw Talax's attention.

He yelled and yelled for water, for food. None came.

Mirdoth had moved Ambrose to the sleeping chamber; the Lord lay on the bed, tossing and turning. His lips grew dry, and cracked, and bled. Mirdoth found a healing balm and applied it.

He fell asleep on the floor, next to his lord. He dreamt of Ithul, his birthplace. Where he had first come to knowledge of magic. And of himself, his own true nature. Where he had first killed. Where he had become something other than himself.

In his dream, he relived those moments. The exultation; the horror. The death, and the destruction. The fall of the Three Kingdoms; the rise of the Black Sorcerer. He pictured the dread mage in his mind, and shuddered, forcing himself awake.

Talax stood over him.

"The girl has escaped."

Mirdoth blinked, and rose unsteadily to his feet.

"What?"

The Titan took another step forward. "The girl has escaped from the Krax. Resumed her quest. Where is she headed, mage? Tell me. Show me."

Even as Talax finished speaking, Mirdoth felt the Titan's presence in his mind; he threw up images then to deflect him. Geni taking lessons from the ladies of the court in etiquette; Geni bursting in on her father, the night the Keep fell. Geni standing next to him as he showed her the Elemscope.

Talax hammered at his defenses; Mirdoth gritted his teeth to keep from crying out in pain.

"I don't know where she's gone," he managed to say. "There's nothing—"

A fire exploded behind his eyes. He screamed, straining to maintain the shields in his mind. Everything went black.

When he looked up, the Titan was standing over him again. In his hand, he held something. A thing that sparkled, and danced, in the candlelight.

Geni's necklace.

"Something of hers." Talax was smiling now as well. "Recently touched. Something of great personal value. Personal meaning. I need not know where she is going now to find her. Thank you, mage."

The Titan raised his arms; a second later the air in front of him began to swirl, and waver, and twist about.

A death-vortex. A death-spell; the demise of any and all who touched it. Mirdoth remembered the enchantment all too well.

He was too weak to counter it.

The whirlpool in the air grew to twice its original size, and then doubled in extent again. It began to move toward him and Ambrose.

Mirdoth stepped forward, into the enchantment's path. Perhaps if he could stand within it long enough, he could somehow—

The vortex roared and leapt forward. Mirdoth braced himself.

Everything went black for a second. He felt himself being wrenched this way and that; felt as if he might almost rip in half.

And then the light returned.

Mirdoth blinked.

He was kneeling; Ambrose was lying next to him, on a hard stone floor, stained with blood.

The dungeons, he realized. He and the Lord were imprisoned in the dungeons beneath the Keep once more.

"I like you here better." Talax's face appeared in the barred window of their cell door. "Where if I need you, I can find you. And if I don't need you . . ."

The Titan's eyes glittered with malice.

"Then nothing more need be done."

A steel plate slid down over the bars then, and Talax's face disappeared. Leaving Mirdoth—and a still-insensate Ambrose—alone in the dark.

CHAPTER FIFTY

The third day since their escape was the day the meager supplies Vreen had gathered for them ran out. Forced again into eating Hutin, they continued to follow the underground river, within Calebethon.

That river had begun to make a sharp turn to the east, much to the distress of Geni and Xander, who were conscious that they were moving farther away from the Henge.

Nym advocated continuing to follow the path, but Geni and Xander were inclined to find a new course. The debate would have remained deadlocked except that Xander found a narrow, dark passage that smelled of fresh air. The passage headed north. Leading the way, Xander urged the company forward.

A few hundred yards on, they emerged into sunlight. Not so much of a shock this time as it had been the last, when they'd left the dim blue world of Calebethon for the bright yellow one of the outside world. In front of them was a lush green valley; a gentle breeze cooled the heat from the blazing sun above. Another hidden world, this one in the high mountain passes of the Spine.

The damp, cool passages beneath the Imperial Spine had chilled Xander's bones during their escape from Kraxis; he stood in the sun for a moment, warming up, thinking of that escape once more, and the journey that had followed. A hurried, rushed thing at first, an uneventful, silent passage these last few days.

Silent, that is, except for Vreen, who had spent so many years with no one to talk to that—it seemed to Xander, at least—he wouldn't shut up at all now. And since Xander was the only one who could actually hear him, he'd had to endure all the little man's talk.

The stories were endless. I'm not just a robber, I'm an inventor. My brother stole my birthright, stole all the money our parents had left us, that's why I became a robber, but truly, I should have been a craftsman, a woodworker, that was always my desire, though I lost the tip of my little finger in an accident—well, a robbery gone bad—and so no one would hire me to be a tinkerer, and on, and on, and on, until Xander thought he would scream.

He tried on several occasions to engage Geni in the conversation—or rather, Vreen's monologue, going so far as to walk alongside the man with his hand on his shoulder so she could see him—but she was, by and large, unresponsive. Xander guessed she was struggling still with a lot of things—how she hadn't believed him, for one. How she'd fallen for Jacob's lies, for another. How the vast Krax army was moving not to help her father, but to seal his fate, and that of Outpost.

They used the sun to gauge their course and their progress through the valley. Hours passed as they descended deeper into the cleft between the mountains. The sparse vegetation thickened, became a kind of prairie grass. Endless fields of it, dotting the mountainside all the way down to the valley floor, broken up here and there by stands of isolated trees.

They stopped to eat beneath one of those stands; an hour afterward they reached the valley floor. Almost at once, Nym—leading the way once more—raised a hand.

"Someone or something lives here."

The Sion was pointing to a well-worn path in the thick grasses ahead of them. The path led into a large grove of short, stout trees. They looked like nothing Xander had ever seen before.

"What are those?" he asked.

"Some kind of fruit tree," Geni replied, pointing to the large pods growing among the thick, long leaves. "It doesn't look like the fruit's ripe enough to eat yet, though."

They continued forward, a little more cautiously now. The grasses disappeared; the forest around them thickened. Intermixed with the short, stout trees now was a handful of much taller ones that towered into the skies. Xander had never seen anything like them, either; the colors were all wrong. The trunks were a deeper orange, the leaves a green shading toward blue.

"These," Nym said all at once, walking to the trunk of one and touching it. "Can it be . . ."

"What?" Xander asked.

The Sion turned to him.

"My Uleri—my brood keeper—told me of them. They are called Hilada. The Titans brought them to Elemental. They thrived here once, all over the world. As did other beasts and plants she spoke of."

The Sion turned and smiled, showing small, pointed teeth that suddenly seemed too large for his mouth. Which itself suddenly seemed too large for his head.

"You don't sense it?"

"Sense what?" Xander asked.

"The magic," he said. "It's thick here."

"I have no idea what you're talking about," Xander said.

"I do." Vreen came up alongside him. "It feels as if I'm . . . tingling all over. The witch's enchantment . . ."

He waved an arm in front of his face; Xander's eyes widened.

The arm was barely visible; it was transparent. Through it Xander could see the trees and the forest.

Vreen himself was transparent as well.

"I feel it, too," Geni said. "It's like . . . the way things should be."

"Perhaps it is how they were," Nym said. "How all of Elemental once was, before the Titans stole the magic of our world."

"There's magic in everything," Geni said. "At least, there's supposed to be."

Xander thought about that.

If this was truly how the world had once been, how it was supposed to be, as Geni put it . . .

He'd never felt anything at all toward the Titans, up until when Talax took the Keep. Never really even thought about them, or the Destiny, or any of those things. He'd only seen the Hiergamenon once, only gone to temple to deliver messages. Those things didn't concern him; they didn't impact his life at all. Or so he'd thought. But now . . .

He began to feel just a touch of resentment toward the Titans. If what Geni and Nym were talking about was true, the Titans had changed the course of the world's history.

Not that he believed anything at all the Sion said.

They moved on, deeper into the valley. As they walked, the shadows around them lengthened; the way grew darker. A combination of thickening foliage and setting sun. In the forest canopy, high above, he caught glimpses of things jumping through the air, from one branch to another. They were too far off for him to make out any details about the creatures. Were they wild animals? Thinking beasts? From this distance, he had no way of knowing.

Nym suddenly halted once more. "Up ahead," he said. "Through the trees."

He pointed; Xander squinted and peered through the bushes.

What he saw filled Xander with dread.

There was a clearing; not a natural clearing, though.

Where flattened earth was now visible had once been the location of a village. A primitive village; the structures had been constructed from straw and the giant leaves of the strange trees.

Nothing remained standing now, though. It was as if a giant storm had torn through the settlement and ripped each home from the ground one by one, turned them over, and scattered their contents to the wind.

"What could have done this?" Geni asked.

No one answered. Xander saw no signs of actual combat. There were no bodies. No blood. The sight filled him with foreboding; whatever had done this might still be around.

He looked up at the sky. They had, by his guess, another hour or so of light.

"We should find a safe place for the night."

The others were quick to agree.

They gathered some of the scattered straw and giant leaves. They moved off the path, trampled a clearing of sorts of their own in the giant grass, and made a primitive camp. Geni charged the golem to keep watch.

As the sun went down, they got first one surprise, and then another.

The giant trees—the Hilada—began to glow. With the same pale blue light that had illuminated their way through the tunnels of the Spine, and Calebethon.

And then the wisps came out.

They danced and skittered about through the trees; Xander looked at them and was reminded of that first time he'd seen them. When he and Geni had first entered the caverns. Before the dragon, before the golem, before Nym or Vreen or Jacob or any of this. When it was just the two of them, struggling to survive.

That day—that time they'd spent together—seemed a long, long way off.

He rolled over in his makeshift bed and settled into an uneasy, dream-filled slumber.

* * *

Nym woke after a scant few hours of sleep, still restless. Full of energy.

He quickened himself and entered the forest. He killed the first half-dozen creatures he came across: three Hutins and a handful of other beasts of the same size he didn't recognize. He found a clearing, made a fire, and ate them all, one after another. Sated, he looked back up the slope and in the light of the moon, saw the very path by which they'd entered the valley. He had half a mind to run back to the Keep this instant, and report in to Talax. He felt he could get there and back before morning. Maybe. The Keep was far away now. This place had recharged him; he felt stronger here, more alive, more full of energy than he had in weeks. Months, even, since leaving Magnar for the north. He felt as if he could run for days on end, without the need for sleep.

Of course that was a ridiculous idea. The second he stepped out of the valley his speed would slacken; he would feel the aches and pains and bruises and burns the Krax had inflicted on him all over again.

No, his task here and now remained the same. Follow the girl. Find the Bane. Bring it to Talax. Was he forgetting anything?

Yes.

Kill them afterward.

A branch snapped. Nym started, and turned, just as the princess stepped out of the shadows behind him.

"Grayskin," she said, which was when he realized it wasn't Geni after all. It was a female, yes, but one he had never seen before. A child of man? No. Nym could sense the subtle influence of the Titans on her. She looked like a child of man, but different than Xander, and the girl. Slimmer; taller. Darker skin, with patterns and swirls that had either been tattooed or painted on. Or perhaps they were natural; in the dark, it was hard to tell.

Some of those patterns were actually glowing. A light blue glow, like the one coming from the trees. Striking-looking creature.

"Who are you?" he asked.

"I am Balu'thia. Of the Iru. I have been chosen to meet you, Grayskin."

"My name is Nym. What do you mean, 'chosen to meet me'?"

"The Pyat has sent me to welcome you to our valley. To invite you and your companions to our village."

Nym, who'd been wondering whether to kill the girl, reconsidered. Village meant fresh food. Village meant clothing, and shelter.

"We would be honored," he said, bowing in return. "Please. Follow me."

It was still dark when he and the girl reached their makeshift camp; the golem stood exactly where Nym had left it; it didn't look like it had moved an inch. Its head swiveled to follow Balu'thia as they walked past.

"What is that?" she asked, when they were past the thing.

"A pet of ours," Nym said.

"You make a joke, Grayskin. That creature looks dangerous."

"Oh, it is—to any enemy of ours."

They'd made a fire the night before; the three manlings had slept in a circle around it. Xander and Geni lay there still, sound asleep beneath the giant Hilada leaves they'd used for blankets. Vreen, of course, was nowhere in sight, but Nym could still smell him.

He woke the others; introductions were made, and the five of them followed Balu'thia deeper into the forest, where they soon reached her village. Nym was expecting a gathering of simple leaf huts, similar to the destroyed settlement they had seen the day before.

Balu'thia's village, though, was entirely different. It was a marvel of elegant beauty. The houses themselves somehow glowed with the same faint blue color that had emanated from Balu'thia. The sun was barely up over the horizon, yet even so there was plenty of light.

As the company entered the village, people began emerging from the huts to greet them. They crowded around the newcomers in curiosity; Nym saw that each of them had the same type of patterns embellishing their skin as the girl had; the same type, but differing in detail and in extent of distribution across the villagers' bodies.

They came to a clearing in the center of the huts. There was another group of villagers there, perhaps a dozen or so, male and female. The group parted as Nym and his fellow travelers approached, revealing a single, elderly male sitting on a wooden throne. Which, as Nym grew closer, he saw was not wooden at all, but rather a collection of leaves from the Hilada trees. Shaped, formed, cut, and somehow fastened together.

"Shhh," the boy said. Nym turned and saw Xander glaring off to one side, glaring at empty space. No. The little man. Vreen. Nym could smell him now. Stupid to bring him; pointless.

"Travelers."

Nym turned back. The man on the throne had risen from it now, was coming toward them. He was strikingly tall; strikingly thin. He wore a black robe, painted with the same patterns as on his dark skin—the same color as the girl's. His hair was white as snow and long, down to his shoulders. He was old, Nym could see. Ancient, even. Although his face was almost entirely unlined. And smooth. Nym could not even see stubble on his cheeks. Just more of the same swirling patterns, even more extensive than on the girl. He wondered if the patterns, the markings on the skin, grew more extensive with age. Did they differ from male to female?

"I am Balu'ki," the old man said. "The Pyat of the Iru."

"The hidden," Geni said.

The man bowed. "Yes."

"What?" Xander asked.

"The hidden." The princess turned to him, catching Nym's eye as well in the process. "It's what *Iru* means in Avostan. That's where we are, isn't it? Iru T'Alavar?"

"This is true." The girl who'd first found Nym spoke now, moving to the old man's side. "You stand in the village of Iru T'Alavar, in the valley of the Iru."

"I'm Xander," the boy said, holding out his hand. Not to the old man, but to the girl. "Pleased to meet you."

She looked down at his outstretched hand and frowned.

"What are you doing?"

"Shaking hands. It's a custom among our people. When we meet friends. Greet friends. Friendly people."

Nym frowned. The boy seemed nervous about something. He couldn't see why.

"Here. May I?" He took the girl's hand and placed it in his.

"See?" he asked, smiling at her. "Now we're friends."

"Interesting," the girl said. "How long do we touch hands in this manner?"

"Stop that," Geni said under her breath, stepping forward, glaring at the boy, and bowing at the same time.

"I am the Princess Angenica, of the house of Aegeon," she said.

"Princess." The Pyat bowed in return. "We are honored by your presence here. You and your companions. It has been a long time since I have seen such a diverse group. So many different lives, so many different beings." The old man turned and looked at Nym. "And never before can I remember seeing a Sion of the world of men and a Sion of the gray skin together."

"Sion of the world of men?" Xander asked.

"Not you." Balu'ki gestured toward Geni. "Her."

"She's not a Sion," Xander said. "She's a princess."

"I'm not a Sion," Geni snapped.

"Forgive me if I have said something to give offense. I meant no harm." The Pyat bowed his head once more. "I have not been outside this valley in an age. Terms and words fall out of favor. In my time—in the time when the outside world and ours communed—*Sion* was a term for those born of channelers. Those of special talents. I can sense, Princess, that kind of special talent within you. That is why I used the word."

"Special talents," Geni said. "What kind of special talent?"

The man walked over to Geni and touched his hand to her cheek.

"I cannot be certain. But there is a fire in your heart," he said. "You are strong, Geni. Your presence here and now, in our time of need—it is truly a gift of the Destiny."

"Time of need?" the boy asked. "What do you mean?"

"Imbazu," Balu'thia said. "You saw what happened there."

"Imbazu?" Nym spoke now. "What's Imbazu?"

"Our neighbors' village. What remains of it." The Pyat smiled. "But now is not the time to speak of our troubles. You must be hungry. Thirsty. We will break our fast together, and talk further."

Nym nodded. That sounded fine to him. Eat. And then talk. And then, perhaps, eat some more.

CHAPTER FIFTY-ONE

He was going to get spoiled, Xander thought wryly, his second bath in as many months. The tub the Iru provided was maybe not up to the standards of the one that he'd used back in the Keep, but the water was at least as hot, and there was more of it. It was sweeter, too, in a way he couldn't put his finger on, its very touch at once soothing and invigorating.

The boy who'd led him to the hut where the filled tub waited had laid out clothes for him to change into: a pair of shorts and tunic, both of the same light, feather-thin fabric. Xander slid them on and left the tent. There was music of some sort coming from outside; drumming. He had seen a great firepit being prepared as well; he wondered how long it would be before the food was ready. He was starving. He—

Stopped in his tracks, a step outside the hut.

Balu'thia stood there, smiling at him.

He'd thought her beautiful before, but the sun had only just risen when they'd first met; her features had been shaded in the dim light. Looking at her now . . .

He couldn't really think of anything to say. He'd heard the phrase "tongue-tied" before, but up until this moment never understood exactly what it meant. Geni was beautiful, but this girl . . .

"Xander." She bowed her head. "I greet you once more."

"Balu'thia. I . . . uh . . . greet you, too." He bowed as well, feeling himself blush.

"Thia," she said. "Please call me Thia."

"Sure. Thia."

She smiled again. Xander tried not to stare. Her eyes . . . they were so brightly blue he felt he could almost get lost looking into them.

"The bath was to your liking."

"Yes."

"Yes. I thought so. The others of your party are already gathered for the feast. I will take you to them now."

"Good," he said. "That sounds good."

Reluctantly, he broke eye contact and fell into step alongside her. He still couldn't think of a thing to say.

"You have come far," she said.

"A long way, yes."

"From the place where your princess rules."

"Outpost."

"The world outside our valley." She shook her head. "I hope to see it one day myself. It must be wondrous."

"Wondrous. I don't know about that," Xander said. "There's a war going on out there now."

Balu'thia—Thia, he reminded himself—shuddered. "War. I cannot imagine. To deliberately take the lives of fellow creatures . . ."

"It's terrible," Xander agreed. "But we didn't start it. The Fallen did."

"What are Fallen?" she asked.

Xander was taken aback.

"Fallen. Grayskins," Xander said.

"You travel with a grayskin," Thia said.

"He's different."

At least Xander hoped so.

"The Fallen start wars," he finished.

"Here. No more talk of war. We must celebrate your arrival in our village."

She gestured up ahead, and Xander saw that they'd arrived at the firepit, where it seemed the entire village had gathered. He caught sight of Geni and Nym—and Vreen? Was that Vreen? The little man looked like he'd been cleaned up, too, sitting on a log near the fire, talking to a handful of the villagers, including, he saw now, the Pyat.

At that instant Geni looked up and saw him, too. Their eyes met and she smiled at him.

Then she saw Thia, and her expression darkened.

Jealous, Xander realized. Geni was jealous.

Thia led him over to the others. Xander found himself staring at Vreen. Cleaned up, the filthy little man looked like a completely new person. In his place was a short, slightly overweight, mostly bald man who reminded Xander of a merchant clerk more than anything else; the type of man who spent the day indoors, sitting, counting numbers.

"Balu'ki—Ki, was just saying how he felt the Destiny had brought us together."

Xander looked up and saw Geni glaring at him, and Thia.

"Is that how you feel, Xander?" Geni asked. "That the Destiny have brought us together?"

"Uhhh . . ."

"I believe it is true," Thia said. "You have come to us at a time of great need."

Ki frowned. "Now is not the time, Granddaughter."

"Not the time for what?" Xander asked.

"We need your help," Thia said. "A great evil has come to the valley."

"Granddaughter . . ."

"But it is true. It must be. The Destiny *have* sent you, Xander." Thia put a hand on his arm. "That you appear in our time of need . . ."

"This is about the destroyed village, isn't it?" Geni said.

Thia looked to her grandfather, who sighed and nodded.

"My fault, I suppose, for bringing up the Destiny at all," Ki said. "Yes, this is about Imbazu. What happened to it."

"What did happen to it?" Xander asked.

"As Balu'thia said," Ki responded. "Evil has come to our valley. A kind of evil that has not been seen since the time before this one. Since the days of Cataclysm."

"Evil." Xander frowned. "What kind of evil?"

"A creature from the mists of the past," Ki said. "An umberdroth."

"What?" Nym barked out a laugh. "You cannot be serious."

"I am very serious indeed, Sion," Ki said.

Nym shook his head. "Those things are fairy tales. Myths."

"It was no myth that destroyed Imbazu," Ki said.

"Wait a minute, please," Geni said. "Will someone tell me what an umberdroth is?"

"It's a legend," Nym replied. "A myth, as I said. A kind of creature the Lady Umber created to terrorize her enemies. Even if they ever existed, they have been gone for a thousand years."

"Then what destroyed our village, hey?" Balu'thia asked. "What killed our people?"

"Some other kind of beast, probably. The hills here are full of them."

The Pyat nodded. "What you say is true enough, Sion. The hills are full of living beings, of all kinds. But we have lived in this valley in harmony with all of them, for a thousand years. None has ever attacked us."

Nym had no response for that.

"An umberdroth," Xander said. Whatever that was, exactly. "And you think we can help you get rid of it?"

"Yes," Balu'thia said. "I believe the Destiny have brought you to us, to do just that."

"Pyat."

Xander looked up and saw a boy standing in front of them.

"I am instructed to tell you the food is ready."

"Excellent." The Pyat got to his feet. "We will talk more of this later. For now, let us eat. Drink. Celebrate your arrival."

Xander got to his feet as well, at the same time as Thia did. He found himself for a second face-to-face with her, the two of them barely inches apart.

She smiled. In that instant, he felt like celebrating indeed.

Not only did they eat, they overate. At least Xander did. And he drank as well; a kind of spiced wine that went straight to his head. The banquet lasted through the day and on into the evening hours. He quickly lost track of time; the last thing he remembered was watching the villagers perform a dance; watching Balu'thia perform.

When he opened his eyes, he found himself in what he could only describe as a nest. Soft, yet firm, it was even more comfortable than the bed he had slept in during his night at the Keep weeks ago.

He was still fully clothed and yet he felt refreshed and clean. In fact, he was cleaner than he could remember ever being. It was as if his clothing and his person had somehow had all their contaminants removed during his sleep.

A sleep that had been wonderful; one of the best nights of sleep, in fact, that he'd ever had in his life. Filled with wonderful dreams. He remembered one of them in particular: himself and Geni, flying in the cavern with the wisps. They soared, hand in hand, just as they had weeks earlier. Then Balu'thia joined them. They flew together as a trio, Xander in the middle, holding hands with both of them.

He lay back in the bed for a moment and closed his eyes, hoping the dream might return. When it didn't, he reluctantly rose and followed the path from his hut out to the firepit. There was no one in sight; judging from the height of the sun in the sky, it was late. Midmorning. A woman emerged from a path in the forest, carrying a bucket of water. She wandered past, smiling. Xander took the path himself and came to a lake. Nestled in the middle of the valley, its calm waters reflected the snowcapped mountains behind it. He splashed water on his face, rubbing the sleep from his eyes. Absently, he picked up a rock and skipped it on the water. He watched the ripples for a moment, smiling. Nine skips. Not bad.

He turned and saw Ki standing at the edge of the path.

"Good morning."

"Good morning. I am glad to see you awake at last."

"Almost awake." Xander smiled back. "Thank you. For the banquet. It was wonderful."

"You are welcome. You slept well?"

"Never better. Where is everyone?"

"A party of our warriors went in search of the umberdroth. The others—your companions—went with them."

Xander frowned. Geni was out there, trying to help these people, while he was sleeping in bed? "I ought to be there, too."

Ki shook his head. "There is no cause for alarm. My people will not attempt to confront the creature, should they find it. They are simply gathering information."

"I suppose," Xander said, still not entirely convinced.

Ki bent and picked up a stone. He threw it then—trying to skip it the way Xander had, but with no success.

"It's all in the wrist," Xander said. "Like this."

He threw another stone himself; this one skipped seven times.

"Ah," Ki said. "I see."

They each tried a few more; Ki was at last able to make one skip three times.

"Always there is something new to learn," the Pyat said, brushing the dirt off his hands. "Every day brings an adventure, if you are open to it."

Xander had to laugh. "These last few weeks, that's certainly been true."

"For you, yes. Your quest."

Xander's eyes widened. "How did you—"

"I spoke at length with the princess this morning. She told me about it. Have no fear. Your secret is safe with me."

"What did she tell you?"

"Enough for me to know that you are on the right path. That you will find your Bane, sooner rather than later. And that you, Xander, will have a role to play when the time comes. A special role indeed."

He frowned. "I thought Geni was the one with a special talent."

"She is. But you, too . . . there is something about you, boy. The Destiny have their hand on you, in some way. They have chosen you."

Xander doubted that—but he left those doubts unsaid, for the moment.

For a full week they sought the creature. Up and down the valley of the Iru, through their forests and villages, their lakes and rivers, the caves and hollows of the mountains that hid their paradise from the outside world. They found traces of its presence; footprints that told Xander that Ki hadn't been exaggerating about the thing's size. Footprints that quieted even Nym's skepticism, as did the partially chewed corpses of the herd animals they came across one afternoon. But that was all they found: traces. Every time they seemed to be getting close, the thing seemed to move away.

They had a plan in place to fight it; the golem was key. Leeland. The creature moved along with them in their search parties, staying close to Geni at all times. Xander stayed as close as he could, too; he found himself torn between wanting to join the hunt and wanting to spend time with Balu'thia. Ki, who assigned members to each search party, rarely seemed to put them in the same one. Was that deliberate? Xander couldn't tell; but certainly the old man knew, in a way that Thia didn't seem to, that Xander was leaving the valley. Sooner rather than later.

He and Geni talked about that more and more as the days passed; as much as they wanted to help the Iru, as grateful as they were for this respite from their quest, they simply could not afford to dally much longer. The Krax army would have reached the Keep by now; Talax would have word of what they were doing. It wouldn't be long before he moved after them, moved to pick up their trail. And even if he couldn't find them, he knew what general direction they were headed in. They had to reach Nit'va'ganesh first; they had to be the ones to find the Bane.

It was only lately that Xander had realized that that was only half the battle; maybe not even half.

They still had to bring the Bane to Tandis, if the captain was still alive. Or to King Galor, if not. All the way across not just one continent, but two. Which meant that they still had a long, hard road ahead of them. A long journey. The valley of the Iru was not on Geni's map, but they still had a few hundred miles to go before Nit'va'ganesh, by Xander's estimates. And then the whole journey back. A matter of months, perhaps, before they could reach the bridge.

He picked up a stone and skipped it across the lake, which was when he realized that perhaps there was another way. A journey to Athica by boat. Capitar maintained trading outposts along the bay; most of them were in Kraxis, but a few, Saren had told him, were on the southern coast of Ithril. If that was true, if they could somehow reach there—

"Xander."

He turned and saw Balu'thia walking down the path toward him.

"I have been speaking to the Sion."

"Nym."

"Yes. He tells me you are leaving soon."

"I'm afraid so."

"This makes me sad."

"It makes me sad, too." He forced a smile. "But we're not going just yet. Another couple of days. We want to make sure the umberdroth isn't coming back."

"I don't care about the umberdroth." She walked closer to him. "I care about you."

Xander's eyes widened.

"I care about you, too," he was about to say, but before he could speak, Thia leaned closer and kissed him on the lips.

Xander was too surprised to do anything but stand there.

"You don't have to go," she said. "You can stay here, with us. With me."

"I . . ." He shook his head. He didn't know what to say. He didn't know what to do. "I'd like that, but . . ."

"I would like it, too."

Balu'thia kissed him again. This time, Xander kissed her back.

Gods, she was beautiful. Like everything else in this valley, life seemed to be practically bursting out of her. Could he stay here? Live with Balu'thia, and her people? Grow old, grow happy? Skip stones for the rest of his life?

Doubtful.

He broke away. "Balu'thia. Thia. I—"

"It is the princess, is it not?" she said. "You have lain with her, and so—"

"No," Xander said quickly. "No, I have not lain with her. We're not even—"

"I will lay with you," Thia said. "If you tell me now that you will stay, I will."

She was wearing a simple shift of white cotton; she reached up to unbutton it.

"No," Xander said, shaking his head, moving her hand away from the dress. "No. I . . ."

He looked at her. Tears were welling up in her eyes. He saw himself reflected in them, for a second. His face, and the forest behind him. The trees. The valley. The village.

In that instant, the world around him seemed to stand still. Xander felt as if he was somehow able to step outside it, and see how connected everything was. How connected they all were. Himself, to Balu'thia. Her, to the Pyat. Him, to the village. The village—

His eyes widened, and he stumbled backward.

He fell into the river.

"Xander!" Balu'thia ran to him, helped him to his feet. "What is it? What's wrong?"

He shook his head, trying to clear his thoughts. Clear his mind of the terrible images he had seen in the instant he'd pictured the village.

Death. Destruction. Misery.

"I saw it," he said, getting to his feet, shaking himself off. "The umberdroth. In my mind. It was—"

The ground trembled.

He heard screams and a chill went up his spine.

"What is that?" Balu'thia asked. "What's happening?"

Xander knew. What he had seen in that instant was no vision. It was real.

The monster was here.

CHAPTER FIFTY-TWO

The hut where he'd spent the last weekend had been trampled flat. So had a half-dozen others nearby.

There was a body on the ground; an old man. For a second he thought it was Ki. The Pyat. Judging from her reaction, Balu'thia thought the same. Then she knelt down next to the man and shook her head.

"Oman. One of my uncles."

"I'm sorry," Xander said. "But—"

"I know. We have to go." She let go of the man's hand and they ran once more.

They found the umberdroth in the village square.

Xander stood still for a moment, unable to believe his eyes. The sheer size of the thing . . .

It looked vaguely like the paintings he'd seen of mountain tigers. Creatures of the time before this one—the days before the Cataclysm. Creatures a full twenty feet long, the length of a Yorish galley, a moving mountain of flesh, only in this case, the flesh looked like rock. Its skin seemed to be made of large stones jutting out in various directions. It was as if its bones, not content to stop growing with it, had grown to engulf the creature living within. Its claws looked razor sharp, like shards honed to a knife edge.

It roared—a screeching call filled with malevolence, and anger—which instantly made Xander want to turn around and sprint away as fast as he could.

"An umberdroth." Nym emerged from another of the many paths that led to the village square. "The old man wasn't lying at that. Gods. Where did it come from? Why is it here?"

Geni burst from the bushes a step later. She looked at Xander and frowned.

"Where have you been?" she asked. "We've been trying to find you . . ."

Her voice trailed off as she caught sight of Balu'thia standing next to him. Her face fell, which was when Xander realized that the two of them—he and Thia—were still holding hands.

He was trying to think of what to say to Geni—if he should say anything—when two Iru warriors burst from the bushes and charged forward. The first came within ten feet of the monster, then threw his spear. It bounced harmlessly off the umberdroth's side.

The second, seeing that, charged straight at the beast.

"Yaaaaahhhhggghh!" the man screamed, and stabbed it square in the side with his spear. The wood snapped; the man stood there for a second, frozen in surprise.

The umberdroth moved then, with a speed that seemed impossible for a creature that massive. It pivoted and then, in a blur of motion, its left front leg slashed outward and struck the two soldiers.

The air turned red with gore; next to him, Balu'thia stifled a scream.

"Leeland," Geni said, and the golem stepped forward and then, instantly and without hesitation, charged.

The umberdroth pivoted to face it.

The golem was taller, but the umberdroth was wider and longer. The creature swiped at it; the force of its blow, the noise of bone on metal, made a clanging sound that made Xander want to cover his ears.

The golem fell to its knees.

"Leeland!" Geni said again, in an entirely different tone of voice.

Xander started forward; Balu'thia pulled him back.

Nym, though, had no such hindrance.

The Sion moved—faster than Xander had ever seen any living thing move, in a way that reminded the boy of something, someone, although for the life of him he couldn't at that instant remember what—charging forward, drawing a knife as he did so. He leapt and grabbed the creature's leg, then stabbed it. The dagger must have struck home; the umberdroth roared and swung him off.

Nym flew through the air, struck a nearby hut, and lay still.

His attack, though, gave the golem the time it needed. The golem put its arms together and swung from its knees. Its clenched fists struck the umberdroth, knocking it back into one of the huts. The structure collapsed instantly but the creature was quickly back on its feet and leapt up high into the air to attack the golem.

The golem leapt, too.

They came together with such force that the shock wave knocked Xander to his knees. He struggled to regain his footing, and did so just in time to see that the golem had jumped onto the umberdroth's back. It had locked its powerful arms on the shoulders of the monster and was pushing forward. Trying to snap its neck. The umberdroth was trying to brace itself in the soft soil; trying but failing.

Slowly, slowly, the creature's head was being forced down. Any moment now, it would snap.

The umberdroth roared out in pain, and frustration. For a second, Xander felt sorry for it.

Then, in a lightning twist, the umberdroth used the golem's momentum against it and sent it flying. The golem landed with a boom, knocking down a series of wooden benches, and toppling a great stone sculpture that stood in the very middle of the village square.

It rolled over, then lay still.

The umberdroth turned its attention to Nym. The Sion was now struggling to his feet, completely unaware of the danger advancing on him.

The umberdroth snarled; Nym's eyes widened.

In that instant, Xander pulled free of Balu'thia's grip and leapt.

His tackle knocked Nym to the ground, just as the creature flew over the two of them.

"Xander?" Nym croaked.

"That's me," Xander said.

Although not for much longer, he thought.

The umberdroth loomed over the two of them. It raised a huge rocky paw off the ground and prepared to stomp them into oblivion.

Xander closed his eyes and felt the earth shake.

He waited for the pain. For the blackness. Neither came.

He cracked an eyelid.

"You can get off me now, I think," Nym said.

Xander rolled over and looked up.

The umberdroth's head was two feet away from him. Its eyes were frozen wide open in shock.

The shaft of the great statue in the village square protruded through its chest. Behind it, Xander saw the golem holding the other end of the statue.

He shuddered in relief, as Geni, and then Balu'thia, helped him to his feet.

*   *   *

From all around, the villagers converged.

"You are very brave, Mr. Xander," Vreen said as he reappeared. "Vreen is not so brave."

"We owe you a great debt of thanks," Ki added.

Xander bowed. He walked behind the monstrous creature that had nearly killed him. The golem stood over the fallen creature. Its task completed, it was absolutely still. It looked a little worse for wear. Some scuffs on its iron exterior. A slight dent where it had landed when thrown.

Xander turned back toward the dead umberdroth. Cautiously he touched it. It felt like it really was made of stone. Walking toward the front of it, he saw something hanging around its neck. A chain of some sort. It was silver.

Ki stepped forward and pulled it off the creature's neck.

"It is jewelry of some sort," he said. "Strange."

Someone let out a gasp.

Xander turned and saw Geni staring at him, eyes wide in absolute horror.

"What is it?" he asked. "What's the matter?"

"That," she said, pointing to the necklace. "Oh, Gods. How is this possible?"

Xander looked at the necklace. "I don't understand. What . . ."

"That's my necklace, Xander. The one that I wore—that night when the Fallen attacked us, in the wood. Remember? My mother's necklace?"

Xander frowned. He didn't remember. And it didn't make sense.

"How could your necklace have gotten here? Why would the umberdroth be wearing it?"

Ki stepped forward. "These are questions that must be answered indeed."

Xander suddenly recalled another question, one that Nym had asked earlier.

Where had the umberdroth come from, after all this time? And why was it here now?

He looked down at the necklace, and then over at Geni.

And an answer to all their questions formed in his mind.

"Talax," he said, and the sound of the word sent shivers down his spine.

"He knows," Geni said. "Where we are, what we're doing. He knows."

Xander nodded.

"Yes," he said. "I'm afraid he does."

BOOK FOUR
GALOR AND MIRDOTH

As long as there are immortals on our world, the Destiny will seek to remove them.

—Hosten

Chapter Fifty-three

"Altar." Hildros pulled the stick out of the fire; the little creature on the end of it was burnt to a crisp. He smiled, slid it off the stick, and onto the flat rock next to half a dozen of its brothers. "You know why they call it that, don't you?"

"No." Calis shivered and wrapped his blankets tightly around him. Spring was late coming to the passes here; the mountainside was still covered with a light dusting of snow. Chunks of ice still clogged the Gandru; they'd been following the river since leaving Ruvenna, sometimes by boat, sometimes on foot. Pushing west as fast as they could. "Why?"

"That's the shape of the valley. An altar. You'll see it tomorrow. Day after at the latest. Here." Hildros sat down next to Calis and handed him a plate of food. Calis ignored the creatures and grabbed a big hunk of bread. The last quarter loaf they had, he knew: he ripped off a chunk and bit into it. Stale. He could taste mold as well. He debated spitting it out, and decided against it. No telling when they'd get more. Hildros said tomorrow for Athica, but he'd said that yesterday as well. The unseasonably cold weather was slowing them down.

"You ought to eat, boy," Hildros said. "The meat. Keep up your strength."

"Not that hungry."

"Hmmmfff." Hildros snorted and ripped into another of the little creatures. The bones crunched; Calis shuddered. He'd seen the little things live; mountain rats, Hildros called them. Even skinned, with the heads cut off, they looked nasty to him, too nasty to eat.

"Reason I say that"—Hildros crunched into another of the little creatures—"is there're supposed to be things in these passes. Larger creatures, if you get my drift."

"Larger creatures?"

"Ogres. Giant spiders. That sort. Monsters left over from the days these were wastelands. From the days after the Cataclysm."

Calis snorted. "You're pulling my leg."

"Yeah." Hildros smiled. "But you still ought to eat, boy. You got demons of your own to face—don't you?"

The smile disappeared from Calis's face at that.

Demons of his own, indeed. As if Tandis's warning hadn't been enough.

There are those who would regard your very existence—the presence of another channeler in the world—as a threat.

Hildros had spent this entire last leg of their journey—the trip from the mountain villages on the other side of the range, through the passes, and down this side of the range—warning him that Galor could be a little difficult at times. Temperamental. A bit eccentric. Prone to anger quickly.

Frankly, Calis thought, it might be easier dealing with giant spiders.

They finished the meal in silence, and turned in. An early start tomorrow, Hildros said. Their last day of traveling, and they wanted to make sure to reach the gates before lunch, so they could be in the city before the sun set. Find a place to stay, and clean themselves up before seeing the King.

Calis, though, had a hard time sleeping. He kept hearing things in the brush, large things. Giant spiders? Nonsense.

But when at last he did doze off, he dreamt of them. Giant spiders, with the heads of old men, chasing him through the streets of Athica.

He woke feeling as if he hadn't slept at all.

Hildros turned out to be right this time. They made the gates of the city by early afternoon. The outer gates, that is. Calis looked up at the massive doors as they passed through. They were made of stone, hundreds of feet tall. They didn't seem so much connected to the mountains as a part of them, as if they'd grown out of the rock. Or been grown. Maybe they had. There were stories, Calis knew, that Procipinee had raised the entire mountain range as a means of protection, in the days after the Cataclysm. Back then, of course, there had been no "Kingdom." No Athica, no Altar, either. There was a collection of city-states with rulers of great ambition.

Now, of course, there was only Galor.

They passed through the outer gates without incident; in the distance the city itself loomed. Athica. A speck of gold and green, nestled up against the edges of the range. It grew larger throughout the day, as they drew closer, as they journeyed along the gleaming white stones of the old Lord Protector's Road. Amazing how different that path appeared as it wound its way across the western continent. In the eastern reaches of Capitar, it was an overgrown footpath; here it was a gleaming highway of commerce. Wagon after wagon rumbled past, heading to or from the city on the wide thoroughfare. Travelers and merchants passed as well, some on foot like the two of them, others traveling on horseback.

All came to a stop about half a mile shy of the city: a checkpoint, a guard station, which all entering had to pass through. This was the reason Hildros had wanted them to get an early start; the gates to the city would close at sunset, and any not yet admitted would have to spend the night in and among the makeshift tent village surrounding the city.

Hildros shrugged off his pack, and set it on the ground. He pulled out a cloth and unwrapped it.

"Want one?" he asked, holding out one of the little skinned mountain rats.

Calis made a face.

Hildros made a crunch.

Someone cleared his throat.

"Knights."

Calis looked up and saw a man on horseback looming over them. He was Hildros's age, lanky, with reddish, thinning hair, and freckles all over his face.

He wore a captain's insignia. A soldier. There was a troop of men—a half dozen of them—mounted up behind him.

"Henrik." Hildros smiled and got to his feet. He reached up and clasped the other man's hand. "It's good to see a familiar face."

"Hildros. Good to see you, too." The other man smiled for a second as well. Then his expression turned serious. "My condolences, Lieutenant. The news reached us only recently; Uthirmancer, Bili, Kesper . . ."

"Aye." Hildros nodded. "These are dark times, my friend. For the Knights, and all of mankind. Outpost has fallen."

"We know."

"What about Ty?" That was one of the other soldiers calling out. "Is he dead, too, then?"

"Ty is fine," Hildros said, looking over Henrik's shoulder as he replied.

"Well, that's a relief," the soldier called back. "He owes me money!"

Hildros laughed. So did Calis.

"He owes us all money," Henrik said. "Not that we'll ever see it."

"Perhaps you will," Calis said, speaking for the first time. "If the King agrees to send his army."

Henrik looked down at him then, and nodded thoughtfully. "Perhaps so. We'll all know soon enough."

"What's that?" Hildros asked.

"He wants to see you," Henrik said. "Now."

The man turned and motioned to his soldiers, who led forward two horses. Saddled, but with no riders.

"These are for you," Henrik said.

"The King knew we were coming?" Calis asked. "He knew we were here?"

Henrik nodded. "The King knows everything, lad."

The city was larger up close than it had looked from a distance; larger and far more spread out. Row after row of houses, and huts; street after small street, a maze through which Henrik and his men led them, always in the direction of the gold that Calis had seen gleaming in the distance, gold now revealed as the paint, the ornamentation, the decoration gilding every building of Galor's palace complex. A collection of buildings, and temples, and enormous sculptures that occupied the very center of Athica.

The sun was starting to set when they finally reached the complex. The soldiers dismounted; Hildros and Calis followed suit as a man—a very well-dressed man, tall, thin, wearing velvet robes of a deep green color, bordering on black—strode forward to meet them.

"Which of you are the Knights?"

"That would be us," Hildros said, motioning Calis to his side.

"Hildros and Calis. Yes." The man nodded to himself. "I am Annas. Protocol minister, of the third rank. This way, please. The King is expecting you."

Without waiting for a response, the man turned on his heel

and strode off. Calis looked to Hildros for guidance; the old man shrugged and started forward.

"Good luck," Henrik called after them.

Hildros waved a hand in acknowledgment.

They followed Annas through an exterior gate and into the palace compound. The man was in a hurry, clearly; more than once he looked back at them with an expression of dissatisfaction. Keep up, keep up, his eyes seemed to be saying. Calis—and even more so, Hildros—had to strain to keep pace. Part of the reason for that, as far as Calis was concerned at least, was that he kept looking up. The interior of the castle was even more impressive than the outside. It was not at all what he'd been expecting; not at all like the great castles of the western coast, the Keeps at Outpost, at Minoch. Galor's palace was more like the library at New Pariden; like the houses of the great Capitaran merchants. Like Baron Mancer's estate, only a dozen times more so. The walls were covered by more paintings than he had ever seen in his entire life. There were elaborate, enormous tapestries; there were statues; there were weapons of all sorts. There were no guards anywhere in sight.

"Gods," Calis said under his breath. "There's a fortune here, Hildros. Carry off one of those tapestries and you're set for life."

"Carry off one of those tapestries, and your life is over. This is the home of the Sorcerer King, lad," Hildros said. "Only the insane would attempt to steal Galor's property in his place of power."

Calis supposed so, although he had no idea how the King could possibly keep track of everything going on in the entire palace, all the time. Could Galor really be that powerful? That all-knowing? Impossible. And yet . . . he had sent those soldiers to meet them. Right as they were arriving.

Best to watch his words, Calis decided. Better safe than sorry.

They arrived at a great set of golden double doors, fully twenty feet tall. One of the doors was open; through it Calis caught a glimpse of what looked like a court of some kind, in session, as they approached.

Annas paused on the threshold and turned to them.

"The Hall of Justice. When we are inside, there are rules that must be followed."

"All right," Hildros said.

"It is forbidden to talk while a plea is being made to the King. It is forbidden to talk while the King is deliberating that plea, or making a pronouncement."

"Sounds simple enough," Hildros said.

Annas held up a hand. "It is forbidden at all times to speak with the King's guards, or the petitioners. You may speak in the interval between pleas, but you must not make comment on the King's decisions."

Hildros nodded.

Calis frowned.

"You may not leave your seats while the King is deliberating, or making a pronouncement. You may not cast prejudicial glances toward the petitioners, nor those accompanying them." Annas looked up. "Is that understood?"

"Absolutely," Hildros said.

"Mostly," Calis said. "Could you go over that part about—"

"It's understood." Hildros looked up at Calis and smiled. "Just keep your mouth shut, boy—yes?"

Fair enough, Calis thought, and nodded.

With that they followed Annas into the hall.

There were galleries for visitors on either side of the chamber; these were filled with men in robes and women in rich gowns. This was the sort of Athica that Calis had imagined he would see. As Annas sat them in the gallery to the right rear of the room, Calis strained to see the King. His view was blocked by the line of petitioners.

"The King will see you when he has finished these hearings," Annas said.

And with that the man bowed his head, and disappeared.

Over the next two hours, Calis watched petitioners come forward to speak to Galor. It was a dizzying, mind-numbing array of cases; one man wanted the King to strike down what he described as an outdated law regarding housing in a town center; another wanted the King to decide between two exchange rates on goods being imported from Kraxis. A third wanted compensation for an injury caused by a horse coming unhitched on a rich merchant's property. Some of the pleas were made by the petitioners themselves; sometimes they were made by hired magistrates.

To Calis, the discussions seemed surreal. The Henge had been attacked and conquered by the Fallen, refugees were streaming into Minoch and elsewhere, and no one in this room seemed concerned in the slightest.

The time passed. The petitioners came and went. Some left the hall sobbing, some smiling. Some were led away by men and women dressed very much like Annas—protocol ministers as well, Calis assumed—and some were taken off by armed soldiers.

As the crowd thinned, Calis, at last, got a look at the King. Galor sat on a throne at the far end of the room, perhaps a hundred feet away from him. Difficult to see his features from that distance, but Calis could hear his voice. Deep and strong. Confident. The voice of a monarch. Galor was dressed in a long flowing robe of white and blue, edged with gold. He leaned forward in his chair intently each time one of the petitioners approached, then leaned back to consider his decision, and leaned forward once more to make his pronouncements.

Truly, he looked no different dispensing justice than any of the other rulers Calis had come across. He was guilty, the boy thought, of ascribing motives and prejudices to the King without ever having met him. Shame on him for doing that.

Finally, the last petitioner was up. The court was already nearly clear.

.The petitioner was a very old man. His robes were very formal but also very old. The man was trying his best to look dignified but his poverty was difficult to conceal. Calis remembered Ty's words:

Look at a man's boots and you know half his story.

If the man's tattered dress boots told half the story, his moth-eaten formal robe told the rest.

"Minister Pintron, your report was of interest and I would hear more of it," said Galor.

"Y-yes, Your Majesty," the man replied. It was clear that he was very nervous. "The academy at Zabril noticed several days ago that our devices that made use of Earth Magic no longer functioned."

"Do you have a hypothesis on this?" Galor asked.

"Yes . . . though . . . I do not like it. No. No. I don't like it at all," Minister Pintron said.

"Speak your hypothesis," said the King.

"Someone has locked the Earth Shard of the East. The Lord Sovereign of the Kingdom, being a channeler, would sense whether this was the case and what it might mean."

"A sound assumption," the King replied. "You can assure the acolytes' temple that I am investigating the matter and, in fact, my next conference pertains to that."

Calis saw the minister and his party turn and look toward Calis and then turn back.

"Th-thank you, Your Majesty. We will convey your message to our peers."

With no one else in line, Calis started to rise but Hildros quickly put his hand on his shoulder and pushed him back into his seat.

"We must sit here until commanded to approach, lad," Hildros whispered.

The minister and his party exited the court. The door attendant left his stand and closed the doors as he exited the room.

At last the petitioners were done, and the Knights were motioned forward.

As they approached, another man stepped to the throne from alongside it.

"The Azure Knights, Your Majesty," he said. "Those named Hildros, and Calis."

And now, at last, Calis got his first up-close look at Galor.

There was no crown upon the King's head. Instead, his long, white hair flowed freely. His face was partially covered by a long beard and mustache. He looked old, but not the least bit feeble. He had not shriveled, either, the way the old sometimes did. He looked strong; Calis would not have been surprised to see him lift a sword, even at his advanced age.

"Your Majesty," Hildros said, bowing.

Calis, following Hildros's lead, did the same. "Your Majesty."

"Rise, Knights. Your service honors me, and the Kingdom."

Calis did as commanded—and when he looked up, he found the King's eyes on him. Staring into him.

"You are he," Galor said. "Tandis's orphan."

"Calis, Your Majesty."

"Calis. I am pleased to meet you at last." The King's eyes were unreadable. He turned them on Hildros. "And you, Lieutenant. I am always pleased to see you, and to have the chance to pass on my thanks in person for your deeds."

"You honor me, Your Majesty," Hildros said.

The man standing to the King's right spoke again. "I am Bester. First minister of the Kingdom. You have been brought here on the King's order and are now commanded to report on the actions in the East—the war against the Fallen, which resulted in—"

Bester stopped talking all at once, and a second later, Calis saw why.

The King had raised his hand.

"Thank you, Minister." Galor smiled. "We need not stand on protocol. Hildros . . . your report. A summary please. Be brief."

"Of course, sire." Hildros nodded and proceeded to outline the situation for Galor in a matter of minutes.

When he mentioned Tandis's name, the King's expression darkened. Something stirred behind his eyes for a second . . .

And then it was gone.

"And this is why, Your Majesty, the captain has sent me. On his behalf, we ask that the third Army of the Kingdom be mustered, to march across the bridge and—"

"To what end?" Galor interrupted.

Hildros looked confused. "Excuse me, Your Majesty?"

"To what end? What good would retaking the Keep do?"

"Well . . . the Fallen, sire."

"The Fallen."

"Yes. They've taken the Keep. Killed hundreds of your subjects."

"They have indeed," Galor said. "And in so doing, have proven that we and those ungodly creations cannot exist together in this world. At least not on the same continent." The King shrugged. "I see no point in fighting over land I am prepared to cede."

Calis looked over at Hildros. He looked as stunned as Calis felt.

Galor intended to give up the East?

"Sire," Hildros said. "I would ask—"

"There is the matter of this Bane, of course. Tandis has mentioned this to me, on several occasions."

"The Bane." Hildros nodded. "Yes, Your Majesty. The captain hasn't told me much about it, but if the Titan obtains possession of it . . ."

"I would like to hear more about it," Galor said. "Perhaps over dinner . . ."

"I would be pleased to share what I know, Your Majesty," Hildros said.

"Oh, not you, Hildros."

"Sire?" Hildros asked.

"The boy," Galor said, and turned once more to Calis.

Their eyes met, and Calis, all at once, felt his heart hammering in his chest.

"I'd like to hear what the boy knows about the Bane. What the boy knows about a lot of things, actually," Galor said.

Hildros's mouth dropped open.

"But sir . . ."

"There is a problem, Hildros?" Galor's tone sharpened; though his voice went up in volume just a hair, the entire hall fell completely silent all at once.

Minister Bester raised a hand to his brow and wiped away a bead of sweat.

"No, sire." Hildros cleared his throat. "There is no problem whatsoever."

"Good." Galor smiled. "You are dismissed, my friend. With thanks for your service. Minister. A token of our acknowledgment."

He snapped his fingers; Bester stepped forward and handed Hildros a small purse. Calis heard coins jingle in it.

The old warrior bowed and walked away.

As he passed Calis, he clapped a hand on the boy's shoulder.

"I'll be in town. The Blue Lion. Come find me when you're done." He smiled. "I'll be curious to hear about your dinner, lad."

Calis tried to smile back. But the tone of Hildros's voice, the look in his eyes . . .

The boy had the feeling the older man was saying good-bye.

Chapter Fifty-four

Annas led him from the hall down a long, carpeted hallway, one lined with marble busts of people Calis didn't recognize. Past the busts, they came to a nondescript door, which led to a bedroom, one bigger than most of the houses Calis had lived in.

"A bath has been drawn for you. Towels are there"—Annas gestured toward the bed, on which half a dozen of the Knights could have fit comfortably—"as well as a change of clothing. Items that belonged to the King's late brother, Prince Arden. Take care with them, young man."

"Oh, I will," Calis said.

Annas eyed him suspiciously for a moment, before nodding.

"Good. Dinner will be served in an hour. See that you are ready."

He bowed and left the room.

Calis sat down on the bed and sighed.

Dinner, with King Galor. Alone. Not what he had planned. Not what he had counted on at all. There was a little golden statue of a dragon on the table next to the bed; Calis lifted it and was surprised at the piece's heft. It was solid gold, he realized. He held a fortune in his hands. Part of him was tempted, then and there, to take the statue, jump out the window, and head for the coast. Catch a ship north to Yoren, and disappear into the frozen wastes forever. Only somehow . . .

He didn't think he'd make it that far.

There are those who would regard your very existence—the presence of another channeler in the world—as a threat.

He bathed and dressed; Annas returned and led him to another building entirely, to a dining room even bigger than the Hall of Justice, to a table large enough to hold a party of twenty comfortably. There were but two places set: one at the head, and one where Calis was directed to sit, a quarter of the way down one side of the table. He was offered wine, which he refused. He wanted a clear head; he had a feeling he would need all his wits about him this evening, if he was to secure for the captain the army he needed.

He waited five minutes, and then ten, growing increasingly nervous. Uncomfortable. The robes scratched him where they touched the bare skin of his arm. He wondered why the King wanted him to wear these; if it was the King who had wanted that. Perhaps it was Annas, trying to embarrass him. Perhaps—

"I thought those would fit you."

Galor stood in an open doorway, near the table's head. He was dressed as he had been before, with a sole difference.

The crown Calis had missed earlier now sat upon his head.

"You are the size Arden was. No sense in letting those fine robes go to waste—yes?"

Calis stood, and bowed. "Your Majesty. I appreciate the honor."

"You are most welcome. Sit, please." Galor turned and spoke to a man who had followed him in—the same man, Calis realized, who had been in the Hall of Justice earlier. Minister Bester.

Bester nodded at something the King said, bowed, and left the room.

Galor sat.

The second he did so, a man appeared at his shoulder and filled the glass next to him.

"Wine?" Galor asked. "You are young, I know, but this is a fine vintage. Made especially for me by the vintners of Ruvenna."

Calis hesitated. He did not wish to offend, but he did intend to keep a clear head. On the other hand . . .

The King's private wine. It would be special, of that he had no doubt.

He was saved from a decision by the King's next words.

"Well. You will ask if you desire. Now. You must eat." Galor clapped his hands then, and a half-dozen other servants appeared from the kitchen immediately, each carrying a platter filled with a meat or vegetable of some sort. Some carried two platters; one man even held three, stacked lengthwise across his arm. They bowed to the King, laid the platters out on the table, and disappeared.

"It all looks delicious," Calis said. "Which do you recommend, sire? Which to eat first?"

"Ah. I do not eat," Galor said. "But don't let that stop you, Calis. Have as much as you want. And if what you see here isn't to your liking, you tell me. The cooks will gladly make something else."

"Oh, no, this is fine. This all looks great," Calis said. The King did not eat? Did he mean tonight, or in general? The latter would make no sense, though he knew of women who would consider a single bean a meal.

"Tylin will serve you," Galor said, and motioned the man who had poured the wine to come forward.

Calis instructed him what to put on his plate, very much aware of Galor's eyes on him the whole time. The King's gaze didn't lift from him as he began to eat, either.

"You are from Kraxis."

"Yes, Your Majesty."

"Obviously." Galor smiled. "It has always been a desire of mine to reconcile the twin branches of mankind, which the War of Magic drove apart. It is part of the reason I have supported the Keep all these years; supplied her with soldiers, and my best men, the house of Aegeon. The great hope of the Kingdom."

Calis didn't know what to say to that, so he just nodded his head once more and offered another "yes, Your Majesty."

"The captain has told me some details of your past. What do you recall of your childhood?"

"Before I joined the Knights? Not much, I'm afraid." Calis, about to wipe his mouth on the sleeve of the robe, remembered at the last second whose robe it had been, and used the napkin on his lap instead.

"Your parents?"

"I don't remember them at all." He returned the napkin to his lap. "I can sometimes picture a woman in my mind. I think maybe it's my mother . . ."

"And what does she look like?"

"I don't know. It's hard to capture the image. Sometimes it's clear in my head, sometimes—"

"There are disciplines. Techniques that can train and focus the mind. They are necessary for the effective use of magic—they will no doubt help in focusing your memory as well." The King smiled. "I am surprised that Tandis has not told you about these. Even begun to train you in such matters."

The King's eyes met his.

"I am even more surprised he did not tell you of your powers before now."

Calis felt himself flush. "He said he wanted me to be able to control my emotions before anything. He said that it wouldn't have made sense, if I wasn't ready—"

"Calm down, boy." Galor laughed. "It's all right. I don't blame you. I don't blame him, either. Not really."

The conversation continued; the King took the lead now,

letting Calis eat while he talked a little about the disciplines re-
quired of a channeler. The disciplines he himself had practiced as
a young boy, the ones he had been taught by his mother, Queen
Magesta, the ones he had been forced to learn on his own, after
her death. Her murder.

"A thing we have in common," Galor pointed out. "Our parents, gone before they had a chance to truly impart their wisdom.
To leave us the benefit of their legacy."

"Yes, sire," Calis said. "I hadn't realized it, but it's true."

"So." The King took another sip of his wine. "To the matter
at hand. Why you are here. You want one of my armies."

"Not me, sire. Tandis—"

"Don't quibble, boy," Galor snapped, and his eyes sparked
briefly with anger. "You are the one here. You are the one I am
dealing with."

Calis's heart pounded in his chest.

The King's expression, so calm before, flickered. For just a
moment his eyes revealed a depth of malice that made Calis truly
afraid. Then, like a memory, it passed and he became unreadable
again.

"Has Tandis told you why he needs this army?"

"To retake the Keep, sir. To find the Bane."

"And you believe him?"

Calis frowned. "Sire? I don't understand."

"It's a simple question, young man. Either you believe him,
or you don't. Either this Bane exists, or—"

"Of course it exists, sire. Begging Your Majesty's pardon.
Tandis wouldn't make something like that up. Wouldn't lie to
me."

"You trust him, then?"

"With my life."

"Unfortunate."

"What?"

"Tandis has been deceiving you for some time now."

"You mean because he didn't tell me about my powers." Calis nodded. "I suppose you could see it that way, sire, but I don't look at it as lying. It's more as if—"

"Boy," Galor said sharply, "it is not your powers the captain has been lying about. It is himself."

Calis frowned. "Sire?"

"Tandis." Galor got to his feet. "You think you know him well?"

"Fairly well, sir. I suppose."

"Where was he born?"

"The captain? I don't know. It hasn't come up when we've—"

"Of course it hasn't come up," Galor said. "Do you know how old he is?"

"No."

"What about his family?" Galor asked. "His parents. Brothers, sisters, uncles, cousins . . . Has he talked about them?"

Calis frowned.

"You haven't met them," Galor said. "No one has. No one ever will."

"I don't understand," Calis said.

"Bah." The King waved a hand and looked off in another direction entirely. He mumbled something and nodded to himself.

Calis became aware that he was holding his breath.

Gods, what to do? What to say? What was the King getting at? He was trying to tell him something about the captain, at least he had been, but now—what was happening? What was the matter with Galor?

The King shook his head and blinked his eyes in rapid succession.

Then he turned to Calis and smiled. "Forgive me. I was . . . preoccupied for a moment."

"Of course," Calis said, bowing his head, averting his eyes from the King's gaze.

Eccentric, Hildros had warned. Temperamental.

That didn't even begin to cover it.

How about insane? Calis thought, and having voiced the word—at least to himself—felt a chill run down his spine.

Galor smiled. "You are finished?" he asked, nodding toward the table and the array of dishes laid out on it.

"Yes."

The King clapped his hands. The same half-dozen servants who'd brought the food appeared once more and cleared it away.

"I will have gansa," Galor said. One of the servants nodded; the King turned to Calis and smiled. "A liqueur. Not for you. But if there is a drink you want, or dessert . . ."

"No, sire. Thank you, though."

The servant returned with a glass of amber liquid. Galor took it and stood.

"Come, boy. Walk with me."

He led Calis through another door and into a wide, empty hallway. The walls on either side were decorated as well with tapestries and paintings; shelves held sculptures and artifacts of all kinds.

"I have heard what happened at the cliffs," Galor said. "How your powers manifested themselves. A version of the events, at least. I would like to hear of it from your perspective."

"Of course," Calis said, replaying the incident with his words as he pictured it unfold in his mind. Halfway through the narrative, Galor suddenly stopped walking and looked up to his right, at the painting hanging there. A head-and-shoulders portrait of a serious-looking boy, not much older than Calis was now.

"Ha!" Galor smiled. "Do you know who this is, Calis?"

The boy shook his head. "No, sire."

"It is me, as a young man. Hard to believe, yes? So long ago." The King sighed. "This was the year before the wars began. Or perhaps the year before that. I was engaged to be married. There was a girl—there were many girls." He laughed. "I should have married and had children. Heirs. But then there would not have been so many girls! So many women!"

The King laughed again, then turned to him. "Have you had the pleasure of women yet, boy?"

Calis felt himself blush, bright red.

He cleared his throat.

"No, sire. Uthirmancer wanted to—"

"Ah. No matter. Before you leave"—the King clapped him on the shoulder—"I will send you Averdeen. She is the finest of my concubines. A beautiful woman. Beautiful black hair. A raven. And she bites, too!"

The King laughed even harder. Calis joined in as best he could. This was more uncomfortable than he could ever have imagined possible. The King, completely out of his mind. Talking romance. He wished to the Gods that Hildros was with him.

"And here is another painting," the King said, taking a few steps farther down the hall. "Myself again. During the wars. This never happened as Duree painted it, but I could not tell him otherwise. 'I do not care about what truly happened, Your Majesty, I care only for the perception,' he told me before I commissioned the piece. And this is the perception—is it not?"

Calis stopped in front of the painting. It showed a slightly older Galor. It was no sedate portrait, though; this art showed Galor at battle. Galor the channeler, fighting another wizard. They stood on differing sides of a great chasm, as streaks of lightning—red and blue, in all shades of the same—burst from their hands.

The channeler the young Galor fought was significantly older than he. He had hair much like Galor's appeared now: long, flowing, ivory white. A contrast to the wizard's eyes, which were like discs of black set into the man's head.

"The Black Sorcerer," Calis said.

"Yes."

"This is the battle between the two of you."

"A version of it, as I said. Gods." The King shook his head. "You know how old I am now, Calis?"

"Several hundred years old, sire."

"Eight hundred and twelve years. And yet sometimes, the events that occurred then—they feel more real to me than those that happened only yesterday. Perhaps it is my mind, going. That tends to happen as one grows older."

He turned to face Calis directly.

"What do you think, boy? Do you think my mind is going?"

The King asked the question in a light, jesting tone of voice, but the look in his eyes belied his manner.

Calis chose his next words very carefully indeed.

"I have no point of comparison, sire," he said, trying to keep his tone light as well. "But your grasp of the situation in the eastern continent seems to me sound enough."

The King nodded thoughtfully. "The situation in the East. Yes. It is time for us to talk of that, Calis. It deserves careful consideration. One does not rule eight hundred years—no matter how powerful a sorcerer—without taking great care in affairs of state like this one."

Galor turned to face him.

"Let us suppose I supply you with the army you desire. The army Tandis needs to retake the Keep. Let us further suppose that the force proves to be insufficient; that the enemy forces now gathered at the Eastern Henge overwhelm ours. Now I have lost a third of my strength; and the defeat is mine, and mine alone. The Lords of the Kingdom will blame me, not Tandis, not you, but me for losing their men, and leaving them open to invasion themselves, perhaps. My support is weakened; the Kingdom itself is weakened. The race of mankind is endangered, perhaps fatally so."

Calis nodded. "I see your point, sire. But—"

"Let me finish," Galor snapped. "Now let us examine the alternative. Let us say I send the army, and it is victorious. It is Tandis who will hold the Keep; not only that, it is Tandis and his young apprentice—by which I mean you, boy"—Galor turned and glared at him—"who will reap the credit. And if you are victorious, it will soon come out that there is a young channeler in the world. A channeler born of Krax, trained as an Azure Knight. A vigorous young sorcerer who some would see, some would suggest, some would dare advocate as a more effective ruler than I!"

Galor's face was inches away from Calis when he finished talking; by that point the King was shouting.

"You see my dilemma. You see my problem. You see how much easier it would be for me to ignore Tandis and his demands entirely."

"And what about the Titan? Talax? And the Bane? Tandis feels there is a great threat . . ."

"The Destiny take Tandis, and what he feels!" Galor shouted. "How many problems has he caused me over the years! Far too many, I say. Far, far too many."

The King began to pace. He began muttering under his breath, his hands clasped behind his back as he walked.

Little streaks of blue light crackled between his fingers.

Calis's heart hammered in his chest.

"Sire," he said, swallowing. "My loyalty is to the Kingdom. To you. I have no intentions beyond that service. I swear it."

"You swear it."

"Yes, sire."

"You swear it now, but later, if you are not here, if you are with Tandis . . ."

The King stopped pacing and turned to him.

"An oath," Galor said.

"Sire?"

"In ages past, in the time before this one—even briefly, during the War of Magic, channelers could make an oath between themselves. A pact, that bound the two of them together. The crossing of essences. The breaking of the oath—the forsaking of the vow—would cause the dissolution of the essences."

"I don't understand."

"A vow, boy. You swear loyalty to me. Eternal loyalty. In return for which, Tandis gets his army. Would you agree to that?"

Calis looked at the King.

There are those who would regard your very existence—the presence of another channeler in the world—as a threat.

He had the feeling, at this instant, that if he refused Galor's request, his presence in this world would come to an abrupt end.

"Yes," Calis said. "I would agree, sire. I am anxious to agree."

There was a wooden table in the hallway. The King laid an arm down upon it and motioned Calis closer.

"Sire?" Calis asked.

"Come, boy," the King said. "Lay your arm down next to mine."

Calis did as he was told.

With his free hand, Galor reached inside his robe and withdrew a dagger.

Calis's eyes widened. "What—?"

He started to back away; the King's hand fastened on his wrist. In that instant, Calis realized that his earlier assumption was right. Galor was old, but he was far from frail.

The King's grip on his arm was like an iron vise.

"Relax," Galor said. "You will feel but an instant of pain. That is my vow to you."

The King's eyes sparkled in the light from the candelabra dangling from the ceiling above.

"Be brave, boy. The pain is necessary. For as you will come to learn—"

Galor lowered the blade to his arm, and pressed it against the most prominent vein.

"—any spell worth its salt requires blood to work."

CHAPTER FIFTY-FIVE

Summer had arrived.

As they left the valley of the Iru behind and returned to Calebethon, Geni could feel it. This far south on the eastern continent, snow was a rare sight indeed—winter never truly descended—but now, with each day that passed, the air grew warmer, the chirp of the insects louder, the height of the grass taller in the slopes that lined the far southern ranges of Iru T'Alavar.

Even inside those mountains, there was a difference.

The blue-green lichen that lit their way was brighter, more extensive. It grew not only on the walls, on the trees, but on the walls of the caverns above them. The light was bright enough that Geni quickly found herself wishing for a bath at the end of each day's journey; the cave dust was everywhere. A few days after they'd resumed their quest inside the caverns, she woke one morning, her hair thick with dirt, and grimy all over, and sawed off a good foot of it with her dagger.

Xander's eyes almost popped out of his head when he saw her.

He had changed as well.

The scruff on his face looked more and more like a beard. He seemed to be filling out before her eyes; part of it, perhaps, was the food the Iru had sent them off with. Salted meats, nuts, fruits, as much as Leeland could carry. Which was a lot. The packs he was carrying had been full to overflowing the day they'd left the village. They were close to empty now. As was hers.

The necklace, though, still lay in the bottom of it. She had long since washed it clean of the umberdroth's blood, yet every time she caught a glimpse of its sparkle, she thought of the thing. And the death she had brought. She would have thrown it away long ago, but for all she knew, it might be all that she had now of her parents. All that was left of not just her mother, but her father as well. She couldn't get rid of it.

And yet . . .

Talax had used it to track them once. He might do so again. She was putting all their lives at risk by holding on to it. The Titan knew now that they were seeking the Bane. That's why he'd sent the umberdroth to kill them. To kill her. Why it had taken such a long time to find her, Geni didn't entirely under-stand. One thing she did know: the lives that the beast had taken before Leeland had killed it . . .

They were on her conscience.

It was, after all, her fault that Talax had found out about their mission. She had told Jacob, and Jacob had told his master.

Even thinking of the prince now made her sick to her stom-ach. Sick, angry, and ashamed of how she'd behaved. No wonder Xander had spent so much time with the Iru girl; no wonder he had been avoiding her. Things between them had changed. Would never be the same again. And was she surprised? No. Their des-tinies were different; no matter what happened with the Bane, or her father, or the Keep, she was bound for Athica, and audience with the King. And Xander . . .

Well. No matter what Ki had implied, his destiny lay along a different path. A more prosaic one. The two of them would part when the quest for the Bane was finished.

And the end was nearing.

Ever since they had reentered the underground city, at the far end of the Iru's territory, they had been traveling downhill. These last few days, the slope had increased dramatically. It was as if they were descending into some great underground valley; the air had grown warm and stuffy. The source of the heat seemed to be coming from beneath them; the stuff of Elemental itself. Nit'va'ganesh. The first—and last—of the great fortresses Morrigan had built. The map that had guided them thus far was no longer necessary.

They had come near the end of the line.

She came around the corner and ran into something.

"Oof."

She stumbled backward and nearly tripped. Which would have been disastrous.

The path they traveled now bordered, on one side, a rocky cliff face, and on the other, empty space. A yawning chasm.

And the bottom was a long way down.

"Vreen." She scowled at the spot where the man had been. "Stay out of my way."

There was no reply. Not that she could have heard it had there been one; despite the fact that she knew he was there, Vreen was still no more visible to her than he had ever been.

She sensed Leeland coming up behind her, and in her mind told the golem to halt. As always, he obeyed. She had been spending more and more time trying to commune with him. Never mind that it was sorcery that had given the creature life: She thought now that she sensed an actual intelligence in Leeland's mind. Was it possible that something was growing in there, that by the very act of commanding it she was nurturing an intelligence? Sometimes she thought so.

And other times, Geni thought—Geni knew—she was only projecting her own wishes, her own desires for a companion onto the golem.

She sighed.

Gods. She wanted this quest to be over; she wanted to be home again. Though of course, the Fallen occupied her home now. Athica was where she had to go, for the testing. She knew people there; it would be a place for her to rest, until . . . she knew not what. Until the Keep was in her father's hands again.

If her father was still alive.

On the other hand, completion of the quest would mean separation from Xander, and that thought made her feel guilty. Guilty because it almost made her want the quest to go on forever.

She rose to her feet and walked on.

The blue-green vegetation that lit the underground world was thinner here, the light dimmer. Up ahead she caught a glimpse of Xander disappearing down the trail; he had picked up a fallen tree limb somewhere along the way, and had been using it as a walking stick these last few days. The aid made his silhouette unmistakable.

Nym was nowhere in sight. Up ahead of Xander, no doubt, scouting the way forward. The Sion had taken to leaving them behind for hours at a time; he seemed, if such a thing was possible, even more anxious than they were for an end to this journey. Certainly it was more than he had signed on for.

She trudged forward. Time passed. She bumped into Vreen again. She was about to yell at him when suddenly Xander came rushing around a curve in the path, his eyes shining with excitement.

"We've found it!" he said, putting a hand out in the air.

Vreen instantly appeared in front of her.

"Sorry about that," the little man said. "Before. I did try to warn you. I had to tie my bootlace, and—"

"Hush," Geni said. "You've found what?"

"Up there." Xander pointed, around the curve. "Nit'va'ganesh. Come see."

Geni nodded. "Nit'va'ganesh." The end of their journey, at last."

It was the mirror image of the fortress at Grazna, a virtual twin of the place where they'd found the golem and fought off the darklings. The same triangular arches on the door, and windows; the same massive size, and shape. But the closer Xander got, the more differences he saw.

The first was the most obvious: the building's color. The stone facing was obsidian. Worn to a dull sheen in most places, it still shone in the area surrounding the huge entranceway. It gave the place an ominous, imposing look.

The second was its condition. Grazna had been deserted, its hallways covered in dust and cobwebs, its passages overrun with darklings and all manner of other creatures, but the building itself was intact.

Nit'va'ganesh was different.

The stone near the entranceway was cracked and discolored. Boulders, huge columns of stone, lay strewn on the ground nearby. There were skeletons there as well, and rusted armor, corroded weapons, arrowheads with no arrows.

One of those skeletons was easily the size of the golem, perhaps larger. A giant. It appeared to have three arms, and three legs.

Morrigan's experiments, Xander thought, and shuddered.

"Let's go," Geni said, pushing past him.

He nodded and followed in her wake. He wished he knew what to say to her these days; about what had happened between him and Balu'thia; about the necklace; about the sense he had that time, somehow, was running out. That Talax was not only on their trail once more, but growing closer with each passing day.

He supposed, given Geni's desire to push forward, that she was feeling the same thing.

They passed beneath the archway and entered the building.

Here, too, it was a twin of Grazna. The same long entrance hallway, only there were no candelabra, no alcoves, no hidden golems. There were more bodies: men; darklings; and others; more of the Usurper's experiments. And was that a surprise? No.

Nit'va'ganesh was laboratory as well as fortress. They could expect, he supposed, far worse before their journey was over.

At the end of the hall, in front of a set of wooden doors, there was the skeleton of an umberdroth. Even larger than the one they'd killed in the valley of the Iru.

They made their way around it carefully, and through the wooden doors. They entered another dome-shaped chamber, identical to the one at Grazna, with dozens of doorways along the walls, and at the far end of the chamber an immense, wide staircase leading down.

The staircase was filled with rubble. Bones poked out from the rock; partial skeletons lay scattered around the floor.

"Where do we go?" Vreen asked. "Which door?"

A good question, Xander thought, stepping farther into the room. There was something strange about a number of the doorways, he saw now. They were unnaturally wide. The frames were unnaturally low.

Not built for men at all.

"We should separate," Nym said. "We will be able to explore more of the fortress that way."

"I don't think so," Geni said. "For one thing, we might lose track of one another."

"I'll find you," Nym said.

"For another," Geni went on, ignoring what the Sion had said, "I'm not entirely sure this is safe."

They took a vote and decided to stay together. Nym was clearly upset.

They began exploring, door after door after door. Dead end after dead end after dead end. Passages ending in rubble, passages looping around to connect with another, passages that seemed to end before they really began.

"It's a maze," Geni said.

"What?" Xander asked.

"A maze. That's what it seems like to me, anyway."

"So we just have to keep trying doors until we find a way forward?"

"Unless you have a better idea."

"We don't even know exactly what we're looking for, if I might remind you," Nym said. "We're not even sure the Bane is here."

"It's here," Geni said. "Tandis said so."

"Where?" Nym asked. "We've tried all the doors."

"Maybe not." Vreen, who was running his hands along the far wall of the chamber they'd entered, spoke now for the first time in a long while.

"What do you mean?" Xander asked.

"You're talking to Vreen," Geni said.

"Yes."

"Can you . . ."

Xander nodded, crossed the room, and touched the little man.

"What I was saying," Vreen continued. "This may look like a wall. But see here."

He motioned to what appeared to be a slight gap in the bricks that made up the wall. Whatever it was he saw there, Xander couldn't make it out.

Geni and Nym stepped up behind him, just as Vreen inserted his fingers into a little gap between the bricks and took hold of one.

The brick moved.

"Xander," Geni said. "It's like the tunnels, in the Keep."

"A hidden passage?"

"Maybe so," she said.

"Definitely so." Vreen pulled the brick toward him. A loud grinding noise was heard from within the wall. Then a plume of dust filled the room; it was so thick that for a second, Xander couldn't see a thing.

When the dust cleared, the wall had moved aside and they were staring at an empty room. A hidden chamber.

"Good work," Xander said, and took a step forward.

Vreen grabbed him by the shoulder. "No."

"What do you mean 'no'?"

The little man shook his head. "Something's not right."

"How would you know? You've been here before?"

"A thief gets a sense about these things," Vreen said. "And I have a sense now . . ."

"I feel it, too." Nym made a sniffing sound. "I smell something . . ."

"Death," Vreen said. "Things have died in here. People have died in here."

"Leeland." Geni motioned to the golem. "Come forward."

"No," Vreen said.

"What?" Geni frowned.

"It might not be safe."

"For him?"

"Maybe. Maybe not for any of us." The little man motioned to Xander. "Hand me your stick."

"What?"

"Your walking stick. Come on."

Xander shrugged. He didn't see what purpose that would serve, but . . .

He handed the stick over.

The little man took a very small step forward, taking care not to cross the threshold separating the room they were in from the hall.

Then he shoved the stick forward.

The hall exploded with sound; Xander caught a flurry of movement in the darkness, a flash of metal . . .

Vreen gasped, and jumped backward.

The stick in his hand was barely a foot long now. The end had been sawed off clean.

"A trap," Geni said.

"That's right. I'll bet the whole place is full of them."

Xander nodded. He would bet so, too, actually. He would bet on something else as well.

There wouldn't be so many traps here—so many traps still working, after all this time—if there wasn't something well worth guarding here.

The Bane.

They were getting closer; he could feel it.

Geni motioned the golem forward. It took a step into the chamber, raising its hand as it did so.

There was a loud thunk, and a flash, once more, of metal.

Xander looked up, and the golem was holding a blade the size of a knight's shield in its hand.

Xander stepped forward, past Leeland, and under the blade, into the chamber. The second he crossed the threshold, on the other side of the chamber, the wall slid aside, revealing a second room.

"Another trap, no doubt." Nym came up alongside him, eyes focused ahead. Xander nodded; another trap indeed.

He walked to the threshold of the new chamber.

It was lit by a dull glow that stopped at the very threshold he stood on. A red glow. Magic.

"What do you think?" Xander asked.

"I don't know. But I'm pretty sure we don't want to go into the red light," Vreen replied.

Xander nodded. He took what remained of his walking stick and slowly poked it forward, into the room. Into the glow.

"Careful," Geni said.

"Believe me, I'm being careful."

The stick began to vibrate in his hands. To move. It was like something had hold of it; not a very strong something. He squinted and peered farther into the dimly lit room.

And gasped.

There were skeletons all over the floor.

He jumped backward.

"What's wrong?" Geni asked.

"A lot of bodies."

"That's not all that's wrong. Look at your stick." Vreen pointed; Xander saw that his makeshift cane was even shorter than before. Something had cut the end off his stick; not a blade this time. The cut was rough, not smooth.

"What could have done that, do you suppose?" he asked.

No one had an answer.

He tried again: walked to the threshold and put the stick back into the room. The others crowded close to see if they could puzzle out what was happening.

The stick began to vibrate once more in his hands.

"This is not good," Nym said.

"What?" Xander asked, pulling the stick back once more.

"I think those are irgots." Nym's pale face seemed, if possible, paler.

"How can you see anything in there?" Geni asked. "It's so dark . . ."

"Dark doesn't bother me," Nym replied.

"Hang on," Xander said. "What's an irgot?"

"A bug. An insect. They're supposed to be extinct." Nym frowned. "Horrible little creatures. They'll feed on anything, living or dead. Trees, animals, you name it."

"Golems?" Geni asked.

"I would think so," Nym replied.

"How do we get around them?" Geni asked.

"Maybe we don't," Nym said. "Maybe we have to go back. Retrace our steps. As I said before."

"Wait. I have an idea. They can't feed on what they can't see, right?" Xander turned to Vreen. "There's a chance they might not see you either. Maybe—"

"A chance? Oh, no." Vreen shook his head emphatically. "I am not going in there on a chance."

"What other choice do we have?" Xander asked.

"Go back. Like he said."

"Just put a hand in," Xander said. "See if I'm right. We'll hold on to you. The golem—"

"Leeland," Geni corrected, glaring at him.

"Leeland," Xander said. "Leeland will hold on to you. If those things attack, he'll pull you right back into this room."

"And the irgot will come with him," Vreen said. "No."

"I don't think that's how the traps work," Xander said. "See how the red glow ends right there. In here we're all safe. You'll be safe, too."

Vreen frowned. He looked over at Geni, and then Nym, and then shook his head once more. More slowly this time.

"I don't know," he said.

"Vreen." Xander took Vreen by the shoulders. "We need your help. You're the only one who can do this."

There was a long silence. Finally, the little man nodded. "All right."

And so saying, he walked right over to the doorway and put his hand through into the next room.

"Wait, wait!" Xander yelled, coming up alongside him. "Wait for the golem—"

But it was too late.

Xander saw them now; the irgots. A little black cloud of

movement, swarming, it seemed to him, out of the very walls. Swarming toward Vreen.

The little man's eyes widened.

And the cloud of insects flew past.

"They don't see you." Xander smiled. "I was right. See? You could walk right in. Nothing to it."

"Nothing to it," Vreen agreed, and fainted.

CHAPTER FIFTY-SIX

When the little man woke up—a tense few moments; Geni had no way of knowing what was happening; Xander was still the only one who could see Vreen; and the whole time while they waited for him to regain consciousness, she kept worrying that the horrible little bugs would stumble on him and eat him as he lay there, helpless, in the chamber—he made his way to the far end of the room with the irgots. Nym had spotted a lever there. Geni watched as it moved—seemingly of its own accord—and then, all at once, the red glow in the room intensified for a second, and vanished. Along with the irgots.

They moved into that chamber and on to the next.

That was how it went over the next few hours. From trap to trap; from chamber to chamber. Mechanical traps; traps populated by creatures the likes of which she had never seen, and hoped never to see again. Morrigan's creatures. Nym helped them disarm several; the Sion was uncannily quick, and had the ability to see things in the semidarkness that the rest of them missed entirely. He would be a dangerous fighter, Geni realized.

She was glad he was on their side.

"How many more of these things do you think there are?" Xander asked. "The traps."

"Not sure."

"Stay back a moment." Nym, on the threshold of another, even more dimly lit chamber, tossed a piece of rubble into the blackness.

They waited for the sound of it hitting the floor, or something hitting it.

There was nothing.

Nym frowned, picked up another piece of rock, and tried again. Same result.

Geni stepped up alongside him, torch in hand; she held it as close to the next room as she safely could.

The light didn't penetrate the chamber at all.

"Send the golem in," Xander said.

"What?"

"Leeland." Xander gestured toward the golem. "Send him in."

"We don't even know what's in there."

"Exactly."

"You're willing to risk his life."

"He's not exactly alive, is he?"

Geni glared and spun on her heel.

She was about to upbraid Xander for being callous when she heard a voice in her head.

Princess.

She blinked and took a step back.

The golem was staring straight ahead.

Had she just imagined that?

"What's the matter?" Xander asked.

"Not sure." She looked up at the golem again.

Leeland.

She felt something touch her mind then; a consciousness. She concentrated again, trying to reach the golem.

Leeland.

Princess. I will go.

Her eyes widened; she hadn't been imagining after all.

And at that instant, the golem took a step forward into the chamber and disappeared.

Princess!

All at once, a series of images flashed across Geni's mind. A sudden, searing burst of flames. A great stone, tumbling toward her. Irgots. A great, freezing darkness.

It was as if the golem—and through him, Geni—was reliving every one of the traps they had just bypassed.

And then everything went black.

"Geni!"

She looked up and saw Xander kneeling over her, concern etched on his face.

She was lying on the floor. How . . .

"What happened?"

Xander helped ease her up into a sitting position. "You fainted. Are you all right?"

"I'm fine, but . . ." Her eyes went to the darkened chamber doorway. "Leeland. The golem. Is he still . . . did he . . ."

Xander shook his head.

Her heart skipped a beat.

"He's gone," Geni said.

"I guess so," Xander said after a moment. "I guess that was a bad idea. My fault."

"No." Geni got to her feet. "No, it was his idea. I know that sounds crazy, but . . ."

She walked to the doorway. She wasn't quite sure how to put into words what she'd seen through her connection to the golem; she wasn't sure the others would believe her.

For the sake of the quest, though, she had to try.

"There were traps in there, too," she said. "A lot of them."

She described the things she'd seen in her mind then, the things the golem had relayed to her, in its thoughts.

When she finished, Xander turned toward the doorway.

"So many traps, all at once . . . they must be guarding something important."

"I think so." She had a good guess what; she wouldn't doubt that Xander was thinking the exact same thing she was.

The Bane.

"Maybe not a lot of traps," Nym said. "Maybe just one."

She turned to face the Sion. "What do you mean?"

"A chaos trap."

"What?"

"A chaos trap. In the records . . . I mean . . ." Nym paused. "My parents. When they wanted to keep us away from the ruins of the old empire, they would warn us that the buildings were protected by a chaos trap."

"Which is what?" Geni asked.

"A kind of trap, obviously," the Sion snapped. "Designed by Titans to protect the things they valued most from other Titans. A series of traps, ones that had to be navigated in a precise pattern to defeat."

"How do you figure out the pattern?" she asked.

Nym shook his head.

Geni knew what that meant. So, from his reaction, did Xander.

"So what do we do now?" she asked.

No one had an answer.

Could it really end here? Gods, had the entire quest been futile? All their sacrifice, all their escapes . . .

"There's nothing *we* can do," Xander said.

"What's that supposed to mean?" Geni asked, turning to face him.

He stood at the entrance to the next chamber.

"What are you doing?" she asked. "Xander—"

"It's up to me now," he said, and stepped forward, into the chaos trap.

* * *

You will have a role to play when the time comes. A special role.

That's what Ki had told him. There was something about the old man . . . Xander had believed him. Then, and now. The dragon had said there was something special about him, too.

It seemed to him that the time had come to prove the two of them right.

It wasn't something he could put into words; he couldn't even really argue the point logically. It was just something he had to do. Now.

He stepped across the threshold, and the light from Vreen's torch disappeared. The darkness engulfed him.

A chaos trap.

A series of traps. A precise pattern to get through them. Could he figure out what that pattern was? He would have to, or—

He felt heat behind him and leapt forward. The darkness lit up with a flash of light—flames.

He landed, but there was no floor beneath his feet.

His hands reached out—not straight, but to his left; he knew, somehow, instinctively, that there was nothing directly in front of him to hold on to; he twisted his body, and—

Grabbed on to a rope.

Something roared beneath him. Something that sounded every bit as big as the umberdroth, and a lot less friendly, if such a thing were possible. He began rocking back and forth to gain momentum. Instinct urged him to move—quickly.

The something roared again. With everything Xander could muster he swung himself higher and higher . . .

And let go of the rope. He felt himself hurtling forward . . .

And landed on something soft, and warm.

Something alive.

A slimy tendril closed on his arm. Where it touched him, his skin burned.

He ripped his arm free and jumped away again.

He landed on stone, twisting his ankle in the process. Tears came to his eyes.

He stood and bumped his head on the ceiling.

He ducked low, and a second later bumped it again.

The ceiling was lowering.

He felt the thrum of energy beneath his feet, and realized the floor was rising as well.

He sprinted forward. The ceiling brushed against his hair.

He bowed. He fell to his knees. He crawled.

He lay flat on his belly, and then felt pressure on his chest.

A few more seconds, and he would be crushed. He would die. Their quest would fail, and Geni . . .

In that instant, Xander felt again the way he had back in Balu'thia's village. Back when the two of them had been talking, and he'd seen things somehow outside himself, seen the world as if he were a thing apart from it altogether. Back then he'd seen the umberdroth, preparing to deal death and destruction to Thia and her people.

Now what he saw was that the way out for him lay not straight ahead, but to his right. Where there was a lever, similar to the ones that had disarmed the traps they'd passed through previously.

He stretched out his arm and reached for it.

CHAPTER FIFTY-SEVEN

They had bypassed Minoch on their journey, traveled past it on the coast from Walderon, heading due north for the western coast of the Henge and the approach to the Great Bridge. Mancer was angry; he sent messengers to Calis and the other commanders of the army, insisting that they stop to pay their respects to him. It was his territory they were traveling through; his citizens had gathered by the hundreds to see the new channeler. The army had to stop.

Calis had sent back word that he did not see it that way.

There was another reason as well, of course, that he did not want to stop in Minoch. The captain. He felt differently toward Tandis now; Galor's words, his accusations, had struck home with the boy, despite the fact that the King had offered no proof of anything. The King, in fact, had offered little explanation at all: of his decisions, of his actions, of the Spell of Binding itself.

Calis, in fact, had not seen the King since that evening.

The last he recalled was Galor cutting his own arm, and then Calis's. He'd placed a hand on the boy's forehead and begun to speak. Calis's vision had blurred; the words had blurred as well. Some of the King's words Calis understood; most he didn't. Most weren't even in a language he could recognize. When the

King had finished chanting, Calis had felt a deep weariness overtake him. It was all he could do to make it back to the room where he had changed earlier.

He slept for two days.

He woke to find Hildros standing over him, holding a fresh suit of clothes, bearing news.

The army had been mustered. The army was to march tomorrow.

And Calis, the King's Ward, the first channeler to emerge from the race of men in the last two hundred years, was to lead it.

Of course, the title was for show, as was the rank that went with it: Knight General. Hildros—and Henrik, whom they had met earlier—were the army's true commanders.

But it was Calis the people came out to cheer. In the mountain villages, along the settlements of the river Gandru, in Ruvenna and Walderon, in the towns along the coast.

It had taken a month to move the army to where it lay now, camped within an hour's march of the bridge and the enemy awaiting them.

Calis had reconnoitered the battleground this morning; it was to be, he saw at once, a suicide mission. Just as Hildros had warned, so long ago. The Fallen had the eastern landing barricaded and fortified; from a rise a quarter mile distant, Calis saw that they had catapults, and archers, and all manner of projectiles prepared. The men chosen for the initial attack would perish quickly; the dead would number in the hundreds. Calis had wanted to lead that first charge himself; Hildros and Henrik had looked at each other and laughed when he made that pronouncement.

"Not much chance of that," Hildros said.

"But I'm the commander—"

"You're his heir now, boy. I let you get yourself killed, Galor'll have my head on a stick and my ass for breakfast."

"And mine for lunch," Henrik chimed in.

"So what am I supposed to do while my men are dying?"

"You're supposed to watch. Do what you can to help."

"Come up with a strategy." He nodded. "Very well."

"No." The old warrior gestured toward Henrik. "That's our job."

"That's not fair."

"Life's not fair, boy," Hildros said. "And then you die."

"Then you die." Henrik laughed. "That's a good one. I'll drink to that."

"Let's," Hildros said, and they had gone off somewhere in camp to do just that.

And now here Calis was, alone in his tent once more. As he'd been alone for most of the month. He'd tried talking to some of the soldiers his own age the first few days out; most had shied away, answering his questions with simple grunts or "yessirs." A few had leeched on, commenting on how smart he was, how quick and insightful a study of military matters he was proving to be. It hadn't taken Calis long to stop talking to those people; things had changed for him, he realized. Galor's heir. People were going to treat him differently from now on. Very, very differently. He would have to be aware at all times of others' motives; who was telling him what, and why.

He was beginning to have an insight, perhaps, into why Galor had become so paranoid. Eight hundred years of keeping his own counsel . . .

"My lord."

Calis turned. One of the boys who had been assigned as his squire (boy—the lad was his age, perhaps even a year or two older) stood in the entryway, holding the tent flap open.

"Yes?"

"The knight, to see you."

Calis nodded. "Show him in."

Hildros. Calis wondered if he had come to talk strategy after all. Or apologize for his behavior. If so, Calis was not in a forgiving mood.

And then Tandis entered the tent.

For a moment Calis was too stunned to move or say anything.

"Sir," he said. "I—"

"I believe it's me who should be calling you 'sir' now, Calis. Knight General. You have done well. In all counts. You have brought Galor's army."

"Yes, sir. I . . ." Calis stumbled for words; Hildros had sent for the captain and Ty the instant they were within marching distance from Minoch. Calis had assumed he would reunite with his former comrades, his former commander, at some point over the next few days. He'd expected to have time to prepare, though, to think about exactly what he wanted to say to Tandis. What questions he wanted to ask. Now, though . . .

"I have been talking with Hildros. Strategy. Though there is not much to talk about, as you know. Little strategy in the attack. Our best hope lies in seizing a moment when the elements will favor us. Or at least handicap our enemy. A cloudy afternoon. A foggy morning. A rainy night. We must move soon, though. I have heard rumors; Talax grows impatient."

"Yes," Calis said. "We must move soon."

The two looked at each other.

"Tell me of the King," Tandis said. "How did he seem to you?"

Calis opened his mouth to reply—

Tandis has been deceiving you for some time now.

—and Galor's words, all at once, popped into his head.

"Well enough," Calis said, suddenly—for no reason he could think of—angry. "Tell me of yourself, Captain."

Tandis frowned.

"What?"

"I'm curious, that's all. All these years we have traveled together, and I know so little about you."

"We have stood together in battle, Calis. I should think that provides you all the knowledge you need of me."

"In some ways. But in others . . . I feel I barely know you at all, sir."

"You have questions." Tandis shrugged. "Ask them."

"Very well. How old are you?"

Tandis laughed—a laugh that did not, Calis saw, reach his eyes. "Old enough," he said. "That is a strange question, boy."

"In years."

"Why do you want to know?"

"What about your country, sir? Where is it you hail from, originally?"

Tandis's face hardened. "He told you to ask me these questions, didn't he? Galor?"

"No," Calis said, which was the literal truth, although of course the King had put the notion in his head. "But it's strange to me that you won't answer them."

"They are that important to you?"

"The truth is important to me. Yes." Calis drew himself up. "I am the King's heir now."

"So I have heard." Tandis's eyes narrowed. "It seems to me, though, you may be more than monarch and heir."

"How so?"

"There is something different about you. I can sense it." Tandis took a step forward, his gaze boring into Calis's eyes. "The King's presence."

"What?"

"The Spell of Binding." The captain's eyes narrowed. "The two of you are linked now."

Calis nodded. He had thought, when the time was right, to

ask Tandis more about the spell; if anyone would know, he reasoned, the captain would. But now that they were face-to-face . . .

Those questions no longer seemed important.

"And if we are?"

"Then the two of you are bound together. Now, and forever."

"We are all of us bound to Galor, Captain. To his service. You have told me that yourself, many times—is that not so?"

"It is."

"Which is why truth between us is so important, sir. So when you will not tell me these things . . . your age. Your origin. Your family. . . ."

Tandis nodded, and sighed. "Very well. You want to know about my family? I will tell you about my brother."

"Good. I did not even know you had—"

"He fights for the Fallen."

Calis's eyes widened. "What?"

"My brother fights for the Fallen."

"He is Krax?" Calis asked. There were reports that the army of Kraxis had marched to the Keep recently, to join the forces there.

"No," Tandis said.

"Then . . ."

"He does not serve. He commands."

"But . . ." Calis was confused. "Talax commands the Fallen."

"Yes," the captain nodded. "Talax commands the Fallen."

Calis looked at the captain, and realized something.

A month earlier, Tandis had been on his deathbed. White as a sheet, thin as a rail, scars on his body from the Fallen's cowardly attack.

The boy saw no scars now. In fact, Tandis looked as if the assassination attempt had never taken place.

Calis could not recall a time when the captain had looked like anything other than he looked now. A man in the prime of his life.

Talax's brother.

And suddenly a thought entered his head.

The captain of the Azure Knights—dating back to the time before this one, from the days of the group's formation in the reign of Morrigan the Patricide—had always taken the name Tandis. It was, Calis and the rest of the Knights had always been told, an honorific. Akin to a rank.

But what if there was only one Tandis—what if there had only ever been one Tandis—what if . . .

Talax's brother.

Calis sat down heavily on his bunk.

"Gods," he said.

"No," Tandis said. "Immortals—but never gods. Hosten proved that."

CHAPTER FIFTY-EIGHT

The instant Xander pulled the lever, two things happened.

The pressure on his chest disappeared.

And light suddenly exploded everywhere: brilliant, dazzling light, bright as the noonday sun, brighter by far than any fire or candle or candelabra could ever be.

As Xander got to his feet, he saw why.

Before him was another chamber, a circular chamber, twice as large as any of the rooms they had passed through previously. In the center of it was a single source of light: a candle of some sort, he supposed, though he saw no flame. It blazed as bright as any thousand candles, but the true brightness of the room came from the reflections of its light. Reflections that sparkled and dazzled everywhere Xander looked.

Because the entire chamber—almost every square inch of wall surface—was covered with mirrors.

Mirrors of all sizes, and shapes. Some as large as the great tapestries that hung in the Keep; some as small as the nail on his thumb. Irregularly shaped pieces of glass, he saw as he stepped closer, even the ones that had been framed. There was not a single smooth edge to be found; they were, Xander realized, shattered remnants of a much, much larger whole.

Mirrors.

"By the Gods . . ."

Vreen came up alongside him, shaking his head. "What is this place?"

"Your guess is as good as mine." Xander turned and saw the others coming to join them as well. Nym. Geni. Who was smiling for the first time in a long, long while that he could remember. For obvious reasons.

The golem—Leeland—was walking alongside her. Its body was burned black, dented, and scratched but otherwise it looked unharmed.

"Look," Geni said, gesturing to the golem. "Do you see . . ."

"I do." Xander felt a little smile on his face as well. "Good to see you," he said to the golem who—of course—said nothing back.

"These aren't mirrors."

Xander turned and saw Nym, hands on hips, standing in front of one of the larger pieces of glass.

"What do you mean?" Xander asked.

The Sion just shook his head: Xander, after sharing a puzzled look with Geni, stepped up alongside Nym to see what he was talking about.

Reflected in the glass was a bright blue sky. A series of clouds, whizzing past. Almost as if he were traveling through the clouds. As if he were flying.

"That is strange." He reached out and put his hand on the surface of the mirror. It sank into it, as if the glass were liquid. A ripple emerged from the contact; the clouds, and the sky, wavered.

The glass clouded over, and Xander found himself staring at his own face.

"Look."

Vreen, on the other side of the chamber, was standing in front of a portrait-sized piece of glass with rusted, rough-cut edges, pointing. Xander crossed to him.

"What?"

"The Fist. Kharrazan's Fist."

Visible in this glass was a desert—an endless vista of dunes, and sand, and rock. Far in the distance, a tall, purple mountain range loomed. "That's the Spine," Vreen said. "Probably north of where we are."

Xander nodded and reached a hand forward once more to tap the surface of the glass.

This time, when he encountered resistance, he pushed through it. All at once he touched something. His hand closed, and reflexively he withdrew it.

And gasped.

In his palm, he held a handful of red desert sand.

"Magic," Vreen said, shaking his head, and backing away. "Magic mirrors."

"Magic mirrors. Magic glass." Geni was walking around the chamber, the golem, standing stock-still in the room's very center, next to the single light source, turning as she moved to keep its eyes on her. "I wonder . . ."

Xander frowned. "What?"

"Curgen's glass." She came to a stop in front of a long, thin mirror; her height, but perhaps only half a foot wide. "Could this be the same material? Although . . ."

Her voice trailed off.

Her eyes went wide.

"What's the matter?" Xander asked.

"Gods," she said, visibly staggering. "By all the Gods . . ."

Xander rushed to her side, almost running into the golem, who was moving forward as well.

He got to Geni and gasped.

Visible in the mirror in front of her were bodies. Dozens of them. Maybe even hundreds. All dead. Mutilated. Burned. All wearing a very familiar uniform: the uniform of the Keep's soldiers.

But that wasn't the worst part of it.

The worst part of it was the man hanging upside down, by his legs, directly in front of him. The man who was even now about to be branded by a soldier of the Fallen who held a hot iron within inches of the bound man's shoulder.

The bound man wore the uniform of the Keep as well, though he was no rank-and-file soldier.

"Lord Ambrose," Xander whispered.

"Father," Geni said.

". . . they head South." As Geni watched, another man came into view. A man in a long black cloak, with boots and trousers to match.

He stood over Ambrose and spoke.

"They head toward Imperium. Now why do they do this? Can it be that the Bane is hidden within the great gates? That all this time while we have sought it, it has been beneath our very noses?"

"I could not tell you why my daughter goes in that direction. And with the boy, you say?" Geni felt tears come to her eyes at the sound of her father's voice; it was at once a wonderful and a terrible thing to hear. Wonderful, that he was alive. Terrible, in that he was clearly in pain. Exhausted, strained, tired beyond belief . . .

"Perhaps the two of them are on a honeymoon. I would not put it past Geni to have gotten married, without my blessing. She has always been a most disobedient child—"

Her father's inquisitor snarled and turned away, motioning to the Fallen soldier with the branding iron, who brought it forward and pressed it to Ambrose's neck.

Her father screamed.

She screamed, too. Someone's hand found hers, and squeezed. Xander.

His eyes glistened as well.

"The branding iron?" Her father forced out a laugh. "Gods, have you creatures no imagination?"

Geni tried to smile; his sense of humor was intact, at least. That was something.

"That is Talax," Nym said.

"What?" Geni felt a chill run down her spine.

"Talax." The Sion pointed to the black-cloaked figure. "The Titan himself."

At that instant, as Nym spoke his name, the image in the mirror—Talax's image—turned and frowned.

"Someone is watching us," he said, and took a step forward. "I can sense it. But how . . ."

He looked straight at them.

"Mirdoth," he said. "You saved a piece of it. Curgen's glass."

Curgen's glass. The Elemscope; her earlier speculation proven right. Curgen's glass was what she'd looked through when she'd seen the villagers, and the blue glow that surrounded them. And the red glow that surrounded the Titan. The glow was there now as well, she realized.

The mirror she was looking at glowed as well. The same reddish color.

Curgen's glass. Was that what all these mirrors were—remnants of something the Dread Lord created?

But this was Morrigan's palace—Morrigan's laboratory. Nit'va' ganesh. Only hadn't the dragon Magor said that it was Curgen's first?

On the other hand, the dragon had said a lot of things. *I will be there if you need me,* chief among them. Well, she needed him now. And where was he?

The Titan's hand lunged forward, straight toward them. The image in the mirror shifted; Talax's face grew huge.

"Ah. Now I can see you," the Titan said, and all at once the image of his hand filled the glass.

And then the hand itself came through into the chamber.

"Ahhh!" Xander jumped back from the mirror. The hand brushed against his shirt and grasped at empty air.

Then it shot out again, and grabbed hold of him.

The glass itself seemed to bend, distorting the image of the Titan's face. Geni lunged forward and grabbed hold of Xander by the waist. She tried to pull him free of the Titan's grasp. It was no use. It was like she wasn't even there.

"You must be that troublesome boy Lord Ambrose mentioned. Come tell me what you know about the Bane, boy. Or better yet . . ." Talax's face suddenly grew even larger. "I'll come to you."

No, Geni thought. Talax, in Nit'va'ganesh. Coming to steal the Bane. It mustn't happen. It couldn't happen. They had to find a way to stop him . . .

"Break the glass!" Xander yelled. "Hurry!"

Even as he yelled that, a sword flew through the air, as if propelled by magic. No, Geni realized. Propelled by Vreen.

The invisible man's blade slammed into the mirror and bounced back off.

Talax's head was through now. Here came his shoulders. Geni continued pulling, trying to free Xander, who had his own legs braced against the wall on either side of the mirror, trying to yank himself from the Titan's grasp.

Vreen's sword swung at Talax, again, and again and again. The Titan was laughing, and cursing, and swearing in words Geni barely recognized, words that sounded like the old common tongue, only different somehow. Ancient, horrible words, which reminded her that the thing before her wasn't a man at all, that—

A form rushed past her then, and slammed into the Titan, who grunted and for the first time, moved backward. Nym, she thought at first, but then saw that she was wrong.

It was Leeland.

The Titan raised an arm and brought it down. The blow

was aimed straight at the golem's head, but at the last possible instant Leeland moved aside. The Titan's fist caught him on the shoulder.

The stone floor itself shook with the impact.

In her mind, the golem screamed.

Geni staggered at the pain. She let go of Xander and fell to her knees.

When she looked up, she saw that Leeland's shoulder was dented. There was some kind of liquid—a thick brown gelatinous substance; it looked like mud—oozing from the wound.

But the golem was still pushing against Talax—whose own grip on Xander had loosened, she saw. Loosened at least enough for the boy to twist free and yank the sword from Vreen's grasp, and turn and stab the Titan square in the chest.

Talax roared in pain, and snarled, and reached down, and snapped the blade off at the hilt.

Xander pushed himself free.

Talax roared in frustration, and anger, and raised both arms high above his head.

Geni saw what was about to happen, and screamed.

"Leeland!"

Even as the Titan's fist was coming down, the golem continued to push Talax backward.

Two things happened then, at almost the exact same instant.

The Titan fell back through the mirror; fell back to the Keep.

And his fists struck the golem, which shattered and splintered into a thousand small pieces.

CHAPTER FIFTY-NINE

"You are one of them," Calis said. "One of the Dread Lords."

"That name." Tandis, who had refused Calis's offer of a drink, remained standing near the tent flap, arms folded across his chest. "It is a corruption."

"What?"

"A corruption. There is a faction of our kind who are called Dred'nir. Somehow—perhaps after Pariden's death, which this faction was responsible for—they were labeled such. Dread Lords."

"So you're not one of them."

"No."

"But Talax is."

"Now, yes. Before . . ." The captain sighed. "It is a long story."

Calis, seated on his bunk, nodded, and took a swig from the glass in his hand. He felt the warming fire of the drink on his throat. The numbness reached, for a second, into his mind.

It was all too much for him. The captain, a Titan. Had he actually known Pariden, the first of the Titans, whose death thousands of years ago had set in motion the first of the great wars, between Titans and mankind, among the Titans themselves? It seemed inconceivable, and yet . . .

"You are the Tandis who slew Lady Umber."

"Yes."

"It was said that you perished then as well."

Tandis smiled. "Clearly not."

"But the Hiergamenon says. In the book of Ezmir. The two of you fought, and then—"

"The Hiergamenon says a lot of things." Tandis smiled. "It is only a book, Calis. A book written by men trying to explain things they saw, things they did not entirely understand."

"Well, I don't understand any of this. Why did you keep it all a secret? Why not tell everyone who you really were? Why all the lies?"

"Only one lie. A lie in service of a greater good." Tandis sat down on the bunk next to him. "The others were all gone. The time of the Titans had passed. It was time for mankind to rule this world. I had no wish to insert myself into your affairs. To become a pawn of those seeking power. I wished only to make amends for what my race had done to your world."

"To my world?"

"Yes."

Calis frowned. "This is not your world?"

"No."

"What does that mean?" Calis asked. "You have to explain that."

Tandis was silent for a moment before continuing. "I am not sure I can. At least, not in a way that would make sense to you."

"I'm not stupid."

"Of course not. But these ideas . . . even to begin explaining them requires a body of knowledge . . . an understanding of science—"

"Of what?"

Tandis turned to him and smiled. "Think of it as a different kind of magic. A kind my people—the Arnor—used to travel from our world to yours."

"It must be a powerful magic," Calis said. "How far away is your world?"

"Far, far away. Beyond the sun, even."

Beyond the sun. Calis's mind reeled at the thought.

He looked at the glass in his hand. Empty. He reached for the cask to fill it again; Tandis stopped him.

"This is not the time to drink to excess, lad. You will be needed, in the fight to come."

"Not true." Calis set down his glass on the trunk in front of him. "The army doesn't need me at all. Hildros and Henrik are in charge. I'm just a figurehead."

"I'm not talking about the army," Tandis said. "I'm talking about Talax. We will have to fight him, and in that battle, your strength—your powers—will be critical."

"You need me to fight a Titan?"

"My strength is not what it was."

"You look—"

"Appearances can be deceiving, lad."

"I know that," Calis snapped.

Tandis sighed. "As I said, Calis, a deception in service of a greater good."

"That's not what the King thinks."

Tandis nodded. "The King no longer trusts me. I have known this for some time. At first, I thought it was because of you."

"Me?"

Tandis nodded. "Yes. When Galor learned of your existence, he thought I planned to overthrow him and install you as ruler of the Kingdom. He has grown only more suspicious over the years."

"And that wasn't the case?"

"No. Of course not. And Galor seemed to understand that

himself. At least at first. But now . . . something is different about him now. He seems not himself."

Calis almost—almost—spoke out then. Almost told Tandis of the King's behavior in Athica, how odd, how eccentric, how disturbing it had been.

At the last second, something stayed his tongue.

And then the tent flap opened once more.

Hildros stood there, with Ty and Henrik behind him.

"Captain. Calis. You'd better come quickly." He spoke to the both of them, but his eyes focused mainly on Tandis.

"What is it?" Tandis asked.

"There's movement in the Keep."

"What?"

"Fallen Armies. Marching out of the fortress, heading for the bridge. Forming up."

"Why?" Calis asked.

"Good question, lad," Hildros snapped, in a tone of voice that suggested just the opposite. "Worth finding out the answer to. Once we're ready for battle ourselves."

"Is that Athican brandy? That cask there?" Ty stepped into the tent, smiling. "Would you mind—"

"Not now. Hildros is right. We must move quickly." Tandis turned to Calis then. "With your permission, Knight General. I will fight by your side, if you will have me."

"Of course," Calis said.

They all left the tent then, Calis pretending not to see Ty duck back inside and emerge a moment later, carrying the cask at his side. He had no desire to stop the man.

He might need a drink again himself, before the day was through.

CHAPTER SIXTY

Xander ripped the mirror from the wall and flung it back into the chamber with the chaos trap. He ran to the lever and pulled it.

The chamber went to black; an instant later, he heard the glass shatter. He yanked the lever again.

The mirror lay in a thousand tiny pieces—shards, and broken bits of glass and plate backing—on the floor.

Safe, he thought, and let out a breath he hadn't even realized he was holding.

"Why did you do that?"

He turned and saw Geni advancing on him, looking as upset as before, if not more so.

"What?"

"Why did you do that?"

"Why do you think? Do you want him to come through again? Find us?"

"No. But my father," she said. "We have to rescue him."

Xander was about to tell her No, we don't, we don't have to do that at all, that would be a stupid thing to do, walk right into the Keep, which, in case you've forgotten, is under Talax's control right now, when he realized that trying to talk sense to Geni at this point wouldn't do any good. She was too upset to think straight; in her shoes, he supposed, he would feel no different.

"We can piece it back together later, perhaps," he said. "Once we have—"

"Xander!"

That was Vreen. The little man stood in the center of the circular chamber now, pointing at the far wall. Pointing at a small mirror; it was glowing. A faint blue light, outlining the jagged glass.

Every other fragment in the room, Xander saw now, had gone dark.

"The second you pulled the lever back there," Vreen said, "this lit up."

Xander took a step toward the little man. In the mirror now, he saw a silver pedestal, on top of which was a small silver ball. The same faint blue glow surrounded that as well.

Magic.

It can take many forms. It is my understanding that currently it is in the shape of a silver orb.

Captain Tandis's words, spoken at the Keep, so long ago, came back to him now.

They must have come back to Geni as well.

"That's it," she said. "The Bane."

Xander nodded; the two of them walked up alongside Vreen.

"That's it?" the little man said. "That little thing? That's the Bane? I thought it would be bigger."

"It can take many forms," Geni said quietly. "That's what we were told."

"Small forms, though," Vreen said. "And what is it exactly? This Bane? The whole time we've been looking for it, and you never really said—"

"Nym," Geni said, ignoring him. "Do you see? We've found it. After all this time, we've found it."

There was no response. Puzzled, Xander turned.

The Sion stood a dozen feet back from the rest of them, staring—as they were—at the Bane. But the expression on his face . . .

For some reason, Nym looked terrified.

For the second time in what felt like as many minutes, he had frozen. Such uncharacteristic behavior. He never froze; inaction led to vulnerability, even for him.

The first time had occurred when he caught sight of Talax in the mirror. The appearance of the Titan had suddenly reminded him, after weeks of near forgetting, of who he truly was. Why he was here. And who, ultimately, he was working for.

That reminder, though, had not translated into action.

Nym had simply watched as the other four members of his party—no, not his party, he was wrong to think of them that way. They were the enemy, the invisible man, the golem, the girl, and especially the boy, who had saved his life back in the village of the Iru for reasons that would become clear soon enough, Nym was sure of that, selfish reasons—and Talax had fought. His paralysis still had not ended by the time the fight had finished.

And now, staring at the Bane, it had returned.

What do do?

He should take the Bane.

With his great speed, he could reach through the portal, grab it, and be gone before the others could even move to stop him. He would make for Imperium on the fastest horse he could find. He would bring the Bane to Talax himself, and be raised highest of all Sions of the reborn Empire. He would . . .

What if Talax had noticed his inaction earlier? The Titan would not forgive. He would take the Bane, and then kill Nym.

"What's wrong?"

The girl was speaking to him now; he rearranged his features, as best he could, into a semblance of nonchalance. He was not in-terested in the Bane. He did not care about the Bane.

"Nothing," he said.

"Go on, Geni," Xander said. "Take it."

The princess shook her head. "I don't know. I . . ."

"Don't be scared," Xander said. "Just reach through and grab it."

She nodded, and raised a hand to the glass.

Nym felt perspiration running thickly on his face.

His body trembled.

Take it.

That was what he should do. What he had to do. He heard Talax's voice inside his brain. Perhaps there was a connection of some kind between the two of them now; when Talax had turned and seen him earlier, when he'd realized he was being spied on, Nym had sensed the Titan's anger. Could Talax sense him now?

Take it, take it, take it.

Was he trying to send Nym a message? Or was it all just Nym's imagination?

Geni's hand stretched out—

And bumped into the mirror.

"What's the matter?" Xander asked.

"I don't know. I can't . . ." The girl tried again; same result. She looked at Xander. "I can't get at it."

"Why?" he asked.

"How should I know?" she snapped.

Take it. Take it.

Nym was moving forward almost before he realized what he was doing.

"Let me try," he said, and before anyone could stop him, he reached forward himself.

His hand hit the glass and bounced off. He tried again, and the same thing happened.

"This glass doesn't work like the others," Geni said. "Why . . ."

"I don't know. It looks the same. Why we can't just reach through and . . ."

The boy's voice trailed off. He'd stretched a hand out, just like the girl had. Just like Nym himself had.

Only *his* hand had traveled through the glass.

And now he had pulled it back. And in that hand, he held the silver orb. The Bane.

The voice in Nym's head grew louder.

Take it. Take it, take it, take it.

Xander looked at the thing in his hand and tried to arrange the thoughts swirling through his head into some kind of order.

"How did you do that?" Geni asked.

"I don't know," he said. "I just . . . I reached through and grabbed it."

"But that doesn't make any sense. Why you were able to, and the rest of us . . ." Geni shook her head.

You have a special destiny.

Ki's words echoed in his ears once more. As, all at once, did Magor's.

I sense nothing from you, boy.

Xander shook his own head then. Time enough to sort it all out later. For now, the important thing was the Bane. Frankly, it didn't feel like anything special to him. It was a lot lighter than it looked—too light in his hands to be made out of silver, or any other kind of metal that he knew about. If this really was Morrigan's laboratory, as Geni had said, maybe the Usurper had come up with a new kind of metal. His own kind of metal, though what the point would be of that . . .

Xander gasped.

The silver ball was melting in his hand.

"Aahhh!" he said, and tried to shake it off.

"What are you doing?" Geni yelled. "What did you do to it?"

"Nothing! Get it off, get it off, get it off!" The silver was flowing down his wrist; flowing not like water, but like molten metal, only it wasn't hot and he couldn't get it to flow in any direction but down his arm.

And then, all at once, it stopped flowing, and snapped back into a rigid shape.

A bracelet—a circlet—of silver, around his wrist.

A single piece of metal.

Xander tried instantly to yank it off. It was tight on his wrist; too tight to slide over his hand.

"I can't take it off," he said.

"Perhaps we could cut it off." Nym stepped forward, holding out his dagger.

There was a look in the Sion's eyes that, all at once, bothered Xander. Scared him a little, even.

"No, no." Geni waved Nym off. "Xander. Maybe you can command it."

"What?"

"The Bane. It may be tied to you somehow—a link. Try to contact it. Tell it to form back into a ball."

Tell a piece of metal what to do? That was the stupidest idea he'd heard in a long time, Xander thought, although he realized instantly where Geni had gotten it. The golem.

"I'll try," he said, trying—and he suspected, failing—to keep his doubts hidden.

He raised his arm before his face, and stared at the Bane.

Ball. Go back to being a ball.

"Concentrate," Geni said. "Focus."

He bit back the reply on his tongue once more.

"Let me try," Geni said, and took hold of his wrist, placing one hand on either side of the bracelet. She stared intently at his arm, brow furrowed in concentration.

"Do you feel anything?" she asked after a moment.

"No," he snapped. "It's not working. Nothing's working. This is Morrigan's laboratory, you said?"

"I think so." Geni sighed and let go of his wrist. "I don't think we've found the lab itself yet, but Nit'va'ganesh is where it's supposed to be."

"So maybe we have to find that. Maybe there's something in the lab that'll help us figure out what to do. How to get this off."

"Do we need to get it off?" Vreen asked. "I mean, I'm sure you might not want to have to carry it, but what's the harm in having you wear it back to wherever it is you need to go? I don't see that as a problem. No one can steal it that way, after all. Unless they cut off your whole hand, right? And who's going to want to do that?"

Xander was about to respond when Nym spoke up once more.

"Actually," the Sion said, "I'm afraid I have an answer to that question. One that none of you is going to like."

Nym raised his dagger then, and took a step forward.

CHAPTER SIXTY-ONE

"What are you doing?"

It was the girl who had spoken. Nym ignored her.

"I knew I didn't like you," Xander said.

"I have a deal for you, boy," Nym said.

"I'm not interested in any of your deals. Your word isn't worth a thing, obviously."

"Nym?" the girl said again. "Xander. What are you talking about?"

"He's been lying to us all along. He wasn't captured at any estate, or anything like that," Xander said. "He's been in the fight from the beginning. He's been using us to find the Bane, and now that we have, he—"

"That's not true," Geni said. "Nym . . ."

"I'm afraid it is, Princess. I *have* been lying," Nym said, and the sound of those words, coming from his own mouth, made his stomach roll over.

Gods. What was wrong with him?

"But I'm telling the truth now, boy. You saved my life." He met Xander's eyes. "And so I will spare yours. I will take your arm, and the Bane along with it, and leave you here to heal."

"That's your generous offer? You'll cut off my arm?"

"Yes."

"I have a better idea," Xander said, and drew his sword.

"Don't be a fool. Consider the offer a little more carefully," Nym replied.

"Nym," the girl said. "Stop."

He shook his head.

"Put down that dagger," Geni said. "It's not the best way to get what you want. Put it down, and we'll talk. All right? Just put it down."

Nym frowned. Put down the dagger? Ridiculous idea. Why would he do that? And yet . . .

Perhaps there was sense in the girl's words. They had traveled together so far, for so long . . . surely there was a better way for things to end than like this.

"Put down the dagger."

His arm wavered.

The princess. She was a diplomat. If she was certain there was a way to work this out, between man and Sion, then perhaps she was . . .

A Sion as well, he remembered suddenly. A Sion of man.

And Nym, all at once, had a pretty fair idea what her power was.

"Put it down," she said, and Nym felt the dagger lower in his hands.

It was, he realized, being helped along. There was some-one tugging on his wrist. Someone he couldn't see. Someone in-visible.

Nym lashed out with his elbow, and heard a satisfying crack! followed an instant later by a cry of pain.

"Vreen!" Xander cried out.

The princess looked concerned as well; she looked away from Nym, and at that instant it was like the spell was broken.

Before she could reestablish it, he quickened to her side and hit her square on the jaw, as hard as he could.

She fell to the ground, insensate.

And then it was just him, and the boy. Xander. Who was looking at him, eyes wide, with an expression of horror on his face.

"It was you," Xander said.

"What?"

"You're the one who was chasing us—back at the Keep. You've been chasing us that long?"

"Guilty as charged." Nym smiled. "But the chase is ended now, boy."

And so, Nym realized, was his offer.

He had no further desire to spare the boy's life; he simply wanted what he wanted. The Bane.

And he wanted it now.

He quickened himself once more, and charged.

Xander had never seen anyone—anything—move as fast as Nym did in that instant. The Sion was a blur, the knife in his hand a shining streak of light. Xander saw it shoot toward him, toward his gut, toward a killing blow . . .

And he stepped, somehow, aside.

Nym screamed in frustration and turned to face him.

"Lucky, boy," he said. "But . . ."

And even before he'd finished, the Sion had charged again.

And Xander, somehow, dodged once more.

Even as he moved, he realized what was happening. It was the same thing that had occurred in the chaos trap chamber, the same thing that had happened back in the valley of the Iru. The same thing, Xander realized now, that had happened when he had saved Tandis from the arrow. When he had fought Morlis, and Vincor, and Oro, even.

Time was unfolding before him, and he had the ability to stand outside it. Sometimes.

Like now.

As he looked at Nym, dagger in hand, ready to charge again, he knew what the Sion's next tactic would be. He would feign a lunge this time, feign a thrust straight ahead, for the heart. Dodging would do Xander no good; he would have to parry, and the instant he tried to do so, Nym would use his speed, would move around to Xander's back to make a killing blow.

He knew something else, too.

Once he was dead, once Nym had the Bane, he would take Geni as well. The princess of the Keep would be of much value to the Fallen Army, to Talax.

He would have to fight to kill, too, Xander realized.

Nym couldn't understand it.

The boy had no skill with a blade. No knowledge of combat. He was a peasant. He might as well be fighting with that frying pan he'd used to block the arrow. And yet . . .

Nym couldn't finish him.

Nym thrust straight ahead, expecting the boy to parry. But he didn't. He let Nym come at him, and then chopped down hard on his arm. The boy's sword cut into his wrist; Nym screamed in pain and backed off.

"How are you doing this?" he hissed, studying his wound. Not a deep one. He would bind it when this was over.

"Just lucky. Like you said. Right?" The boy smiled.

The sight of that smile caused Nym to lose control.

He leapt right at the boy, dagger thrusting forward, and then, at the last second, twisted his body around to administer a killing blow.

But the boy wasn't there. The boy had moved.

His sword, however, had not.

The blade dug into Nym's chest. Blood began to flow.

This cut, the Sion knew, was far deeper than the first. He

would have to see to it immediately. Finish the boy, and bandage himself.

He quickened himself once more, and dove at Xander. The boy, somehow, dodged him again.

Nym found himself on his hands and knees.

No, he thought. Get up. Get up.

But he couldn't.

A shadow fell over him. He looked up and saw Xander.

"Sorry," the boy said. "But—"

"Don't be," Nym shot back. Or at least, that was what he had intended to say. But the words came out all garbled.

His mouth was full. A warm, wet liquid.

He spat it out onto the floor. Blood. A lot of it. It was coming from his chest as well. And his wrist. It was all pooling together.

He sank down to the floor, into its warm, welcoming embrace.

CHAPTER SIXTY-TWO

Ambrose coughed, and gagged. His head rolled to one side and he threw up the gruel that Mirdoth had so laboriously spoon-fed him not half an hour ago.

Mirdoth sighed, rolled his lord back over onto the cot, and cleaned up the mess as best he could.

The Titan and his torturers had not killed Ambrose, though they had come close. The Lord had lost much blood; he was in a great deal of pain. Worse yet, though, he was still not sensible. Mirdoth was beginning to worry that he never would be again.

After Talax had been forced back through the glass, the Titan had raged throughout the dungeons. He had killed dozens more, and then he had turned his anger on first Mirdoth, and then Ambrose.

Mirdoth had been prepared; the shields in his mind were strong. He feigned injury, of a severity great enough, he believed, to convince the Titan that he had truly done damage.

Had he known what Talax intended, Mirdoth might have held out a little longer. Might have even, perhaps, used the knowledge he had amassed—knowledge he had recovered, actually, knowledge that at one point had been as much a part of him as the hairs on his chin, the spell of *a'dam'ash ashturay,* the Spell of

Condemnation, the most potent of all death magics—to defend his lord, though such defense would ultimately have been futile. Talax was the most powerful being in the world—or at least, the second-most powerful, after the mysterious figure whose orders Mirdoth had watched him surreptitiously receive those many days earlier.

More powerful than Galor certainly—and a dozen times more powerful than himself. At least, as long as he withheld himself from accessing the full power of the shards.

He did not know how much longer that would be. How much longer it could be, or even should be. Seeing Geni and the boy in the glass, if only for that brief instant . . . they were close now, he knew. Close to finding the Bane. Avalan's circlet of power. Close to thwarting the desires of Talax and his lord. Yet Talax had come dangerously close to capturing them once already; the Titan would no doubt make as many attempts to do so as were necessary. Mirdoth had to help them, no matter what. Didn't he?

Footsteps, all at once, sounded outside his cell. Many footsteps, racing through the hall.

The same mystic barrier that Talax had placed on the observatory was here, too. If Mirdoth wanted to find out what was happening . . . he would need to ask.

He stood and went to the door.

"Guard!" he yelled, hammering on the door with one fist. "Guard! What goes on out there? Guard!"

He kept yelling and hammering—nearly a minute—until the plate slid aside and a soldier—Krax—appeared before him.

"What?"

Mirdoth didn't even bother responding.

He simply reached into the man's mind, and took the information he needed.

A summons from the Fallen commander.

Soldiers rousted from their barracks.

Talax standing before them, raging.

". . . *we will seize the initiative. If Galor's army is here to support the girl and her expedition, we will make that support impossible. If Galor's army is here to rescue them, we will make that rescue impossible. Their army is unprepared; their positions are not fortified. We will move across the bridge, we will attack them, all will move as I direct, not a man is to be left alive, not a soldier is to make it back to Athica with a word. We shall leave the Keep immediately.*"

Mirdoth frowned. Talax had left the Keep?

The guard let out a gasp. His eyes rolled back in his head, and he fell to the floor like a shadow puppet whose strings had been cut. Dead, Mirdoth knew. A death he was responsible for, a death he had caused by his careless disregard for the frailty of the man's mind.

Mirdoth stood there for a moment, shocked at what he had just done.

How easy it was.

How much he wanted to do it again.

He closed his eyes, and sank down to the floor.

And in his mind, the shards called to him once more.

CHAPTER SIXTY-THREE

Geni sighed and got to her feet.

At one end of the chamber lay Nym. Dead.

At the other end stood Xander, the Bane in a circlet around his wrist.

And a thousand miles away, in the dungeon of the castle he had once ruled, the castle that had once been their home, her father was being tortured.

Leeland gone. Broken into a million pieces. The golem was becoming a person. She knew it.

It was all too much for her—mentally, physically, emotionally . . .

She rubbed her jaw where the Sion had hit her, and tried to focus on what Xander was telling her.

"Say it again. You what?"

Xander threw up his hands. "I don't know how to describe it. I stepped . . . outside of myself. Outside of time."

She frowned. "What does that mean?"

"I don't know what it means. All I know is, that was what happened before, too. At Balu'thia's village. When I saw the umberdroth. I think it was what happened when I saved Tandis."

"You saved Tandis."

"Yes. Vreen, wait. I'll be right there."

"All right. Stepping outside of time. We'll find out what that means." Geni nodded, casting her eyes across the room. Vreen. Where was the little man?

Not that she could figure it out by looking.

"Maybe it's the Bane doing it," Geni suggested.

"I don't think so. I don't know why but I don't think whatever it is supposed to do works on or for me. It is almost like it's sleeping."

Geni frowned.

"I was thinking," he suggested hesitantly. "Maybe I'm a Sion, too."

"I don't know. I've never heard of any power like that. Doesn't mean it's not possible, I suppose, but . . ." She shrugged. "We'll have to talk to someone."

"Yeah, I guess so. After all this is over." He nodded, and crossed to the far side of the chamber, where they'd first entered. Where they'd taken off and set down the packs they'd been carrying: their remaining supplies, their weapons, what spare clothing they had.

Xander bent down now and began rifling through them, pulling things out as he went.

"Okay. We've got a few days' worth of food, at the most. Vreen, hold on a minute. I'm in the middle of something. Another day's worth of water, if we're careful. But that's all right, because we know where the river is. And we'll be back to the forest in a week or so, and we can get supplies enough to last until we reach the Iru again. Or not." He flushed. "I mean, we don't have to stop there. We could stay in Calebethon, circle around the valley, and . . ."

Geni looked at him, looked at the supplies he was consolidating, thought about the packs they had been carrying for weeks, and the weeks more they had to go before they reached home, and she sighed heavily. She was so tired. Tired of it all.

"I can't do it," she said.

"What?"

"I can't make that journey again, Xander. Not right now. I don't have it in me." She shook her head. "I'm sorry."

He got to his feet and crossed the room toward her.

"I understand. I'm tired, too. And after all this"—he gestured about the chamber, at the corpse, the shattered bits of glass and metal—"after everything that happened here . . . I know it seems like a long way away. The Keep. Or Athica. Wherever we have to go. But Geni—we did it. Don't you see?"

He smiled. "We started out to find the Bane. That was your idea, and we did it. We'll take a day or so, if you want, but then . . . we have to go back. Tandis needs us. The King needs us. Your father."

She sighed again. He was right, she knew it, but the thought of all those miles . . .

"Is this about Balu'thia?" he asked. "I mean. Like I said—we don't have to stop there. I said that already. Maybe we don't even have to go that way. We can try for the coast. There might be free traders—Vreen, not now."

He turned at the last, and glared behind him.

"It's not about Balu'thia," Geni said. "It's not about anything. I'm just . . . It's too much."

"I'm not leaving you," Xander said, coming closer.

"You have to."

They stood there for a moment, a couple of feet apart.

"You have food in your beard," she told him.

"Sorry." He brushed at it and missed.

"No. Here. Let me." She reached out her hand; before she could touch him, he took it.

"Geni," he said, and pulled her closer, "I . . ."

His head leaned in toward hers.

"Will you look at this already?"

Geni almost jumped a mile.

Vreen was standing right next to Xander. As close to her as he was.

"Ahh!!" She started and jumped back.

"What are you doing?" Xander shouted.

"Trying to get your attention!" the little man said. "Look."

He held up something in his hand. Something long and thin and shiny. At first Geni thought it was a weapon. A dagger. Then she realized she was wrong.

"It's part of the glass," she said.

"Yes. It was lying on the floor there, and I picked it up, and—well, see for yourself." Vreen tilted it in his hand. "If you hold it the right way . . ."

Geni leaned in closer to see what he was talking about.

There were but four known shards left in the world.

The closest was in Capitar, but that was Air. The shard Mirdoth needed to do what had to be done was Fire—named as such a thousand years ago by Magesta. Fire, which was across the western continent, in Athica. The most powerful of the shards, in many ways. The one Mirdoth had drawn upon, more often than not, when performing spells like the *a'dam'ash ashturay*. Back before he had been bound, his powers circumscribed in the aftermath of battle.

But the bonds were loosening. With each passing moment, with every act contemplated, with every act of magic undertaken, the bonds were slipping free.

And having killed the guard . . .

They were slipping away faster than ever before.

He would have to kill again, most certainly, if he and Ambrose were to survive. But the barriers Talax had placed around their cell were powerful indeed; his powers could stretch only so far with them in place. It seemed to him an unnecessary precaution, unless . . .

Not for the first time, Mirdoth found himself wondering how much the Titan knew of him, his history. A determined scholar could piece together all the facts that were necessary to uncover what the King and Mirdoth had hidden for all these many years; Talax was no scholar, of course, but the Titan had his ways, of that Mirdoth had no doubt.

On the cot behind him, Ambrose lay still, his breathing peaceful and easy. That was a function of Mirdoth's powers as well; he had reached into the Lord's mind and soothed, as best he could, the chaos he'd found there. Ambrose was sleeping now; not the kind of sleep that came at the end of a day, but the kind that came at the end of a season, the kind that lasted for weeks, even months on end. A hibernation, such as the bears and other forest creatures enjoyed. Mirdoth was uncertain how long he could make his lord's hibernation last; what would be necessary, what was safe.

Talax was not in the Keep. The opportunity for desperate action was now. But his lord was in no condition to make a journey unsupported. Mirdoth couldn't do what was necessary and carry Ambrose, too. And he wouldn't leave him behind.

Ambrose was a strong man. His adventures as a youth were legend in the Kingdom. But this ordeal was beyond anything the Lord had encountered. He needed a healer, not just for his body but for his mind; there were several Mirdoth could think of, but it would be best if they could reach Galor, in Athica. And soon.

Which made escape necessary. It was now or never.

Perhaps with enough power he could escape with Ambrose.

But for that, he needed the shard. Fire.

He concentrated, and reached out, and the world opened up to him.

Every living thing in this world possesses magic.

He had told the princess as much, not long ago, and it was true. There was magic in the trees, in the creatures of the air, and the sea, and the forest. Accessing the shard, he was able to touch that magic. To access the energy that bound this world together. And now that he had access to all that power . . .

In the middle of reaching out to that energy, in the middle of preparing a spell that would enable him to free himself and Ambrose from the dungeon, Mirdoth stopped, and frowned.

As he reached out to the magic . . .

Something in the magic was reaching out to him.

The piece of the shattered Elemscope.

There was something visible in the little piece of glass. Something that had been partially obscured at first by smoke, or a cloud, but was now coming clear. What that something was . . .

Xander leaned closer, trying to figure it out.

"It's a ball of some sort," Vreen said helpfully. "Like the kind children play with."

"Shinier than a ball," Geni said. "More like a marble."

Shiny, yes, Xander thought. But the sheen didn't come from the ball. There was some kind of coating on it. A black sphere, with a coating around it.

He pushed closer, pushed his eye up as near to the glass as he could get, and squinted at it.

The thing in the glass looked back.

"It's an eye," Xander said, and his heart thudded in his chest. Talax.

"Break it!" he yelled. "Break the—"

Mirdoth blinked.

Geni.

And two others.

They were seeing him, as he was seeing them. Through the shard; through the remnants of the Dread Lord's glass. The glass from the Elemscope; the glass Talax had somehow used to nearly capture them not even an hour earlier, while he had been in the midst of torturing Ambrose. Curgen's glass; there were those who said that once, long before even the Cataclysm, the glass had been part of something else, a doorway, a portal, between that place where men lived and that place where the Titans had existed before coming to Elemental. It was a bridge of some kind, the glass; a way to travel from place to place, from here to there, in the blink of an eye. Without horse, or wagon, or harnessed beast.

Talax had done it.

Perhaps . . .

Mirdoth closed his eyes and concentrated.

"No!" Geni yelled.

"What do you mean, 'no'? You want him—"

"It's not him," Geni said.

"How do you know?"

"I know."

"Well, who is it, then?"

She shook her head. "I can't tell. But—"

"We have to break this piece, too," Xander said. "Smash it with a hammer, or something. Before—"

"Let me put it down first," Vreen said. "I'm going to put it down."

And he did. On the floor, between the two of them.

Both Xander and Geni dove for it. For a second they each had a hold of sorts, a finger on the top surface, a thumb on the edge.

And then the glass, all at once, had hold of them.

He made a vortex of sorts, an energy field, to bring them through. Geni was the key. His familiarity with her essence made it possible to bring her, and hence them, through.

She was the first to recover from its effects.

She saw him, and a smile as wide as any Mirdoth had ever seen from her burst forth on her face.

She got to her feet, and rushed to him.

The second they embraced, her body stiffened in his grasp.

She knew something was wrong. He was not surprised; they were too close for such a change as had come over him to go unnoticed. She pulled back and looked at his face, and her eyes widened.

That told Mirdoth that the change had begun. He was not surprised at that, either.

"Where are we?"

"You're back in the Keep, or what's left of it."

Behind her, the first of the two men who had come through the glass with Geni got to his feet. A short, fat man, who . . .

"You are bewitched," Mirdoth said.

"Yes." The little man nodded. "Yes, I am."

"This is Vreen," Geni said. "He was in Kraxis. He helped us find the Bane. Vreen, this is Mirdoth. My father's counselor."

"You can see me," the little man said. "Does that mean—"

"Quiet." Mirdoth snapped. "Geni. You found the Bane? Where . . ."

His voice trailed off as the third traveler rose to his feet.

"Mirdoth," the traveler said, and stretched out his hand, and the wizard's eyes widened.

It was the boy. Xander. A boy no longer.

And on his wrist was the Bane.

CHAPTER SIXTY-FOUR

Calis rode up and down the lines, next to Hildros, a length behind Tandis and Henrik. Surveying the men of Galor's army. Standing by as the captain eased his horse forward to speak to this man or that one, to lend a word of encouragement. To strengthen a line here, to move a regiment there.

As much as the men had come to know and trust him, and Hildros, for as long as they had ridden with Henrik, it was clearly Tandis who commanded their respect. Their allegiance. Their devotion.

Calis wondered if they would feel the same way if they knew the truth.

"Not long now." Tandis had turned; he came up alongside Calis now. "They'll have to attack in the next hour. Two at the most."

Calis nodded. The Fallen at the front of the ranks were packed in tightly; had been so since early morning. Standing there, with only their swords and shields for company . . . the captain was right. They would have to break ranks to eat soon.

The bridge lay a quarter mile in the distance; the Fallen Army was massed up a few hundred yards on the other side of it. Henrik had lent him a looking glass earlier, to watch as the battle line formed: the different armies, the different creatures, as they came together. Urxen at the front. Sions there as well, a handful of them, placed—by ability, no doubt—throughout the ranks. Trogs behind, massed by the hundreds. Foot soldiers. Henrik's guess was that they would be the first ones to charge the bridge; there would be a volley of arrows, several volleys, no doubt, and cannon fire, and then the Trogs would come. Perhaps the Urxen and the Sion would charge with them, or right behind.

And the army of Kraxis would be there as well.

It made Calis angry. It made him embarrassed. It made his face burn red with shame to see the black and yellow of his country's sigil amid the Fallen Army. He'd looked quickly away and handed Henrik back the glass. The captain had looked away as well, avoiding Calis's eye.

Throughout the day, though, there were murmurs along the line. And suspicious glances cast his way.

Krax.

"I still don't understand," Hildros growled. "Why would they even think about attacking us, Captain? It's suicide for them as much as for us, trying to fight their way across that." He gestured toward the bridge.

"They may want the initiative. They may want something we have. Or perhaps . . ." Tandis frowned. "Something they think we have."

"I don't understand," Calis said.

The captain shook his head. "It's not important that you do. For now, just . . ."

Tandis broke off abruptly.

"What is it?" Calis asked.

"Someone is coming. There." He pointed toward the bridge. "Several someones, in fact."

Calis squinted off into the distance.

"I don't see anyone," he said.

"Nor do I." Tandis's face was grim. "But they are there, nonetheless."

"Sir?" Calis asked.

Tandis didn't answer; he simply continued to stare off into the distance, in the direction of the bridge. Calis turned and exchanged glances with Hildros, who was shaking his head and frowning. Clearly he didn't see anything, either.

"Some movement in the ranks," Henrik said. Calis turned and saw that he had taken his glass out once more. "Some of the Urxen . . . they've broken formation. Can't quite tell why . . ."

"Can I see?" Calis asked.

Henrik nodded and handed him the glass.

"Better ready the men," Tandis said, and drew his sword.

"Captain?" Hildros frowned. "What are you doing?"

"Going to meet them," Tandis said. He turned his horse and came up right alongside Calis.

He leaned across his saddle and lowered his voice.

"Keep yourself safe, boy," he said, so that only Calis could hear. "Keep an eye on the King."

"What?"

Tandis straightened; his horse reared up.

"You heard what I said."

And with that, the captain was off. Riding at a full gallop, straight for the empty bridge.

Calis stared after him, dumbfounded.

There was movement in the Fallen lines, on the other side of the bridge. Shouts; soldiers pointing at Tandis as he rode toward them.

"What's he doing?" Henrik asked.

"I'll be damned if I know," Hildros said.

Calis nodded. He had no idea what was happening, either.

But all at once he was seized by a desire to find out.

He tossed Henrik his glass and spurred his horse forward.

* * *

Four of them, all at once. The Spell of Masking was not a difficult one, but added to the effort, the energy he had already expended on freeing them from the dungeon . . .

The strain was telling on Mirdoth. And on the others as well. Geni alongside him. Xander—Gods, he had barely recognized the boy—who had Lord Ambrose slung across his shoulder and was carrying him as best he could.

Vreen seemed more relaxed than his companions. Mirdoth supposed that was because he was used to being invisible, or, more precisely, unnoticed. Walking right up to a cadre of Fallen soldiers, walking right past them without fear was, the sorcerer supposed, a skill in its own right. One they were all growing practiced at.

They had now passed through the Fallen lines entire without being noticed. They were on the very cusp of the bridge. Almost there. Almost safe. Although *safe,* in Mirdoth's case, was a relative term.

In Athica, the King waited.

"Mirdoth?" The question came from Geni, who walked alongside the boy, on whose shoulders Lord Ambrose rested. Still unconscious; doing as well as could be expected under the circumstances. What concerned him more was the boy. The boy, and the Bane.

In the Hiergamenon, the artifact sang; it broadcast its presence far and wide to any and all able to sense its energies. Here and now, though, wrapped around the boy's wrist, in the form of a circlet, its song was muted, such that Mirdoth could barely hear it himself, and he stood a mere handful of feet away from the lad.

There was something odd about him. Xander. When he had time—if he had time—he would have to find out what.

"What is it, child?" Mirdoth asked.

"Look." The girl pointed straight ahead. Mirdoth squinted off into the distance, where a lone rider approached. "Isn't that—"

"Tandis. Yes." Mirdoth managed a smile, for the first time in what felt like forever.

And in that instant, a roar—an inhuman, ear-shattering exclamation of rage—sounded from behind them.

Even without turning, Mirdoth knew what that sound was. And who was making it.

"Hurry," he said to the others, quickening his stride. "Fast as you can."

The captain had ridden to the very center of the bridge, and held there for a moment.

And then he had dismounted, and started walking toward the eastern approach. Calis slowed his own horse, completely and utterly baffled by what he saw. The Fallen lines were close enough now that he needed no glass to see the confusion of the enemy. The rank and file, looking about for orders. Wondering what to do. He could imagine the scene behind them as well, the archers with bows drawn, waiting for the command to fire on the single unarmed figure approaching them.

A horrible thought occurred to him in that instant.

Galor was right. Tandis could not be trusted. There was no Bane. He was working with the Fallen, had been so all along, was intent on only one thing, delivering the army of the Western Kingdom to Talax for slaughter, and having done that now, he was returning to his master.

No, Calis thought. That was nonsense. That was insane. He knew it for a fact, and yet . . .

It was almost as if the King himself was in his mind, whispering that it was true. Urging him to . . .

Calis's eyes widened.

Four figures had suddenly appeared on the bridge, directly in front of Tandis: a woman; an old man in a robe; a younger man, carrying a fourth on his shoulder, a fourth whose legs seemed, somehow, to be supported in midair.

He spurred his horse onward to them, and dismounted.

". . . right behind us," the older man was saying. "I can stay him a moment, but . . ."

"No." The captain shook his head. "I will deal with him. You take the princess, and Ambrose. And the boy. Above all the boy. Get him to safety."

"You will deal with him." The old man shook his head. "Captain, you know not—"

"*You* know not, Mirdoth." Tandis stepped forward. "Let me share with you."

The two locked eyes; a second later, the old man staggered backward, shaking his head.

"Tandis," he said. "All this time, and I never . . ."

"I deceived you. And many others." The captain turned then and looked at Calis. There was an instant of reproach in that look—an instant of *did I not tell you to stay*—but then it lifted.

"This is Knight General Calis. He commands the King's army. Calis, this is Mirdoth—counselor to the Lord of the Keep. Ambrose here. Who is badly injured." He gestured to the man being carried. "Princess Angenica, Ambrose's daughter, and her companion, Xander. You will note the circlet on his wrist, yes?"

Calis nodded. "Yes."

"This is the artifact we have been seeking. I charge you with this single task, Calis. Deliver it to Galor."

"I don't need anyone to babysit me," the boy, Xander, said, coming forward.

"It is not you I am concerned about," Tandis said. "Calis.

I have your word? You will make the boy's safety your first priority."

"Yes, sir," Calis said.

As he spoke he studied the thing around the boy's wrist. The Bane. It looked wholly unremarkable—a simple metal bracelet. A silver bracelet, its surface entirely free of scratches, or dents, or blemishes of any kind.

"Tandis!"

On the other side of the bridge, Talax was coming. Striding toward them slowly, confidently.

The Fallen Army was moving, too. Sions stepping to the fore, forming a wedge behind their leader.

"Come," Calis said. "We have to hurry."

"Let's get him on your horse," Xander said. "Him" meaning Ambrose. Calis had glimpsed the Lord of the Keep months earlier, when the Azure Knights, whole then, had passed through Outpost on their way south. He had barely recognized the man when Tandis identified him. Ambrose was a shell of his former self, physically and mentally. Calis could sense it; something had been done to the Lord's mind.

Xander had a grip on one of Ambrose's arms, and one of his legs. Calis went to grab the other.

He bumped into something. Someone.

He frowned and took a step back.

"What sorcery . . ."

"Sorcery named Vreen." Xander smiled at him. "It's a long story."

Calis felt vulnerable. The western edge of the bridge was now several hundred yards behind them. The east was filled with the Fallen, who were no doubt readying archers to deal with the unexpected intruders on the bridge.

"Come," Calis jumped up into the saddle. "Take the captain's horse, and—"

At that instant, he felt the bridge beneath him shake.

At the eastern approach, Talax had taken a step onto the span.

"Gods save us," the princess said.

"The Gods are not here." Tandis stepped forward. "But I will do my best to act in their stead."

Chapter Sixty-five

"To the west," Tandis said. "To the far side of the bridge, all of you. Now."

Geni, her father safely on the knight general's horse, nodded and turned to go. Xander was backing away already as well.

Only Mirdoth, standing next to her, hesitated.

"I can help," he said. "Captain . . ."

"No." Tandis spoke without turning. "This battle is mine."

Geni put a hand on her teacher's shoulder.

"Mirdoth. Come. We must hurry."

The old man turned to her and nodded reluctantly.

Clearly there was something wrong with her teacher. Her friend. For all that he was exhausted, for all the energy he had expended freeing them from the cell and guiding them safely to this point . . .

She sensed within him even more power . . . something threatening to erupt.

He seemed to her on the verge of losing control.

"You are a fool to come here." Talax remained at the far eastern edge of the bridge, one foot on the rock of the cliff face, the other on the timbers of the span. "To face me, now. Weakened, as you are."

"Even weakened"—Tandis took a step forward himself now—
"I have always been your master, Talax. That will never change."

"Why fight, though?" Talax asked. "We want the same thing.
An end to our time here. Give me the boy. Give me the Bane.
And let this world be free."

"The only freedom that would be served by granting your request would be the freedom for your armies to slaughter."

"Always you have favored the race of men," Talax said. "You
cannot see that the Fallen have a destiny, too. We must let both
alone, to find their path."

"You speak part of the truth, at least," Tandis said. "You must
let these people alone. You, and your army."

"I can see there will be no talking sense to you on this," Talax
replied. "But there is one point I must correct you on." The
Titan smiled. "This is not my army."

For the first time, Geni saw Tandis's confident smile waver.

And in that instant, Talax raised and then quickly lowered his
arm.

Behind him, the Fallen Army surged forward.

"Back!" Calis yelled. "Back!"

He spurred his horse into a gallop, one hand on the reins, the
other on Lord Ambrose to keep him from falling. The others—
the princess, the boy, the magician, and somewhere, he supposed,
the invisible man—hurried as best they could toward the western pass, even as the first line of Galor's soldiers—foot soldiers,
spears and shields held out before them—came charging across
the bridge.

Hildros was there, in the front of their ranks, motioning fran-
tically to Calis and the others.

"Boy! Here! Quickly!"

The old warrior's presence was that of a rock in the midst of a raging river; Galor's soldiers streamed around him on either side.

Calis and his charges made their way to him; they pushed back across the bridge to the other side and struggled toward a hilltop not a thousand feet from the fighting, the very hilltop from which they had surveyed the Fallen Army earlier.

"Who in the name of the seven devils are all these people?" Hildros yelled. "And why—"

"I'm Xander," the boy said.

"Xander." Hildros shook his head. "Fine. Well, listen, Xander, why don't you—"

"This is Angenica. Princess Angenica," Calis said as he dismounted. "We'll need a healer here immediately."

"Healer. What—" Hildros's eyes widened as he recognized the body lying across the back of Calis's horse. "Lord Ambrose! What happened?"

"A healer, Hildros," Calis repeated. "Now."

He turned away from the others and surveyed the scene on the bridge. What he saw disheartened him.

The Fallen were pushing Galor's army back.

"Healer!" he heard Hildros yell behind him. "We need a healer here!"

It was the Sions, Calis saw. A half dozen or so of them in particular. They moved like whirlwinds through the men before them; cutting them down like scythes, as the bridge groaned and strained beneath the weight of the assembled armies.

The odds needed evening up.

"Hildros," he said, turning. "The boy here. He needs to be protected."

"The boy." Hildros said. "What boy?"

"Me," Xander said to Calis. "But I'm not a boy. I'm the same age you are."

"Doubtful."

The two glared at each other for a moment.

"He carries the Bane," Calis added.

Xander held up his arm to show Hildros the circlet around it.

"Me protect him?" Hildros frowned. "Where are you going?"

Calis drew his sword.

"Down there," he said, and charged.

Chapter Sixty-six

Another man joined them. An officer named Henrik. Xander listened in as Hildros and the newcomer talked strategy. At least that was what he supposed they were doing. Xander didn't see that there was much strategy to this fight at all.

The two armies couldn't really get at each other. The bridge was like a bottleneck; they fought, two or three at a time, in the middle of it, trying desperately for some advantage. They were packed in so tightly that use of archers or catapults was impossible. Early on, for a few moments, it had seemed that the Fallen were going to break through, but then the knight general—Calis—had joined the fray and helped beat them back.

The man was a good fighter. Fearless with a sword. Xander wished he'd had the opportunity to learn the blade. Maybe when this was all over. When this thing was off his wrist.

"Healer," someone said. "Who called for a healer?"

"Here," Geni said, rising to her feet. She and Mirdoth had been alternately standing and kneeling around her father's body these last few moments; wiping Ambrose's brow, propping up his head with a wadded-up blanket Hildros had given them.

The newcomers—there were two of them, one a soldier, the other, in a long off-white robe, the healer, Xander presumed—

strode quickly to Geni's side. The healer knelt down next to Ambrose; he and Mirdoth began talking in hushed tones.

"You're the princess," the soldier said. "Princess of the Keep."

"That's right," Geni said.

"Yeah. I saw you a few months ago. Rode through." The soldier—a short, barrel-chested man with very bad teeth, who suddenly looked very familiar to Xander—smiled. "We engaged in a conversation."

Geni frowned. "I don't recall that."

"Well. I remember you," the soldier said, his smile growing broader.

"Wait a second." Xander snapped his fingers. "I remember now."

The soldier looked up at him. "What? What are you talking about? Who are you, boy?"

"Xander. We've met."

"Don't think so."

"Yes, we have. You're the one from the bar."

"The bar."

"Needles," Xander said. "We played a game of Needles. Ty, yes? Your name is Ty."

The soldier frowned. "Uhhh . . ."

"You were taking on all comers," Xander said. "You said best five throws for a hundred gildar. Twenty gildar to play. I played. I beat you. You went upstairs to get the money, and you never came back."

"This is not ringing a bell," the soldier said.

"You owe me money." Xander said. "Where's my money?"

A shadow fell over his shoulder then: Xander turned and saw Hildros standing there.

"Ty," the old warrior said. "What are you doing here? In case you hadn't noticed, there's a battle going on."

"Ty." Xander folded his arms across his chest, and smiled. "Aha!"

"I fully intended to pay you," the soldier said. "I was waylaid by a team of ladies. And—"

"So pay me now," Xander said.

The soldier frowned. "Best two out of three?"

His sword was slick with blood, as was the bridge. Slick with blood and gore, covered with the screaming, sobbing bodies of the dying and the dead.

Whatever enchantment held the bridge itself up (and Calis had little doubt in his mind now that such enchantment was real; the thin timbers that formed the crossing could not possibly hold the accumulated weight of those fighting on it now), it did not protect the railings on either side of the span; many of those timbers—thicker, and reinforced every few feet with cross ties— had splintered in the first few minutes of battle. Some remained clinging to the bridge by a handful of nails; others had fallen away entirely, into the ocean a thousand feet below.

Dozens of soldiers on either side of the fighting had joined them.

Calis himself had almost fallen on two occasions: through his own clumsiness on one occasion, through an opponent's skill on the other. A Sion, whose strength seemed beyond belief. A warrior of Calis's own height, who nonetheless was able to lift a man in each hand and toss them aside as if they were no more than throw pillows from a lady's bedchamber.

Calis charged him and brought his sword down on the Sion's armor. Not without effect; the creature screamed, and backhanded Calis, who flew a good ten feet through the air before slamming into something that splintered behind him. One of the rails, Calis thought, even as he heard the crack and landed, flat on his back, on the bridge once more.

He felt the rushing wind beneath him in his hair.

He looked up and saw the Sion standing over him. The thing reared back to kick him the rest of the way off the span.

Calis caught the creature's foot in his two hands and heaved, and it went screaming, spinning, arms flailing off the bridge.

He got to his feet and began moving forward once more. Moving through the Fallen, moving east, in search of the captain. Tandis.

He slew Urxen and Trog alike. Slew without thinking: operating, he realized, on instinct more than anything else. Instinct that told him what the enemy was, what it was capable of doing, and how best to attack it. Was it magic? Some outgrowth of his powers? Or was he doing, at last, what Uthirmancer had been trying to tell him to do all along? The man had been his closest, most constant teacher in the Knights, and after every lesson, after every technique of swordplay or grappling he'd demonstrated, after every sparring session, he would always tell Calis:

Now forget what I told you, and fight.

He raised his shield in time to parry a killing blow from a Sion who wore the uniform of an officer; the creature drew a dagger with its other hand and moved to gut Calis with it.

Calis felt the power stir within him then, as he'd felt it at Imli's Swamp weeks earlier. He saw the shards and held his hand up like a shield, and from it a blue-green light emerged, one that met the dagger and held it at bay.

The Sion's eyes widened in shock, and fear.

Calis charged with his shield extended, and slammed the creature backward, off the bridge.

It fell without a sound, and as he traced its descent with his eyes, he saw two figures, fighting on a cliffside, a few hundred yards from the eastern approach to the bridge.

Tandis and Talax, he realized. Not that he could see their faces from this far off. But it was them, he was sure of it.

The extent of the destruction surrounding the fighters was proof enough.

Calis had seen war before; had seen ruin, and suffering, and devastation on such a scale that he thought rebuilding, recovery, impossible. Burned villages; rubble where great towers had once stood. Dead bodies stacked like cordwood; dams broken, houses flooded, whole cities lost.

Never, ever had he seen destruction on the scale he was witnessing now.

A whole chunk of the cliffside was missing. Burned away; granite blackened and shattered by whatever eldritch energies the two fought with. The ground nearby was blackened as well; that entire slope had been covered by grass and flowers and even small trees barely moments earlier. Now it was gone; even the topsoil, Calis realized, was gone. All he could see was rock. Two Titans had done this in mere minutes?

Given how many centuries the Arnor had been here, Calis was surprised the world itself had lasted this long.

In the distance, Talax raised his arms over his head, then lowered them, as if he were signaling the start of a chariot race. As they came down, tendrils of energy—red, orange, yellow—erupted from them.

The tendrils hit Tandis and the captain staggered.

Calis leapt forward and began cutting his way to Tandis's side.

The shards in Resolyn and Imperium were blocked to him now. Mirdoth knew not when that had happened, but it meant that in order to restore his energies, depleted by the struggle to maintain the Spell of Masking, to get them to safety, he would need to access the shard of Fire, in Athica.

Which meant he would need, at last, to reveal himself to Galor. So be it. The Bane had to be kept safe.

He reached out with his mind.

"Are you all right?"

He looked up and saw the boy Xander—boy no longer; he was clearly a man now—frowning at him.

"Leave me, boy," he snapped, and at that very second, a voice sounded in his head.

Mirdoth.

It took him a second, but then he placed it.

Galor.

Along with the voice, there came now an image: the King, alone, in the center of the great labyrinth he had built to house the shard of Fire. The most powerful of all those shards remaining in the world.

He had not seen the King in nearly a century; had not spoken to him in this manner—through the power of the shard—for much, much longer.

After all this time, Galor said. *you would break our pact? The agreement we made? Why?*

The King was thinner than Mirdoth remembered, the bones of his arm visible beneath paper-thin skin. He is old, Mirdoth realized. Old, as I am old. Our time has passed and yet, the King, as always, seeks to hang on.

Mirdoth wondered, in that second, if the desire for power—the desire to remain the center of all things—had not unhinged Galor just a little bit.

Only to destroy your enemies, King.

Liar! Galor's eyes blazed fire. He opened his mouth to speak again, but Mirdoth cut the link between the two of them. He needed the shard, not the King. There was no sense in arguing further.

The die had been cast.

CHAPTER SIXTY-SEVEN

In the Hiergamenon, the two had been friends.

More than friends, in fact. Talax had served Tandis in the first of the wars against the Dread Lord Curgen, before turning from the Arnor's side. They had been as brothers—and now, like brothers betrayed, they fought with all the viciousness and desperation they could muster.

The ground shook with the fury of their combat; the air swirled with mystic energy. Calis could not tell which way the fight was going; first he thought Talax had the advantage, then Tandis. A certain death blow here was dodged, a bolt of energy there deflected.

The tide of battle on the bridge was no easier to judge; pockets of Fallen had made their way to the western side of the bridge, but a squad of men stood on the east as well. Though both approaches provided a larger field to fight on than the bridge, the ground there was still a bottleneck. Only so many Fallen at a time could reach the men who had battled their way to the east; only a few of Galor's soldiers could attack the Trogs who had reached the west. It was stalemate as well. For the moment.

A Trog landed, flat-footed, on the ground directly in front of him, ax raised high over his head. Calis raised his shield just in time; the ax came down, and he felt the shield shatter.

The creature screamed, and yanked the ax back, and Calis's shield went with it.

He drew his sword and stabbed forward; the Trog dodged out of the way. Once. Twice. Then a third time.

"You move too slow, manling," it said, smiling.

"Really?" Calis smiled, too, and as he did so he lunged forward again. The creature dodged, but Calis's lunge was a feint; even as it jumped sideways, he was twisting and raising his sword, slicing upward.

The blade caught the Trog at the neck and dug deep.

And then cut completely through.

The creature's eyes widened, and it opened its mouth in surprise, perhaps to say something, perhaps not, but talk was impossible by that point, for its head had toppled off its body.

The head hit the ground and began to roll backward, down the hill. Toward the waiting cliffs.

Calis stepped forward, off the bridge, and onto the eastern slope.

A hundred yards ahead of him, at the very cliff edge, he saw the Titans.

Tandis lay on his back, on the ground. Talax stood over the captain, hands raised together into a single fist.

The Titan brought his arms down for what Calis was sure would be a killing blow; at the last second, Tandis rolled aside. Talax, unbalanced, wobbled on his feet.

Tandis kicked out; Talax went sprawling.

Tandis charged. Talax raised a hand, and within it there suddenly appeared a glowing ball of red energy. The air swirled around it like a vortex; he fired the ball at Tandis, who raised a hand of his own and formed the same kind of shield Calis had seen earlier; a halo of blue light.

The red ball struck the halo and bounced off. It spiraled toward the nearest soldiers, a group of Urxen warriors, on the very edge of the battle.

The ball of energy hit right in the middle of them, slamming into the shield of one. It splintered into a thousand glowing bolts of energy; some of those bolts hit the ground, or flew up into the air and vanished.

Some hit the Urxen; those that were struck seemed to light up with power for a second.

Then their armor glowed and melted away.

They were skin; then bones; then dust.

Calis turned back to the Titans. Tandis and Talax stood a dozen feet apart; energy flew from their hands, and met in the middle, exploding in a kaleidoscope of color.

Calis moved toward the two.

"No!" Tandis cried out without turning away, without taking his eyes or his focus from the Titan in front of him. "This battle is not for you, Calis! This is too dangerous. Stay back!"

But even as Tandis spoke, Talax's head swiveled; his gaze fell on Calis. Keeping his right arm raised, keeping the energy from that hand streaming toward Tandis, the Titan moved his left arm in Calis's direction. The wave of energy streaming from that hand moved as well. Moved like a searchlight, moving across the ground, moving inexorably toward Calis.

The boy took a step backward and his foot touched empty space.

He turned and saw the sea a thousand feet beneath him.

He dropped his sword and raised both his own hands, and concentrated, trying to find the power within himself once more. The power he had felt at the swamp, and on the bridge. The power to form the same kind of mystic shield that the two fighting before him had created.

It began to take shape in front of him.

And then the beam of energy from Talax's hand slammed into his chest, and he staggered backward.

His foot wobbled in empty air once more; a second later, the other joined it, and he fell.

He reached out with both arms; his chest slammed into the cliff face.

His hands scrabbled for purchase; he found a cleft in the rock and held on tight.

He began to pull himself up; as he did so, he looked over at the Titans and saw that Tandis had seized the advantage. The captain loomed over Talax; the blue glow overwhelmed the red.

Talax cried out in anger, and frustration; the red glow suddenly burst out, brighter than ever before.

Then there was a sudden explosion of brilliant, near-blinding white light. Calis shielded his eyes; he felt wind tear at him, a hot, burning, acrid wind that smelled of death, and dying things.

The ground shook; the cleft in the rock moved and grabbed at his left hand. He yanked it free, seconds before the gap closed entirely.

And now he was hanging by one arm, dangling over the edge of the cliff.

He yanked himself up and rested his elbow on the rock.

The ground where the Titans had stood was empty. All that remained there was a crater, gouged into the rock itself.

Gone, both of them. Along with the soldiers who had been nearest the explosion.

The Titans were both gone. Dead? Could it be so? Titans die?

He'd have to worry about that later. For now . . .

I charge you with this single task, Calis.

The artifact. Deliver it to Galor.

He shut his eyes and strained to lift his body the rest of the way up.

Keep yourself safe, boy.

Keep an eye on the King.

His arm shook with the effort; Calis felt, all at once, the strain of the last few hours. Felt it in his right arm, his sword arm; his left, which had held the shield.

He felt himself slipping.

Don't look down, he told himself. Don't look down.

He looked down.

The rock face was almost sheer beneath him; there was a handful of outcroppings to his left and right. There might have even been one or two far, far below. Doubtful he would hit any of those when he fell. But the ocean, the whitecaps in the distance . . .

Those, he couldn't miss.

The muscles in his right hand ached; he scrabbled again with his left, trying to insert it into a gap in the rock. He missed, and his right hand slipped, and then it came out of the cleft as well.

He felt himself, for a split second, beginning to fall.

And then something grabbed his left hand.

"Easy."

He looked up and saw Tandis.

"I've got you."

The captain smiled and pulled him the rest of the way up onto the rock.

"Thank you," Calis said, sitting on his knees for a second, catching his breath.

Tandis smiled. "That was—" he said, and then his eyes opened wide, and the point of a sword emerged from his chest.

Calis scrambled backward and almost fell off the cliff again.

The rest of the blade came through the captain's body.

Behind him, Talax came into view.

The Titan placed a foot on Tandis's back and yanked the sword he'd driven through the captain's body back out.

Tandis fell forward. Talax gave him a kick to help him on his way, over the cliffs.

And then he was gone.

Chapter Sixty-eight

Something had changed.

The men of Galor's army, who had established a foothold on the other side of the bridge, were suddenly being forced back. Cut down. Not one at a time, but handfuls at a clip. By a single figure, who was brushing them aside as if they were straw men, scarecrows propped up in a field to scare the birds away.

It was, Xander thought, like watching Saren play that game with which he used to occupy himself while he waited for customers. He would line up the little wooden markers on the counter before him, stand them up next to one another all in a row, dozens of them at once, carefully arranged into a pattern, and then he would knock over the first in line, and it would knock over the second, and so on, and so on, so that the first little push he gave eventually sent the entire line of markers tumbling.

Dominoes. That was it; the game had been called dominoes.

That was how the men of the Kingdom were falling now. Only the sounds they made as they fell were not the gentle clicks of markers hitting table, wood on wood.

The sounds they made were screams. Cries of pain, and anguish, and surprise.

"Talax," Mirdoth said. The old man stood next to him on the little hill, hand raised to his brow to shield it from the noonday sun, high overhead. "He is coming."

Xander squinted. He couldn't see anything, really, besides Galor's army as it came stumbling backward, back across the bridge.

"You have to go now." Geni, still kneeling next to her father, turned and looked up at Xander. "You have to get out of here."

"The battle's a long way from over, miss," Hildros said. "We've got four thousand of King Galor's best men here, and Captain Tandis—"

"Tandis is dead," Mirdoth said.

"Ha! I've heard that one before," Hildros said. "He'll be along, soon enough. I'm sure of that."

"No," Mirdoth said. "He will not."

There was a ring of certainty in his voice, so much so that Hildros's smile faltered.

Xander and Geni exchanged glances.

"You have to go now," she said again.

Hildros turned and glared at her, and then Mirdoth, as if they were responsible for the captain's disappearance. "All right. No harm in being safe, I suppose."

He turned and cupped his hands. "A horse! Someone bring me a horse. The fastest horse we have. And the best horsemen. The best soldiers. We have to get this boy to Minoch."

"Get him to Athica," Geni said.

"One step at a time, little miss," Hildros said.

Geni got to her feet.

"I am many things," she snapped. "I am a princess. I am a Sion. I am the heir to the Warden of the Keep, and I may even be a channeler, but one thing I am not is a little miss. Is that understood?"

Hildros mumbled something under his breath, and looked to the sky. "Begging your pardon, Your Majesty. Where's that horse?" he shouted, turning away. "Ty? I want you here, too. Ty?"

Xander scanned the horizon for the little man as well—and at that second caught sight of Talax, who had at last reached the eastern approach to the bridge.

He waved the Fallen soldiers behind him back, and cupped his hands over his mouth.

"Send me the Bane!" he yelled. "No more fighting is necessary. Just send me the boy!"

The Titan's voice dominated the scene. Despite standing hundreds of yards away, Xander could hear him as if he were standing nearby.

The fighting on the bridge paused for a second.

Hildros snorted. "Send him the boy. I'll send him something all right."

The old warrior turned and motioned to a company of archers, who stood atop a second hill, fifty feet or so behind them, a dozen or so feet higher above the battle.

"It's not going to work," said Geni. "When he attacked the Keep—"

"Fire!" Hildros yelled, shooting a sideways glare at her as he did so.

A split second later, the archers shot. A flight of arrows that looked, to Xander's eye, to be soaring true, to be soaring straight for the Titan.

In midair they disappeared.

"This is not good."

Vreen was standing next to him, wringing his hands, shaking his head. "This is not good at all."

"Please." Geni turned to Xander. "Please. We went all that way to get that thing. You have to keep it safe."

He looked at her, and then down toward the bridge.

Talax raised his hands like a club over his head, and brought them down.

The bridge shook, like a leaf in a storm, wobbling back and forth. There was a handful of fighters left on it; men and Fallen alike.

All struggled to keep their balance; all failed, and fell.

"Gods," Hildros said, shaking his head. He turned toward Henrik. "Catapults?"

"Aye." The other man nodded. "Catapults. That should do it."

But the tone in his voice as he spoke . . . the look on his face even as he turned to obey . . .

He knew it wouldn't. Just as Xander did.

There was no stopping Talax now.

"Somebody needed a horse?"

The little man—Ty—was walking up the slope toward them, riding one horse, holding the reins to a second.

"Me." Xander sighed, and held up a hand. "That would be me."

His fault.

His peril had distracted Tandis, had allowed Talax to come up from behind and deliver the killing blow.

Now it was his duty to make things right.

Talax stood at the eastern approach to the bridge; Calis came at him from behind. The Titan was distracted. Calis seized the moment and tackled him. Talax fell forward; Calis drew his sword and brought it down.

The blade halted a foot shy of Talax and snapped in half with an ear-shattering crack.

Talax reared back and slapped him with an open hand. The blow nearly ripped Calis's head from his shoulders. He saw stars, and flew backward, and landed on the ground.

Keep the boy safe.

Get the boy to Galor.

But all he could see was the captain's face.

He got to his feet, screamed, and charged again.

Talax caught him as he came, caught him with a hand on the knight's tunic, lifted him in the air, and threw him.

Flying, Calis thought. He was flying.

There wasn't time for a proper good-bye, Geni realized; there wasn't time to say everything in her mind. In her heart. It wouldn't be a good idea to do so anyway, she realized.

Xander would try to stop her.

Even as he mounted the horse alongside Ty, she turned toward the bridge, and Talax.

And gasped in surprise.

Mirdoth stood there, blocking the Titan's path forward.

CHAPTER SIXTY-NINE

"Old man." Talax stepped up onto the bridge. "Today is a day of surprises, indeed. You seek to pit your strength against mine?"

"Your strength." Mirdoth shook his head. "There is nothing more pitiful than seeing an Elas'nir trying to play the role of the Dread."

"You are the pitiful one," Talax said. "A wolf that pretends to be a sheep."

The Titan raised his hands; energy danced between his fingers.

But it was Mirdoth who struck first.

A beam of bright red light; energy powerful enough to cleave rock. Energy he had channeled from Fire, in Athica. Energy he had bent to the *a'dam'ash ashturay,* the most potent of all death-magics. The spell he had studied long and hard these last few days.

The beam struck the Titan and he vanished into thin air.

At least, that was the scenario that had played out in Mirdoth's mind.

In reality, Talax simply groaned and fell back onto one knee.

And then rose to his feet once more.

Mirdoth was stunned.

"Impressive, sorcerer," Talax said. "I have not felt such power from a mortal since the Usurper himself. But as long as you only have access to two shards, you are a shadow of the might he had. And I have power at my disposal that no Dread has ever possessed."

The space in front of Talax began to swirl with energy; energy that came not just from the Titan, but seemed to flow through him from somewhere else entirely.

He had been a fool, Mirdoth realized in that instant.

Tandis had been weakened, that was true. But with the young man—Calis—fighting alongside him . . . he should have been strong enough to hold Talax to stalemate, at the least. To keep the Bane safe. There was only one explanation.

There was a further power behind Talax. Someone lending the Titan strength. It took no particular genius on Mirdoth's part to realize who; the mysterious figure he had glimpsed earlier, through his magics, in the Keep. The figure Talax feared; the voice that had demanded news of the Bane.

Light flew toward Mirdoth, and filled his world.

And then everything went black.

You have a special destiny.

Xander reined his horse to a halt.

"No," he said.

Ty looked up at him. "What?"

"No. I can't run away. Not now. Not while Geni's risking her life back there."

"She's a magician, she said." Ty shook his head. "She's got a chance of slowing him down. Giving you time to get away. So—"

"She might be a channeler." Xander jumped down off the

horse. "She might be able to slow him down. But even if she does, you think he won't catch me? Catch us?"

The little man glared at him. "All I know is what Hildros told me to do. Which is to get you someplace safe."

"There is no place safe," Xander said. He turned his horse around.

Her turn, Geni thought, stepping up onto the bridge.

"Halt," she said, focusing all her energies on Talax. "Come no farther."

The Titan shook his head.

"I grow tired of this. Stand aside."

Geni ignored him and focused her mind.

It was a matter of concentration, Mirdoth had said. Of aligning the wishes of the mind with the mechanisms of the body. Lending power to her voice; channeling the energies around her, and then bending those energies to her will, and then imposing her will on others around her.

"Turn around. Call off your army. Abandon the Keep." Geni fixed her eyes on Talax's. "I charge you—"

The Titan barked out a laugh. "Impressive. You have promise, girl. A budding talent. Stand aside—"

The smile disappeared from his face.

"—and I won't kill you."

And with that he began walking forward once more.

Combat-magic, Geni thought.

Mirdoth had mentioned it, in passing. In their lessons. Spells of attack. Spells designed to mortally wound an opponent. That was for later, he had said. And not for such as him to teach. She would undergo the testing, and Galor would decide. Her promise, her potential, her training. The spells she would learn from the ancient texts.

Geni had, of course, peeked on occasion.

She raised her arms and tried to touch the shards.

Talax made a casual motion with his hand that sent her flying backward.

She got to her feet, and Xander was standing alongside her.

Oh, no.

"What are you doing here?" she yelled. "Why aren't you . . ."

She felt like crying.

"I couldn't run. I couldn't leave you."

"Oh, Xander."

She took his hand.

They turned and faced Talax.

"By the Mithrilar themselves." The Titan's eyes were focused on Xander, on the thing on his wrist. His expression was one of mingled surprise, and puzzlement. "How is this possible? I can see the Bane, wrapped around your wrist. But I cannot sense it at all. No. I cannot sense it one bit. You are fortunate, boy. *He* would be here right now if I could sense it. If I could sense you."

Geni shook her head. He? Who was "he"? And what did Talax mean, he couldn't sense Xander?

The Titan strode toward them, still shaking his head.

Xander stepped in front of her and brandished his sword.

"Stay back."

"Send the girl away, boy," the Titan said, and the bridge shook with the force of his footfalls as he drew nearer. "Send her to safety, and come with me. He will be very interested in meeting you indeed."

Gods, Geni thought. *Gods. Hear my plea. Keep us safe. Keep Xander and the Bane—*

Xander charged forward, sword high over his head.

At that instant, the bridge beneath her feet shook once more.

Shook, and shattered.

"Xander!" she screamed.

Eyes wide, he turned and reached for her—

Their hands brushed against each other, fingertips barely touching—

And then they fell. Xander. Geni. Talax.

And then she landed on something, landed hard enough to knock the wind out of her. A split second later, Xander landed right next to her.

"What—" she began.

"Hold tight, little things!" Magor said, and the dragon roared, shaking the splinters and cracked beams and remnants of Amarian's Folly from its head and shoulders. "Hold tight as you can!"

CHAPTER SEVENTY

A dragon.

Calis returned to consciousness and the first thing he saw was a myth come to life—a dragon approaching him.

Calis had seen much this day that he had never imagined possible. But a dragon?

Truly these were miraculous times.

It landed in front of him.

"Unless you plan to stay here in the East, you should come with us," said the boy on its back. Xander.

Without hesitation, Calis leapt onto the back of the massive beast. With its great wings the dragon was in the air again.

Fallen archers soon recovered from their shock and were firing bolts at the dragon. The arrows harmlessly bounced off its scale armor.

It landed on the western approach, and the princess, Xander, and he jumped from its back, safe. Miraculously so.

The creature—Magor, he thought he heard the girl call him— had snorted, flapped its wings, breathed fire, and then taken to the skies once more. Seeking his own kind, the girl had said. There were rumors of more of the legendary beasts elsewhere in the world, but in all his years of traveling, Calis had found no substance to those rumors. He wished Magor better luck.

The dragon had saved them all: the army, the princess, and the Bane. True, the Keep—and the East—were lost to them for the moment, but Calis felt oddly philosophical about those things. A bridge had been raised across the chasm once. He saw no reason it could not happen a second time.

"Still think you ought to give me a chance at getting that thing off."

Ty was holding up Xander's wrist, staring at the Bane.

"Might be some kind of trigger on the inside of it. Like a latch." Ty smiled. "I knew a lady once—well, a girl anyway—her father had put this belt on her, and she wanted—"

"We'll leave that for the King, you," Hildros snapped. "Make yourself useful, Ty. You can start by helping the men get in order, for the march back."

The little man shrugged and walked off.

"How about you?" Hildros said, spying Calis looking on. "You all right?"

"Fine. I suppose." The boy sighed. "I can't believe he's really gone, though. The captain."

"I know." Hildros nodded, gazing toward the cliff. "I keep expecting to see him climb up, brush himself off, and start telling us what to do."

Calis nodded. Part of him expected it as well.

Part of him, though, knew better.

The healer helped them lift first Ambrose, and then Mirdoth into the cart. They would be seen to in Minoch first, though the healer had come right out and told Geni that the cure for what ailed the two men was beyond his powers—or those of his colleagues in Baron Mancer's city—to provide.

Only in Athica. Only at the King's own hand, he had said.

The capital. Xander was looking forward to seeing it himself. Looking forward to meeting Galor, and getting this thing off his wrist. The Bane.

Perhaps Galor would be able to enlighten him on a few other matters as well.

He would be here right now if I could sense it. If I could sense you.

Who had Talax been talking about?

"Hey."

He looked up: Geni had turned away from the cart, which was even now beginning to pull away.

"Hey."

"What are you thinking about?"

"A lot of things."

"Well, stop." She slipped her hand into his. "We'll figure them out."

"Them."

"Your abilities. Your destiny. No point in worrying so much."

"Okay." He smiled. "What should we think about?"

"Let's think about tomorrow," she said. "What do you want to do tomorrow?"

Acknowledgments

I would like to particularly thank:

Dave Stern, my partner in crime on this project. His mentoring, editing, and writing help were instrumental in making Xander and Geni's adventures come alive. His help in fleshing out the long history of *Elemental* from an outline of events into the epic backstory contained in the Hiergamenon provided me with a wealth of new directions for this story as well as for *The War of Magic*.

Keith Clayton, whose dedication and project management helped bring together all our assets into a single cohesive narrative. He provided the driving force to make sure I kept on time and would bring Dave and me back into reality when we got too into writing the Hiergamenon epics.

Mikita Labanok, the unsung hero of this entire affair. It is he who got the ball rolling. I've spent two decades working on the universe that *Elemental* takes place in, but it was Mikita who saw the value of teaming people with complementary talents to create something that is wonderful in different media.

Paul Boyer, whose work on the map and cover were something that I am very grateful for. His work on both the book and *The War of Magic* helped guide much of the spirit of the story.

Kristin Hatcher, my friend who instilled in me the motivation to make sure that I quit procrastinating and started writing the stories of Tandis, Xander, Draginol, and the rest.

Thomas Pitoniak, the brave soul who copy edited this book. Thank you for your patience and input.

And to my lovely wife, whose love and support made it possible for me to run a company, develop a game, and write a book at the same time.

PHOTO: ANGELA MARSHALL

BRADLEY WARDELL, president & CEO of Stardock, a Midwestern software company, is the lead designer of Elemental: War of Magic, and is active in software development, designing, and coding for many Stardock products. His other activities include being a Microsoft MVP, blogger, podcaster, and featured columnist. He is a graduate of Western Michigan University, where he met his wife, Debbie Wardell, with whom he has three children. In his free time he enjoys beekeeping.